RAID BY NIGHT

I heard a series of strange sounds. I tried to identify them.

Suddenly, I knew! Ladders! They had ladders!

Along various spots in the wall were small bundles of grass and twigs that could be quickly lit. Taking one from its cubbyhole, I struck a light and touched it off with a spark. As it sprang into flame, I held it over the wall.

In the brief flare of light, a dozen savage, painted faces glared up at me. Then the ladders started to rise.

An arrow struck near me. Aiming at the nearest man's chest, I fired.

They came with a rush.

D0974613

Bantam Books by Louis L'Amour
Ask your bookseller for the books you have missed.

BENDIGO SHAFTER
BORDEN CHANTRY
BOWDRIE
BOWDRIE'S LAW
BRIONNE
THE BROKEN GUN
BUCKSKIN RUN
THE BURNING HILLS
THE CALIFORNIOS
CALLAGHEN
CATLOW
CHANCY
THE CHEROKEE TRAIL
COMSTOCK LODE
CONAGHER
CROSSFIRE TRAIL
DARK CANYON
DOWN THE LONG HILLS
DUTCHMAN'S FLAT
THE EMPTY LAND
FAIR BLOWS THE WIND
FALLON
THE FERGUSON RIFLE
THE FIRST FAST DRAW
FLINT
FRONTIER
GUNS OF THE TIMBERLANDS
HANGING WOMAN CREEK
THE HAUNTED MESA
HELLER WITH A GUN
THE HIGH GRADERS
HIGH LONESOME
THE HILLS OF HOMICIDE
HONDO
HOW THE WEST WAS WON
THE IRON MARSHAL
THE KEY-LOCK MAN
KID RODELO
KILKENNY
KILLOE
KILRONE
KIOWA TRAIL
LAST STAND AT PAPAGO
    WELLS
LAW OF THE DESERT BORN
THE LONESOME GODS
THE MAN CALLED NOON
THE MAN FROM SKIBBEREEN
MATAGORDA
MILO TALON
THE MOUNTAIN VALLEY WAR
NIGHT OVER THE SOLOMONS
NORTH TO THE RAILS
OVER ON THE DRY SIDE
PASSIN' THROUGH

THE PROVING TRAIL
THE QUICK AND THE DEAD
RADIGAN
REILLY'S LUCK
THE RIDER OF LOST CREEK
THE RIDER OF THE RUBY HILLS
RIDING FOR THE BRAND
RIVERS WEST
THE SHADOW RIDERS
SHALAKO
SHOWDOWN AT YELLOW
    BUTTE
SILVER CANYON
SITKA
SON OF A WANTED MAN
THE STRONG SHALL LIVE
TAGGART
TO TAME A LAND
TUCKER
UNDER THE SWEET-
    WATER RIM
UTAH BLAINE
THE WALKING DRUM
WAR PARTY
WESTWARD THE TIDE
WEST FROM SINGAPORE
WHERE THE LONG GRASS
    BLOWS
YONDERING

Sackett Titles by
Louis L'Amour

---

1. SACKETT'S LAND
2. TO THE FAR BLUE
    MOUNTAINS
3. THE DAYBREAKERS
4. SACKETT
5. LANDO
6. MOJAVE CROSSING
7. THE SACKETT BRAND
8. THE LONELY MEN
9. TREASURE MOUNTAIN
10. MUSTANG MAN
11. GALLOWAY
12. THE SKY-LINERS
13. THE MAN FROM THE
    BROKEN HILLS
14. RIDE THE DARK TRAIL
15. THE WARRIOR'S PATH
16. LONELY ON THE
    MOUNTAIN
17. RIDE THE RIVER
18. JUBAL SACKETT

LOUIS L'AMOUR

TO THE FAR BLUE MOUNTAINS

BANTAM BOOKS
TORONTO · NEW YORK · LONDON · SYDNEY · AUCKLAND

*This low-priced Bantam Book
has been completely reset in a type face
designed for easy reading, and was printed
from new plates. It contains the complete
text of the original hard-cover edition.*
NOT ONE WORD HAS BEEN OMITTED.

TO THE FAR BLUE MOUNTAINS
A Bantam Book

PRINTING HISTORY
E. P. Dutton edition published October 1976

Bantam edition / June 1977

2nd printing . . . . . July 1977	11th printing . . January 1981
3rd printing . September 1977	12th printing . . . . . May 1981
4th printing . . February 1978	13th printing . . . August 1981
5th printing . . . . April 1978	14th printing . . . . April 1982
6th printing . . January 1979	15th printing . . October 1982
7th printing . . January 1979	16th printing . . . . . May 1983
8th printing . . . . . May 1979	17th printing . December 1983
9th printing . . . . . May 1980	18th printing . September 1984
10th printing . . . . . June 1980	19th printing . . . . April 1985

All rights reserved.
Copyright © 1976 by Louis L'Amour.
Cover artwork copyright © 1985 by Lou Glanzman.
*This book may not be reproduced in whole or in part, by
mimeograph or any other means, without permission.
For information address: Bantam Books, Inc.*

ISBN 0-553-25272-0

Published simultaneously in the United States and Canada

*Bantam Books are published by Bantam Books, Inc. Its trade-
mark, consisting of the words "Bantam Books" and the por-
trayal of a rooster, is Registered in U.S. Patent and Trademark
Office and in other countries. Marca Registrada. Bantam
Books, Inc., 666 Fifth Avenue, New York, New York 10103.*

PRINTED IN THE UNITED STATES OF AMERICA

H   28 27 26 25 24

To Oscar and Marion Dystel

△ △ △

∆ 1 ∆

My horse, good beast that he was, stood steady, ears pricked to listen, as were mine.

When a man has enemies he had best beware, and I, Barnabas Sackett, born of the fenland and but lately returned from the sea, had enemies I knew not of.

The blackness of my plumed hat and cloak fed themselves into the blackness of the forest, leaving no shape for the eye to catch. There was only the shine of captured light from my naked blade as I waited, listening.

Something or somebody was in the forest near me, what or who it might be I knew not, nor was I a believer in the devils and demons thought to haunt these forests.

Devils and demons worried me not, but there were men abroad, with blades as keen as mine, highwaymen and creatures of the night who lay waiting for any chance traveler who might come riding alone . . . to his death, if they but had their will.

Yet the fens had trained me well, for we of the fens learned to be aware of all that was happening about us. Hunters and fishers we were, and some of us smugglers as well, although of these I was not one. Yet we moved upon our hidden ways, in darkness or in light, knowing each small sound for what it was. Nor had wandering in the forests of Raleigh's land among the red Indians allowed my senses to grow dull.

Something lurked, but so did I.

My point lifted a little, expecting attack. Yet those who might be waiting to come at me were but men who bled, even as I.

It was not attack that came from the darkness, but a voice.

"Ah, you are a wary one, lad, and I like that in a man. Stand steady, Barnabas, I'll not cross your blade. It is words I'll have, not blood."

"Speak then, and be damned to you. If words are not enough, the blade is here. You spoke my name?"

"Aye, Barnabas, I know your name and your table, as well. I've eaten a time or two in your fen cottage from which you've been absent these many months."

"You've shared meat with me? Who are you, then? Speak up, man!"

"I'd no choice. It is the steps and the string for me if caught. I need a bit of a hand, as the saying is, and the chance to serve you, if permitted."

"Serve me how?"

He was hidden still, used as were my eyes to darkness, yet now my ears caught some familiar note, some sound that started memory rising.

"Ah!" It came to me suddenly. "Black Tom Watkins!"

"Aye." He came now from the shadows. "Black Tom it is, and a tired and hungry man, too."

"How did you know me then? It is a time since last I traveled this road."

"Don't I know that? Yet it is not only I who know of your coming, nor your friend William, who farms your land. There are others waiting, Barnabas, and that is why I am here, in the damp and darkness of the forest, hoping to catch you before you ride unwitting into their company."

"Who? Who waits?"

"I am a wanted man, Barnabas, and the gallows waits for me, but I got free and was in the tavern yonder

8

studying upon what to do when I heard your name spoken. Oh, they kept their voices low, but when one has lived in the fens as you and I . . . well, I heard them. They wait to lay you by the heels and into Newgate Prison."

He came a step nearer. "You've enemies, lad. I know naught of them nor their reasons, but guilty or not they've a Queen's warrant for you, and there's a bit in it for them if they take you."

A Queen's warrant? Well, it might be. There had been a warrant. Yet who would know of that and be out to take me? We were a far cry from London town, and it was an unlikely thing.

"They are at the cottage?" I asked.

"Not them. There's a bit of a tavern only a few minutes down the road, and they do themselves well there while waiting. From time to time one rides to see if you are about at the cottage, and I think they have a man in the hedgerow."

"What manner of men are they?"

It was in my mind that my enemy, Captain Nick Bardle of the *Jolly Jack*, was out to take me, but he himself was a wanted man, and he'd have no thought of Newgate.

"A surly lot of rogues by their looks, and led by a tall, dark man with greasy hair to his shoulders and the movements of a swordsman. He seems the leader, but there's another who might be. A shorter, wider man . . . thicker, too . . . and older somewhat if I am to judge."

My horse was as restive as I. My cottage was less than an hour away . . . perhaps half that, but the night was dark and no landmarks to be made out. My situation was far from agreeable.

My good friend and business associate, Captain Brian Tempany, was aboard our new ship, awaiting my return for sailing. It was off to the new lands across the sea, and for trade with whom we could. And perhaps, for Abigail and me, a home there.

A Queen's warrant is no subject for jest, even if he

9

who had sworn to it was dead and the occasion past. The warrant should have been rescinded, but once in Newgate I might be held for months and no one the wiser.

Once back in London, Captain Tempany might set in motion the moves to have the warrant rescinded, or my friend Peter Tallis might, but to do that I must first reach London and their ears.

"Go toward the cottage, Tom, and be sure all is quiet there, and along the hedge as well. Then come back along the track and meet me. Lay claim to a boat."

"I'll do it."

"A moment, Tom. You spoke of a favor?"

He took hold of my stirrup leather. "Barnabas, it is hanging at Tyburn if I'm caught, and it is said that you are lately home from the new lands across the sea, and that you sail again soon. There's naught left for me in England, lad, nor will there ever be, again. I am for the sea, and if you'll have me aboard, I'll be your man 'til death.

"If you know aught of me you know I'm a seaman. I've been a soldier as well, and am handy with weapons or boats. Take me over the sea and I'll make out to stay there."

There was sincerity in him, and well enough I knew the man, a strong and steady one, by all accounts. To be a smuggler in Britain was to be in good company, for the laws were harsh and many a churchman or officer was involved in it, or looking aside when it was done.

Our fens in Cambridgeshire and Lincolnshire were havens for smugglers, for there were many winding waterways by which a boat could come from the sea, and a score of towns the boat could come to with no hint that it came from the sea.

"Think well of what you ask, Tom. It is a far land to which I'll go. There be savages there, and forests such as you've never seen. It will be no easy time."

"Whenever was it easy for such a man as I? The scars I carry speak of no easy times, lad, and however bad it may be it will be better than the steps and the noose, and that's what awaits me here."

When he had gone I sat listening for a time, untrusting of the darkness, but heard no sound for the slow dripdrip of raindrops from the leaves. Black Tom would be a good man in Raleigh's land . . . a good man.

My horse started of his own volition, impatient of standing, and sheathing my sword I let him go, then loosened the flap of my saddle holster on the right side. As we drew near the tavern I turned my mount to the grassy border along the track that we called a road.

A tall man who moved like a swordsman? A man with black and greasy hair? I knew of none such.

Before me appeared the lights from dim and dirty windows, and I remembered the tavern. An old place, with a stable for horses. The door opened and a man came into the darkness as I drew rein. He closed the door behind him, and I waited.

He stood a moment, then went around the house to the stables. After a moment he emerged, mounting the horse he led, and turned along the track ahead of me. At a respectable distance, I followed.

This must be the man who would ride to the cottage to see if I was about. Would Black Tom mistake him for me?

My stay at the cottage need not be long. It was a thing of sentiment as much as business that had brought me back, for the feeling was on me that I'd not again see the home my father had been given for his service in the wars. My father was Ivo Sackett, yeoman, soldier, first-class fighting man . . . a decent man, too, and as good a teacher as he was a fighter.

There was William to see, for he would care for the land whilst I was gone over the great waters, and we had a few small matters to speak of. He was a man to be trusted, but in the event something happened to him . . . after all, all men are mortal.

My father had schooled me well, and although he left me a fine stretch of fenland, I had no desire to remain there, nor had he wished me to. He had trained me well

11

in the use of arms, of which he was a master, and taught me better than he knew of reading and writing.

"Lad," he would say to me, "I know a weaver who became a great merchant, and the men who rode with William the Norman had only their strong arms and their swords, but with them they became the great men of the kingdom. For some men an acre and a cottage are enough, but not for you, Barnabas. I have tried to fit you for a new life in the new world that's coming, where a man can be what he's of a mind to be."

This cottage and the land in the fens was what my father had done. Now was the time for me. Deep as was my affection for the cottage and the fens, I knew there was a broader, wilder world. I had my father's contempt for the courtier who suspends his life from the fingertips of those in power, looking for morsels. I would be beholden to no man.

The rider I followed was slowing down now as he drew nearer the cottage.

He drew up suddenly, listening, but sensing he was about to halt I had myself pulled up close under a tall hedge, and he could not see me.

He stared down the road behind him for a long time, then he started on, but I held my horse for I had a feeling he would stop again. And he did so, turning in the saddle to look back. After a moment he started again, seemingly reassured.

When he was near the lane that turned down the slope to my cottage, he drew up and dismounted. Purposely, I let my horse take two steps that he could hear.

Instantly, he froze in position, staring toward me. But I sat silent, knowing he was worried—frightened a little, or at least uneasy—and this was what I wanted.

He led his horse into the opening of the lane leading to my cottage, and what he saw or failed to see satisfied him, for he mounted again. But he rode on to where he could look toward the water side of my cottage, and then it was that I started to hum a tune and walked my horse toward him. He was around a turn of the lane but

12

he heard me, as I knew he would, and as I turned the corner I saw him, halberd in hand.

"Ho, there!" I said, not too loud. "Is this the way to Boston?"

"Ahead there, and you'll see the marker." He leaned toward me, peering. "You came up the track?"

"Aye, and a start it gave me, too! Something was there . . . I know not what. I spoke to it, but had no answer, and came on quickly enough. Damn it, man, if that be your way, be careful. I liked not the smell of it."

"Smell?"

"Aye, a fetid smell . . . as of something dead. I saw no shape or shadow, but . . . have you ever smelled a wolf?"

"A wolf?" His voice rose a little. "There are no wolves in England!"

"Aye . . . so they say. Not wolves as such, I suppose, but I have smelled wolves . . . not your ordinary wolves, you understand, but huge, slinking creatures with ugly fangs. Bloody fangs! And they smelled like that back there. Have you heard of werewolves, perhaps? I sometimes think—"

"Werewolves? That's just talk . . . campfire talk, or talk by peasants. There are no wolves in England, and I—"

"Well, I've had a smell of them. That was in Tartary where I went for Henry the Seventh—"

"Henry the Seventh!" His voice was shrill. "Why, that's impossible! It has been almost a hundred years since—"

"So long?" I said. "It scarcely seems so." I leaned toward him. "Werewolves! I'd know that odor anywhere! The smell of graves opened! Old graves! Of bodies long dead!" Pausing, I said, as if puzzled, "But you said King Henry the Seventh was nearly a hundred years ago?"

"Nearly." The man was edging away from me.

"Well, well! How time goes on! But when you have passed, you know, when you're no longer subject to time—"

"I must go. They await me at the tavern yonder."

"Ah? A tavern? I was tempted to enter, but you know

how it must be. When I enter the others leave. So I—"

"You're mad!" The man burst out suddenly. "Crazy!" And he clapped his heels to his horse and raced away.

From the hedge there was a chuckle. "He didn't know whether you were crazy or a ghost, Barnabas." Black Tom shivered. "On a night like this a man could believe anything out here in the dark." He gestured. "Come quickly! We have a boat."

Down the lane I rode, with Black Tom trotting beside, hanging to my stirrup leather. There was time for only a glance at the cottage, dark and silent, its small windows like lonely eyes. I figured William was at the hut, some distance away. I felt a twinge at my heart, for the cottage had been my boyhood home, this place and the fens. Inside was the fireplace beside which my father had taught me my lessons. No man ever worked harder for the future of his son, teaching me all he could from what he had seen and learned.

No more . . . my father was gone, buried these several years. A wave of sadness swept over me. I started to turn for another look . . .

"Quick! Barnabas, into the boat! They come!"

It was no common boat, but a scow, and I took my horse quickly across the plank, and we shoved off upon the dark, glistening water. We could hear the hoofbeats of horses.

Looking back, I felt warm tears welling into my eyes. It had been my home, this cottage on the edge of the fen. Here I had grown to manhood, and here my father had died.

And where, in my time, would my body lie?

△ 2 △

We of the fens knew every twist and turn of the water-ways that formed an intricate maze where a stranger might soon become lost. A man might believe the fens, seen from West Keal, utterly flat and without a hiding place. But there were many islets, hidden coves, willow-sheltered channels, and occasional fields.

Over the years the fens had changed much, while seeming not to change at all. Roman efforts to drain them had largely failed, due to changes in the sea level and long periods when no effort had been made to continue the work. Now Elizabeth was considering a new effort at drainage, for once drained the fens became the richest of farmland.

We who lived in the fens had small concept of their actual area, and no doubt felt them larger than they were, for they seemed vast, extending into several shires, although boundaries meant little.

The Romans had come, even, it was said, to the place where we now rent. It was an islet of no more than three acres cut by several narrow, winding waterways. There were few low-growing oaks, gnarled of trunk and thick of branch, but not tall, and some birch trees. Backed against a limestone shoulder was the hut, a place already ancient when my father played there as a child, and how ancient no man knew. Many times had the thatch been renewed, and long ago I had watched my father replace the door. I had come here before first sailing for America, but now, almost a year later, nothing had changed.

Even Black Tom, who knew the fens, had not known of this place. William knew, and I. Black Tom looked around, admiringly. "A tidy place! A man could live here on the eeling alone."

"Aye, but I am for America, Tom, love it though I

15

do. It is a good place, with the cries of the marsh birds and the glow of the last light on the yellow water lilies. Nor shall I forget the sound of oars as a boat moves through the fens, or the way the morning mist lies close above the grass."

"You were born here?"

"In the cottage we just left. My father was a soldier home from the wars, given this land in respect of things done. It was what he wanted, I think, land of his own and a free, honest life. He had lived by the blade and bow in many a land. He taught me much the schools teach, and much that no school could teach, and I honor him for it. He wanted a better life for me, and I shall have it, in America."

Black Tom nodded.

"My father finished his life," I continued, "and made a better foothold for me. And I in my time shall do the same for my sons. Yet it is honor I wish for them, honor and pride of person, not wealth. Nor do I wish for titles, or a place near a Queen or a King, for pride of title or family is an empty thing, like dry leaves that blow in the cold winds of autumn."

"You have a wife?"

"Nay . . . but soon, if all goes well. A bonny lass who will go with me to America." I considered, and smiled. "It is not so much that I wish to take her to that wild land, but that she will not be left behind. She's a lovely lass, and we sail well together. I've a fine ship waiting, a cargo loaded, and she waits upon the wind . . . and me."

"She must be a strong lass, to risk a wild land."

"Aye, and I've thought much upon that, Tom. It is well for men to risk dangers, for we have broad backs to bear the blows, but I marvel at the courage of women who go with us, and must think of bearing children alone, and in a far place.

"I wonder sometimes. Why do I go, Tom, when I have this? If Queen Bess drains the fens I would be a man of wealth, for much of this about us is mine. But I will not stay for it."

"With me it is different, lad. There's the noose at Tyburn waiting for my neck," said Tom.

"Perhaps, Tom. But think you: others like you stay. How many men in Britain today would sail for America? How many do you know that have lurked in the towns, hiding or moving from place to place rather than try a new land? They hide from change. They fear it. We do not."

"What of the savages there?"

"I have known but few, and as their lives need strength, they respect strength. As they must fight with their enemies, they respect a fighter. As a coward is a danger to them, they despise a coward.

"There are honest men among them, and dishonest, even as with us. One must deal fairly, and watch himself against weakness, for they despise that. Give no gift without reason or they will think it an offering from fear, and kill you out of hand.

"In the forest they are masters, craftsmen as sure and true as men can be, and there's much to learn from them. Vast areas of the land seem to be uninhabited, for they are few in proportion to its size. They are a different people, of different backgrounds, and you cannot expect them to react like Christians. They have not heard of turning the other cheek—"

"And well enough they haven't. I never got far with that myself."

We came upon William. He and I had much of which to talk, of plantings and harvests and what to do with the money earned from the produce of my land, little though it was. In all I owned but some small pieces of tillable land, and some from which rushes might be cut —enough for a man's living and a bit over. William was a solid man, and I'd promised him half. When there was sufficient earned, he was to buy another small piece of land.

"And what if you come not back, Barnabas?"

"Leave it in the trust of a good man. For if I come not back, a son of mine surely will."

William and I had known each other from boyhood,

17

although he was the older by some seven years, a strong, resolute man who had land and crops, and worked hard with his hands.

I said to him, "And if the time comes you wish to cross the sea, come to me and I shall find a place for you."

"I am an Englishman, Barnabas. I want no more than England."

Was he wiser than I? My father had lived through wars and troubles, and it left him with a sense that nothing lasted but what a man made of himself. "Be wary," he advised me, "of trusting too much. Men change and times change, but wars and revolutions are always with us.

"Own a bit of ground where you can plant enough to live, and be not far from fuel, for days and nights can be cold. Be friendly with all men and censure none, tell nobody too much of your affairs and remember in all dealings with men, or women, to keep one hand upon the doorlatch . . . in your mind, at least.

"Men distrust strangers, so have a few places where you are known . . . but not too well. Not even a marsh-rat will trust itself to one hole only, so always have an escape route, and more than one, if it can be."

So in the days of my growing up we had used more than one market town, to become somewhat known in each, and we went to church now here, now there. My father did no smuggling as many fen-men did, but we knew the smugglers. We of the fens were a close-mouthed lot, not given to talking to strangers, but with a strong loyalty for one another.

The mysterious swordsman, if such he was, might ask in vain and learn nothing to help, nor would he find me now, for a myriad of watery routes led to many towns and villages in several shires.

With a warm fire going William and I talked much, and at the last he said, "Do not worry about your fields. I shall handle them as I would my own, and will take one-third."

"One-half," I repeated.

He shook his head. "You give too much, Barnabas."

"One-half," I insisted. "I wish you to have the reward of your care, and with what you have and what you can make of mine you can become a man of consequence."

"You go to a far land, Barnabas. Are you not afraid?"

"The forest seems safer than the London streets, William, and there is land for the taking—forests, meadows, and lakes. And there is game."

"Poaching?"

I smiled. "There are no lords there to bespeak the deer or the hare, William. There is enough for all. I shall take seed to be planted, William, and tools for working the land and cutting down the forest. I shall build what I need. My hands are cunning with tools, and necessity will add to their skill."

He shook his head, slowly. "No, Barnabas, it is for you to do this. I have not the courage to risk all upon a chance. My own land is here. I shall plough my own acres, sleep in my own cot."

"I wonder what it is?" I said. "I wonder what chooses between us, that I go and you stay? Our situations are not too different, one from the other, nor is one less or more the man than the other, it is only that we are different."

He nodded. "I have thought much upon this, Barnabas, and asked of myself the reasons. I do not know. Perhaps it is something in the blood of each of us that you go out upon the sea and I cling to my small holding here.

"You will allow me to say I think it a foolish thing you do? What will you do for drink, Barnabas?"

"I will drink water."

"Water? But water is not fit for men to drink. For the cattle, for birds and beasts, but a man needs ale . . . or wine, if you are a Frenchman."

"The water of the new world is wine to me, William. I ask no more. The water of the streams is cold and clear."

And so we parted, we two who were friends but strangers, we whose paths would diverge, yet cling. As he waved good-bye from the island, I thought there was a little of wistfulness in his face. Perhaps something deep within him longed to follow me to the far lands. But that may have been my own pride in what I was, and where I was going.

The route we took to London must be roundabout. I decided upon Thorney. It was a lovely fenland village, a place I'd loved since boyhood when my father had told me stories of Hereward the Wake, the last man to hold out against William the Conqueror. Thorney had been one of the last places he defended. From here I would ride on to Cambridge, and then London.

So easily made are the plans of men! We poled our clumsy craft down the watery lane, reeds and willows tall about us. The dawn light lay gray-gold with the sun and mist upon the fens, and around us there was no sound or movement but the ripples of water around our hull and the small, intimate sounds of morning birds among the leaves. My horse had no liking for the scow, and the uncertain footing worried him, yet the craft was strong if not swift.

Seated in the stern, I turned my eyes ever and anon toward our wake, but there was no sign of pursuit. Nonetheless, I was uneasy. It disturbed me that I knew not my enemies, for these were no common thief-takers. There was motive here.

Well . . . soon I would be abroad upon the seas, and if they wished they might follow me to Virginia and to those blue mountains that haunted my days and nights with their unfathomable promise and mystery.

Unfathomable? No. For I would go there. I would walk the dark aisles of their forests, drink from their streams, challenge their dangers.

The last shadows wilted away to conceal themselves shyly among the reeds and under the overhanging branches to wait the courage that night would bring them. The sun arose, the fog lifted, sunlight lay gently upon the fens. Some distance off we saw men cutting reeds and grass for thatch, then they were blotted from view by a thick stand of saw-sedge, seven to ten feet tall, but giving the appearance of a simple meadow if looked upon from distance. Passing through it was quite another thing, and I recalled returning from those meadows as a boy with cuts upon arms and legs from their wicked edges.

What memories would my children have? Would they ever know England? They would be far away and in another land, without schools, without books. No. There must be books.

It was born then, this idea that I must have books, not only for our children but for Abigail and myself. We must not lose touch with what we were, with what we had been, nor must we allow the well of our history to dry up, for a child without tradition is a child crippled before the world. Tradition can also be an anchor of stability and a shield to guard one from irresponsibility and hasty decision.

What books then? They must be few, for the luggage of books is no easy thing when they must be carried in canoes, packs, and upon one's back.

Each book must be one worth rereading many times, each a book that has much to say, that can lend meaning to a life, help in decisions, comfort one during moments of loneliness. One needed a chance to listen to the words of other men who had lived their lives, to share with them trials and troubles by day and by night in home or in the markets of cities.

The Bible, of course, for aside from religion there is much to be learned of men and their ways in the Bible. It is also a source of comments made of references and figures of speech. No man could consider himself educated without some knowledge of it.

Plutarch also. My father, a self-educated man, placed much weight upon him. He was, I quote my father, urbane, sophisticated, and intelligent, giving a sense of calmness and consideration to all he wrote. "I think," my father said, "that more great men have read him than perhaps any other book."

"Barnabas?" Black Tom was watching the riverbanks. "Is your boat anchored in London?"

"Aye. And there is a man in London with whom I speak. I shall be gone for a long time, and there are things he must do for me here, business he must handle when I am far from England."

"Do you trust this man?"

"Aye," I said, after a moment of thought, "although he has the name of one gifted at conniving. Yet we have things in common, I think."

"What manner of things?"

"Ideas, Tom. We have shared large ideas together, Peter and I. There is no greater time than for young men to sit together and shape large ideas into rounded, beautiful things. I do not know if our thoughts were great thoughts, but we believed them so. We talked of Plato, of Cathay and Marco Polo, of Roman gods and Greek heroes, of Ulysses and Jason."

"I know nothing of these."

"Nor I, of some of them, but Peter did. And I learned and became curious and someday I shall know more of them. Peter spoke also of a strange man who came once to his booth in St. Paul's Walk to sell some ancient manuscripts, a man who spoke of the wise Adapa and the Hidden Treasure of the Secret Writing. He spoke as if he expected somehow that Peter would respond, but although it disturbed him, Peter knew nothing of Adapa.

"We talked of many things, Peter and I, and it is he who will handle all sales of furs and timber for me when I am gone away. When my ships return to England, he will dispose of their goods and order things for me.

"Also, he has books I must have, and charts of land where we go."

"They are new lands. How can there be charts?"

"A good question, yet those lands may only be new to us because our knowledge is limited. They may have been old lands to those before our time. Although much history remains, much more has been lost. Men have always gone out upon the sea, Tom, and some few of them have made records. And if we do not leave records, who will know where we went or what we did? I shall try to write of these things, Tom."

"I cannot write."

"Nor could others who went abroad upon the world. So much was done, so little recorded. And much was recorded and then lost. Peter has talked to me of men and nations, of deaths and battles of which I never heard.

"Avicenna? Who is he? Somewhere I heard the name, but Peter knew. A great man, a great writer, a man of knowledge in many areas, a very great man, indeed. If such can live and we not know of him, how many others might there be?

"The strange man who came to Peter and then never came again . . . who was he? Where had he found the manuscripts and charts he sold? Who was the one he called the Wise Adapa? Even Peter had never heard of him, nor scholars at Cambridge whom he knew.

"I have myself seen the chart of Andrea Bianco that shows well the coasts of Brazil, and the chart was drawn in 1448, and it is said that Magellan found the straits named for him because he, too, had a chart . . . drawn by whom?"

"This all may be as you suggest," said Tom dryly, "but I worry less about charts of a distant land than a road to London that will keep us free of the Queen's men."

"Worst of all," I said, "I do not know my enemies. Someone stands behind them with a well-filled wallet, or they would not have come so far upon a chance."

We slept in turns, and when I last awakened our scow had brought us in the late afternoon to a point of trees where there was an opening in the reeds lining the shore.

"We will leave the boat here." I stood and stretched, liking the feel of my muscles underneath my shirt. I could feel the ripple of them and sense their power, and before we were once more aboard ship I would have need of them . . . this much I guessed. We glimpsed the steeple of a church, and a ruined tower. Thorney should be near.

"The point," I said to Tom. "We will land there."

Leading my horse ashore, we went along the lane

toward the road that led to the village. No one was in sight. Already shadows were long and dusk was upon us.

The street was almost empty, and only a few heads turned to look as we passed along the cobblestoned street. Outside of the village I mounted, and with Black Tom trotting beside, we made good time for a mile, then changed places.

Willows lined the track we followed to Whittlesey. The market square was empty, shadows everywhere. A few lights showed.

"I've a friend here," Tom said. "We'll knock him up and have a place to sleep the night and a quick start come morning."

Glancing up at the tower of St. Mary's, I knew I'd miss the bells, for we could hear them far across the fens when out for eels or cutting thatch. Many a time I rested from labor to hear them.

We shared work, we of the fens, and I'd worked in many parts of Cambridgeshire or Lincolnshire, travelling along the narrow waterways to meet friends with whom I fished. We of the fens were much less likely to remain close to home than others of our time, who knew little of any place more than a few miles from their homes.

Even now change was upon us. Ours was a restless as well as a violent age. Men from the villages had gone out upon the water with Drake, Hawkins and Frobisher, with Gosnold or Newport, and some of them returned with gold and all with tales.

Tom stopped before an ill-looking cottage on the edge of the village, a cottage set well back in the trees and close to the river.

A rap brought no response, nor did another. Tom was growing irritable when a shadow loomed at the corner of the cottage. A voice growled, "Who comes?"

"Richard, you're a poor host if you do not open your door and trot out the ale. You've two quiet men here who would remain quiet, wanting food and a quick start before the day breaks, and no bothering with keepers of taverns who remember too well. Will you have us in?"

24

"Aye, Tom. I'll have you in, and collect the two shillings you owe from a fortnight past."

He disappeared. After a moment there was the rattling of a chain and the door was opened. Once inside, Richard stirred the fire to a blaze, lighting up our faces.

He was a long thin man with a dour expression. Yet upon a closer glance, when the light caught the side of his face, I saw that the wrinkles of ancient laughter had woven a net of humor around his eyes and mouth.

"There's a horse outside, Richard, that will need rubbing down, and care. You'll see to it?"

"I will . . . when I've put something on." He puttered about, filling two flagons of ale and pushing out a plate of bread and cheese. "There's apples, too," he added, "if you'll be asking no questions how they was come by."

While we ate he went to the stable, and when he returned Tom said, "There might be some asking about, Richard, and we'll be wanting no word of our passing."

"Not likely I'd be talkin', Tom, but I do wish you'd stay on a day. There be a fine piece of bog oak close by that will bring a pretty penny, but I'll need a strong hand or two."

Such a find was not uncommon, and was like the finding of a treasure trove to a poor man. Sunken ages ago by a falling of the land or rising of the sea, many great trees had been buried in the peat, and perfectly preserved by it, and if sawed immediately into planks and timbers were worth a good bit to the finder. But if let to lie about, the wood decayed, so the work must be done at once and the planks allowed to dry and season in the air.

"Is it true, Tom, what they be sayin' about drainin' the fens?"

"It is. And when drained it will be the richest farmland in the kingdom."

"Aye," Richard grumbled, "but it ruins the eeling, and there'll be not so many birds. We live well enough now, with no drainage done, a goose to the table whenever we wish, eels and pike for the eating or the market, and our patches of crop land no tax gatherer can find. If

25

the fens be drained, strangers will come in. Wild and lawless they say we be, and that we stink of our fens, but we are free men and better it is to remain so.

"Once the gentry ken how rich is the land they'll have it from us by hook or crook, or they'll come on with their laws to interfere with the hunting, the digging of peat, or the cutting of thatch. They'd have us bound out to labor on their farms instead of us living free."

True enough, and well I knew it, for most of the fens were held in common. Once the fens were drained the fine, free life would be gone and the birds and eels with it. We lived well, often better than a lord in his castle, for it was all about us, for the taking.

Yet I was leaving this for a new world, new ways of living. Was I the fool? Was I leaving a certainty for a chance? No matter. My way was chosen. Not for a minute did I consider not going.

Was it some impulse buried deep within me? Was there in my blood and bones some selective device that chose me and a few others like me to venture? To go on? To penetrate the strange and the new? Were we something chosen by nature for this purpose? Had we control over our actions, or were we mere tools of the way of things that must ceaselessly go forward?

William would stay, Richard would stay, even Peter Tallis would stay, yet I would go. My friend Jeremy Ring would go, and Black Tom Watkins. You might say he was fleeing the noose, aye, and how many others here in Britain were likewise fleeing, yet did not go?

"We will sleep now, Richard," I said, "for tomorrow Tom and I must travel far . . . and fast."

△ 3 △

Dark were the London streets, and wet with rain. We walked my horse along the narrow lanes, keeping free of streets where we might be seen and spoken of.

"We will do well to stay clear of taverns," Tom suggested.

"We've a place, Tom, a sure place. It is the house of a sailor's wife, a clean place and the food is good."

"Women gossip."

"Not this one. She's a good lass. The house was left her as an inheritance. She lets rooms and feeds folk who want something better and cleaner than the taverns, and waits for her sailor to come back from the seas."

"A lonely life."

"Aye, but Mag is the girl for it."

Rounding the corner we saw the tall house before us. Dismounting, I tapped on the door.

"Who's there?" It was Mag's voice.

"A friend of Jeremy's, whom you know. I've a horse and a man with me."

"I'll open the gate."

The window slid softly shut and we led my horse around the corner to the gate in the dark lane. The gate swung open. Mag whispered, "I'll get something on. There be hay and grain in the stable."

"She does well, this sailor's wife," Tom suggested.

"She's a good woman." I wanted to put him straight on that. "And there be many such. You know a sailor's life."

"Aye," he said, without bitterness. "I've been left ashore once, near drowned several times; taken by pirates twice and, when I come ashore, robbed by landlubbers. It is better to smuggle than work the deep seas."

Mag held the door for us. "I've drawn some ale. It

27

is on the table, and there'll be some'at to eat in a bit." Her eyes searched my face. "You're all right?"

"There's a Queen's warrant up for me, Mag, but it will be recalled, I am thinking. In the meantime I must sleep, and in the morning would get word to Peter Tallis in St. Paul's Walk."

"I know the man. How is Jeremy?"

"Well enough. I left him aboard ship. We sail for Virginia."

"Ah? It is far, I think. Jack was wishful of sailing there, and he spoke of it often. He knew Captain Newport, and was wishful to sail with him. My Jack is a gunner, and a good one."

We ate, and then we slept, yet scarcely had my eyes opened in the morning than Mag was at the door. "Get dressed," she whispered through the crack. "Peter will be here. There's some'at of which we must speak."

Tom was awake. "Morning is it?"

"Peter will be here later. Mag got word to him, somehow," I said.

Mag sat with us over her own glass. "I sent the lad next door to Peter. He's a bright one and for a tupence he'll run any word for you, and keep both eyes and ears open. He also brings me the news. Lord Essex is at York House awaiting the Queen's pleasure, but the word is that she'll not see him, she's that angry and put out. And there's been fighting down the country and a man named Genester is dead . . . murdered, they say."

"Killed in a fair fight," I replied.

She glanced at me, and Tom, too.

"We went to get a sick man he'd taken away to let die," and they were waiting for us. We were all in it, Jeremy as well, but it was I who killed him, man to man in a duel.

"The old man he'd taken there to die had been a friend to my father, so we went to bring him back for proper care. Genester expected to inherit if the old man died, and Genester intended to let him die. But Genester has friends at court, and I have none."

"They'll throw you into Newgate until there's a trial,"

Tom warned. "And it's a pure hell, filthy and crawling with lice. There's good people in there for debt, and every kind of human vermin you can find mixed in among them."

"I did only what had to be done," I said. "Now I must see Peter and board my ship."

"Won't they be watching it?"

"They will." I looked over at Mag.

She leaned her forearms on the table. "Virginia," she said, "Raleigh's land. Is it so grand a place, then?"

"A broad land, with forest and running streams and meadows the like of which you've never seen. A beautiful land, Mag, a place in which to rear tall sons."

"I have no sons," she said.

"You've time, lass. Get that sailorman of yours and come to America. Raleigh is said to be making up a group to settle there, and if all goes well my ship will be back. Peter will know when it comes, for he's to buy and sell for me. Come, I will find a place for you."

"My father sailed with Hawkins in '67," she said. "He talked much of the new lands, the savages, and the Spanish to the south."

A thought came to me. "Mag, you've others here?"

"One man only now. A fortnight or more he's been here. Paid in advance, he did, and well."

"A seafaring man?"

She lifted a shoulder. "Who knows? Conrad Poltz, he is, and polite enough, but he does not stop to talk. Not after the first day."

"What, then? He asked questions?"

"He claimed knowledge of Jack, that he'd known him. But I do not think he had. He was asking about others here. He rises early and spends the day along the river, watching the ships."

Conrad Poltz. I knew not the man.

My friend Coveney Hasling might know this Conrad Poltz, but Hasling was also known to be my friend and might be watched. It was Hasling who had, in a way, given me my first chance. He was a kindly old man who was interested in antiquities, and wandered about the country buying old things found by diggers of ditches, cutters of peat, and such like. When I found several ancient gold coins, I had taken them to him, and he bought some, and saw to the selling of others.

Tallis might also know this Conrad Poltz.

Peter Tallis was a man of parts, a man of many strange talents. He was a skillful forger, and had been known to prepare documents, alter others, connive in many ways. It was to him I had gone when I wanted a copy of Leland's book on the old places of England. The book was known to exist in manuscript, but no printing had as yet been made, and until I went to America, I'd thought of searching for antiquities to sell.

Little happened in England that Peter Tallis did not know, and his booth in St. Paul's Walk was well situated to hear all that went on, and was the clearing house for information and gossip in all of London.

London was a vast melting pot, changing rapidly from the somewhat provincial city it had been. Ships were coming and going from the new lands, fishing, trading, attacking Spanish vessels. They brought strange wares to the market places of London, and stranger stories. Men who had been prisoners returned with their tales of the Barbary Coast, of the Levant, of the Guinea coasts and the islands of the sun. And it was Elizabeth who pulled the many strings from behind the scenes as well as in the open.

More than one vessel that went out to the Spanish Main was secretly financed by the Queen herself. King Henry VIII, who desperately sought a male heir to carry on his building of the English empire, died not knowing what an heiress he had sired in Elizabeth. From his seat in the Valhalla of dead kings, he must have looked back with amazed pride to see what Anne Boleyn had given him in that small red-haired daughter he had seen but rarely.

My father had often talked to me of kings and men, of governments and battles and the leading of peoples. "A king must think not only of today," he had told me, "but of tomorrow and tomorrow. When a law is passed,

30

he must understand its consequences. Moreover, he must always think of the succession.

"Henry the Eighth saw very clearly all the enemies England had, and that he must have a strong hand to follow him. We are a small island in a stormy sea, and there are many enemies for such. King Henry knew that we must have the strength to stand alone, and as the years passed and he had no heir, he saw all his work coming to nothing.

"He married again and again, but there was no son who lived. Of course, Elizabeth . . . a daughter by Anne . . . he had her, but he had no faith in the ability of a woman to stand against the storms that would assail England. There were women enough for Henry without marrying them. What he wanted was a son, an heir, one who could sit upon the throne of England with wisdom and power. He died not knowing what he had sired in Elizabeth."

Peter Tallis had echoed many of the things my father had said, and we had talked much in those days before my first voyage to America. Now I would see him again.

We went to our room to wait for Peter. As we lay half asleep, a faint stirring came from the room above me, as of someone moving quietly, not wishing to be heard. It was very early still, and at that hour anyone might move quietly, not wishing to awaken those who wished to sleep. Yet I listened and gradually my ears became familiar with the natural creakings and stirrings of the old house, and could easily distinguish those other sounds, however faint they might be.

A door above closed softly, and faint creaks on the stair told of someone descending.

Mag had returned to her room across the hall. Whoever it was came softly along the hall to our door and paused there, listening. I could hear his breathing and was tempted to leap up and jerk open the door, but instead lay very still.

After a moment his footsteps retreated along the hall and I heard the outer door open, then close.

Instantly, I was up. Tom's eyes opened and I explained. "I don't like it," I added. "He may be a spy."

I rose, buckled on my sword, and went across the hall to Mag's room. She opened at my knock.

"Mag, tell Peter to meet us at the Prospect of Whitby. This man Conrad Poltz worries me. We shall be at the Prospect by eleven of the clock, and we will wait one hour. No more. If Peter does not find us there, or cannot come at that hour, let it be at The Grapes. We will stay there. Then we must be off for the ship."

Hurriedly we went to the stable. My horse was gone!

A glance was all that was needed. Turning swiftly, we went out the gate. At a fast walk I led the way to the river.

"If it is a boat you have in mind, he would have thought of that," Tom warned.

"Upriver then, quickly."

By divers lanes and alleyways, we wove between buildings and across barnyards, which were many in London. We came suddenly to the old tavern where I had first met Jeremy Ring.

A man was leading a horse to the water trough and I knew him at once as one of the rowdy crew who had been drinking with Jeremy Ring that night when first we met.

"You'll be remembering me?"

His smile was wry. "If need be, but I can forget as easily."

"Well, then. Remember me long enough to tell me if there's a boat about, and then forget you've seen me."

"I've a boat at the old dock below, but I'd not wish to lose it."

"Do you know The Grapes?"

"Aye."

"You'll find your boat there, when we're done with it, nicely tied. In the meanwhile I'd not have you visit The Grapes without a drop of something. Spend this, or a piece of it." I put a coin in his hand.

"What of Jeremy? We miss him about here."

"We've been about together, and he'll be waiting aboard ship. We've a voyage coming."

"Ah? I have given thought to it myself."

"Give more thought, and if it is to Raleigh's land you come, be asking of me discreetly. There's a new land yonder where there are no lords nor gamekeepers, and the air has the flavor of freedom in it. And there's a wide land all about, fit for a man to move and breathe in."

"The savages?"

"They be few and the land be wide. They plant a little corn and live much by hunting. I think we can live together, for some I have met were good people, although they love the ways of war."

"Here I know what to expect and where to turn."

"Aye, but there's no press-gangs yonder, nor any debtors' prisons."

"Give them time," he said grimly, "and they'll have both."

"It may well be, but I think not. There's a different temper in the minds of those who go over the sea. There will be abuses, for they are only men and not angels, but they will be the better for starting afresh."

Once in the boat we pulled strongly for the Prospect, holding close in shore where we might not quickly be seen. My ship was waiting for me, and I was keen to reach and board her again.

"We must sail for America, Tom, to forge a new land, you and I and others of our like."

"Others of *my* like?"

"Why not, Tom Watkins? Why not, indeed? There are no privileges there, and let us not have them. You are a man, Tom Watkins, and you have lived. You have erred as have we all, but we know what is right and just. The land yonder is fresh, wide open for such as you and me, and if we make again the old mistakes the fault will be ours. If we see clearly we can build something new."

"I am a simple man, Barnabas. I have given no thought to such things. It's for my betters—"

"Betters? Who is better unless he makes himself so? You can be one of those for whom laws are made if

33

you so will it, or you can be a maker of laws yourself."

"I cannot read, Barnabas. I have no learning."

"You have lived, Tom. You have done good things and bad, you have seen others who did likewise. You know what you respect and what you do not, so all that is left is to weigh each law, each idea against what you know, decide how you would like things to be, and then work to make them so."

"The great lords will own the land. There is talk that the Queen will grant them land."

"You have not seen it, Tom. This is no tiny island bounded by the sea, but a vast land stretching westward. If you do not like what they do you may go west, but once you breathe the air in America, you will no longer worry about great lords. England itself will change, but she will change first over there where the land is new."

We bent to the oars then, and there was no time for talking, and truly I had much to think on that had no part of kings or lords or free air or land. I had first to wonder who it was that pursued me and why the Queen's warrant was still out for me. It was easier to swear out a warrant than to recall one sworn, and this might be the very same one caused by Genester, my old enemy. But I had a feeling there was another reason, of what I knew not.

Again the thought of those blue mountains came to me, and as much as I loved England, the lure of them was a challenge, making me forever restless. But had I the right to take Abigail to that far country? Yet had she not lived aboard ship with her father? And she had few ties in England.

I had not the right, yet even as I told myself that, I had to smile at my foolishness, for I had not the choice, either. Abigail had said she would not be left behind. She would be there beside me.

We moved alongside the small dock, tied the boat to an iron ring, and walked up to the Prospect. I entered. Black Tom waited without.

Two men sat within, and one of them was Peter Tallis.

34

The other man was stocky, with a scar on his right cheekbone. He wore a black cloak.

We moved to a table in a corner, and spoke in low tones.

"We have but little time," Tallis said quietly. "If you are found we will both be in Newgate and you on the way to Tyburn."

"Tyburn!" I was startled.

"Genester had friends, and they have stirred the Queen to anger. You have been pictured as a dangerous rebel, a murderer, and a mutineer. They say you attacked your ship's captain, that you stole a ship's boat, that you looted cargo."

"But I was taken forcibly! I was knocked on the head! My own goods were stolen!"

"They will say you were pressed. You will be taken up for murder, for piracy on the high seas and several other charges."

"Cannot the Earl help me?"

"He is an old man, and ill. He is in no condition to do anything. There is one thing he has done, however. He has given you the ship. He has made it over to you, from topm'st to keelson."

"*Given* it to me? I understood it was simply to carry me over the sea, and my goods back."

"It is in your name. She is an old vessel but sound. Captain Tempany is aboard with a full crew, but the ship is watched, although they do not yet know you own her. But they will have you, no matter how."

"I don't understand. With Genester dead, I thought—"

"You sold some gold coins to Coveney Hasling?"

"I did."

"You found them, you said, on the dyke near Reach?"

"What has that to do with it?"

"Barnabas, you are in more trouble than you know, and I see no way out for you. Those coins you found were gold, and Roman. It so happens some such coins were in the royal treasure, along with the Crown jewels when King John lost them in the Wash."

"But—"

"It is believed by the Queen, and undoubtedly by some more loyal to themselves than Her Majesty, that you have found the Crown jewels."

"*What?*"

My voice raised somewhat, and the other man in the common room turned to look at us.

"Why, this is foolishness! The jewels were lost in the Wash!"

There was irony in Peter's tone as well as his glance. "And who comes from the fens near the Wash? You do. Who suddenly appears with gold coins? You do."

Every Englishman knew the story, but we of the fens had cause to know it best, perhaps, because it happened right at our door.

King John's forces were moving up from Weisbeck to a crossing of the Willestrem. In the train of supply wagons that followed were the Crown jewels, all the royal regalia, along with many ancient possessions of England, valued as greatly as the jewels themselves. Much gold and silver plate, gems beyond number, gold coins stamped with the symbols of many royalties and kingdoms, and also the sword of Tristan.

All he possessed was there, and King John moved forward toward their stop for the night, which was to be at Swineshead. The King was in pain from the gout, impatient to be at ease and off his horse, and the Willestrem was a simple enough stream that seemed to offer no danger.

If they considered the tides of the sea at all, they did not understand how fierce they might become where the rushing force of the sea suddenly narrowed at the river's mouth.

What happened was sudden. The supply train was in the water, fording the river, when the full rush of the tide swept in. In an instant they were engulfed, and in another they were gone—only here and there a man or horse fighting the rush of water, a few splashing ashore.

In an instant the accumulated treasure of the Crown of England was gone, swept away by the tide. Buried in mud, perhaps, or floated into the deeper waters of the Wash, only to sink into the mud at the bottom.

The blow was a bitter one. Within hours, King John himself was dead, poisoned some said, but more likely dead as a result of the cold and wet, combined with gorging himself on the good food at Swineshead.

The treasure had never been found.

And now, because of a few gold coins happened upon when washed from the mud of the dyke, I was accused.

"That is nonsense," I said. "The coins were obviously lost by some traveler, or dropped by some looter after a battle. I found them in the mud, washed out by a heavy rain. They had been in a leather bag."

"I believe you, but there are those who do not."

My thoughts raced ahead. Even to one as relatively inexperienced as I, it was plain to see what would happen. I should be imprisoned and questioned, perhaps tortured. There was nothing for me to tell, so the torture might continue for a long time, and surely imprisonment would follow.

How could I convince them that I had found nothing beyond the coins I had sold?

I was suddenly sick and empty. There had been other coins, too. Following upon my little success with my first find, I had obtained the Leland manuscript and set out to investigate another place I recalled from my travels. There, too, I had been fortunate.

"Believe me, Peter, I know nothing. Only that I must escape, and now. If I do not, I see no way to avoid prison."

My voice lowered. "Peter, I cannot longer wait." In my mind came something my father had told me. It was a chance. "Peter, go to Tempany. Tell him to sail at once."

"And you?"

"Tell him to watch for a boat from off the Bill of Portland."

"All ports will be watched, you may be sure of it."

"Tell him to sail, but to take his time when passing the Bill and to keep a sharp lookout. I have a thought of what I can do."

Turning my head to look, I suddenly noticed that the other man was gone!

Instantly, I was on my feet. "Peter, I shall send you goods. You market them and buy for me. You'll do this?"

"As we planned. Of course."

In an instant, I was out of the door, and in two strides across the narrow stone wharf. Peter followed me. Black Tom took one look at my face and unloosed the mooring.

From in front of the Prospect, we heard a rush of feet and a rumble of voices. Peter stepped quickly into the boat with us. "I do not think they know me," he said, "and if I can get away—"

We shoved off, but not out into the stream. Hugging the shore where we would not be immediately visible, we eased away from the Prospect—first under some looming houses beside the Thames, then under the reeds that grew along the bank. We were strong men, Tom and I, and we bent to our oars with a will. Behind us we heard curses and shouts, but looking back we could see nothing but the green of the bank, those lovely banks of the Thames that I might never see again.

"Where are you for?" Peter asked.

"The Grapes. I promised to leave the boat there."

"Good! In Limehouse I have friends."

"Can we trust them?"

Peter chuckled. "With everything but your money or your wife. Rob you, they might. Betray you, never!"

It was an old building, patched up and vine-grown, with willows, and in back of these, elms. We left the boat at The Grapes, and went down a lane from the river.

Peter's friends were a motley lot, as pretty a bunch of rogues as it had ever been my fortune to see—and better seen by daylight than after dark.

"Horses? Of a surety! Anything for you, Peter! We have excellent horses, and if you'd not be seen, we have covered lanes leading in all directions."

He leaned toward me, an evil-looking man with a hatchet face and a bad scar pulling down one eyebrow. His breath was foul, but his manner genial enough. I noted a dagger in his waistband. "You might," he said, "leave some'at on the table for the poor o' Limehouse . . . the poor being me." He spread wide his mouth in what I took for a grin and looked at me slyly from under his brows. "You be one o' Peter's friends, be ye? Peter it is who knows the gents. Peter's a smart one, a shrewd one, knows a thing or two, he does. He's had me out of Newgate twice, lad . . . twice! I owe him for that, and a thing or two else."

The horses were brought around, two fine geldings, and a mare for Peter, who would be riding into the heart of London. We parted, leaving a silver crown.

We rode north, following devious country lanes. We saw few people, herdsmen who waved at us as we passed, and once a girl milking a cow, from whom we begged a draught of the fresh warm milk.

At nightfall we came upon a small tavern, and rode into the yard. A swarthy, hard-faced man faced us inside the gate. He looked from one to the other of us, and liked not what he saw.

"It be a lonely road for travelers," he said.

"Aye, but a pleasant way to see the land," I replied. I think it was of shillings and pence that he thought, and little else beside.

"It's a bed we want, and a bit of something to eat," I said. "And we've enough to pay."

"Aye. Get down then. The woman's inside."

"The horses will be wanting a rubbing down," I said, "and oats."

"If there's a rubbing down, you'll do it yourself," he replied. "As for oats, we've none about."

"Hold up, Tom," I said to Watkins. "We'll go down the road a bit. There's grass a-plenty there, and our horses will fare the better for it."

The tavern keeper saw his pence leaving and it upset him. "Oh, be not so much in a hurry," he protested. "Maybe I can find a bit of grain."

"Find it," I said, "and the rubdown, too. I'll pay for what I get, but I'll get it, too."

He liked me not. There was a hard, even look to his eye, but the thought of a bed was on me, and a warm meal, else we'd have gone down the road to whatever lay ahead.

The door opened under our hand and the common room of the inn. The woman who came out drying her hands on her apron was pleasant-faced.

"A place to sleep," I said, "and something to eat."

She gestured at a table. "Sit. There's a bit of meat, and bread."

The bread was good, freshly baked and tasty. The meat was likewise. Whatever else he did, the man lived well. With such food before him, he'd little reason to growl.

He came into the room, drew a draught of ale, and sat at another table. He'd have a swallow and then he'd stare at us. Finally he said, "Do you come far?"

"Far enough for hunger," I said.

"From London town?"

"London!" I said. "Hah!" Then I added, grimly, "I've no liking for towns. I'm a country man."

That he had no liking for strangers was obvious. I wondered if it was the way here, or whether he had another reason.

He looked at Tom. "You be lookin' like a man from the sea," he ventured.

"Aye," Tom said, "I've been there."

"So have I," he said then. And to our surprise, he continued. "I did m'self well on a voyage with Hawkins, so I left the sea and came here to where I was born. I've the inn," he said, "a few cows and pigs and some land of my own out yonder. It is better than the sea."

He took a draught of ale. "But I liked the sea, liked it well, and Hawkins was a good man. No trouble made him show worry."

A thought suddenly came to me. "Did you know David Ingram?"

He turned and looked at me sharply. "I knew him. Was he by way of bein' a friend to you?"

"I did not know him," I said, "but I'd give a piece to talk to him. He made a walk I'd like to hear about."

He snorted. "It took no trouble to hear him. He talked

of little else. Browne . . . now there was the man. He saw it all, but had little to say."

"From the land of Mexico to Nova Scotia is a far walk," I said. "It was a time to see what no white man had seen before."

He took his ale and moved to our table. Putting it down, he leaned forward. "Ingram was a fool," he said. "He was always a fool, to my mind, though there were those who thought much of him. He was good enough at sea, only he had a loose mouth. Browne was the better man."

He went into another room and came back with a sheet of parchment. "See this? He drew it for me. Drew it the year after he got back. He's gone now, but this he drew with his own fist."

He pointed at a place on what was the coast of the Mexican gulf. "They walked from there along the shore, traveling at night to avoid Indians, much of the time. They crossed a big river here," he put his hand on a spot, "on a raft they built. It landed here. They saw some big mounds . . . walked north by east."

I watched his hand. "*Here.*" He put his finger on a point almost halfway up the river and east of it. "They found some of the finest land under heaven right here. Great bulls . . . shaggy ones . . . wandering about in grass to their knees. Streams flowing down from mountains . . ."

"Mountains?"

"Aye . . . mountains to the east. They found a way through those mountains, but that was much farther north, I think."

The parchment lay on the table before us, and I looked long upon it as we talked. This man Browne had been beyond the blue mountains of which I had heard. He had seen a fair land, and great rivers. I had no need to copy the sheet before me, for it was engraven in my mind.

△ 4 △

We rode westward.

Yet soon we were angling off to the south, into areas I knew not of. Here Black Tom had the advantage of me, for he had traveled to Bristol ere this, and even into Cornwall.

"They're a rum lot," he commented, speaking of the villagers. "Some are fine people, friendly to strangers, but others will have nothing for him, not even a word. You'd think they'd be curious and wanting news, but no such thing. They are content with what is about them.

"It is changing," he continued. "Twenty years ago it was much worse, but with Drake, Hawkins, and all the talk of them, many of the country folk know as much of what goes on as do those in London."

After a bit our course changed, to the south. There was only the small beginning of a plan in my thoughts, something of which my father had told me in one of his odd bits of talk, although nothing he said was ever a careless thing. He had lived too long, close to wars and rebellions, not to expect such things to occur again, and there were times when a man must take shelter. It was with this in mind that he had told me of various places, caves, ruins, coves . . . all manner of spots where a man might go in need of hiding.

When I had told Peter to have the ship pick me up off Portland Bill it was this I had in mind, for there was a cave on the seaward side of the Portland isle of which few men knew, a cove large enough to hide a fair-sized vessel, as it had on one or another occasion.

Even local fishermen knew little of it. Although some were aware of a black opening there, they had better things to do than prowl about against the face of dangerous rocks. If I could get there I could remain out of sight

42

until my ship appeared offshore. Then a quick dash, and with luck we'd be aboard unseen.

Tom talked much as we rode, yet I listened with only half an ear, for I'd a feeling there was a troublous time before us. If it was truly believed we had found King John's royal treasure, the search for us would be wide as England. Riders would have gone out to all the ports and towns, and it behooved us to hold to the back ways, as we had done.

Another night we stopped in a village and bought cheese, bread, and ale. Then we found ourselves a wood-cutters' hut in Pamber forest, built a small fire on the hearth, rolled up on the floor in our coats, and went to sleep.

Suddenly, I heard a faint creak. How long had I slept? In an instant my eyes were open. There was someone at the door. Slowly the door was pushed open, and a head appeared, a head and a hand, then a blade.

A man stepped in. Behind him was another. With my left hand I threw back my blanket and with my right I lifted the pistol from my saddle holster.

I heard Tom stir.

"Come in, gentlemen!" I said. "But please, no quick movements as I've no wish to be cleaning scattered brains from the wall, and my pistol never travels alone. It has a mate."

Tom came to his feet near the wall, a cutlass in his hand.

"If you wish, Barnabas, I'll carve a bit of meat for you," he said.

"Now, now!" The man in the door came a step farther into the hut. "No need to get your backs up."

"Stand fast!" I said quietly. "Tom, throw some fuel on the fire. We'll want to see our guests in a better light."

With his left hand, Tom threw a handful of brush to start the morning fire on the dying coals. When the fire flared up, he added sticks.

The man in the doorway was blond and smiling, al-though his leather jerkin was scarred and torn, his shirt almost gone, and there were bloody stains on both shirt and jerkin. The light in his eyes was cheerful.

"Aye!" he said, "A lucky chance is this! You'll be Barnabas Sackett, and a lot of the devil's trouble you've brought us!"

"Us? Who might you be referring to?"

"Let me get closer to the fire and I'll do some talking. You've naught to fear from us, though we're perhaps the only men in England can say that. What a noise you've raised, my friend! Why, the woods and roads are alive with men, all searching for Barnabas Sackett? What is it you've done, man? Stolen the Crown jewels?"

"Are you followed?" Tom asked. "Speak up, man!"

"No. We gave them the slip, the ruddy beggars. But not by much, and I'd say that before the day is broad you'd best not be about here. They've roused the country to search for you."

He squatted by the fire. "Not four hours agone they came suddenly upon us, rushed in with halberds and blades, even some with forks. We'd a lively set-to there, for a bit, and we lost a lad, but accounted for two or more of them, and some hurt. We drove them off, then we went through the hole in the wall of an old abbey and escaped." He laughed with satisfaction. "They thought us surrounded, snug and tight. Tell us, Barnabas. Are you guilty?"

There was no use lying. "Almost a year back," I explained, "I came upon a rotting leather purse, buried in mud on the Devil's Dyke, nigh on to Reach. There were some gold coins inside. I sold them."

The blond man stared at me, his eyes twinkling a bit. "And they think you've found the royal treasure! Have you?" He searched my eyes.

"The gold coins was all, and I think them lost by other means at another time," I replied. "But they'll have me hidden deep in a dungeon at Newgate, trying to torture it out of me, and I have other plans."

He held out his hand to me. "Pimmerton Burke is the name. Pim to my friends, and you'll be among them, I hope. I am afraid I cannot vouch for all the scruples of

44

my companion here, but he's a likely lad in a bit of trouble. Sam Cobbett's his name yon. He took a wicked blow on his pate with a club, and he's been addled ever since."

"Addled? Who says I'm addled?" Cobbett grumbled. "I'm not so addled as you, Pim, but I'll confess the head aches something fierce."

Outside, the wind was picking up. Wind blew down the chimney and guttered the fire. We added fuel and huddled closer. These were landless men and probably thieves, wanted, maybe, by the law. Or, worse still, wanted by no one.

Pim looked a good man, but I wanted to test him.

"You know the country about here?" I asked.

"I know it." He drew in the dust of the floor. "See? There's an old place, some earthworks . . . ditches and a rampart. It is a mile or so, perhaps two miles this side of the village."

"I think," I said abruptly, "that we'll go west." I got up. "And we'll go now."

"Now?" Pim was reluctant.

"Now," I said.

Sam Cobbett looked up at us. "Leave a place like this? It's blowing out, and there's rain a'coming. You go if you like. I'm snugged in here, and here I'll stay."

Pim shrugged. "I'll go along."

Outside, we saddled quickly. Pim led off, but when we were scarce a half mile out, I stopped him. "Now for your earthworks," I said.

He stared at me, then laughed. "You don't trust easily," he said.

"I don't," I said.

"Well, now. There's a man," he said, and led off into the driving rain, our cloaks billowing about us, the track slippery beneath.

We came to the earthworks, low green mounds and trees covering several acres. With Pim and Tom I went to the top of the wall, just our heads rising above it. Pim pointed a way that led down lanes among trees, a way that would keep us free of people unless there was a chance meeting on the road.

"It would help," he said, "if I knew exactly where you were going."

It was then I took a risk. This man could help me with his knowledge of the people and the area, knowledge I did not possess. "I am for the New World," I said. "I love England, but my destiny lies yonder . . . over the seas. Come with me, Pim."

"I have thought of it," he agreed. "It is a temptation when all else is gone. I have only strength and ingenuity, and neither trade nor land."

"It is a far land," I said, "and a dangerous one."

"I'd venture it," he said, "though a simpler land would be more to my wishing."

He pointed. "A track lies yonder. The road is traveled by few, and will take us well on our way."

He looked at me. "Is it Bristol, then?"

"A likely place," I agreed, "with ships for any land, but mostly for ships to the west."

We mounted once more. It was a weary time, for neither Tom nor I had slept but the least bit, and our eyelids drooped. Pim Burke led the way, pausing from time to time as he approached a turn in the lane to look before him.

It was scarcely light when we came up to the door of an inn, in Odiham, a fine-looking timbered building scarcely fifty years old, and Tom led our horses around to the stable while Pim Burke opened the door and led the way inside.

A stout, red-faced man was kindling a fire. He turned to look. "Ah? Is it you again? You are a rascal, Pim. Will the Queen's men never take you?"

"I hope not," Pim said cheerfully, "although Newgate might be better than some places my head has lain this past fortnight. Can you have something put on for us, Henry? My friends and I have a hunger two days old . . . or so it feels."

"Sit yon." Henry pointed toward a table in a corner

near another door. " 'Friends,' did you say? Are there more?"

"One more. He stables the horses now."

"We will pay," I said.

"Ah? Did you hear that, Pim? Did you listen well? Such words are music to an innkeeper's ears. You would think we held open house here, the way you come by to eat whenever you're near."

"It may be the last time, Henry. I am for Raleigh's land, across the sea."

Henry turned and looked. "Well. I shall be sorry to see the last of you, Pim, but you're a good man, too good to be strung up at Tyburn, and that's where you'll end if you stay on here."

Henry went to the kitchen and emerged with a large meat pie which he served with a quick stroke of his cleaver. "It is cold," he said, "but good. There's some lentils, too, and a bit of pudding. You have the look of travel behind you, and you'd best eat whilst you can."

He put his hands on his hips. "I'd be about it quick, too, if I were you, for there's two or three of the locals who come in, and they're curious."

He turned away. "I've ale or beer, but if you want it there's milk and buttermilk. We be country folk here, and there's milk in plenty."

"Milk," I said, "by all means. There's always beer."

He looked at Pim. "Get your man in here. I'd like you to be off before the locals come."

When Pim disappeared through the door to the stable, the innkeeper walked back and planted his big fists on the table, one of them still clutching the cleaver.

"He's a good man, Pim," he told me. "I've known him twenty year. Strong . . . a fierce fighter at the fairs and such like, always in trouble but nothing bad. There's not an evil bone in him. He's my wife's brother, and I love him like he was my own, but I fear for him. Is it you he'd be going with to America?"

"Likely," I said. "I've a ship coming."

He looked at me again, for after a few rough nights of

47

travel in rain and wind I looked like no man who would have a ship.

"As you see," I said quietly, "all has not gone well. Pim is not the only one with troubles, but the ship awaits and I've been over the sea before."

"You're not from about here. Your voice has a twang to it."

"I'd say the same of yours."

He did not speak his doubt but I could see it plain enough. It mattered little. He was not anxious to know, nor I to tell.

We ate then, and we ate well. When scarcely an hour had passed, we were gone.

We rode on, avoiding traveled roads, avoiding inns. At last we rode into a lovely village in a hollow of the downs, a place called Rockbourne.

There we took rooms for the night. We brushed and cleaned our clothes.

Pim sat on the floor near the window, watching me. "Something worries you, Barnabas."

"Aye."

"Do you know a place called Durdle Door?"

"Aye."

"At daylight then."

We had come far, but not fast, for we had skirted around villages and towns instead of riding through.

Where would our ship be? Had it been seized by Her Majesty? That well might be.

I walked to the window and looked down onto the cobbled street.

"Tom?" I said.

Something in my tone drew him, and he stepped near, looking onto the street where I looked.

A man in cloak and boots stood across the street. A stocky man, well set-up. And as I looked down, he looked up, and we saw each other plain. He lifted a hand to me, and started across the cobbled street toward the door.

I had seen him before!

△ 5 △

It needed no guessing to know this was indeed the man. The air of assurance, the stride in his walk—all carried an air of purpose.

"What will we do?" Tom asked.

"If he wishes to talk, then talk I will."

"Be careful," Tom advised.

"We shall want a small boat," I said to Pim, "a boat with a sail and with some speed."

Pim looked up at me, his feet against the wall. "To go where?"

"To sea, perhaps," I said. "If we must, we will buy it. If you find what we need, return here, but keep a sharp eye out, for there may be trouble brewing."

I went downstairs.

The man waited in the common room with two flagons of ale, one left standing on the table for me. My flagon, if I sat where it was, left my back to the door.

Taking up the flagon I moved it to where I could sit and see the door.

He smiled, with genuine appreciation. "Good! I like a cautious man." He leaned forward. "Now Barnabas Sackett, let us talk."

"Talk, then. I shall enjoy the ale, the quiet of this room, and the view of the river yonder."

"You are in a delicate position, Barnabas."

He proceeded to present the Queen's case against me. I listened patiently, hearing him out. I was wondering what he wanted. When he had finished, I told him of the leather bag, and the contents therein.

The man smiled. "And the other coins?"

"What others?"

He smiled, but he was not amused. "Do not take me for a fool! I took you for a shrewd young man, but yours is the story of a fool."

49

"Nevertheless, a true one."

"No more of this!" He slapped a hand upon the table. "You have found the treasure. The Queen wants it. England owns it." He paused. "Others want it, too. If you are caught, the Queen will have it from you, have no doubt of that. You will get Newgate or Tyburn for your trouble."

"And—?"

"There are others. Such a treasure could give a man wealth, and such wealth is power. If you deal with those others, you could get something . . . enough to make you rich. Also, you could be given a chance in some other country."

"Who are you?" I asked suddenly.

He paused only a moment, then looked up at me, for his eyes had been on the backs of his hands. "I am Robert Malmayne."

I knew the name.

For a moment all was cold within me, for he was a man known, yet unknown, a man of secret power, a man who moved in the shadows of men close to the Queen, yet it was whispered that he was a Jesuit. It was also whispered he was a secret agent of the Queen herself, that he was the right hand of the Pope. Such stories were common, a fabric of gossip and lies and rumor. Yet one fact remained. He had power.

"You will deliver the treasure to me," he said, his voice as cold as ice. "And you will have a share. Otherwise, I shall destroy you—like that!" He snapped his fingers. "You think you have a ship, but my men are aboard her, and in command. We know you were to join her in Falmouth, so undoubtedly the treasure is there, waiting."

Falmouth? I had said nothing of Falmouth, nor had it entered my plans. My intent was to join her across the bay from where we now were, off Portland Bill.

Somebody aboard, Tempany, perhaps, or Jeremy Ring —possibly even Abigail—had let Malmayne's men believe Falmouth was the place, and an obvious one it was, too.

Abigail, perhaps, but why? She believed I could do

50

anything, never reckoning with impossibilities or the limits of strength.

But what could we do against Malmayne's men? I knew neither how many there were, nor how armed or how cunning.

"One thing you can be sure of, Malmayne. The treasure is not in Falmouth now."

Well, that was honest enough. So far as I knew, it was still at the bottom of the Wash, no doubt beyond the reach of men. Certainly, I did not lie.

"Why should I believe you," Malmayne persisted.

Let Malmayne believe what he wished. What I needed was a chance to escape.

I stood up. "Malmayne," I said, "let it be Falmouth then. You say you have my ship. You say I have the treasure. A little of something is better than nothing at all, so let it be Falmouth."

"Where is the treasure?"

I smiled contemptuously, and hoped I did it well. "Do you think I will tell you that? And then be dropped off a cliff with my throat slit? Falmouth it is, or nowhere, and you or your men come about me and all will be thrown to the winds."

He did not like it. Or me.

He stared at me, drumming his fingers on the table. "Betray me," he said at last, "and you will die . . . when I choose to let you die."

I took up my flagon, finished my ale, and went back upstairs.

He was looking after me, smiling.

Closing the door of my room behind me, I called for Black Tom and Pim. They had disappeared.

I thought swiftly.

What must be done must be done quickly. I looked out the window, searching for some sight of Tom or Pim. There were many people about, fishermen, sailors, tradesmen, but I saw nothing of Tom and Pim.

I was turning from the window when suddenly my attention was caught by a girl tugging a two-wheeled cart, piled with bags which looked like laundry. She had stopped around the corner from the street and close under my window, and she was punching the bags into some kind of shape. As I looked down, she suddenly looked up.

"Jump," she said, just loud enough for me to hear.

Clutching my scabbard, I stepped to the sill, glanced left and right, then jumped. I landed easily, rolled over, and was immediately covered by a bag of laundry.

"Lie quiet now, or you'll cost me a crown."

Taking up the shafts of the cart, she began to tug it along the street, walking easily along, then turning.

I smelled the river.

She lifted one sack and looked down at me. "Ah, but you're a handsome lad! Glad it is I've saved you, although I wish you could stay about a bit. There's a boat casting loose. It has one brown sail and is called *The Scamp*. You'd best get aboard and go below. No need to thank me, your friend Pim did that. What a lad he is, to be sure! And a crown with it. Well, a girl can't have every day like this or she'd get no washing done at all!"

She lifted the sack. I swiftly rolled over the edge of the cart and to my feet. The boat was there. In a few quick strides I was aboard.

I saw Pim forward, and saw him cast off, heard the complaint of a block as a sail was hoisted.

Below my eyes grew accustomed to darkness and I saw Black Tom. All three of us were safe—at least for the moment.

Black Tom Watkins looked at me, then mopped his brow. "Cold, I was! Cold, with the fear of death in me. Thank God, you came. Was it the lass?"

"Aye." I told them of Robert Malmayne. "It is nip and tuck for all concerned now, since Robert Malmayne thinks I have the royal treasure."

"You mean there's trouble still?"

"It's only begun, Tom. Malmayne and his men will try to follow. But we've a ship to take, an ocean to sail, and a new land to make our own!"

"You've an appetite," he said grimly. "I hope your teeth are big enough!"

"They'll be," I said, and felt the bow dip and the spray splatter my face, run down my cheeks.

I touched my tongue to my lips.

We were at sea again.

Δ 6 Δ

The waters of Lulworth Cove were quiet. Only a few fishing boats were about. Looking back toward the shore, I saw no unusual activity, no evidence that what had happened aboard had attracted attention.

Pim saw me looking at the hills and gestured at one. "There's a stone forest yon. Trees, or something very like them, buried long ago and turned to stone."

We slid easily through the opening and into the longer swells of the sea. This was a wide bay, and yon lay the Bill of Portland.

The Durdle Door was out of sight now, and only the high cliffs were visible. The sea was picking up. I glanced at the sky.

Tom Watkins nodded grimly. "Aye, she's coming on to blow, Barnabas, and a bad thing it will be for us. An ill wind, to be sure."

I took the tiller from him and he went forward with Pim.

The salt taste on my lips was good, and I liked the wind on my face. The place toward which we went would be no easy place to find, and a dangerous one with cliffs and rocks close aboard. Yet it had to be.

How long our wait would be I could not know, but we must wait, and watch, and hope that the ship would not pass us by in the night and storm. Chesil Beach lay off to the west of us, a curving, shelving beach of gravel and sand, of pebbles rolled up by the sea; and no more dangerous stretch lay along the coasts of England than that innocent-seeming shore.

Good ships had been lost there, and not a few of them either. Good ships, and good men aboard them, their bodies washed up and left by the sea. After every storm a man could find old coins, old timbers, all manner of odds and ends back to the time before the Romans. Who knew what lay under that water? What yet undiscovered treasure?

Again I looked toward the shore, misted over now with the thickening air. That was England, the land of my birth, my home. Even now I was a wanted man there, but that was circumstance and no fault of the land nor the people. I was sailing away, but I would love her always, and wherever I went a bit of her would be with me.

To disbelieve is easy; to scoff is simple; to have faith is harder. Yet I had faith in the intentions of my countrymen, no matter how far they might at times stray from those intentions.

At last we moved in toward the Bill, rounded in, and among scattered rocks we found our way, and then a dark opening, darker now. Carefully, I eased the tiller, and the boat slid through the portals into a vast cavern, literally a cathedral of stone. From far above came a faint glimmer of light. There were holes, I had heard, from sheep pastures atop Portland Island that looked into the cavern, and the holes had been ringed with rocks to prevent unwary sheep from falling through.

Pim Burke looked around, awe-struck. "How did you know of this place?" Staring around, he asked, "Is there another way out?"

"Nobody knows," I told him. "Two passages lead off from here. One winds back for a ways, to a gravel beach at the end. My father was there once, and found a Roman sword laying. He left it lay."

Outside, rain began to fall. Our boat rocked quietly upon the water, feeling only the gentle swell, an afterthought of the waves outside. Even the sea sounds were muted here in this vast, domed cavern, and we heard only the lap of water, the murmur of our own voices. Yet we could see from the cavern mouth, and could watch for ships.

Would she come? Had they received my message? Were they free to come, or had they been taken and imprisoned, too?

A slow hour passed, and I knew it was but the beginning, for we might wait many hours, even days.

Slowly the hours drew by. We took turns sleeping, yet kept a watch from the cavern mouth where we could not be seen. Visibility was poor, and we would not have much time.

Waves broke against the rocks, snarled and sucked their teeth against the black rocks. While the others slept I watched and held my sword and thought of what lay before me.

I dozed, awakened, dozed again, yet was awake again at last to watch the sea darken. Dipping both oars into the water I rowed the boat through the wide entrance into open water. Waves broke furiously over sharp-toothed rocks nearby. One huge pinnacle, already worn and ravaged by the sea, stood a grim and silent sentinel against the wind.

Black Tom sat up, then moved to shake out the sail. He glanced at me and grinned. "God ha' pity on the poor sailors on such a night as this!"

Pim Burke sat up. "They'll see us from the cliffs yon," he warned.

"Aye, if they're out and standing in the rain, they'll see us, but he would be a fool indeed who had a warm fire on his hearth to be standing on the black cliffs looking upon the sea. A fool or a poet, I'm thinking!"

"Or a wife with a husband still out," Pim Burke added. "My ma has watched from such a cliff, and many a time, for sons and husband . . . and watched in vain, more times than not."

"England's given enough of her blood to the sea," Tom Watkins said, "time and again. Since men first walked her shores, they have gone down to the sea and left their hearts there, and their bones on the bottom."

Talking had become hard with the wind upon us, and

blown spray and spume in the air, so we desisted from speech and I clung to the tiller, meeting the heavy seas as well I could. She was a good craft that and, bad as the seas now were, no doubt the boat had known worse. Yet as our bows were splattered with foam, I could not think of the dead men's skulls below, and wonder if we three might add ours to the lot.

All the night long we fought the sea, and there was no sail against the sky, not even a bare pole. So with dawn we put about and ran in for the cove, and it was a bitter thing we did to make that cavern mouth at all, but make it we did, riding the crest of a big one that took us safely over the last rocks and left us there, just inside the mouth.

No longer was the water calm within the cavern, for the storm outside brought great, rolling seas within, swells black and shining that rose until we feared our mast would shatter against the roof. But of course it was not so high at all, just in our fears.

It was no good place to be, even so. Yet such is man that soon we became used to our lot. I broke out some biscuit and passed it about, and as we lay there upon the rise and fall of the swells and the booming of the sea within, we chewed our biscuit and wished for an end to the storm.

At last the wind changed, the swells became less, and once more we could see out across the stormy sea. The wind howled like all the banshees in Ireland, but no ship showed herself upon the sea. The long day through we watched, and when the night came weariness lay heavy upon us, and occasionally through the broken clouds the moon shone down.

Next day, again we fought the sea and schooled our boat to take the waves, and a gallant craft she was. And then, with the dawn breaking clear, we saw her bare poles black against the rising sun, rolled and tossed and smashed about, and I knew her for what she was, the ship we were waiting for.

"There'll be a line overside," I said.

They watched as we drew nearer and nearer, our two courses becoming one. She was down to just enough canvas to hold her nose into the wind, and I glimpsed at least two men on the deck as we closed in.

"It's her or Newgate," I said. "And if we miss, at least we'll lie clean upon the sea's bottom."

"Aye!" Pim balanced to the roll and rubbed his palms down his shirt to dry them for a clean grip. "Take us to her, man."

The ship came alongside as our courses became one, and a line was tossed to us. We took it sharply and bent it quickly to make fast; and then a ladder was over and I glimpsed the face of Sakim—my friend the Moor.

We made fast the painter that would tow the boat after we were aboard, and Pim took the ladder by its side and went up like a monkey and over the rail.

"Tom?" I knew he could not hear in the wind and the creaking and groaning, but my gesture spoke.

He looked with no favor on the swinging ladder but it was no new thing to a man who had boarded many a smuggling craft, so he grabbed the ladder, slipped badly, then went up.

I held the end of the line I must pull to release her so she'd fall astern on the painter. For an instant I held it, then tugged and grabbed for the rope ladder. One foot missed, the other toe landed fair, and up the ladder I went, banging a finger badly against the hull, and over.

When our boat fell back to the painter's end I thought it might snap, but the line held and she towed there behind us, a gallant craft, handsome, sturdy, and sure. I blessed her in my mind for a good little ship, and turned to the deck with my hand on my sword.

"You've no need to worry." It was one-eyed Jeremy Ring at my side. "We got rid of Malmayne's gang in London. And you can thank your lady for it."

"Abigail?"

"Aye! She smuggled them rum from the ship's locker and we lugged them all ashore."

He showed me to the after-cabin. I opened it to the light, and stepped in.

She was standing there, her hands out to me, and her lips bright with a smile, her father behind her.

With me they were at last, England on our beam, and America yonder across the sea, and a fit lot of men with me to start a new land. If they lived. And if I did.

We went into the cabin and Captain Tempany got to his feet from behind the table where he had spread his charts. "Lad, lad! It is good to see you! We were afraid, especially when they came aboard in London, and we knew them for Malmayne's men."

"Are we safe?"

He looked up from under thick brows. "Have you forgotten the Queen? There'll be ships out for us when they know you've escaped."

I had thought myself secure once aboard ship. Now my confidence was gone. But the boat was fully crewed, with my old friends Sakim, Jublain, and Jeremy Ring. There was also a crew of good craftsmen, to homestead the new American world.

The ship was also heavily laden with munitions.

Abigail was quiet, obviously worried. "Barnabas, if they should ever take you to prison I do not know what I should do!"

"Go on as you have and leave the matter to Jeremy and to Tom Watkins."

"What could they do?"

"Men have escaped from Newgate, and I think escape would be my only chance. You see, nobody will believe the truth about the coins. It seems too much luck for one man to have. Tell me, is my chest aboard? With the charts?"

"Yes. There are some other charts and some papers that Peter Tallis brought, too. They say he is dishonest, Barnabas, but I like him."

"And so do I. Abigail, if anything should happen, you go on with your father to Raleigh's land, and wait for me. I shall come."

"Nothing will happen."

She said it, but she did not fully believe it. Nor did I. I would not feel entirely safe until we set foot on American land.

"My place is with you, Barnabas. Do you think it is only men who wish to see new land? I, too, want to see those shores again. I, too, want to see what is beyond them."

I was silent, for I knew what she said was true, and I did not want to persuade her otherwise. In that I was selfish. I wanted her with me always.

"It's no land for a gentle, lovely woman," I protested feebly.

She looked at me, laughing. "Barnabas, when I was not yet fourteen and off the coast of India, I used a pistol repelling boarders off my father's ship."

Later I spoke of my worries again to Captain Tempany.

"All we can do is what we can," I began, "and when we have done that it rests with God. I do not want you to risk a shelling of this boat by refusing a command to lay-to. If they take me, go on about your business. I'll find a way to come to America."

He shook his head. "Lad, lad! You do not know what you risk! I visited a friend in Newgate for debt. A foul and ugly place it is, and every privilege you get you pay for."

Then we talked long of trade, of Indians and goods, of the buying and selling, for we had much planned.

"It is the new lands for you, my boy," said Captain Tempany, "and for my daughter, too, I hope."

Suddenly there was a dull boom. For a moment my heart seemed to stop.

"We had better go on deck," Tempany said. "I fear for you, lad."

We opened the door and stepped out on the deck, and at once we could see her, not two miles off, clearly visible ahead, a Queen's ship and a big one, holding a course that would take her across our bows.

Jeremy Ring came toward us. "She fired a warning gun, Cap'n, shall we heave-to?"

"We must, I fear."

Abigail came quickly to my side and took my hand. Her cheeks were pale, as mine must have been. We stood there, shoulder to shoulder, seeing the ship come down upon us.

"Forty-two guns," Ring said grimly. "We couldn't fight her, Cap'n."

"I'll fight no Queen's ship," he said.

A boat was already bobbing upon the waves, and Sakim stood amidships with a ladder. It seemed only a moment until the emissary was aboard. For such he was, I knew.

"I have orders to search you," he said. He was a handsome young man, obviously impressed by Abigail. "I hope I shall offer no inconvenience, but I must seize the man Barnabas Sackett, if he be aboard."

"I am aboard, Lieutenant," I said quietly, "and there is no need for a search."

"I must search," he said. "It is said there is treasure aboard."

He was thorough, I grant him that, and he gave us such a search as few ships have been subjected to, but he found no royal treasure.

At last I stood by the ladder. "Abby," I said, "Abby, I—"

"Go," she said, "but come to America when you can. I shall be waiting."

They stood about, Brian Tempany, Jeremy, Tom Watkins, Jublain, Pim, Sakim, and the others.

I looked around at their faces, spoke my thanks to them, and then went over the rail and down to the boat.

From the deck of the Queen's ship, I watched the other one sail away, her canvas drawing well.

"She's a fine craft," the lieutenant said, beside me.

"The best," I said, choking from the sadness in me. "They are good folk, loyal and strong."

"Come!" he took my arm. "You must go below. I regret the necessity but you must be held in irons for the Queen's officers."

"Wait," I pleaded, "let me see her out of sight."

He took his hand from my arm and left. And so I stood, alone upon the deck of the ship that would take me to prison, watching all that I loved sail away into the misty distance of a wind-blown sea.

Soon there was no topm'st to be seen, only the gray line where sea and sky met, and an emptiness in my heart.

They took me below then, and they clamped irons upon my wrists and ankles. They chained me to a bulkhead, and they left me there.

I was fed a little. I was given water. And I was visited by no one.

△ 7 △

Of Newgate prison I'd heard a great deal of talk, but it in no way prepared me for what it was. To a free man living in the fens, with fresh air to breathe and going about when he chose, where he chose, it was a frightful thing to be confined, and worse to be confined amid filth and the filthy.

No sooner was I brought into the prison than I was loaded with irons, shoved about, and abused. Then the prisoners came to me with demands for garnish, which I provided, having hidden money about me.

One lingered. He was a bold-faced rascal, a thief, he added, and occasionally a highwayman.

"You can have the irons off," he told me, "for a bit of something to the jailer, and for a bit more you can live well, but never let them think there's an end to what you have, for then you will be thrown into the worst hole they have and left to rot. There's no bit of human feeling in them. Many a man has died here."

His name was Hyatt. I found myself liking the man. I was in sore need of somebody with a knowing way about Newgate.

"It is Croppie you must see," he advised with a knowing wink. "Henry Croppie is the one, and he's a brute, mate, a bloody brute who'd kill you with his bare hands."

"I also have two hands," I said.

"Aye, but there's a sinister power in his, and delighted he is to put it to use on some poor soul. If he kills you it is no loss to him, but if you kill him it's Tyburn or Execution Dock."

A wicked gleam lit up his face. "It is said you know where there's treasure . . . gold, mayhap, and gems. Is it true then?"

Now a man who has nothing is of no use to anyone, but if there is a chance of gain even the best of men are sometimes swayed, so I merely shrugged. "Let them believe what they want," I said. "I admit nothing, deny nothing."

With a bit of coin placed in the proper hand I had my irons removed, was changed to better quarters, and found choicer food available. It was not in my mind, however, to remain long where I was.

The questioning would begin. "It is like so," Hyatt said. "They will speak gently at first, try to get what they want without effort, and if they do not get it, they will bear down."

For a week I went about the prison, my nostrils repelled by the vile stench, yet taking in all that went on, and all who were about, for help may come from strange quarters and I was in no position to hold back from the roughest hand.

Men and women mixed together, some children ran about, all in the filthiest rags, faces and hands dirty, with the worst of criminals mingled with debtors and those thrown into gaol for heresy, which was an easy thing if one talked but loosely of Queen or Church.

One day I was called to a private room where two men sat. One was a slender man with a tight, cruel mouth and a tightly curled wig. He looked at me with an aloof and distant expression.

The other man was square and solid-looking, a man of the Army, I would have guessed, or perhaps the captain of a warship.

"You are Barnabas Sackett?" this one asked.

"I am, and a loyal yeoman of England," I added. "I am also an admirer of Her Majesty."

"There be many such," he replied shortly. "Now to the matter at hand. You have traded certain gold coins to Coveney Hasling and others?"

"I have."

"Where did you obtain these coins?"

Relating the events of the day on which I found such coins was simple, and then I followed by relating that once I knew antiquities might have value, I went to another place and found more.

"So quickly? So easily?"

"It was chance. One in a thousand, I suppose, although there are many places in England where old coins are found."

"Your home is in the fens?"

"It is."

"You live near the Wash?"

"Some distance from it, actually."

"But you know it? You've sailed on it?"

"Many times."

"You know the story of the loss of the royal treasure?"

For hours they questioned me. The man with the wig had a cold, fierce eye and there was not one whit of mercy in him, nor any belief in my story.

He turned at last. "Damn him for a liar, Swalley!" he said. "I told you this would do no good. I say the rack . . . or a thumbscrew. He'll speak the truth fast enough. His kind have no belly for pain."

"How is yours?" I said roughly. "I think you have no stomach for it, either. Have done with this. I have spoken the truth. If you do not care to believe, do what you will, for I have nothing else to tell you."

He looked at me for a moment, and then he struck me across the face with the back of his hand. It was not much of a blow, and I smiled.

"If we each held a sword," I said, "I'd have your blood for that."

"What? You threaten *me*? Why, you—!"

63

"I am an Englishman. I am freeborn. A man who strikes a prisoner so is a coward, and you, sir, are doubly a coward."

"Here! That will be enough of that!" Swalley came to his feet suddenly. "I am sorry, Sir Henry."

He pointed a finger at me. "You! You will tell us where lies the royal treasure or, by the Lord, you shall be put to the question."

"I have told you all I know. You waste time. Would I be going to America if there were such a treasure?"

Swalley stared at me, then smiled with thick lips that repelled me. "How do we know you were not for Spain? Or for Italy? We know you have the treasure, for word has been given us that you have it, that you took it from the Wash this past year. It is sworn to."

Appalled, I stared at him. Then I shook my head. "That is obviously a falsehood. There is no treasure."

"Think of it," Swalley said quietly. "We will talk again."

So I was returned to my cell. I looked about the bare room with its cot, its white-washed walls and bare ugliness, and felt hatred for the first time.

What right had they to seize and confine me in this manner? Taking me from all I loved, from my chance at a future of some worth, and bringing me to this horror? Yet moaning and wailing was not my way. I had never complained, for who cares for complaints? If something is wrong, one does something.

Hyatt . . . I must see Hyatt. I went forth from my room, guessing very well that once questioning began there would be no longer such freedom, even though many a malefactor enjoyed it. I should be taken, held, confined, tortured.

Suddenly I stopped. Before me was Peter Tallis, talking to a thin, wiry little man whom I had seen about before. He glanced my way but gave no indication that he knew me. I walked swiftly past him, looking about for Hyatt.

He spoke as though talking to the small man. "Barnabas, this is Feghany. In prison he is known as Hunt, for

64

Feghany means a huntsman or something like. He is a good man, and will help.

"I have word. If you escape, it must be now. No delays. You are to be taken to a dungeon and they will have the treasure out of you or you shall die. It is in the hands of the men you saw."

"I will need a horse . . . three horses."

I was standing, looking about as if for someone, seeming not to be aware of his presence or that of Feghany. Others moved about us. Across the larger room I saw Hyatt.

"There will be horses at a house you know, a house you once visited after the theatre."

Tempany's!

"Go there when you leave. Waste no time. Ride far north and west. The Queen will be desperate. Her men will be everywhere searching for you. You can rely on Feghany."

He moved on to talk to another prisoner, while Feghany loitered near me. "Have you got a Kate?" he said, low-voiced.

"A Kate?"

"A pick, for opening locks. You're going to need one. I'm thinking they'll have the cramp rings on you before night."

At my blank look, for I knew nothing of thieves' cant, he said, "Cramp rings . . . irons . . . shackles." He looked disgusted, "Don't you know *nothing?*"

He promised to bring me one.

Whatever else happened, I had to be away from this place. The stench on the main floor was disgusting. Crossing the floor I went to my own cell.

Once inside, I looked at the window. Six feet from the floor, over four feet wide and slightly arched at the top, it was crisscrossed with iron bars. The bars were at least six inches apart, and there were two horizontal bars that crossed also.

There was a bench and a bed in my cell, and a wooden bucket. The bench was heavy to move, and could not be moved back quickly, so I upended the

65

bucket and stood on it to get a better look at the sill.

The bars were set into the stone, but I noted with satisfaction that weathering had worn the stone on the outside. Peering out, I could just make out a wall beneath my window. If I could lower myself to that . . .

Footsteps alerted me and I stepped down and moved the bucket. I was sitting on my bed when the cell door opened amid a rattle of shackles.

A guard was there, and Feghany was helping him carry the irons.

The guard grinned. His teeth were broken and yellow. "You git the cramp rings again, lad! Tomorrow."

"But I paid you!" I protested.

"Aye, so you did, but there's a voice louder than mine that says back you go, so into the irons it is."

"Sorry," Feghany said to me, "but it's no doing of the guard's. Remember him. Later he may take them off, if you've a bit of the necessary."

"Now hold up there!" the guard protested. "Not so loud!"

Feghany slapped me on the shoulder and something cold touched my neck below the collar. "There! Don't worry now!"

When they had gone I put my hand inside my collar. A thin bit of metal. A Kate with which to pick the lock.

There was no time to waste. I was bound for a dungeon and more questions. I was headed for torture that could only end in death.

So what was to be done must be done tonight.

I heard the yowlings and screams that came from the cells and the larger rooms below where the prisoners mingled.

I checked the bars at the window again. Rain and wind had done their worst with the exposed walls, and some of the bars were loose in their sockets.

I was devoutly grateful. Gripping the pick in my hand, I went to work to break away the stone, scratching away with my lock-pick at the crumbling edge of the socket.

Then, putting down the pick, I took the bars in my

two hands and strained, pushing them out. The bars gave a little, then held. I worked longer, then hearing footsteps in the passage I sat down on my bench, leaning my elbows on my knees, my back to the door. There was a momentary pause outside my door as the guard peered through the tiny window, then went on.

Once more I returned to the bars. If I could but remove two, at most three, of the uprights, and one of the horizontal bars, I could get myself through. I worked, picked away very carefully. Then I tested one of the bars. My strength served me well now, for the bar gave. Then as I exerted more pressure, the bottom moved outward.

Very carefully I extracted the top from its socket and placed it on the floor. The second bar was more stubborn. Again and again I strained and worked at it. At last the bottom came loose and it joined its mate on the floor between myself and the door.

The horizontal bar was not so deeply set, and the grains of rock came loose each time I scraped with the pick. The wall was old and crumbling. By this time I was soaked with sweat and my knuckles were scraped and torn. It was after midnight before I had removed the third bar, and by that time the prison was quiet.

Carefully, I moved the heavy bench under the window. I sacrificed my coat to cover the irons on my bed and give some shape of a man lying. My foot was on the bench when suddenly a key rattled and the door behind me opened.

"Ah!" It was Henry Croppie. "Caught!"

He sprang to seize me from behind, but his foot landed on the iron bars which rolled under him. His feet shot up and he fell.

Turning from the bench, I met him as he rose to come at me, and I hit him.

My fist was a hard one. It caught him on the nose and I felt the bone give way. He went almost down, then lunged up, reaching for me with his hands.

Seizing one of his hands, I wrenched it quickly behind his back and shoved up in a hammerlock, an old

67

wrestling trick. He started to cry out and I slammed him down upon the floor and knocked him out.

There was nothing for it. To try rushing away down the passage would but lead me to another heavy door, and to more guards. The window it must be.

Leaping up on the bench, I thrust myself through and pulled my legs up while behind me I heard grunts and spitting and coughing amid the rattle of chains.

I looked down, and the stomach went out of me. The wall on which I pinned my hopes was at least twenty feet down and scarcely two feet wide. I might drop and reach it, but the chances were greater that I would slip off. For a moment I hesitated. To slip from that wall meant a drop of at least thirty feet. I looked up.

The edge of the roof was scarcely four feet above my window top. Gripping the bars I turned my back to the outer night and stood up on the outside sill, shifting my hands higher. Gripping a bar with one hand, I reached up, let go the gripping hand, and caught the roof's edge. Very carefully I pulled myself up and over the edge, to lie gasping on the leads.

Sweat was dripping from me. I rubbed my hands as dry as might be and began to edge myself along the leads. It was very wet and slippery, and if I started to slide there was small hope for me but death on the rocks almost sixty feet below.

Edging along, I reached the far edge of the building. And there just below me was another leaded roof, not six feet down. I went over the edge and I ran along the peak of the roof for at least fifty feet. There was a small attic window and I tested it with my hands. The wood frame was old and crumbling and I managed to force the window, and stepped into what seemed like an empty room, musty with long dead air. A faint light came from another window. I crossed and opened the door into a hallway.

If I was still within the bounds of Newgate it must be the quarters of the gaoler. Yet I believed the building was one adjoining the prison. At the end of the hall the door was shut and tight. I couldn't force it in the time allowed me. Turning swiftly, I went down the hall to a window at the far end. In a moment I was once more in the cool night air with a faint mist of rain on my face, and I was on the leads of another roof.

Some distance off, on still another roof, was a dormer window. I went swiftly along the roof. Time was running out and I must be away, to Southwark and the house of Brian Tempany where horses awaited.

From roof to roof I went, then to the window. It was slightly open!

Pulling it wider, I stepped in.

There was a sudden gasp.

I pulled the window shut, turning as I did so. Somewhere beyond the clouds there was a moon, and a vague light entered the room.

A girl was sitting up in bed, clutching the bedclothes to her. I made out what seemed to be a young and pretty face, tousled hair, and wide eyes.

"Please! Don't be frightened. I am just passing through."

"You are from Newgate," she said.

"I won't be long," I said cheerfully, "if I do not keep moving, or if you should scream to warn them."

"I shall not scream if you do me no harm," she replied coolly. "My father died in Newgate, for debt, and I have no love for them.

"Go down the stairs." She pointed. "The door opens on another street. Cross it and go down the side street. I wish you luck."

"Thank you," I said, and did as she suggested, closing the door softly behind me. Once in the street, all was dark and still. I ran, swiftly and on light feet.

Soon I crossed a square, then another. St. Paul's loomed. I slowed to a walk and crossed the street, moving toward the bridge to Southwark.

Tempany's house was dark and silent. For a time I waited in the shadows, studying it. There seemed to be nobody about, yet it might be a trap. It was unlikely that anyone would suspect that I would come here, yet on the other hand, they were none too sure of Tempany's loyalty, either, because of his association with me.

Must it be always dark and raining when I came to this house? I entered the paved court and suddenly saw a thin thread of light from a window. Someone was here. Should I go directly to the stables? Or should I rap on the door? Yet who would be here? Tempany was gone; so was Abigail.

At the door I tapped lightly, and almost at once there was a response from within the house. The door opened and a tall figure loomed. It was Lila, Tempany's housekeeper and sometimes maid to Abigail.

"Ah? It is you is it?" she demanded accusingly. "If you have come for horses they are there, in the stable."

Lila was a big woman, strong as an ox and just as formidable. But she was expecting me. She led the way to the kitchen and waved me to a table. She had a pot on, and she filled a tankard with ale. Then she put food on the table, working swiftly and smoothly. I fell to, hungry as a maunder's child, and the food was good. Nay, it was excellent.

She went into another room, and when she returned she had a black cloak, voluminous and warm, a hat, and a sword, as well as a brace of pistols and a bag of silver. "You'll be needing these. Peter Tallis let me know."

Overwhelmed, I could only thank her.

"Bother!" she said sharply. Then she turned on me. "How's my young lady? Have you seen her at all?"

"She's at sea, bound for America," I said, "where I hope to follow."

"You'll take me with you?" she asked, suddenly.

I could only gulp, then swallow. "What . . . what did you say?"

"You must take me to America," she said. "I will not be left here with herself off across the world needing nobody knows what, and she alone with all sorts of man-creatures and no woman by. She wouldn't let me go, but you will. Take me, Barnabas Sackett."

"Take you?" I repeated the words stupidly, appalled at the thought of traveling so far across the country with

70

this large woman, not fat mind you, but broad in the shoulder and beam, and strong. "What of the house? Did not Captain Tempany leave you in charge?"

"That he did, and a lonely life it is, so I sent for my brother, and he has come along. He will stay whilst I am gone."

"A brother?" Somehow I had never grasped the idea that there might be another such. One I could accept, but two?

"Aye." He came in from the hall then, a man as big as two of me and with hands like hams. "I'll guard well the house, Sackett, as well as if it were my own, and you be takin' the lass here. She'll be happier in America with her mistress, for she's done nothing but worry since they left."

"You don't understand," I said patiently. "We go where there are savages. To a wild land. I do not know how I am even to get there myself, let alone take a woman with me."

"Wherever a man can go, I can go," Lila said calmly. "And whatever the hardships, I'll put up with them. My folk were fisher-folk and well I know the way of boats and sails. I can do as much as any man . . . as any two men."

"As for the savages," her brother said, "if they molest my sister, God have mercy on them, for she will not!"

No protest I could utter stirred her resolution one whit. She would go with me, and not only that but she had already packed and had our horses saddled.

Still arguing, I got to my feet, belted on the sword, and took what she had handed me. I donned the cloak.

"It may be months before I see Abigail. We must somehow cross the sea," I said, "and sail along a dangerous, unknown coast. And if we find her we shall be very lucky indeed."

"We will find her, worry none of that," Lila said.

"There will be storms and danger. There will be bloody fighting. And the law is upon my path, Lila."

"I shall be no burden," she replied calmly. "And I

can cook better than the sort of victuals you'll be after having."

"Come then, Lila, and if you cannot ride all night, do you stay behind."

"I'll ride the nights and days through," she said firmly.

And so she did.

△ **8** △

North and westward we fled through the wind and the rain, driving along lonely lanes, plunging through the darkened streets of villages, our black cloaks billowing out behind like wings of great bats, the hooves of our horses striking fire from the cobbles.

Out of the night and into a village, then on again. At dawn we rested our horses in a grove beside the way, and sitting under a tree, ate a bit of the food Lila had put up, and it was good food, tasty and lasting. Meanwhile the horses grazed.

"Be they hunting you then?" she asked, looking at me from under her thick brows, "like Peter Tallis said?"

"They think the coins I sold were part of King John's treasure, lost in the Wash. It did no good to tell them nay."

"We go to Bristol?"

"I did think of it. But now . . . no. I am for Ireland now, to one of the fishing towns."

She was silent for several minutes, and then said, "Do you know Anglesey?"

"I do know of it."

"I am from there."

I was astonished, for I had no idea her home was anywhere but London, and said as much.

"My father was a friend to Captain Tempany, and worked for him. Before my father died he found me a place with him. You wish to go to Anglesey?"

72

"I do, and to Ireland from there, and from Ireland to America."

"It is an old old way," Lila said, "but traveled often of an olden time."

A mist lay upon the grass and wove itself in cobwebby tendrils among the dark trees. The dawn was touching the mist with pink, but very lightly yet, as the hour was very early.

"I spoke hastily when I said I knew Anglesey," I explained, "I have not been there, but my father was, and he told me much of it . . . an island of bards and witches, where the Druids were a time long since."

She gave me a straight and level glance from under her dark brows. "And live yet, if you know to find them."

"Druids?"

"Aye . . . and the bards, too."

She was a strange woman, this Lila. Looking at her brooding face, I was minded to think of the story of Boudicca, of huge frame, the fiery Celtic princess who with flaming red hair and spear led the Iceni against the Romans, the Iceni, some of whom it was said had been among my ancestors. But who could tell? That was long ago.

We rested there, while the dawn painted the clouds with a deft brush. The warmth felt good to my muscles, and at last I got to my feet. "It is time, Lila. We have far to go."

She mounted with ease, and we rode on, again keeping to the lanes and byways, avoiding the traveled roads.

We walked our horses now and again not wishing to attract attention by seeming pursued. We walked, trotted a bit when the way was easy, now upon the open moor, then under the shade of old beeches.

At dusk of the second day we came up to Cricklade, following the old Roman road, at times a mere path, often a lane, yet running straight as the eye can see. We walked our horses beyond the town to Ashton Keynes where the Thames winds about, a small stream there, of no size at all.

73

There was an inn, and it looked neat and clean. "We'll try to sleep inside this night," I said. "I shall have a room for you if there be one, and I'll make do below stairs in the common room."

A room there was. To preclude curiosity, I said, "The girl is tired, strong though she is, and I'd not have her worn out for meeting the man she is to marry."

Lila looked at me, but said nothing.

"I am her cousin," I explained, "and she's betrothed to a lad in Shropshire. A sturdy one, too!"

"Aye." The innkeeper looked at Lila and shook his head approvingly. "That he'd better be."

There was some idle talk, and the innkeeper's wife showed Lila to a room under the eaves, small but tidy, and I rolled up in my cloak by the fire when the guests had gone and it was bedding time. It was a small place, and there was but one other there, a short, stocky man with a pleasant smile and a careful eye. He worried me some, for he asked no questions nor made comment, but listened to all spoken as he smoked by the fire.

When I was rolled in my cloak he said, "You've good horses there."

"Aye," I said, not wishing to talk.

"They've come far," he said.

"Aye," I repeated.

"And they'll be goin' farther no doubt. 'Tis in my mind that you should have fresh horses, sturdy ones, too."

Now I was alert, for this was leading somewhere if only to a horse trade. The man was no fool, and such worried me.

"Mine are strong," I said. "They are good for the distance."

"No doubt," he said, "but what if they're in for a run now? How long could they last?"

"As long as need be," I said, "and so they must. I've no silver for others. They'll go the way," I said, "and to the green pasture when the run is over, to rest awhile."

"Aye, but you'll still be needin' others, or I miss my thought." He leaned over and knocked out his pipe at

74

the hearth's edge. And then, low-voiced, he said, "You give your friends a de'il of trouble, man."

"What do you mean?"

"Would the name of Feghany sound true? Or that of a man named Peter?"

"There is a Peter in the Bible," I said.

"This is a different Peter," he said dryly. "You're in sore trouble, lad, for they be askin' questions in Oxford an' Winchester an' Bristol, too."

"You were speaking of horses?"

"Aye."

"Take them up the road to Cirencester . . . the old Roman road. Hold them there and we'll be along."

He reached inside his shirt and handed me a sheet of paper. "Read it," he said, "and then put it in the fire, yonder."

I read. Then I looked straight in his eyes.

"How did you find me?" I asked .

"We almost didn't," he said grimly. "We were looking for a lone man riding, and we'd men out at villages along every way northwest. Ah," he said, shaking his head, "that Peter! He should have been a general! He thinks of everything."

"But here? In this place?"

"I was in Cricklade when you passed through, watering my horses at the river, so I followed, saw you giving a look to the inn, so I came here before you."

"My thanks." I looked at him. "You've a name?"

"Call me Darby. They all do."

We slept then, and when in the cold light of another day my eyes opened, he was gone. The innkeeper was stirring the fire.

"Your cousin is awake," he said. "What a woman she is! Why, she'd make two of me!"

"And stronger than any three," I said. "I do not envy the lad. He'd better be one who keeps his eyes from the others or she'll have him over her knee."

He laughed. "Little thought he'll have for others with her to take care of," he said. "I'll put somethin' on for you."

An hour later, in a patch of woods and under the old beeches near the Thames, we traded horses with Darby. There were saddlebags on my horses, and a brace of pistols in case I had none.

"There be this, too," Darby said, and from a roll of skins he took my own sword, the blade of my father than which none were finer. "How he got it from the gaol I shall never know!"

"Nor I," I said, "but I feel a new man now."

I put out my hand. "Someday, Darby, in America mayhap?"

"Na, I be a busy one here." He shook his head. "It has a sound to it, though. America! I like it. Savages they tell me, and forests and land wherever you look."

"And running streams, Darby. Keep it in mind, if the worst comes. If you've a thought of finding me, follow a river to the far mountains and ask for me there."

"Barnabas Sackett, is it?"

"Aye, and by the time you get there the name will echo in the hills, Darby. The Indians will know of it if the white men do not. It is a fair land, Darby, but a raw, rough land that will use up men until it breeds the kind it needs. Well, I will be used, and I hope to have a hand in the breeding, too."

Westward we went, riding easy on strong, fresh horses, through Cirencester to Gloucester over Birdlip Hill, and when I dipped into the saddlebags there was a purse of gold there, a dozen coins, and some silver.

"May I have the other sword?" Lila asked.

"A sword?" I was astonished. "It is a man's weapon."

She looked at me coldly. "I can use it as well as any man. I've five tall brothers, Sackett, and we fenced with swords upon many an hour. Give it to me, and if trouble comes, stand aside and watch what a woman can do!"

"Welcome!" I said cheerfully. "I did not doubt that you could do it, but only that you wished to."

"I do not *wish*. I do what becomes the moment. If it be a cook-pot, I cook. If it be a needle, I'll sew, but if it be a blade that is needed, I shall cut a swath. To mow

76

arms and legs and heads, I think, is no harder than the cutting of thatch."

In the Cotswolds and the valley of the Severan there were Roman ruins all about, nor was I a complete stranger to them for I'd been led their way by Leland's manuscript, and remembered much of what I'd read.

We camped one night in the ruins of a Roman villa, and drew water from a mossy fountain where Roman patricians must once have drunk. Where we lay our heads that night, Roman heads had lain, though in better fare than we. But now they were gone, and who knew their names, or cared? And who should know ours, ours who had but the green grass for carpet, and the ruined walls of a once noble house for shelter?

Lila was a quiet woman. She spoke little and complained none at all, yet she was woman—too much woman to go off to America with no man of her own. I said as much, and she looked at me and said, "A man will come. Where I am, he will come."

"You'll see few white men in America, or any other but Indians. Good folk some of them, but they do not think like we do."

"I shall not marry an Indian. I shall marry an Englishman or perhaps a Welshman."

Then we forded a stream and rode up a narrow pass between rocks, and when night came we were in a wild and mysterious land, a place of long shadows and great rocky battlements and rushing cold streams and rich green grass around hard black rocks that shone like ice in the dim light of the after-sunset. It was a primeval landscape. Suddenly, they came upon us, a dozen or more of them. Wild, uncouth creatures, some clad in skins, some in rags, wild, mad things wielding all manner of weapons.

They came up from the rocks where they had lain in wait. Screaming wildly, they came down upon us. Lila drew her sword and wheeled her horse to meet them. I tried to yell that flight was our best chance, but she was beyond hearing. She did not scream, but yelled some wild Welsh shout, and light caught the flashing blade of her sword as she swept on toward them.

I barely had time to draw and fire a pistol, and then she was among them.

But what had happened? After her wild Welsh yell they had suddenly frozen, mouths wide to scream, staring at her. Then as one man, or woman, for there were women among them, they fled.

Her sword reached one, I think, before they were gone into the rocks from which they came. Then Lila wheeled her horse, towering in her stirrups, and shouted after them, a hoarse, challenging cry.

Her sword was bloody and she leaned from her saddle and thrust it into a hummock of earth and moss, once . . . twice. Then she sheathed it.

Awed, I led us away up the trail to where it went through a pass in the mountains, and she followed quietly.

Later, when the road widened, we rode side by side. "What did you say that frightened them when you called out?" I asked.

"It does not matter."

"It was a curious thing. They stopped as if struck, then they fled as if all the terrors were upon them."

"Indeed, they would have been. They well knew when to fly. That lot! I have heard stories of them! Poor, misbegotten, inbred creatures that live in caves and murder innocent travelers. The soldiers have come for them a dozen times, but they disappear. Nobody finds them . . . at least no Englishman."

She was silent then, and I as well. More than two hours had passed since we had seen even the slightest sign of life, and nothing at all but the wild mountains and the rushing cold streams and the rocks that lay like chunks of iron on every hand.

"There's a cottage yon," she said, pointing ahead.

"You have been this way before?"

"No."

"You are from Anglesey, Lila, and you spoke of Druids."

"Did I now?"

78

"It is said there are people on Anglesey who have the gift."

She rode on, offering no reply. We were ascending a pass through wild, heavily forested hills. Suddenly it came to me.

"This is the pass from Bettws-y-Coed!"

She turned her head. "You know it? You have not been to Wales before?"

"I have not. Is this the pass?"

"It is." Now it was her turn to be curious. "How did you know?"

I was not exactly sure, only somehow it had come upon me. "I was told of it once . . . long ago."

"And so you know it in the dark?" For night had fallen.

"I was told of how it looked in the dark, and how it . . . felt."

She looked at me again, but now we were approaching a high place in the pass, and down the far slope we saw something white against the blackness, and then a dog barked.

"The cottage," she said. "We will stop there, I think."

"As you will. It is better than the damp hills and the rocks."

"They are Welsh hills," she said sternly, "and Welsh rocks."

Our horses had been growing more and more weary as we moved on, and now as they saw the faint glow of light from a window, they moved forward eagerly. At the door I dismounted while a huge dog barked viciously, his hair on end, teeth bared.

Lila spoke sharply to him in Welsh and he cringed and moved back, but snarled still. We heard the sound of a bar being removed, then a voice spoke from a crack. "Go away! The place is closed!"

Lila spoke sharply and the door crack widened and a girl thrust her head out. "Who is it that speaks thus?" she demanded, in English, then added a word in Welsh.

"We have traveled far, and have far yet to go," I said quietly. "It is myself and a woman."

79

"Are you wed, then?"

"We are not," I said. "She is a friend to my betrothed."

"Hah!" The door opened wider. "Then the more of a fool is your betrothed to let you out upon the Welsh hills with another woman. De'il would I be so generous!"

Lila had stepped down from the horse and she towered above the girl in the door. "We would eat and sleep here," she said, "and have our horses fed."

It was spacious enough inside, a wide room with a low ceiling and a stone-flagged floor, washed clean enough to eat from, which was not all that common.

There was good furniture about and a fire on the hearth, and beside the hearth an old man smoking a pipe. A churn stood in a corner near a sideboard with several rows of dishes.

The girl, seen in the light inside, was dark and pretty, with quick black eyes and lovely lips. "Come," she said, "sit and be rested. My brother will see to your horses."

She looked again at Lila. "You look Welsh," she said.

"I am from Angelsey," Lila replied.

They eyed each other, taking a measure, respectful but wary.

"He speaks of me as a friend," Lila said. "I am in service to the one who will be his bride. She is on her way to America. We go to her now."

The girl looked at me, hands on hips. Then she said, "We've eaten, but there's a bit of bread and cheese and I'll scrape about and see what else."

The old man looked at me thoughtfully. "You are also Welsh?"

"English," I said.

"Ah? I would have said you were Welsh."

Lila turned and looked directly at me. "Who was your mother?"

"I know little of her, only that she was gentle, very beautiful, and that my father rescued her from some pirates in the western isles, and that she had told him she was not frightened because she knew he was coming for her."

"She knew?" Lila looked at the old man, and the girl,

who had come back into the room, had stopped also, listening.

"Aye." I loved that part of the story. "Father said she was very calm, and she told one of the men who started to lay hands upon her that he would die before the hour was gone, and he stopped, and they all stopped, frightened.

"One of the others then asked her, sneering, 'And I?' He was a young man, and very bold in his youth and his strength. 'You will live long in evil, but my son shall kill you one day.'

" 'Your son? Where is he? I shall kill him now and be sure what you say is a lie.'

" 'I have no son. Nor have I husband yet, but he is coming now. It is his sword,' she looked at the first man, 'which will draw your blood.'

" 'What are you?' that first man asked. 'A witch?'

" 'I am of the blood of Nial,' she said.

" 'If you be afraid,' the younger man said to the other, 'I will take her. She's a handsome wench, and witch or no witch, I'll have her.'

"And then my father was there, and my father's men. He came into the room sword in hand. The first man died, and the younger escaped with a sword cut, and my mother called after him, 'Do not forget your destiny. You will die by the sword in the flames of a burning town!' "

"It is a fine story," the old man said, "a grand story! And you, the son, have killed this man?"

"I am the son, but I have killed no man in the flames of a burning town, nor am I likely to. Soon I shall go where there are no towns, but only forests and meadows and mountains. I fear the prophecy will not be complete."

"Be not sure," Lila said. Then to the old man and the girl. "Did you hear what he said? That his mother was of the blood of Nial?"

"I heard," the girl said. "I believe it."

"It was in his face when he came into the room," the old man said, "I know the look of those who have the gift." He looked at Lila. "You have it."

81

"What is this gift of which you speak?"

"It is the gift of second sight, the gift of looking beyond or back. Nial was a *spaeman,* one of those who foretell events. The story is ancient, and from Iceland, and the mother of Nial was the daughter of Ar the Silent, master of a great land in Norway. But Nial was a gifted man, a great talker, and a pleader for his people."

I was tired, and it was late.

"We must to bed," I said, "for in the morning we cross the Menai."

The old man tapped out his pipe. "Put them in the loft," he said. "They'll sleep warm there."

"I shall stay by the fire," I said, "for to sleep too sound would not please me."

The old man turned his head to look. "You are followed, then?"

"It may be. If so, we would not wish to have it known that we were seen. We are good folk," I added.

"Sleep," he said, "and rest. We will let no harm come to the blood of Nial."

I added sticks to the fire when he had gone to his bed, and rolled in my cloak upon the floor near the hearth. It would be a cold night, but the cottage was snug and warm.

I took two pistols under the cloak's edge near me, and my naked blade. Its scabbard lay to one side. I hoped the night would be quiet, but I was not a trusting man, and the hilt of a sword has a good feel.

Oft times a blade across the room beyond the reach of a hand means that death is nearer. I closed my eyes, and heard the rain fall upon the thatch, and against the walls. Drops fell down the chimney and the fire sputtered and spat.

The wind curled around the eaves, moaning with its loneliness, and listening to wind and rain half slept.

Where, O where was Abigail? How far out upon the sea? Did she sleep well this night? Did the ship roll? Was all well aboard?

Outside a stone rattled, and in the darkness my hand tightened upon the sword's hilt.

△ 9 △

We came over the hills to Bangor in the morning, with shadows in the valley and sunlight on the sea. The mist was lifting from the trees, clinging wistfully as if reluctant to leave—like the smoke of ancient Druid fires which once burned in this place.

We came over the hills, and I knew it well from my mother's tales of Taliesin, the great Welsh bard. The village lay upon the hills where once the Druid's upper circle had been, overlooking the Menai Strait that separated Wales from Anglesey, once called Mona, and before that other names as well.

Bangor had been a place of ritual for the Druids, but that was long ago. Something stirred in me when I saw the view from there. Was it some ancient racial memory? Something buried deep in my flesh and bones?

Lila rode behind me into the village. My eyes were alert for trouble. From here our destination was clear: from the north coast a boat to Ireland; then to lose ourselves in that war-torn island where marched the armies of Lord Mountjoy.

Eyes turned upon us when we dismounted, for we were strangers, and Lila as tall as any man here, and as broad in the shoulders. She looked the Viking woman whose ancestors had once raided these shores, then settled here and across the water as well. They had founded Dublin. What was it the name first meant? Dark Pool, if I recalled correctly.

Recalled? How could I recall? But so I did . . . no doubt something heard, something read, something dimly remembered from another time.

Yet I seemed to have passed this way before. Too many strange memories came to me now, too many whose origin I could not recall.

There was a roadside inn where fishermen and sailors stopped, or travelers like ourselves. And we went there now and sat at a table and were brought without asking—fish, bread, and ale.

The people were Welsh. Yet there might be spies among them, although I hoped my pursuers were far from us, seeking in Bristol, Falmouth, or Cornwall.

Traveling with a woman may have helped to fool them, for that they had no reason to suspect—nor that I would go into Wales. Yet I was ever a cautious man.

A distinguished-appearing man sat near us, with a thoughtful but stern face. That he was a man of the Church was obvious.

"You travel far?"

Smiling, I said, "It is my hope."

"It is not many who come here," he continued. "I come for my health. It is the air of the sea, the smell of the ocean."

"It is a place for poets," I said, "or warriors."

"Are they not often the same?" He looked from Lila to me. "Your accent is strange," he said, "yet your companion, I'd say, is of Anglesey."

"You'd be right," I said. "She lived here once." About myself I said nothing. He was curious, yet I liked the man. He was someone I should have liked to spend a few hours with, talking over the ale, and watching the ships, feeling the wind in my hair.

"I am Edmund Price, of Merionethshire," he said.

"You are a poet," I said, "spoken of in London and Cambridge."

"So far off? I had not realized my poor talents were known."

"The tongue of Wales is music, and you write it well."

"Thank you. That was well said. You are a poet also?"

I shrugged. "I am nothing. A man of the sword, perhaps. A man yet to shape his way." I looked at him with respect. "You, they say, are a man of vast learning, familiar with many languages."

He shrugged. "The more one learns the more he under-

84

stands his ignorance. I am simply an ignorant man, trying to lessen his ignorance."

"I spoke of travel," I said, "and not lightly. I go to Raleigh's land."

"Ah, yes . . . Raleigh. Well, he has acquired a name these last few years, has he not? Men speak of these new lands. I wonder if they are new."

"Who knows? Where man is able to go, man has been. The Irish, they say, sailed over the sea long since, and the Welsh, under Madoc."

"The Irish at least," he replied. "Do you know the tale of Gudlief Gudlaugson, who sailed from the west of Ireland in 1029 with a northeast wind, and was driven far to the southwest, and finally found shelter upon a lonely coast and found there Bjorn Ashbraudson, who had left Ireland thirty years before? It is a known story among us, and many another like it.

"There were Danes settled in Ireland who heard the old Irish stories, and for many a year the land now called America was called Greater Ireland, and the stories were the Irish had been to far western lands even as they had to Iceland."

"I know nothing of these stories. I only know what I have said, that where men can go, they will go, and what is so hard about crossing a sea? It is sailing along shore that is dangerous, and men had sailed from Egypt to Crete and even to the western ocean shores of Spain in the time of Solomon, which is a farther distance than from Iceland to America."

We talked of many things, and it was a pleasure. But the time drew on, and Lila nudged my foot under the table.

"Now we shall go," I said.

"Go," Edmund Price said, "and may the Good Lord go with you."

"Thank you," I said.

I turned toward the door, where Lila already was, and reached for my purse. Edmund Price lifted a hand to stop me. "Please! Allow me, Barnabas Sackett."

And I was in the saddle and riding out of town before I realized that he had called me by my name!

Anglesey was a lower land, a flatter and sunlit land. And we rode swiftly up the coast toward the point from which we must take to the water, and there were behind us no apparent pursuers.

Where now was Abigail? Where was our ship? How far at sea? Whose hand was at the helm? Who lined up the fo'm'st on a distant star?

We rode across the moors, past quiet farms and between stone walls that guarded fields to right and left. We rode at last to Trearddur Bay, and to a small house there of sticks and plaster, a cozy and warm cot, under low trees with vines all about and some flowers, and it had a view over the bay, and of the mountain that towered to the north.

At the door we drew up. Lila called out, and the low door was opened by a tall man, a very tall man, for when he straightened up from the door he was taller than Lila, a man with a red beard and shoulders rolling with muscle under a flimsy shirt.

"Ha!" He looked at Lila. "You've come home, have you? And who is the man?"

"His future belongs to my mistress. We seek a boat, Owain."

"A boat? To where would you sail, sister?"

"To Ireland to find a ship for America."

"America, is it? You'd go there?"

"It is my destiny."

"Well, look for cousins there. We had those who sailed with Madoc, long, long ago. And others who went looking for them later. And once I talked to a Dane who had gone there in an Irish ship. He was an old man, very old, yet he spoke of wonderful things, palm trees like those in Africa, and great stone buildings, and people who wear feathers. You go to a wild land, but it is at a good time you come, for a ship lately here lies now off Ireland, if you can catch her. She is small, but seaworthy. Her captain is from Iceland. But how to get there? I do not know how it will be done."

"Is it far?"

He shrugged a heavy shoulder. "If you wish to know, you must ask the wind." He looked closely at me. "Is it because of the girl that you hurry? Or are there those behind you?"

I smiled at him. "A little of both. The girl, of course, for I love her very much, and would be with her. As for those behind me, if I am caught it goes hard with me and I do not think I will let them take me. The sea is too close, and my sword too sharp. There would be a fight, I think."

He chuckled, deep in his heavy chest. "There speaks a man. Go within." He gestured. "Your mam will see you, Lila. Feed him. He will need his strength where he goes now, and if he sails with the Icelander, he will need it well. Go. I shall find a boat, and if there be strangers coming, I'll give a call in time.

"Eat . . . rest . . . talk to Mam and let her listen to your voice so in the years to come she will have it to remember."

We ducked our heads under the low door, but not so much as he had ducked when he came out.

Inside it was cool and still. There were pots and kettles about, and a good smell of cooking, and a woman there, tall and thin with gray hair and a face unlined by the years, her eyes as old as the stones outside, but not cold.

"Is it you, Lila? It has been long, girl."

"I am passing."

"I heard you speak. So you come and go. Well, it is a far land to which you go, and so has it always been with us. So many have gone, so few have come back. It is the sea that takes them, or the farther shores. I do not know."

She moved easily, putting food on the table. "There's a slab of mutton from the moors beside the sea. The sheep eat salt grass and theirs is the best flesh of all. Eat, boy, and do not stand on time. The food will stay with you and the memory of it where you go. My mam

87

said always to take a cargo of memories, whatever else, for when all is lost the memories remain."

She looked at Lila. "Your mistress is a good woman, girl?"

"She is that. And this one a good man, although I doubted him at first. I did not think any man good enough. Nor do I fear to sail with him. Only the Icelander must be wary or this one will own the boat."

"You have the gift, girl. What do you see?"

She looked up. "I will not speak of that, Mam."

"Come! Is it so bad, then?"

"No." She hesitated, smoothing her strong white hands on her skirt. "Only dark times lie before and about us, dark, dark times. I will marry there, Mam, and die there, too, with a son to leave behind."

"And this one?"

"Four sons, Mam, that live. Some others will die, and she will die in England, and he . . . alone . . . he will die alone with a weapon in his hand, and there will be fire around and howling madness with the flames. It is not a good thing of which to talk."

Somberly I looked at her. "And will I die old or young, Lila?"

"Old," she said, "old. Your sons will be men, one of them lost afar off whom you will not see again, far, far off in a strange place. But he will live to leave his blood behind, as will the others."

"But Abigail will come again to England? She will leave me, then?"

"Not like that. I see love always. But she will leave. I do not know why, nor when . . . and she will not come back. I see blood upon the shore, and some people already in America are gone . . . gone. . . ."

I ate in silence then, brooding upon what she had said. I believed only a little, but they believed, and that worried me.

Yet, what was there in what she said to worry about? I should live to an old age, I should have four sons to leave behind, and I should have sewn my seed in a new land, under new trees.

"Old," I said. "Well, we must all grow old, and die when the hour comes. But what of the Queen? Will she relent? Will she learn I have no treasure?"

"She will not relent, nor will he who comes after. You will be sought always, for this is fixed in their minds: that you have found the royal crown, and you have kept it for yourself. When it is found that you are in America, some will come seeking you, and you will hide . . . you will go far."

"To the blue mountains then?"

"To the very mountains. You will lose yourself in them, and they will give you food, shelter, all that you need. You will live in their bosom."

"Ah, well. It is what I want, after all."

For I was contented then. The mountains would be mine. I would go to them, wander among them, know them. Was not that my destiny, after all?

Footsteps, an opening door, and then the huge frame of Owain was standing there.

"Men come. Four men upon horses."

"Are they strangers?"

"Aye. Would I come if they were not?" He looked at me. "The boat makes ready. You will go then?"

"I shall, and take your sister there. First, I must stand in the road and see what manner of men they be."

"I would stand with you. I'll get my axe."

My hand lifted. "See your sister to the boat. Did you not say there were only four?"

Sword in hand, and two pistols belted on, I walked out upon the road of gray pounded shells, and I stood there, dark against the road, watching them come.

The mountain was behind me, dark against the sky, a piece of the sea was on my right. Under my black cloak was my sword. My hand on the hilt, the sword half-drawn.

I waited for them there, and hoped they would be strong.

△ 10 △

A rough-looking man now stood in front of the cottage. He looked both at me and the men coming toward me. He called out something over his shoulder. Two other men came from the house.

Across the road near the shore, a man was mending a net. As Owain passed, going to the boat, he spoke. Then the man left his net, holding a long pole.

The riders were coming nearer. Several other people appeared and stood, watching.

The riders drew up, facing me, some thirty feet off. One of them was Robert Malmayne!

"So? We meet again!"

"There is a sadness on me," I said, cheerfully, "for we meet only to part."

"Not this time, I think. You are my prisoner, Sackett."

"You say that to me when you have only three men behind you? And what men they are! I think they have no stomach for steel, or you, either."

My sword slid easily from the scabbard, the point lifting.

There was a whispering of sandalled feet upon the shell road, a whispering around me. "Go!" A voice spoke in my ear. "The wind does not wait!"

"And leave these gentlemen?" I said.

There must have been fifty people around us now, both men and women, with a few children. They were saying nothing, but crowding closer and closer. Some had spears, others had poles or sticks. Some had nothing. One at least held a scythe and there were several with wood-axes.

"Back up there!" Malmayne shouted. He waved at them.

"You are in Wales, Malmayne. They do not speak English."

"Tell them to get back."

"I don't speak Welsh, and what are they doing? You are strangers, and they are merely curious."

"By heaven, I'll teach them who is strange!"

He started for his sword but found a large hand already on the hilt. He looked down into a smiling, bearded face. Malmayne cursed, but the hand on the sword hilt would not be moved.

"Careful, Malmayne!" I warned, smiling. "These are good folk, but somewhat rough when stirred."

Now they were crowded tightly around all four horsemen, so close the horses could not move. One fellow had a hold on a rider's leg. He was smiling, just holding the leg, but the implication was clear—one heave and the rider would be sprawling in the road.

"Come!" Owain shouted. "The wind is for the sail! Come quickly!"

Backing away, I sheathed my sword, then ran lightly to the shore. Lila was with me. I caught the gunwhale of the boat and we leaped aboard. We shoved off. The wind took the sail and it bellied out.

"I shall see you die by fire!" Malmayne shouted. "I shall have a warship after you!"

With Holyhead behind us, we held a course to the southwest for Wicklow Point, far and away across the Irish Sea.

"What will they do?" I asked, gesturing behind us.

"They? Nothing. After a bit they will drift back to their work and your Malmayne can do as he feels, which will not be much on Anglesey. He'll get no boat there, nor for miles away, and by that time we shall be along the Irish coast, which none knows better than I."

We had a strong wind, a following wind, and the sea went well before us. After a bit I went below and lay down on some mats and sails and slept. When I awoke, our vessel was south of Wicklow Head and off the Horse Shoe Bank which we kept inland of us.

"When you sleep, you sleep!" Owain declared. He pointed ahead and to starboard. " 'Tis an easy coast here, if one be watchful. Yon lies a rock . . . Wolf Rock, 'tis called, and she bares her teeth when the wind blows.

There are banks along the coast, no place for a ship to be caught, so a man must hold well out upon the sea. Most of the dangers lie four to six miles out, along here."

We stood together, watching the sea ahead. "Landsmen!" he said. "Such fools, they are! Why, a month ago in Dublin town I heard one talk in a tavern, a wise man, they said he was, and he was saying how ancient seafaring men were afeard to venture to sea, that they always held close along the coast for safety. I laughed at him, and he became angered."

"Did you tell him?"

"I did, but what good to tell fools? I told him the dangers of the deep ocean were one in ten to the risks along an unknown coast, or even a known one. He looked at me with pity for my ignorance, he who had never set a sail nor held a hand to the tiller. Look you! Ahead of us lie the Arklow Bank, the Glassgorman, Blackwater and Dogger, and any one a death trap—be you not knowing them. Yet the sea looks innocent enough to a landsman."

"The Icelander you spoke of. Where will he be?"

Owain considered that. "He may have moved, yet I think in Castlehaven or Glandore. He does not like busy places, that one."

Green lay the coast and gray the sea, and the wind whipped whitecaps from the wave crests and stung our faces with blown spray. Our craft lay over on its side and cut the waves handily as if playing with the sea, like a porpoise. We saw only a few fishing boats closer in, and one square-rigged ship, afar off.

From time to time I took the tiller.

It was Glandore Bay to which we came at last, rounding Galley Head and Foilsnashark Head and keeping Adam Island well off our port beam. The Bay was small, but it penetrated well into the land and was thus well-protected from all winds.

There were two castles in view. This was, or had been, a seat of the O'Donovans.

The gray walls of Castle Donovan arose on our port side.

We dropped anchor there, close in, and the ship we looked for was there, the Icelander standing by the rail watching us as we steered into the harbor.

"Hoy, Thorvald!" Owain called. "I have two for your ship!"

"Ve sail for Newfoundland!" Thorvald called back. "Ve sail at first light!"

"It is my sister who goes, and an Englisher. We have followed you from Anglesey!"

A skiff was lowered and Lila climbed down, then I. Owain rowed us over, and we climbed aboard.

"A woman aboard my ship? I would do it only for you, Owain!"

Thorvald was broad and thick, heavy-boned and blond. He looked at me with piercing blue eyes. "You are a sailor, yes?"

"I am."

"Vhere is it you go?"

"To Virginia, but Newfoundland is a step upon the way. We thank you."

"Somevon looks for you?"

"Aye, mayhap a Queen's ship, but if you do not wish to risk it, we will find another way, or buy our own boat and sail it together."

Thorvald chuckled. "You'll find that hard, very hard! And cold, too." He smiled wryly. "If a Queen's ship will follow vhere ve go, she may have you, und velcome."

The hills were green and lovely around the Bay of Glandore, and the crumbling ruin of Castle Donovan looked wild and strange among the thick-standing trees above the bay. We went ashore in the skiff, and at a place to which Owain took us, I bought some provisions.

Curiously, I glanced around the old building. It was a combination warehouse and shop, a place I suspected where a goodly portion of the merchandise had been smuggled. We bought what we needed, including some additional stores for the ship, and then returned to our boat.

It was no great craft, at all, but built somewhat on the lines of a Norwegian *bojort* with a square topsail above the spritsail, a lateen mizzen and a small spritsail under the bowsprit. It was called the *Snorri*, and I liked the look and the feel of her. She was steered with a whip-staff, which gave the man at the helm a chance to observe the sails.

There was a small cabin aft and a section was curtained off for Lila.

The sky was gray when we left the emerald-green harbor of Glandore behind and sailed past the islands into open sea. Standing amidships I looked back at Ireland. Would I ever again see the isles of Britain?

The wind blew smartly from the south, yet Thorvald crowded on what sail we had to make good time toward Iceland. A sound of distant thunder with far-off streaks of lightning warned us what trouble lay ahead, but Thorvald had grown up on a ship's deck, and the man on the whip-staff was a burly fellow of forty years or more, who looked the Viking he was.

Shortly before noon I relieved the helmsmen, and Thorvald stood by, keeping a close eye upon me for he was no man to trust his ship to an unknown. But I was a fair hand from the boating down off the fens. After a bit he no longer watched so closely, trusting my hand and judgment.

Most of the time, Lila stayed below. When the weather was mild enough and the ship steady, she cooked with supplies from the stores, always warm, nourishing food.

Thorvald looked at her and shook his head. "You spoil us all, Lila. It is not good for sailor to expect too much!"

He wasted no time, but laid a course for the northwest, pulling steadily away from any area where a search might be directed, steering toward the cold northern waters.

At midnight I awakened and came on deck to stand beside Thorvald. "If you wish to sleep," I said, "you can leave her to me."

"I am tired," he said simply. "The course is northwest-by-north."

He went below, and I was alone with the man on the whip-staff, whose face I could not see under his cowling.

The wind had grown colder with the days, and when

94

at last the mountains of Iceland loomed ahead we gathered amidship to look at land again, and Thorvald took us easily into a small cove where lay his home.

Three days we lay in port, and then once more set sail. Now the wind was steady but cold. And on the night watch it grew suddenly colder. Wary of some change, I awakened Thorvald.

He came on deck, sniffed to smell the wind, waited a bit, and then said, "Ice!"

We changed course toward the south. Suddenly I saw something white and glistening in the water. It was ice. Soon we saw several patches of broken ice and then, looming, a huge berg.

We passed her, several hundred yards off, a vast white tower pointing an icy finger at the clouds.

The days passed swiftly. It was a gray and overcast day when we sighted the birds of Witless Bay, and turned north along the coast, for we'd made our landfall a bit to the south of our port.

We moved into St. John's harbor and dropped our anchor there. Many boats were about, Portuguese, Basque, and Icelandic fishermen, and some others, just as obviously pirates. The pirates loved the rugged bays and small harbors of the island. They liked to recruit seamen there, for the Newfoundlanders were hardy men, skilled in all the work of ships and the sea, welcome aboard any ship, but doubly so aboard pirate craft for whom speed and seamanship were a prime requirement.

"Ve'll go no further here," Thorvald said. "Ve sell vhat ve have brought and ve load fish for home."

"I wish I could tempt you. I've traded for furs along that coast." I indicated where the large land might lie beyond the island. "There's a fortune to be had for the taking."

Thorvald shook his head, although his eyes held on the western horizon.

"Think, man," I suggested, "you could take back as much in one voyage as in four."

He shook his head again. "I vill find a boat for you," he said, "I know all here, und they know me."

It was a bold island to which we had come, and there were bold men about, ships fitting for the sea. And boats came in to dry their fish or to replenish supplies for another spell upon the dark water.

An eagerness was upon me now. I had come far upon my way, and I thought only of Abigail and our ship and my friends. Always the blue mountains hung like a mist at the back of my dreams, and there was no challenge that called to me as they did.

We went ashore and moved among the fishermen, Thorvald, Lila, and I, buying what things we needed, for it was a goodly port of supply.

Suddenly a huge man stood before me. He was bigger than I by breadth and height. A strong man he looked, and certainly he felt himself so.

"The wench, there," he gestured at Lila. "Fifty English pounds for her!"

"She's a free woman," I said.

"Bah!" he sneered. "What woman is free when money is offered? I want her! A hundred pounds, then!" His eyes bulged a little as he leaned toward me. His face was red with drinking.

"No," I said. "Now stand aside."

"Stand aside!" he shouted. "You say that to *me?*"

He was a big man and drinking. A dangerous man, I thought, and I was of no mind to fight with him then. I was impatient to be off to the south, hungry for a ship to take me there, and irritated by this great oaf who stood there, breathing his foulness upon me.

He reached for his sword, so I dropped one hand to stay the drawing of it, and with the fist of the other I smashed him in the wind.

It hit him hard and his breath left him with a gasp. But knowing a hurt man is not a whipped man, I spread my legs and swung both fists to his jaw.

Both landed . . . and as I have said, I am strong as two men . . . or three.

He sat down hard in the mud, blood streaming from his smashed nose and mouth. He was stunned by my blows. So I walked by him and went on. Thorvald stared at me.

"There is power in you," he said. "But do you know who he is?"

"No."

"Nor I . . . but he comes from yon ship," he pointed to a Dutch *fluyt* that lay in the land-locked harbor, "and he is a pirate."

"No matter," I said, but I lied. For suddenly there was a great envy upon me. The *fluyt* was a neat, compact, and handsome vessel, every line of her speaking of speed and good handling.

"He comes," Lila said quietly.

Turning, I saw the big man had gained his feet. A half dozen were gathered about him, all looking toward me. He pointed, then took a step toward me but staggered and almost fell again.

A lean-faced man with dark, pleasant eyes stepped up to us. "Yon's a quarrelsome, trouble-making man. We'll be well rid of him when he goes."

"Is that truly his ship?" I asked.

"It is."

"And is he truly a pirate?"

"He is . . . and fresh from robbing good fishermen upon the Banks, and making ready to sail for the Antilles when he is finished with his drinking."

"I am Barnabas Sackett," I said, "from England, and this is my good friend Thorvald."

"I know him," the lean man said. "You travel in good company."

Now the pirate's men were approaching.

"I will stand with you," said Thorvald.

"Lila," I said, "when this is over we must move your goods. Now we shall have a ship."

"A ship?"

"Aye."

They were coming up to me now, rough-looking men, at least two of them rascals.

They started to draw their swords, but I lifted a hand.

97

"If you draw on me, it will be mutiny. When did a good crew mutiny against their captain?"

"Captain!" They stared at me, startled.

"Had you rather sail with that great, drunken booby yonder?" I gestured at him. "If you like him, keep him. I want no part of him. But if you sail with me there'll be no brawling ashore."

"Why should we sail with you? Do you have a ship?"

"The *fluyt*," I said, "is now my ship. I say we leave him to his drink and go aboard of her and make ready for the sea. If he is no better a master than he is a fighter, she'll need work."

One of the men, who appeared to be a fisherman, laughed. "He has courage, this one!"

"If I go aboard," I said, "you'll obey me."

They knew not what to think of me, looking from me to Lila and then to Thorvald.

"Come!" I said abruptly. "That one is finished. You can see it for yourself. He'll lead you to your death, or capture and a Spanish prison."

"And where would you take us?"

"To rich prizes, and an even division all around with no giant share for the master. And then I'll go ashore in Virginia and the *fluyt* is yours."

Oh, I had properly guessed my men! I was not speaking into the wind, for they were men who appreciated courage and little else. They wanted profit, but it was the game, too, and they had just seen their master put down in the mud by a man a third smaller, and easily at that.

Some of whatever fear they had felt of him had gone with his fall. Now he fell again, and had stumbled up again, whether from drink or the effects of my blow I neither knew nor cared. He was hauling at his sword hilt.

To be a leader of pirates demanded not only courage but gall, the daring to challenge anything, and these were the men for it.

"He will kill you," one of them said. "He comes now."

He was coming, with a naked blade, but I waited, barehanded, measuring his movements. There was ugliness in him, and fury. He would be rash and overly confident, because I stood with no weapon in my hand.

My father had little to leave me in goods of this world, but he had what he had learned of men and weapons, of horses and women and ships and towns. He taught me well, and I knew what I could do.

"He means to kill you," Thorvald warned. "Do not mistake him. He will be quick."

They drew a little aside, knowing this was between us, for this is the way of men. One fights one's battles alone, not asking mercy nor expecting help.

The giant lifted the point of his sword toward my belly, and he was steadier than I had expected. My blows had jolted some of the drunkenness from him, but I knew the memory of it was in his muscles yet.

His was a flat, single-edged blade, the cutting edge down. His grip would be strong upon the sword, his concentration hard upon it. He was thinking now of what he would do to me. He was already tasting his revenge for the blows I had struck him.

Suddenly, he lunged. It was perfect—the move, the lunge. How many times had I done this in practice?

With a quick slap of my palm I knocked the blade over, out of line with my body. Then I took a quick step in with my left foot, my right leg hooked behind his, and my right hand smashed up, the butt of my palm under his chin.

His head snapped back and my leg tripped him. He half-turned and fell again into the mud, his grip loosening on the sword. As he hit the mud I kicked it from his hand, then took it up. He lay staring . . . shocked . . . expecting death.

I broke the blade over my knee and threw the pieces to the earth.

"Come, Lila," I said, "we will go to our ship."

"You are a bold man," Lila said. "I begin to see what she sees in you."

The closer we came to the *fluyt* the better I liked her— a neat three-master with nice lines. Yet when we went up the ladder to board, I was shocked.

Her decks were dirty and she looked unkempt and down-at-heel, certainly no proper look for a trim Dutch vessel. Several hands were loitering about and one man stood upon the quarter-deck staring down at me and at Lila.

"Who be you?" he demanded.

"Your new master," I told him, mounting the ladder to stand facing him. "Your former master and I had a bit of a difficulty, and those who were ashore decided they'd prefer me as master."

"They did, did they?" He scowled at me. "They said naught to me!"

I smiled at him. "There's the ship's boat alongside. Go ashore and talk to your former master, if you like."

"You'd like that. To have me go ashore and leave you to command!" He stared at me from under bushy brows. " 'Tis an unlikely thing."

He peered at me. "Who says you can handle a ship? Or a crew?"

"Ask them below there," I said, gesturing. "Now go below and get yourself a clean shirt, clean pantaloons and a trim for your beard after a shave. Don't appear on this quarter-deck without them."

He started to argue, his eyes peering at me. "Go," I repeated, "or you'll find yourself among the crew."

"You'll need a new sailing-master then," he said, "unless you can lay a course yourself, for there's no other aboard can do it."

"Show up here looking the way an officer on the poop deck should look, and you'll keep the job," I said harshly. "Otherwise I'll do it myself."

"You can lay a course, can you?"

"Aye," I said, "but I've no wish to displace you."

Grumbling, he went down the ladder, and with Lila following I went into the aftercabin.

Surprisingly, it was not so bad as I'd expected. But it was still not good enough to suit Lila. "Go! Leave this to me! And the cooking, too! Just see there's enough aboard to do with!"

Out on deck again I turned the crew to, late as it was, and set them mopping decks, coiling lines, and making things shipshape. There were enough good Newfoundlanders aboard so that the job was not a great one, but it stirred them about and let them know a new hand was at the wheel.

All the while I was thinking. I'd no wish to be a pirate, only to be ashore in Raleigh's land with Abigail, at the same time I'd grown up in an England of the Armada, of Raleigh, Drake, Frobisher and Hawkins. Sea-fighting was in the English blood, and the Spanish were sailing their great galleons up the coast from the Antilles, loaded with gold, some of them.

With the crew at work I went to the aftercabin and spread out the charts on the great table there. They were old, none so good as those aboard my own ship, yet good enough, and I'd a memory for the charts I'd left behind. Yet I studied them, supplying what else was needed from the memory of those other charts.

Westward and south, along the shores of the Gaspé then south past Nova Scotia and down the coast, holding well out to sea.

I was still at the charts when an hour had passed and the sailing-master returned. He'd done a good bit to himself, and looked fresh and clean . . . at least, cleaner.

When he saw me studying the mouth of the great river of Canada, he shook his head. "Do not think on it. A strange ship has newly come there, a ship with many guns that flies no flag I've ever seen. He who commands is a

101

pirate also, but like none I have ever seen. He owns but one hand. Where another was there is now a hook, sometimes a claw or talon. He is a young man, very strong, very quick, and I believe he does not leave. An Indian told me he is building a great house, a castle, perhaps, on a hill in the mountains."

"We will avoid him then." Looking at the men down on the deck, I noticed one, a strongly made fellow with fine shoulders and a well-shaped head. "That one down there. Who is he?"

"A Newfoundlander, and a good man, too. His name is Pike. Or so they call him. He was a fisherman before he came with us, and a hunter of whales."

"And your name?"

"Handsel. The first name is Peter, but I am called Hans or Hands . . . it does not matter which."

"You know this man Pike?"

He nodded. "He works well, and he fights well." Then he added, "I think he is the best seafaring man aboard. He knows the sea and he has a love for the ship."

That night the food upon the table was food Lila had prepared, and it was good. The men ate, and ate, and pushed back from the table with a sigh. Watching them, I knew my struggle was over, for it is rare that sailors have such food and they would not risk losing her, even if they wished to lose me.

After a few days, I mused, I would have no trouble. Whoever heard of a revolution of fat men?

Long I studied the charts while the crew worked upon the deck, repairing lines and sails and simply dressing her up for sea. As the beauty of the ship became evident, their pride in her grew.

On the third day I was upon the deck and the man I had inquired about passed me. Within the hearing of several, I stopped him.

"Pike?"

He turned squarely to face me.

"Starting today you are sailing-master. You will direct the deck work, and the handling of sails. You will report to me . . . and only to me."

"Aye!"

"The ship is our home, Pike. It is also our fortress, our refuge. I wish it treated so. If there comes a time when we must sail through the eye of a needle, I want her ready. Do you understand?"

"I will do that. She will be ready, Captain."

On the fifth day we sailed out of the harbor and set our course for the coast of the great land to the west, but I chose a route that would hold us far at sea and clear of the Gaspé.

Whoever the pirate was who had the claw hand, I had no quarrel with him. Let him go his way, and I mine, and mine was for Raleigh's land.

For three days the wind held true and we made good weather of it, seeing neither land nor ship, nor wishing it. My intent was to reach for the south, closer to home, and perhaps a Spanish ship.

On the sixth day in the morning watch there was a cry, "Sail ho!"

With the glass I'd found aboard I studied her. It was a small fishing vessel, nothing aboard, no doubt, but hardworking fishermen and their catch, and I'd rob no such man.

"The other would have," Handsel said grimly. " 'Twas said he passed nothing!"

"And wasted his time," I replied shortly, "judging by what's below."

Twice during the next few hours we sighted craft. One was another fishing vessel; the second was an Icelandic boat. Having been dealt with so justly at their hands, I had no intention of returning the favor by looting a craft that might belong to some friend of Thorvald's.

Now we moved in closer to the coast. It was a dangerous practice, and this I knew, but I believed that most Spanish craft came north along the great warm stream that flows along the coast of America until nearly opposite Raleigh's land, when they turned eastward for Spain.

We were still far to the north, but there was ever a chance . . .

Pike was at my elbow. "Captain," he spoke for my ears only, "there's a vessel beyond the island there." He indicated the direction with a nod. "Over the trees? Can you see?"

"Aye." I directed my glass that way and saw it plain, only the tips of her masts visible above the trees on the low, sandy island. Those masts should be showing well above the trees, and I had an idea about that.

"Pike, have a look. What do you think of her masts?"

He peered through the glass, then turned to me. "She's stepped her topm'sts, Captain. Whoever she is, she's stepped her topm'sts not to be visible. For some reason she's lying up."

"Aground?"

"She's on an even keel. She's making repairs, I'd say, or being looted."

Taking the glass I studied the shore. The island was low and sandy with a few sandhills covered with coarse grass, and the sandy ridge along the backbone of the island was covered with pines.

There was a mild sea running and we eased the whipstaff to guide her in closer along shore. I saw no sign of life anywhere.

Night was coming on and I liked not the look of the shore.

"Captain?" Pike said. "We've a man aboard knows this island."

I lowered my glass, incredulously.

"Aye, we call him Blue, for there's an odd color to his skin. He was fishing off the Banks and was blown away for several days ahead of a storm. He once landed here for water . . . there's springs on the other side."

"Have him up. I would speak with him."

Still no sign of life or movement. Was she a dead ship, then? Or some trick of the eye and no ship at all? Or were we watched from beneath the pines, yonder?

Blue was a lean, long-armed man with a face scarred by powder or some such thing, giving it a blue cast.

"I know her," he said, "and there's a fair anchorage

beyond the island, good holding ground if the weather be good. More than one ship has watered there."

It was growing dark, but through the glass which I handed him he could barely make out the masts. "I've a feeling about her," he said, taking the glass from his eye, "and I'd be hard put to say the why of it, but I am certain sure she is Flemish. My eyes are better than most and I seem to see a heart-shaped dead-eye in her rig—and the Flemish do like them so."

Under his guidance, and with careful use of the lead, we worked our way about the end of the island, with no lights showing.

In a small cove Blue knew, we dropped our anchor and lowered a boat. With a dozen men, I led a reconaissance.

Up the low, sandy shore, over the sandhills and along the edge of the trees. Walking quietly was not an easy thing, for there was much debris—fallen limbs, broken twigs, and leaves. Yet we managed it, and slowly, warily, we made our way through the trees.

Blue caught my arm, pointing.

Not one ship, but two! Closer to the shore was a Flemish galleon, a fine craft of a type they'd been building no more than ten or a dozen years, beautifully ornamented along her gundeck. Obviously her masts had been stepped to avoid any sudden escape, but her way out of the inlet was blocked by the other ship, of which we could make out very little in the darkness.

An awning had been spread and several men were seated under it, drinking. At least, three were drinking and the fourth sat opposite them, his hands tied behind him. Further along the beach another fire had been lighted and we heard shouting and laughter from there, drunken laughter, it seemed.

"A fine place!" One of the men was saying. "A dozen times I've used it, and a dozen good ships looted and their loot taken aboard our own craft at our leisure."

He pointed a finger at the bound man. "Come now! We know there's gold aboard, and the gold we will have, or we'll take your hide off, an inch at a time."

He was a big man, by the look of him, although he was seated on a cask. He had a dark, saturnine look about him, with a taunting, evil face, and his companions looked no better. I glanced toward the beach to see how many men were there . . . a dozen? More . . . many more.

At least thirty, and there might be fifty. How many were left aboard? And was there anybody on the captured vessel?

Abruptly, I turned and led the way back out of the brush. "Blue, keep an eye on that ship." I pointed to the captured vessel. "Let no one see you, but keep an eye on them. If there's any move, come to me at once."

On the shore we got into the boat, and in a matter of minutes I was sitting in the aftercabin of the *fluyt* with Pike and Handsel.

"You will stay with the *fluyt*," I told Handsel. "At the first light, bring her off the mouth of their cove, and have her ready for action. Can you do it with a dozen men?"

"With this craft I can. The Dutch build their ships to be worked by few hands."

"Bring her around at daylight, then, and train your guns on the pirate ship, but do not fire unless fired upon."

Turning to Pike, I said, "You take a dozen men and seize the ship. Go around by boat . . . 'tis all in darkness yonder by their ship. Slip aboard and take over. When you have her, run up a white flag or any bit of white cloth on the fo'm'st."

"And you?"

"We'll go the way we went before, meet Blue, and take the master of the ship and his prisoners. Be wary now, I want to lose no men, but if you move with swiftness and silence you'll have them. Most of the crew is ashore and drunk."

Pike turned to leave. "Pike?" He stopped. "I trust in your judgment. If at any point you think the job cannot be done, return to the *fluyt*. You'll get no argument from me."

All was dark and still when we next came through the pines. The fires still flickered on the beach, but few men stirred. Most were already in a drunken sleep.

106

Under the awning the three men sat, still baiting the captured captain. "You have until daybreak. Think it over," the pirate was saying, "or else we'll skin you alive."

Softly I came to the edge of the pines. The wind had swept clear the sand upon that side, and it was but a dozen steps to the side of the awning. A moment I hesitated there, drawing my sword from its scabbard. Blue moved off to my right, drawing his cutlass. Three other men were with us, and we moved in closely.

"Skin you!" the dark man repeated drunkenly. "We'll skin you alive! There's gold. I know there is gold."

"There is no gold," the prisoner replied calmly. He had a fine look of contempt for them. "I am a merchant venturer. We have cloth for trading with the Indians, and we hope to obtain furs. We have some knives, some tools. We are none of us wealthy men."

I had walked quietly forward. "I believe you, my friend, and I shall be content with your cargo. You may keep your vessel and your hide."

"Wha—*what?*" One of the men came to his feet, the others just stared. But their captain did not move. His back to me, he simply spoke quietly.

"Whoever you are, you had best leave. The ship is mine, the cargo is mine, and this man's skin is mine."

"Yes?" I touched the back of his neck with my sword point, denting the skin.

"Yes," he repeated, and he moved not a hair. "And your skin, too, if you do not put that sword aside. You see," he said calmly, "I know who you are, I know what ship you had, I know what you plan to do . . . and you are now *my* prisoner. Though it is possible," he added, "that we might reach an agreement, Barnabas Sackett. We just might."

For once I knew not what to say, nor which way to move. A quick glance toward the pirate ship . . . no white flag.

A glance back toward the opening of the cove, and my vessel was not there, either.

Blue was with me, but where were the others?

"Taking over a pirate ship," the captain continued,

"is never as simple as it seems. You see, your man Handsel used to sail with me. He knew I used this island, knew what ship you had seen, and saw a chance to become master of a vessel serving under me. When you came ashore the first time, he sent a message to me, and since then we have been simply waiting. Surrender. Surrender now, or die."

"You have nerve, my friend, but nerve is not enough when I have a sword. If one wrong move is made, I'll lean on this blade. Will you but feel the needle point? It is razor sharp. One move, and no matter what happens after, your spinal cord is severed."

He held very still, but he laughed softly. "So what do you do now?" he asked. "Kill me, and you die next. If you do not kill me, my men will surround you and take you. What will you do now?"

With my left hand I drew a pistol from my waistband. Was Blue with me or against me? I gambled that I had judged him right.

"Blue, keep them covered with your pistol and shoot the first one who twitches. And cut loose the unfortunate captain."

△ 12 △

Blue did not hesitate, but moved swiftly behind the prisoner and cut him loose.

The man stood, tottered, and almost fell, then braced himself, chafing his wrists to restore circulation. "Thank you," he said quietly. "I am grateful."

"You have a crew?"

"Yes . . . a few are left. They are prisoners aboard my ship."

"We must free them." I glanced toward the pirate ship . . . and still no white flag fluttered from the masthead, nor had my vessel appeared off the cove.

And what of Lila, still aboard the *fluyt?* She was a strong, capable young woman, but there were evil men aboard the Dutch ship, and Lila was alone. What would the Newfoundlanders do?

"Take that line, Blue, and let's put some lashings on our friend here."

"You're acting the fool," the pirate said calmly. "I am the only one who can help you now. You live or die as I decide. As for the gentleman you so kindly released, do you suppose he will help you? He wishes only to take his ship and escape. You can expect no help from him, and your own crew have sold you out."

"One of them has," I said, "or so it seems. But I had no ship or crew when first I came upon them, and what I've done once I can do again."

Blue lashed the pirate's wrists snug and tight, and then those of the other two, who sat quietly under the muzzle of my pistol and the threat of my blade.

"My name is Duval," the pirate said. "You have heard of me?"

"I have not," I replied shortly, "but no doubt there's a noose waiting for you somewhere."

"If you've not heard of me," he spoke contemptuously, "you're no seaman."

"I know little of pirates," I said, "except for one called the Claw."

He gave me a sharp look. "Talon, you mean. That is what they call him now. Ah, yes! He was the one. But he has retired now. He swallowed the anchor and built himself a place ashore."

"He still has ships on the sea."

Duval shrugged. "It may be true. How do you know of him?"

I ignored his question, gathering up the weapons that lay about. There were several pistols and cutlasses.

The sky was growing gray in the east. There was no sign of the *fluyt* and I knew I must do what had to be done without her.

And whatever could be done must be done at once,

swiftly. I glanced upward and the thought came to me with the wind.

"We should fly our flag," I said, "and that will be our mast." I indicated a tall, almost bare pine that towered high.

They stared at me, unsure of what I meant. "We will use Duval for our flag," I said. "Get a line over that big bough and we'll hoist him up there."

Duval's face went white. "You can't—"

"Oh, we're not going to string you by the neck," I said. "We'll just hang you up there out of harm's way. Of course," I added, "if you struggle too much you might work yourself loose, and if you do that, you'll fall."

From the ship's stores brought ashore from the captured vessel, Blue took a heaving line. Bending the end of it to a stronger line, he threw the heaving line over the branch on the second try, then pulled the heavier line over.

Rudely he pulled Duval around and, taking a turn around his ankles and another around his bound arms, they laid hold of the line and hoisted him aloft, nearly fifty feet in the air, hanging face down from a limb.

At the last minute Duval twisted, turned, and tried to fight. "Damn you! Turn me loose and I'll give you a thousand in gold! Two thousand! Anything! I'll get your ship back!"

"Hoist away," I said, and we hoisted.

"Looks right pretty up there," I commented. Then I glanced at the others. "Will you lie quiet or shall we hoist you aloft?"

"We ain't makin' no trouble. Just leave us be."

Thrusting two spare pistols in my waistband, I led the way toward the water. There was in my mind no thought of what might be done, only that somehow I must have the men free who were in that vessel, and somehow I must come by a ship.

Such carrion as Duval interested me not, nor his talk of gold or ships. I would be a trader in a new land, and perhaps at a later day, a farmer. Many a pirate had I known of, and most found their way to a gibbet. I had no such wish to be dancing on air at the end of it all. What was it Black Tom had called it? "The steps and the string." And well he might, for that was it.

Drunken men sprawled upon the sand, and we looked at them from a distance off. There were not enough of them.

"They be waiting aboard there," I told my companions. "Waiting for us, belike."

"Aye," Blue chuckled, "I wonder if they've sighted our colors yon."

"If they have," I said, "it will give them something to think on."

I turned on the man we had freed. "And your name is what?"

"My name is Hanberry. James Hanberry. English to my father's side, Dutch on my mother's, and I live mostly in the Netherlands. I've a good cargo aboard there," he said, "one I'll fight to keep."

"You lost it," I replied coolly, "and if we get it back, I shall claim a part."

"Then do what you have to do by yourselves! I'll be damned if—"

"Be damned then," I said cheerfully. "You'd be skinned alive by now had it not been for me. You will either help or go your own way."

We walked, and when we had gone some thirty yards, he ran to catch up. "You shall be damned, Sackett! The Good Lord will send you to the lowest hell!"

"Let him, then," I replied. "In the meantime, we have work to do."

Turning to Blue I said, "What think you of Pike?"

"A true man, say I, and I have known him these twenty years, boy and man. If he has not flown the white flag it was because he could not."

The wind was growing colder. Whitecaps showed themselves, cresting each wave. The tops of the pines bent before the wind, and I did not envy the captain, hanging on high.

The two ships lay off the shore, almost side by side. We climbed into a ship's boat and pushed off. Pistol poised, I watched the rail of the pirated ship and saw no movement.

There was a rope ladder over the side. As we drew up we made fast to the bottom of it and I climbed swiftly and swung over the rail.

A faint creak warned me. A door stood partly open. The ship moved gently upon the water, but the door did not swing.

Blue hit the deck behind me, Captain Hanberry a moment later. "The door," I whispered. "There's somebody back of the door."

Turning sharply as if to the ladder to the afterdeck, I wheeled quickly as I reached it, grasped the latch, and jerked the door open.

A man sprawled upon the deck, then started to rise, "Get up if you're friendly," I told him, and shifting the pistol to my left hand, not wishing to waste a shot on so vulnerable a target, I drew my blade.

He got to his feet slowly, a thick-lipped man with blue eyes and a florid face. "I be one of the crew," he said, "Cap'n Hanberry will speak for me."

"He is that," said Hanberry, "and a good man, too. Where are the others, Rob?"

"Below decks," he said, "workin' theirselves free. I was the first. I come above decks to see how the wind blew. There be two men in the aftercabin, Cap'n, scoffing an' drinkin'. There be another for'rd, I'm thinkin'."

"I'll take the one for'rd," Blue said.

He left me, moving swiftly along the deck, and I stepped into the after passage, which was a short one, with a door to right and left, and the main cabin straight aft. I walked on, opened the door, and stepped in.

There sat a man with his feet on the table, tipped back in a chair. He suddenly slammed his feet to the floor and I shot him as he reached for a pistol.

The ball took him fairly in the chest as he started to rise, and I turned swiftly as a second man heaved a bottle. Dodging the bottle I sprang past the table. He came up, cutlass in hand. Then he looked across his blade at me and suddenly threw his weapon down.

"No," he said, "I'll be damned if I do! I'll not fight for Duval. I'll not risk my neck."

"Then out upon the deck, man, and take that with you." I indicated the body. "There's more outside."

Flemish galleon she was, the forem'st stepped forward of the forecastle as on most galleons, decks narrower than her sides because of the Danish tax, which charged according to the width of the deck. A good, solid vessel which I liked not so well as the *fluyt*, but almost as much.

Her topm'sts had been taken down so she'd not show above the trees and could be looted in security. She carried thirty guns, and how she had been taken I could not guess, for the pirate vessel opposite carried only twelve, although obviously a fast sailer.

From behind the mainm'st I looked over at the pirate vessel, scarcely a cable's length off. She looked dark and sullen, low upon the water as if crouched to spring. There was no sign of Pike, nor of any of the others, nor was there movement upon the shore opposite.

I turned upon Hanberry. "How is it to be, Captain? Do you follow my lead in what happens now? Or, when your men are free once more, will you leave us?"

He flushed somewhat. "Do you think me ungrateful? We shall carry on, although my men are not schooled in fighting."

"If they trade in these waters, they'd better be," I replied.

Beyond the pirate ship the pines were a dark huddle against the white of the sand—a thicker patch and deeper than those we'd come through to capture Duval.

Was that where Pike waited? Was the watch kept so well he dare not attempt an attack?

Well, then. If we could attract the attention of those aboard the pirate craft, then he might have his chance.

"Open the ports," I said, "and run out your guns. First, make sure they are charged."

"You'd fight here?" Hanberry's voice shook a little. "In this cove?"

"Why not? At such close quarters both ships will be battered to kindling, and they know it. And we've fifteen guns to their six. Charge every gun, six with chain and grapeshot to clear the decks, nine with heavy shot. Four to aim at the gun deck, five at their waterline."

Hanberry's face was pale, but as his men streamed on deck, he gave the order. They rushed to the gun deck and their guns.

"What's her name, Captain? I cannot see it from here."

"The *Hayda*."

"Ahoy, *Hayda!*" I called. "Surrender at once or be blown out of the water!"

There was a long moment of silence. Then a voice called out, "Who speaks? Where is Captain Duval?"

"Barnabas Sackett is the name, and your Duval hangs from the pine yonder, where you will hang also unless you give up the ship."

A man stepped into the rigging in plain sight. "I'll see you in hell first!" he shouted. "We took your ship once and we'll do it again!"

There was no sign of Pike.

"Is that what you all say?" My voice carried easily across the narrow gap between the vessels. "If you don't want to die for the man who spoke, then throw him into the water. If he isn't in the water by the time I count three—!"

From over the bulwark I could see crouching men running to man the guns.

"Just a minute here," he called. "Let's talk this over!"

"Fire!" I replied.

The galleon jolted sharply with the concussion and the broadside's recoil rolled us over, then back. Bracing myself, hand gripping a stay, I peered through the billowing smoke.

"Load numbers three, four, and five with grape," I ordered, "and stand by to fire."

Hanberry rushed to me. "They'd have surrendered!" he shouted angrily. "They were ready to surrender!"

"They were preparing to fire," I replied shortly, "while he talked."

A man ran forward and dove into the water, then two more.

As the smoke lifted somewhat we could see that the mainm'st was down, that portions of the rigging had been carried away, and that great, gaping holes had been ripped in the gundeck. Five holes at the waterline were pouring water into the hold.

"Damn you!" Hanberry shouted. "Damn you for a scoundrel! They'd have surrendered!"

Pike and other men were rushing from the pines toward the shore. Beyond our view, and along the shore, there was a sudden clash of arms, the sound of guns and yells.

As suddenly as they began, the sounds ceased. Then moments later, a boat appeared around the stern of the *Hayda*.

Turning to Hanberry, I covered him with a pistol. "I will take your weapons, Captain," I said politely. "After this is over they will be returned."

"I'll be damned if you do!" he said.

"Would you rather be aloft there?" I asked mildly.

Swearing, he handed over a pistol and his sword. It was a gentleman's dress sword, hardly what one needed in such a place as this. Still, it was a weapon.

Pike and the others had reached our deck. "Sorry for the delay, Captain Sackett, but they had a party on the beach there, and we'd have lost men trying it. As you wished, I waited."

There was still no sign of the *fluyt*. "Gather all the weapons," I said. "Do what you can for the wounded."

They worked swiftly. Turning to look about me at the galleon, I could see no evidence of damage. Duval and his men seemed to have taken the Flemish ship without a struggle.

The *Hayda* was listing heavily to the starboard.

Pike returned. "What happened to the *fluyt*, Cap'n? Did she na come around?"

"We'll find her, Pike. Let us speak with Hanberry, and do you stand beside me when the talking is done."

It was no easy thing to sort out what remained. The *Hayda* was a wreck, not that good seamen could not put her into some kind of shape, but it would take much time, and much hard work.

A dozen or so of the *Hayda*'s men had been killed in the broadside we loosed upon them, and most of those killed were the ones who had rushed to line their guns upon us. A dozen and a half were wounded, more or less, and some of the Flemish lads had cuts and scrapes from the fighting, but nothing to speak of.

Hanberry was in no good mood when we sat down together. "This is foul treatment!" he protested. "I am an honest merchant, with an honest crew. Who are you, anyway, Sackett?"

"For the moment, a pirate, it would seem. A privateer, perhaps, although I confess I have no letter of marque."

"Return my ship to me or I shall see you hang!"

His remark made me smile, for was I not already in risk of my neck? The problem facing me was a perplexing one, and I was in no mood for problems. I wished only to have a good ship under me and to be again on my way to Raleigh's land. But the only available ship was Hanberry's vessel. With it in my possession, I might retake the *fluyt*, rescue Lila—if she needed it—and then be on the way to our rendezvous with Abigail and Captain Tempany.

"Return *your* ship?" I said. "You have no ship, Hanberry. It was taken from you, and when I came here you were in danger of being skinned alive. You had lost your ship, Captain. You had almost lost your life, and the lives of your men as well. I took not the ship from you, but from Duval, who hangs up above us.

"You have water for blood, Captain. You were afraid to fight, afraid to fire, afraid to resist or not to resist. I suggest when next you come to shore, if you live to do so, that you stay there. That you find yourself a shop in a town that has a good night watch, and always be under cover with the doors locked by sundown.

116

"Understand this, Captain. You lost your ship. You have no ship. Duval had it, now I have it. What happens to you now depends upon what I decide, and I may leave you here with Duval, to settle it between you."

Oh, he hated me! He hated me not only for what I said but for what I had done that he had not done.

Whether I was a good man I did not know. I knew I was a man who wished to survive, and that to survive I must use both wits and strength.

"If I can use this ship to retake my *fluyt*, I shall. There are reasons why the attempt must be made. If I cannot, I shall sail in it where I am going."

"And what will you do with us?" he asked. I left that to his imagination. He had seemed, when I had first seen him sitting there, bound and facing Duval with contempt, a brave man. He was nothing of the kind, only a good talker and a hater without the will to fight as he must.

I now had sixteen men. Hanberry had at least twenty, but several of his had already lined up with mine in the fighting and the work.

Later, I put it to them honestly. "I want my *fluyt* again. If I get it, I shall not want this craft. The cargo is mine as a prize of war. If you choose to sail with me, and to leave with me when we have the *fluyt*, you shall be rewarded. I can promise you fighting, hope of rich reward, and a chance to go home. If you choose to stay with him, I shall give no argument."

Nine of the twenty chose to join with me, several quibbled and were uncertain. I merely told them, "We will strip the damaged vessel of her cargo, her guns, whatever is aboard of value. We will do it now."

One of those who had declared for Hanberry said, "And if we've no mind to work?"

I smiled. "I hope, then, that you're a good fisherman. There are fish to eat, and shellfish, too, by the signs along the shore. So try your luck. Those who do not help will not eat."

He shifted his feet, glowering at me.

The men available I turned to on Duval's ship. We

dumped three guns over the side to right her a bit, although it did but little, then we opened her hatches and went to work.

The several ships Duval had looted had netted him little, yet there was much powder and shot, a great store of lead, some foodstuffs the water had damaged already, but much else still of value.

When we had gathered much of it on deck, Pike took several of the men and warped Hanberry's galleon alongside. Rigging a sling and tackle, we began transferring the loot from Duval's *Hayda* to the galleon.

It was not a rich cargo, as such cargoes go, but the powder, shot, and lead were worth much more than their weight in gold to me.

Finally, we lowered Duval from his pine tree. He stared at me with such hatred as I have rarely seen. "I'll have your heart out for this!"

"Hoist him aloft," I told Blue.

Duval grabbed at my arm. "No! My God, man, you can't do that!"

"Then keep a civil tongue in your head."

Turning to Blue, I said, "Put him in the brig on his own ship, and put a man on watch. If he tries to escape while you do so, shoot him."

At last I stood on the beach, facing Hanberry.

"You have the *Hayda*. If you have resolution enough you can patch her up and sail her out of here."

He stared at me, choked with fury. By the rules of war, his own ship was mine, and his cargo also. Yet I promised myself that if I could find the *fluyt* and retake her, then I'd return his ship to him with those of his crew I had aboard.

We left him there upon the shore.

On the afterdeck I met with Pike and Blue. "You know Handsel best. What do you think he would do?"

"I have been thinkin' of that," Pike said. "He'd but twelve men aboard . . . not all of them able. He can handle the *fluyt* with the number, but he'll not be able to fight her. Nor will he return to Newfoundland, for well he knows they'd be askin' of me there, and of

118

Blue here. I think he would sail on down the coast."

We talked of it until the day was gone and the stars were out, trying each possibility and the arguments against. Finally, I sent Pike below for sleep and held the watch alone.

She was a neat craft, this Flemish galleon, not large but easily handled as were the Dutch craft. With so many ships upon the water, the Dutch had learned they must make their ships easier to handle, and had done so. They were cracking fine seamen, the Dutch.

Midnight was long past when I awakened Pike.

The clouds had cleared away and the stars were bright in the sky. There was a mild sea running, and enough wind to carry canvas without worry. We were making good time at last, heading south and a little west. At this point the coast of America slanted away to the south-west, and I knew from the charts there were scattered islands off the coast.

And somewhere far down the coast, without me, was Abigail, in what kind of weather I knew not.

But first I must find Lila and free her . . . or them!

△ **13** △

Now being at sea again, and south-bound, my spirit was at rest, for though much trouble might come, I had my destination before me.

The continent lay west of us, just beyond the horizon, and we kept a man aloft at all times, alert to see any vessel that might hove into sight. But mostly we looked for the *fluyt*.

It was not in me to go a-pirating, nor was it large in the minds of my crew, for well they knew we had a goodly store below decks and if a port was made with what we had, all should do well.

Soon we sailed closer to the shore. Twice we sighted

small boats, but they fled on seeing us, taking their cargoes of fish into shallow waters where we could not follow. Yet one fellow was close enough that we hailed him.

He came alongside, wary of us, but curious. I traded some line and canvas for fish, and asked about the *fluyt*.

"Aye, see her we did! She's lying up in the lee of a high, rocky island a half-day's sail to the south, or was before daylight. We saw her before, and not likely to forget it, either, with a great, tall woman at the wheel, hair flying in the wind!"

"A *woman?*"

"You think me a liar? Well, I am neither a liar nor drunk . . . a woman, I say! And such a woman as you never saw!"

So now it seemed we were close, and all my troubles might be resolved at once, yet I was not one to count money before it was paid me. I bade good-bye to the fisherman and we had up some canvas and took our way south, with me sore afraid the *fluyt* would have flown before we had sight of her. Yet for once good fortune was with me, and we rounded into the cove to see her lying there, waiting.

We came in close enough and let go our anchor, and a boat to the water almost as quickly.

She was at the rail when I came alongside.

"Is it you then?" she asked. "Full long enough you took!"

"What in blazes happened? Where's Peter Handsel?"

"He's below . . . confined in the rope-locker. The crew liked my cooking better than his sailing, so I've been sailing-master and cook as well."

She looked closely at the Flemish craft. "A good ship," she decided, "but I like this one better."

We wasted no time with further talk. If it pleased the Lord that I come well home again to Raleigh's land, I'd be happy, and if it were soon, happier still.

It was true I had done well with my fishing in troubled waters, but more by good fortune than by my own efforts, although I had not hesitated when it was time to act, and sometimes that is the whole face of it.

With Pike and Blue in the cabin, I spoke them fair. We'd rich cargo below, and I'd taken them to it, and so I told them I should take the powder, lead, round-shot, and the beads and trade goods. The richest of the cloth they might have.

So I divided the cargo there, and they had no word to say against it, and my portion was shifted to the *fluyt*. Much of what I wanted most for Raleigh's land they could easily come by in Newfoundland, but the cloth was a rich thing.

"And the Flemish ship, then?" Pike asked.

"I give her to you," I said. "Sail, sell, or sink her, she's yours, but if you decide to sail her, come along down to Raleigh's land with such cargo as I am taking, trade goods for the savages, and powder, shot, and some food for us, and we'll make trade together."

"I never thought to have a ship nor become a merchant," Pike said, "but I shall do both."

So we parted there, clasping hands at the last, and I went about the galleon and shook each hand and thanked each man for his help, and we parted, one sailing south and one north with the first light.

Some of my men went with Pike, and some of Pike's with me, I taking only those who dared the new land.

We sighted three ships that gave us chase, but we, perceiving their intent, clapped on all sail and fled away to the westward, and having the wind of them we were well away and they gave up the chase, not knowing what we were or whether worth their effort.

Dearly now, I needed sight of the land. My charts were out upon the table, but what use a chart without a sighting? We had come from Newfoundland over to the coast, and followed it down some distance, but not nearly so far as Raleigh's land.

So we edged in close, and I caught a cape in my glass that had a familiar look, then a rivermouth and a queer tuft of trees, all marked on one of my charts. So I made us several days sail to the north of my thin sandy islands that divided the sounds from the sea at the place I sought.

Meanwhile, Lila made nothing of her story. She had barricaded herself in the galley with the keys to the storeroom in her pocket, and denied anyone entry or food until Handsel was in shackles and the key in her hands. Meanwhile she set to work to cook, letting the aroma of her cooking drift over the ship.

It has been said there were iron men aboard the wooden ships, and well there should have been—and for the most part they needed iron stomachs as well, to handle the cooking. Salt meat as hard as iron and biscuit full of weevils. Lila had cooked much for strong, hearty men and knew the weapon she possessed.

Two days it needed, and then they had brought her the key, led by a man named John Tilly, a fine seaman who liked not Handsel nor his kind. Although young, he had already been long at sea.

I was on the afterdeck, watching the sea, my glass ready to pick up any unusual thing upon the far waters, when Tilly came to me.

"Captain," he said, "we've a man aboard to whom you must speak. His name is Jago, and he comes from Anglesey as does the lass."

Something in his manner was odd, so I asked him, "Who is this Jago? Does he have a complaint?"

"None at all! From the first he stood beside me for taking Handsel. He is a fine seaman, Captain, and a good fighting man, but there is a strangeness on him at times and now there's a fear on him."

"A fear?"

"Of the waters ahead. He knows the coast you speak of, the place where we go. He has been in both the sounds and up one of the rivers, but it is the sea itself that he fears, the sea that lies off the coast of the place called Raleigh's land."

Of sailor's tales there is no end, nor of enchanted islands, vanishing ships, or mysterious places in the sea, and of this we who are of the Celtic race have understanding, so I had this Jago up to the deck and he was

122

no kind of a priestly man, nor a poet, either, but a strong fellow of middle size with a square head upon a solid neck, and two fine, strong hands.

"You are Jago?" I said.

"So they have said since I was old enough to listen, and I've no choice but to believe them. However, one name is as good as another, and if you've another you like, call me it and I will come."

"Jago is a fine name, and it pleases me. Do you know these waters, Jago?"

"No, nor any man for long. They be not twice the same. But you are safe enough this week. Next you will be south too far. You must steer clear of fogs and land on no strange islands. You know there are islands?"

"I do. I spoke of them with a friend of mine named Peter Tallis. They were discovered by Juan de Bermudez in 1515, and are said to be enchanted isles."

"Well they could be. Where else does coral be found so far north? Where else so many dangerous reefs? Enchanted the isles may be, but they be a hell for mariners, with their ugly reefs rising unexpected-like from the depths.

"There and south of there is the sea of which I speak. Beware it. Many ships have vanished. . . . There's an opening there sometimes, it comes and goes, sometimes it is in fog, and sometimes a spot of bright sunlight, but those who sail through never come back. Beware of a day when there's no fish around, for then it's to open, and well they know it and off they swim."

"I'll take your advice, Jago. Now tell me, do you know a stretch of coast with long thin outer islands? Banks that form a natural breakwater for two great sounds into which rivers flow?"

"I know the place. 'Tis west and south . . . two days more, I think."

"You've been there?"

"Twice, and once on a Spanish ship. I was a prisoner of them but spoke their tongue and am a good Catholic, so they used me as a seaman and I had freedom, of a sort . . . until I escaped. If it is there you'll go, I can be

123

taking you, and to whichever river you wish, for each has a different smell. One smells of freshness and the mountains, and two of swamps, and one of fish."

Far into the night I studied my charts.

It would be my second voyage to the sounds, and pausing in my study of the maps I thought again of that buried hulk in which I had taken shelter and where I had fought the alligator.

Whose ship might that have been? And what of its crew? If ships disappeared in these waters, as Jago said, then men vanished also. The Roanoke colony and Grenville's men . . . gone.

Many were the tales that came from the sea, but I had little faith in enchanted isles or haunted ships or the like. Those were sailor's tales to be told in port to goggle-eyed landsmen, and rarely believed of themselves. Yet . . . what Jago had told, Jago believed, and he was a no-nonsense sort of man, and a good seaman.

Many in the England of our good Queen Bess thought of this land as unknown, and indeed, much of it was, but where there are riches to be had, men will go, and the ships of Gosnold, Weymouth, Newport, and others had already cruised the coast. To the north were the ships of the French, and Cabot had sailed here, and Verrazzano, Corte-Real, and many another.

All the knowledge we had of such places was from the few men who could write and keep records, and how many could write? Among my crew, there were but three who could write, and if something happened to us, then what record could be left by the others?

I studied even my secret ones, which had far more detail, and I made a chart of my own from memory of what I had seen.

My plans must be simple, to be augmented with time. First, to find Tempany and Abigail, second to establish a trading post, third to cultivate friendship with the Indians, and fourth, to establish a base deeper into the country from which we could explore toward the mountains and to which I could retreat if a British ship with warrants for my arrest should come.

After a bit, I slept, awakening to go on deck for the morning watch. We had hove to during the night, simply taking in our sails and drifting.

Jago was on watch when I came on deck. "It will be a fair day, Cap'n, a fair day." He glanced at me. "Will we be making a landfall today?"

"Aye." I glanced toward the clouds that lay low along the horizon, and nodded to indicate them. "What do you make of them, Jago?"

"Cap'n," his voice shook a bit, "we'd better head in toward land. That's no natural cloud."

"Hail the men on deck," I said, "and shake out some canvas. Put a good man on the whip-staff for we'll be looking for our opening in the outer banks."

Taking my glasses, I studied the cloud. It seemed neither nearer nor farther off. The sky above was blue and lovely, but the white clouds, possibly a fog, lay close along the face of the sea, and once inside that cloud we should be able to go neither north, south, east, nor west.

The cloud hung there, turning slowly lighter as the sun arose. How easily, I thought, when the mind is prepared can one begin to believe!

It was only a cloud . . . a bit of fog that would clear with the day.

Only it did not.

There was little wind, and we moved but slowly. I looked again at the fog bank and it seemed closer. Jago was staring at it, obviously frightened. With my glass I lifted a strong dark line, like a thread. Land!

"Aye," Jago said, "and none too soon."

Lila came on deck and walked to the rail and looked astern. As she stood there the fog seemed to thin toward the center and dimly we seemed to see an island.

A mirage? My chart showed no island there. It suddenly seemed clearer. Were those houses? Temples? I walked to the after-rail and stared.

"See it, Cap'n?" said Jago. "See? Look, but never

speak of it, men will think you daft, as they have thought me. Look . . . something moves! Do you see it?"

Indeed, I did, or thought I did. I pointed my glass toward it again, and the figures leaped at me. Men . . . and women, all in strange costumes . . . temples of a sort not seen before . . .

"Captain," Tilly was speaking, "we're closing in on the shore. There seems to be an opening yon."

With an effort, I took my eyes away and looked shoreward. A long white beach, gleaming in the sun, a sandy shore stretching north and south as far as the eye could reach . . . and yes, there seemed to be an opening.

"Jago?" I said. He did not turn and I spoke again, more sharply. "*Jago!*"

"Aye, aye."

Indicating the opening, I said, "Do you know that one?"

"I do that. She's shoal, Cap'n, but with the lead we can go in yonder."

He looked back over his shoulder, and I over mine. The opening in the mist had closed, the mist was thinning, the fair vision of a city was gone.

Was it a mirage? For a moment it had seemed we looked into another world, as through a magic window or door.

Was that where the vanished ships had gone? Through that door? Into that mirage?

▵ **14** ▵

Cautiously, using the lead, I took the *fluyt* into the passage between the sandy islands, using only such sail as needed for steerage way. If we ran aground here and a storm blew up we would be at the mercy of wave and wind, and all my great hopes might vanish in what followed. If I ran aground, I wished it to be not too forcefully, that we might the easier escape.

Lowering a boat, we let it proceed before us, and thus found our way through and into deeper water, when we took the boat back aboard once more. Remembering my one-time meeting here with my old enemy Bardle, I had two guns prepared and gun crews standing by.

Blue, having the sharpest eyes, was posted aloft to look out for ships and savages, or any smoke which might hint of activity ashore.

Now that we were so close, Lila was silent, eyes wide with apprehension, fearful her mistress might have been killed, drowned, or otherwise lost. I scoffed at this, and kept still my own fears, for better than she I knew what dangers the country might hold.

Calling John Tilly aft, I told him I wanted the men to go below, two at a time, and arm themselves each with a cutlass, and then I wanted muskets charged and kept in a rack conveniently placed inside the door to the main cabin where they would be ready to hand.

Worried, I paced the afterdeck. I had armed myself with my sword as well as a brace of pistols, yet it was not of weapons I thought, for indeed, they were but a precaution. Captain Tempany was a fine seaman, and he'd a good crew aboard . . . but supposing he had been overhauled and forced back by a Queen's ship because of his connection with me?

What if pirates had taken his ship? Or storms?

Hour by hour my anxiety grew, and still no sign of the ship.

Darkness came, and rather than venture on we let go the anchor to wait for daybreak.

The ship should be here, yet if I recalled rightly there were four big rivers flowing into the two sounds, and a number of lesser streams. There were any number of coves and inlets in which the ship might be lying. I tried to think of all the reasons we had not found her, all that could be done, yet nothing gave me rest.

Alone I stood by the rail, looking shoreward. Restless, unable and unwilling to sleep, I had told Tilly to let the crew rest and when I was ready to turn in I'd awaken one of them to take my place on lookout.

Hearing a step, I turned. It was Lila. She came to the rail and stood beside me. "Will we find her?"

"I think so. If she is here, we'll find her."

"It is a vast land. I could not imagine it so big, so empty."

"There are Indians over there . . . many of them." I paused. "Not so many people as in England, of course. The way they live, mostly hunting and gathering berries, roots, and nuts, they need much land to support only a few."

"They do not plant?"

"Some of the tribes do. They plant corn, a few other things. Mostly they live by hunting, fishing, and gathering, so they move from time to time, going to new areas where they can find more game, and more food."

"Our coming will change them, I think."

"I don't know, Lila. Perhaps it will. Yes, I believe it will, and perhaps not for the better. They have a way of life that is not ours, beliefs different than ours. We will learn much from them about this country, and they will learn from us, but I am not sure whether what they learn will be good for them.

"All I know is that it is inevitable. If not us, then somebody else, and all change is difficult, all change is resisted, I think. No people can long remain in isolation, and men will go where there is land, it is their nature, as it is with animals, with plants, with all that lives.

"Since the beginning of time men have moved across the face of the world, and we like to believe this is a result of our individual will, our choice, and it may be so, but might it not be that we are moved by tides buried in our natures? Tides we cannot resist?

"Whole nations and tribes have moved, suddenly, always with some kind of an excuse. But was not the excuse sometimes found afterward? How do we know we make these moves by our own decision?

"Men like to believe themselves free from nature, free of the drives that move animals and plants, but wherever there is open space men will come to occupy it.

"The Indian himself has moved, pushing out other

resenting

The

LOUIS L'AMOUR

ollection

Explore

FLINT

Your first handsome hardcover
Collector's Edition
for 15 days
FREE

FLINT
IF HE HAD TO DIE, AT LEAST IT WOULD BE ON HIS TERMS.

Get a taste of the *true* West, beginning with the tale of *FLINT* FREE for 15 Days

Hunted by a relentless hired gun in the lava fields of New Mexico, Flint *"settled down to a duel of wits that might last for weeks...Surprisingly, he found himself filled with zest for the coming trial...So began the strange duel that was to end in the death of one man, perhaps two."*

If gripping frontier adventures capture your imagination, welcome to The Louis L'Amour Collection! It's a handsome, hardcover series of thrilling sagas by the world's foremost Western authority and author.

Each novel in The Collection is a true-to-life portrait of the Old West, depicted with gritty realism and striking detail. Each is enduringly bound in rich, Sierra-brown leatherette, with padded covers and gold-embossed titles. And each may be examined and enjoyed for 15 days. FREE. You are never under any obligation; so mail the card at right today.

Now in handsome Heritage Editions

Each matching 6" x 9" volume in The Collection is bound in rich Sierra-brown leatherette, with padded covers and embossed gold title... creating an enduring family library of distinction.

SILVER CANYON · LOUIS LAMOUR
THE DAYBREAKERS · LOUIS LAMOUR
FLINT · LOUIS LAMOUR

**Nobody writes
adventures like**

**Take "FLINT" for
15 DAYS
FREE!**

Bantam Books, Hicksville, N.Y. 11802

☐ YES! Send FLINT For 15 Days Free! If I keep this volume,
I will pay just $10.95 plus shipping and handling. Future
Louis L'Amour Westerns will then be sent to me, one each
month, on the same 15-day, Free-Examination basis. I
understand that there is no minimum number of books to
buy, and I may cancel my subscription at any time.
60533

Print
NAME_____

ADDRESS_____

CITY_____

STATE_____ ZIP_____
L82

**SEND NO MONEY.
JUST MAIL THIS CARD
AND RIDE INTO THE
REAL OLD WEST.**

BUSINESS REPLY CARD

FIRST CLASS   PERMIT NO. 2154   HICKSVILLE, N.Y.

Postage will be paid by addressee:

The
Louis L'Amour
Collection

Bantam Books
P.O. Box 956
Hicksville, New York 11802

NO POSTAGE
NECESSARY
IF MAILED
IN THE
UNITED STATES

Indians. I heard of this on my previous voyage . . . it is inevitable."

Long after Lila went to sleep, I paced the deck, wandering from bow to stern, alert for any moving thing upon the dark water. At last I awakened one of the men, a Newfoundlander I knew only as Luke, and left him on lookout.

Yet sleep did not come for a fear was on me, a fear for what could have happened to my love, she who had given up all for me to come to this far, strange place. How deep, how strange is the courage of women! Courage is expected of a man, he is conditioned to it from childhood, and we in our time grew up in a world of wars and press-gangs, of highwaymen and lords sometimes as high-handed as they. We grew up to expect hardship and war. But a woman?

I'd seen them follow their men to war, seen them seeking over battlefields to find their lonely dead, or the wounded who would die but for them. I have seen a woman pick up a man and carry him off the field to a place where he might have care.

Abigail, for all her life aboard-ship with her father, had given up all a girl might have for the hardship of life in a new, strange land, without comforts, without the chance of care if she came to a child-bearing time. At least, no care other than I could provide.

At last I slept, and it was full dawn before my eyes opened again, and when I came out upon deck we got under way, making our way past the tiny coves and inlets, the rivermouths and the bays.

No ship . . . nothing.

Had not two colonies disappeared here? Had not the men Grenville left vanished?

Into what limbo? To what awful death?

The green and beautiful shores took on a horror with their blank, unyielding, unspeaking faces. We looked, and our eyes told us nothing, for we could not see beyond the leaves, beyond the vines.

My eyes sought the stream where lay the old hulk where once I'd taken shelter. What brought that vessel to its end? Where were its crew? Where its cargo? To what mysterious end had it come at last, in this lonely place?

How lonely? How many eyes might peer from behind that screen of branches? How many might lie in wait for our coming ashore?

The *fluyt* was alone. No help would be forthcoming if grief came to our side. There was no warship to come, no signal could bring help. Whatever might be done we must do.

"Blue," I said at last, "let's go south to the other sound. They might be awaiting us there."

"Aye," he said gloomily, and I loved him for his sadness.

All aboard were strangely silent. No voice was raised in ribaldry or song, no loud hails were given out. Men walked quietly, understanding my worry and my doubt.

We edged again past Roanoke Island and into the larger sound. We saw no sail, no masthead beyond the trees. Two large rivers opened into the sound. Cautiously, we ventured into the nearest. Scarcely had we entered the mouth of this river that flowed from the west than another appeared, flowing down from the north. We held to the center of the river, taking soundings as we moved, and passed the point where the two rivers joined. We had gone past it only a short distance when suddenly, Blue, who was aloft, shouted.

"Cap'n? There's a wreck on the starb'rd beam! Burned ship, two points abaft the beam!"

I ran to the rail. It was there, lying on the western side of a small inlet or rivermouth. The current was not strong, yet there were mudbanks on either side.

"I'll go ashore," I told Blue, "and do you stay with the ship. Drop the anchor and wait, but keep a sharp lookout."

John Tilly came with me, and six good men, armed with musket and cutlass.

As the boat drew nearer we could see the ship's bow was firmly wedged into the mudbank. Either she had come in under some sail, driving hard on the mud, or else

130

there had been a good deal of a pile-up after she struck.

Only the hulk remained, burned near to the water-line with the charred butt of a mast over-side and some broken spars about.

Tilly pointed. "She was under fire, Captain. See the hole?"

There was a hole in the hull, right at the waterline, and I could see the top of another just below the water's edge. She had been hard hit, probably aflame before she struck.

"They drove her in a-purpose," Luke said suddenly. "They were wishful of getting ashore, I'm thinkin'."

Suddenly, I had a rush of hope. We edged in close and made fast to the hull, then Tilly, Luke, and I climbed over the wreckage to the shore. There had been a hard rain, and what tracks had been left, if any, had been washed away.

Slowly, we wandered about. Nothing . . . no single sign of anything that might have lived beyond the wreck, beyond the fire. Yet, the fact remained. Somebody *could* have made it ashore. There had been a daring lot aboard. For fearlessness in the face of danger, for ingenuity at survival, for skill in hand-to-hand combat, I could have wished Abigail in no better hands than those who sailed with her . . . if they had lived long enough to help.

"Go back to the boat, Tilly," I said. "We have come too late."

"It was your ship then?"

"Aye, and a fine lot of men aboard, and the girl who was to be my wife, and her father, a good man, a fine man. All gone."

"They might still live, Barnabas."

It was the only time he'd ever used my given name, and I looked up at him, seeing the sympathy in the man.

Luke had started back to the wreck. Now he called out, "Cap'n . . . look!"

I turned at his outstretched arm and pointing finger. They stood there, a small and haggard band, on the

131

edge of the forest. Some were still within the trees, but Jeremy Ring was there, and Sakim, and Black Tom Watkins, and—

She came from the forest and walked through the small group and stood there, staring toward me, a shabby, soiled, woebegone little figure.

Abigail . . .

△ 15 △

Her face was burned by the sun, her nose was peeling, she was scratched and torn, and her dress was in tatters. She stood quietly looking at me, surrounded by her ragged, half-naked band . . . all armed.

"I knew you'd come," she said simply. "I told them you'd come."

I went to her then across the sand, and took her in my arms, and so we stood for several minutes while the others filed past us, not looking, not speaking.

How many there were or who they were I did not know until later. At that moment I could think only of Abigail. Yet one question I did ask, and feared for the answer.

"Your father?"

"He is dead. He was killed in the attack. He told me to run her aground, to get away, and to wait for you. He told me that you'd come. He had great faith in you, Barnabas."

"I should have been here before, but so much has happened."

"Was it so very bad . . . in Newgate?"

"Nothing. Nothing to this, to what you have been through."

We turned then and walked to the boat, hand in hand.

For the first time I looked around. Pim was there, a wicked scar across his face now, and Sakim, looking no

132

different than I saw him last, only a little thinner. And there, too, was Jublain, the companion of my first venture from the fens.

"We shall go aboard now," I said.

Hours later, when Abigail had bathed and changed to fresh clothing we found aboard (for there was much loot in the hold), the story was told.

Their voyage had been smooth, easy. They had crossed the Atlantic in sixty-five days, making their first landfall far to the north, and seeing no other sails until close in to the coast of Raleigh's land when they saw topm'sts over the horizon that soon disappeared.

Knowing that if I did join them it might be many weeks, they had looked about for a location for a trading post, aware that such was my intent. They found several, one of them on a creek just a little farther along the river from where we were now anchored.

It was a few square miles of solid earth among the swamps that lay all about, with thick forests of cypress, bays, and myrtles, laden with Spanish moss and tropical vines. It was a place with a good breeze down the river, easy of access by boat or canoe.

They had run some lines off to a couple of huge old cypresses, and going ashore, had begun felling logs and clearing land.

They had been so occupied when Nick Bardle and his men appeared. They had left the *Jolly Jack* anchored out of sight in a small bay, and had slipped through winding waterways to the river above the ship, crossing the river at night and concealing themselves under overhanging cypresses. Just before daylight they pushed off and drifted down upon the silent ship.

Unknown to Bardle, Jublain and seven others had slept ashore to be prepared for an early start, trimming logs for the fort they were to build. When the attack began they had already gone into the woods to select trees for felling.

With only an instant's warning, Tempany cut his lines and attempted to get away downstream, hoisting canvas, and trying to deflect his guns to bring them to bear on the boats. Yet this Bardle had expected, and suddenly the *Jolly Jack* appeared in the rivermouth, cutting off any retreat. A broadside toppled the mainm'st and holed the ship in three places. With water rushing in, no chance of escape, with her father badly wounded, Abigail had herself ordered the ship run aground.

Her father died within those last minutes, and as the ship struck, what was left of the crew jumped to the mudflat and headed for the surrounding jungle.

Sakim, one of the last aboard, touched off two guns aimed at the *Jolly Jack*, then helped Abigail to escape from the ship. Fleeing into the woods, they joined forces with Jublain and his hastily gathered men, but there was nothing to be done. Their ship was in flames, Tempany was dead, and escape into the swamp was their only chance.

The vast and dismal swamp covered over two thousand square miles, a dense forest of black gum, cypress, and juniper, tangled with Virginia creeper, honeysuckle, and reeds. Much of it was deep, dark water, threatening and still. Sunlight filtered through the boughs overhead, and only here and there was there solid ground.

A ship's boat had been taken into the swamp for use on some of the winding waterways in hauling logs to the building site. Into this they climbed, slowly gathering up a few stragglers, then escaping into the depths of the swamp.

The only food they had was a little brought ashore for the men working on the fort.

Yet there were many deer, occasional bears, and many kinds of birds. Using much ingenuity they had somehow managed to exist.

Bardle, after putting out the fires, had looted the ship, then set fire to what was left and finished the burning. He had hunted for them, but a few well-placed shots from the swamp itself had dissuaded him. After a while, he had sailed away.

"You have not seen him since?"

"No," Abigail said, "and we kept a good watch because

we were expecting you. We did not know how you would come, or when, but we all believed in you."

"He will come back then," I said, "and we must prepare for that."

Long we talked that night, over the table and after, and I told her of my escape from England, and the part Lila played, but adding little about the difficulties on the island or my dealings with pirates. Yet as I spoke there came a little hint of warning: I had another enemy now in Duval . . . and Hanberry, too, when it came to that.

"For me," I said at last, "there can be no question of returning. All that is behind me, and from this moment we must build a new life in this land."

With sadness, I looked at her. "Abigail, I thought of none of this when you agreed to come with me. I had no idea I would forever cut off from all we know of home, so I want to say now you are free to go. The *fluyt* is here. We've a good crew. Tilly is a most able sailing-master and he can return you to England."

She filled my glass with ale. "You talk foolishness. I am no child to want only the glitter and the glory. There are enough women in England for that, and for all else, and good people they be, but I made my commitment to you long ago. If you stay, I stay . . . and I want to stay.

"Bad as it was out there in the swamp, I came to love it, although I, too, long for your blue mountains."

"But you must realize that I must avoid contact with other Englishmen. The order for my arrest will remain in force, and any ship that comes might bring those who would take me back. From now on we are not only exiles from England, but from Englishmen."

"So be it, then. I am content."

The night was filled with small rain. We had dropped down the river a bit and anchored out of the current in the sound. Because of the darkness and the rain I kept two men on watch, wary of what might befall.

Long I lay awake, considering what must be done. With Abigail to consider, I had also to think of ways to divert her, to keep her content with our life, and I thought of several. The first and most obvious I did not think of at all.

Lila did.

At daybreak I was in the cabin, charts spread out upon the great table, studying the courses of the rivers. The place Tempany had chosen I liked full well, but it was a place known to Bardle, a place where we might soon expect trouble, hence it was in my thoughts to move.

Once again we set sail and returned to the northern sound.

We were seeking out a river of which I had some small acquaintance on my previous voyage when Lila came to me with John Tilly.

"Here he is," she said.

"I see . . . and a good man, too."

"Of course he is a good man. He is a man of God."

"Aren't we all?" I said gently.

"I mean," she said severely, "that John Tilly is a minister of God."

Startled, I looked at him again. "Is this true, Tilly? I had no idea."

"You had no reason to suspect it. You found me upon a ship of pirates. I was a prisoner there until they discovered I was a capable seaman."

"Well, we can always use a man of God. Nice to have you aboard, Tilly."

"Captain Sackett," Lila said severely, "you do not seem to understand. John Tilly is a minister of God. As such he is empowered to perform *marriages*."

I do not think I am unusually dense, yet the thought that sprang immediately to mind was the wrong one. "Lila! You don't mean to tell me! You've found a man?"

She flushed. "That is not what I mean. I am thinking of you and Miss Tempany."

Well! For a moment I just stood there looking stupid, and then I said, "Of course . . . of course, Lila. I was thinking of other things, I—"

"You had better go ask her," she said gently, then.

"The Reverend and I will discuss what is to be done."

I looked around at the grinning sailors. Jeremy, who was chuckling, Jublain with his mocking smile, and Pim Burke. "Don't look so damned superior!" I said irritably. "That's why she came out here. It is just what we've planned."

"She's down in the waist," Pim said, grinning like a pleased ape. "Tell *her* about it."

Abruptly, I turned my back upon the lot of them and went down the ladder to where she stood alone near the rigging, watching the riverbanks not so far off.

She looked up as I drew near. "You know he liked you very much," she said.

"Who?"

"Father. He spoke to me of it many times."

"He was a good man, a strong, kindly man."

We stood by the rail looking shoreward. A heron flew up from the swamp back of the trees and banked away on slowly flapping wings.

"I want to build a stockade," I said, "with the buildings all inside, a place on a hill with a good field of fire all around. It will have to be close to the river so ships and boats can come in close.

"Then I want to get a vegetable garden and some grain growing, and to plant a small orchard."

"I'd like that."

"By the way, there's a man up on the afterdeck you should know, a very special kind of man."

She turned and looked at me. "You mean there's somebody I haven't met?"

"Well . . . you've met him, I'm sure, but not in his official capacity, and that's the only way to really know him. Come . . . we'll go aft and see him."

"Now? I was enjoying this."

Taking her by the arm, we started toward the ladder to the afterdeck. We were almost at the top of the ladder, and John Tilly was waiting near the whip-staff with his Bible in his hand. Lila was there, and most of the crew were arranged in respectful rows on either side.

"What does this man do?"

"What does he do? Why, he marries people. He's a minister of the Church."

She stopped abruptly. "Barnabas . . . ?"

"We mustn't keep the man waiting, Abigail. You can marry me now and resent at leisure."

"I shall never resent it or you." She looked around quickly. "Oh, Barnabas! You . . . I must look a sight."

"You couldn't be lovelier. Come on now."

She looked up at me. "Why! You're laughing!"

"It is a fault I have. There is something about solemn occasions that always stirs my humor. I like them, I respect them, but sometimes I think we all take ourselves too seriously."

"You don't think marriage is serious?"

"Of course, I do. It is the ultimate test of maturity, and many find excuses for avoiding it because they know they are not up to the challenge, or capable of carrying on a mature relationship."

We stopped in front of John Tilly.

Out upon the sound a slight wind ruffled the waters. The morning sun was bright upon every wavelet, and on the shore-side trees the leaves stirred occasionally in the slight wind. Three gulls winged their way overhead on slow, easy wings.

The deck tilted slightly under our feet and Tilly's low, well-modulated voice began the service.

I looked at the girl beside me, saw her hair stir slightly in the wind. Her fingers clutched at mine and held on, very tightly.

She was far from home, her father was dead, and she was marrying a man whose future was bound to a strange, lonely land.

When the brief ceremony was concluded we walked to the taffrail and stood there together, not talking, just looking out over the water.

"This can only be our first home," I told her, "for later we must go to the mountains and build there. We must have a place to go when the Queen's officers come . . . and they will."

138

That night we remained aboard the *fluyt*, which we now christened the *Abigail*.

We stood together under the stars, smelling the strange, earthy smells from the shore of rotting vegetation, of flowers and the forest, and some faint smell of woodsmoke from the fire of some of my men, who stayed ashore.

"My mother," I said, "made a prophecy before I was born. It is thirty years ago, I think, or near to that. A man was about to attack her, and before my father came, she told the man he would die by the sword of her son, in the ruins of a flaming town."

"Lila told me the story, as you told it to her. She also told me you had the gift."

I shrugged. "I think nothing of it. It comes and it goes, but my mother, I think, was only trying to frighten the man, for how could such a prophecy be? That I should kill the man in the ruins of a burning town? I, who shall never see another town?"

"Who knows?" Abigail said. "Who can read what is in tomorrow's wind? Shall we go to the cabin?"

△ 16 △

Green lay the forest about us, brown and silent the moving river . . . the land lay still, brooding, expectant. Now was the time for dreaming past, now was the time for doing.

Oh, what a fine and handsome thing it is to sit in taverns over flagons of ale and discourse bravely of what daring things we will do! How we will walk the unknown paths through lands of sylvan beauty, facing the savage in his native habitat, far from the dust of London crowds!

Warmed by wine, the rolling poetry of words and a fine sweep of gesture, a young man feels the world is his, with a pearl in every oyster, a lovely lass behind every window, and enemies who fade from sight at his very presence! Yet the moment of reality comes, and no eloquence will build a stockade, nor will a poetic phrase fend off an arrow, for the savage of the woodland has his own conception of romance and poetry, which may involve the dreamer's scalp.

Forever the dream is in the mind, realization in the hands.

An easy thing it had been when England lay about us to scorn the vanishing men of Roanoke, the disappearance of Grenville's men, for the giving up of Ralph Lane's colony. That was all very well for *them*. They had failed where we would succeed.

We had gone beyond help. If a man here should take a misstep on a path and fall with a broken bone, he need expect no doctor, no litter. If savages closed about him, no Queen's men would come with banners in bold ranks marching, nor would there be a skirl of pipes and the movement of kilts and the claymores swinging. One would be a man alone, and alone he must fight and die, or fight and live.

The entry into a new land is a hard, hard thing as Black Tom Watkins said, and upon me lay responsibility for all of these who came with me. All men wish to be captains, but few men wish to shoulder the burden of decision, and in coming here with these others, I had staked a claim that I must wall against misfortune.

First, our food. We had come well-provided, but for how long? Well I knew how precious were the foods of home, so these must be carefully used, and we must hunt, gather, and plant, to prepare for the cold winter to come.

At once I drew a plan for a stockade, showed it to Jublain, John Tilly, and the others. A change was made here, an addition there, then the men went forth with axes. With Black Tom and Pim Burke I went to the woods, for meat.

Two were left with the ship's boat, and they were to fish.

We were twenty-seven men and two women, and to feed such a lot is never a simple thing.

Steadily, we walked into the woods, for I had no wish to hunt close to camp and so frighten away what game was near. Several times we saw wild turkeys, but it was deer I wanted, and more than one.

Yet each such venture was more than a hunt for food, it was an exploration, and after each venture of my own or others it was in my mind to note down what was observed and to piece together a map of the area for all to see.

Suddenly, we came upon deer, a half dozen of them feeding in a meadow, some hundred and fifty yards off. It was far to risk a shot upon which so much depended, so I began my stalk. Having hunted deer in England I believed these would be no different.

All were feeding. Indicating the one I would attempt to kill, I suggested to the others that they choose their target and shoot when I shot.

Slowly, silently I began moving upwind toward them. Suddenly I saw their tails begin to twitch, and knowing they were about to look up, I stood fast. Their heads lifted and they stared at me, but I made no slightest move, and waited. Soon they decided I was harmless and resumed their feeding.

Moving on, I closed some fifteen yards closer before their tails began to twitch again. They looked about, looked longer at me for they must have realized that strange object out there was closer, then back to feeding. Again I moved, again I stopped.

Now I was within less than a hundred yards of my target, and lifting my gun, I took aim. My ball took the buck through the neck just forward of the shoulders. He leaped, fell to his knees, then rolled over.

Tom and Pim had come closer also, and instantly, both fired. Pim's was a clean miss as his target, startled by my shot, made an abrupt move, paused, then began to walk away.

They came up to me and we waited, hoping the deer might stop not far off, but they continued to move on

141

into the brush, and we let them go.

"The neck shot is best," I commented, "if chance allows. If shot through the heart or lungs they will often run a mile or more before dropping."

Tom was the most skillful butcher among us, so he began skinning the animals out, while Pim and I followed in the way they had gone. A deer will rarely travel more than a mile from his home grounds if it can be avoided, so we hoped they had but circled around. Whatever they had done, we saw them not again.

With our meat and the skins we returned to our camp, killing three turkeys on the way.

So there was meat that night, but scarcely enough, and I knew we must go far afield, must kill and dry the meat and prepare for the winter to come. Supplying my small force was to be no small problem.

The days went swiftly by, working, hunting, clearing and planting land. During this time I kept several men aboard the *fluyt*, now rechristened the *Abigail*, cleaning her up, making minor repairs, and adding to her armament two guns recovered from the burned vessel.

The stockade was completed and four swivel-guns were mounted on the walls. Two more of the recovered guns from the burned-out wreck were hauled to the hilltop where the stockade had been built and mounted to cover the river itself.

We saw no Indians, yet from time to time their tracks were seen, and twice we saw canoes passing swiftly along the river in the dark.

"I do not trust them," Jublain protested irritably. "These, if I mistake them not, are Chowanokes."

"I know nothing of them," I said.

"Nor I," he admitted, "but I served with a soldier who came with Lane, and he spoke of them with no favor. They were allied to Wingina, who was a chief to the south and a great enemy to all whites.

"If the Roanoke colony vanished, he would be the likely culprit."

"And not the Spanish?"

"Aye, mayhap the Spanish, too."

It was a lovely land, alive with flowers and richness of soil, but except when cutting logs we avoided the swamp. There were alligators there as well as snakes, and a dismal place it was. Yet it was the easiest way for us to procure the timbers we needed, for a tree felled there could be towed by a boat easier than it could be moved upon land.

Nor had we any wish to make our position more obvious by cutting trees. Taken from the swamp they left no gaping holes, nor any sign of activity likely to be seen.

If the Indians left us alone we were content that it be so, although it was trade with them I most desired, I preferred that we make our own position secure first, for in dealing with a people of so vastly different a culture and background we must ever be wary, for their understanding is not ours, nor is it based on the same considerations.

Now I was indeed thankful for the long talks with Captain Tempany, with Coveney Hasling, and with others, for each had served to broaden my viewpoint and the depth of my understanding.

There was much to learn of people, much to learn of the art of government, which had suddenly become my responsibility. I had already learned to listen to the advice of others but to act only on my own beliefs, and to make my own decisions.

The days went swiftly by, but soon there was on my table a growing map of the area in which we lived. Along with it I began to note down what I knew of Indians and what signs we had seen of them.

What of Potaka? On my earlier voyage we had met, and instantly had become friends. He was an Eno, of a tribe from somewhere inland, I knew not exactly where.

It had been a year, perhaps somewhat more, since I had seen him. The Eno were good hunters, but careful farmers and shrewd traders, and if any might have a surplus for trade it would be the Eno . . . from the little I knew of the Indians about here.

Our catch of fish was excellent, so I put more men to that service, and soon we had racks of fish drying in the sun and had to maintain a guard to keep off the

143

birds. We killed many pigeons, of a kind that roosted in great numbers in the trees and could be taken easily.

Inside our stockade but backed up against the outer wall were our cabins. One for Abigail, Lila, and me, another for an armory, one for the storage of meat, another for grain, a third for our trade goods, and the largest yet a barracks for the men, although we maintained a crew of seven men aboard the *Abigail*.

We ate at a common table for I wished no stories to circulate that better food was served us than was prepared for all.

When would winter come? It worried me that I did not know, and could only guess, which made for bad planning. Despite the poor success of our hunting, for we found little game, the fishing went well, and our crops came readily up, promising a late but good harvest.

At the table, I explained the situation. "There are Indians up the river whom I know, they are called the Eno. There are other Indians a little way off called the Tuscarora, and I do not know them but other Indians fear them and they are spoken of as fighters.

"There are Indians near us called the Chowanoke or Chowanoc, but they are a small tribe. It may be that we can arrange an alliance that will offer protection for both.

"Avoid Indian women. It may be some of you will wish to have Indian wives, but first you must learn the Indian way, and to approach the father first and agree upon the present you will give him.

"We are very few here, and must walk with care, always respectful of these people."

"They are savages," Emmden muttered, "only savages!"

"But people, just as you and I, and they have customs as good for them as ours for us. Treat them as equals."

Emmden looked his disgust, but spoke no word against my order. Yet his manner worried me. He had been a sailor aboard the Flemish ship and I liked not his manner, and I spoke of him to Tilly and Jublain.

"Aye," Jublain agreed, "yon's a surly dog, and he's found others of his kind. They talk continually of going a-pirating and I doubt not they'd try if they could find men enough."

Despite the fact that our fort was on a low hill it was shielded from view by the tall trees that made up the forest around the hill. That hill was stripped of brush and trees that might offer concealment and prepared a good field of fire for our weapons.

Meanwhile, those of us who knew how to use the bow resumed its use in our hunting. In the fens we had grown up as archers, each of us skilled in hunting with bow and arrow, so among us we numbered ten skilled archers and some who were good enough. Our hunting, to save powder and lead, was now done with bows and arrows.

The English longbow was a formidable weapon and despite the coming of firearms we in the fens and others in rural parts of England kept our skill in its use, competing in shooting at fairs and sometimes at markets. In the fens, where hunting was less restricted, many a fenman kept meat on his table with the bow.

In the evenings we made arrows, improved our bows, and sharpened axes and saws against the work to be done. They were quiet, busy times but we were in better condition to survive than had those who came before us, for all were accustomed to work, and aware of the need for it.

Nevertheless, we cut mast timbers and piled them above the ground to season, and some of the men were riving shingles, working with a froe and a maul to split them off the larger chunks or logs. It was in my mind that sooner or later a ship would come, and then we might sell our timber or trade to good effect.

Yet we had our own quarters to furnish as well, so we made stools, benches, and chairs as well as buckets, ladles, spoons, and baskets.

And then we found the Indian.

It was Abigail who saw him first. She had gone with Lila to the edge of the forest to gather herbs. The morning was warm and still, but under the trees that bordered the swamp it was dark, mysterious, and very still.

Abigail had stopped inside the edge of the timber, to listen. Somewhere out across the swamp a woodpecker was working on a tree. Out upon the ship someone was hoisting something with a block and tackle. She could hear the squeak and groan of it. At the fort she could hear someone sawing . . . here all was very quiet.

She saw the big alligator first. He was a huge, old fellow, all of ten or twelve feet long and when she saw him only his eyes and snout were above water. He was moving toward the shore, moving toward where she stood with a purposefulness that told her he was coming for something, or somebody.

"Lila?"

"I see him."

He was coming toward her. Maybe if she threw something into the water . . . ?

She stooped to pick up a stick or chunk of bark . . . and then she saw the hand.

For an instant she stood silent, holding her breath. It *was* a hand, a man's hand, and it lay half-clutching the damp leaves at the edge of the brush.

The hand had an arm. Then, half-concealed by the low-hanging leaves, she made out the body. A man's body, a man terribly wounded, bloody.

"Mam? We'd better go. He's coming!"

"Throw something at it. Anything."

Abigail looked quickly around. There was nothing. Catching hold of the hand, she pulled. It was all she could do to stir the body, but she did, she drew him slowly from the brush.

"Lila? Help me!"

Suddenly, Lila screamed. She had never heard the Welsh girl scream and she dropped the hand and ran quickly.

The 'gator was a big one, and he was coming out of the water, evidently drawn by the scent of blood from the man's body.

Abigail, who had lungs of her own, screamed also.

There was a shout, then running feet, and I was the first to reach them, running, sword drawn, expecting to find Indians or Bardle men.

146

Jublain was only an instant behind me, and Watkins came from the woods further along the shore.

"Look out for his tail," I warned. Where had I heard that? "He'll use it to knock you into the water or break your legs."

The big beast stood, half out of the water, staring at us with gleaming reddish eyes, his jaws opening and closing. The smell of blood and death drew him, yet our increasing numbers must have brought some thread of caution into his brain, for he stared at us, his eyes going from one to the other until I thought he might charge.

At my feet was a broken, rotting chunk of wood, and picking it up, I dashed it against his head. My shot was good, and it struck hard. He snorted and made an angry dash of no more than two feet, then retreated slowly, reluctantly, into the water.

"What is it, Abby?" I asked.

"There's a man . . . he's not dead, I believe."

I walked past to where her finger pointed, and Jublain, sword still in hand, came to stand beside me.

The wounded man was an Indian, and of a type I had not seen before. He was a big man, well made, but from the marks upon his body he had been wounded, then tortured, and had somehow escaped.

"Get four men," I said, "and have them bring a litter. We'll take him to the fort."

"A savage? *Inside* our fort?" Jublain protested. "If he lives he'll betray us."

"Nonetheless, we'll try to save him. He escaped them somehow; he's come a long distance. If a man in such condition can do so much, he deserves to live."

△ 17 △

That the Indian had lost much blood was apparent, for he had been shot with an arrow in the back of the head, the stone arrowhead almost burying itself in the bone behind one ear.

From the looks of his skull he had been struck with a club. His black hair was matted with blood. There were many minor wounds and burns.

When he was bathed and cleaned and his wounds treated as well we might, I spoke to him, in the few words of the Eno tongue that I had learned, and he grunted something in reply, from which I gathered that he understood.

Then, touching my chest, I said, "Barnabas," very slowly. Indicating Lila, who stood over him, I said, "Li-la."

Then I pointed to him. "You?"

"Wa-ga-su," he said.

He was wary as a trapped animal, but he was not cringing.

"Abigail and Lila," I said. "Be very careful. We are strangers, and to him every stranger is a possible enemy. He does not know why he is here, or why we try to make him well. He may think that we make him well only to torture him again."

"What kind of Indian is he?" Lila asked. "He seems to understand you."

"Aye . . . a word or two. Perhaps we can learn from him about the country to the west, for I do not think him an Indian of this area. I think he is from far away, for his stature is different, and even his facial structure, and he is of larger frame than the Eno that I have seen."

For three days, then, I saw him but rarely, for my work was great and the time of the season was short. Our gardens were growing, and there was hope in me that we would make a good crop. For I was worried about winter.

Of furs we had but few, for most of the skins were needed in the preparation of clothing for the winter. Yet we had the skins of several foxes and some small dark animals of the weasel type that were called mink.

On the fifth day after the discovery of the savage, I went to the room where he was kept and cared for. Jublain had come with me, and suddenly the Indian began to speak in broken Spanish. It was a language Jublain well knew, having been a prisoner among them at one time.

"He is a Catawba . . . whatever that is, from the west." Jublain paused, listening. "From the edge of the mountains."

"Ah!" I exclaimed, with pleasure. This was what I had wished for. "Ask him about the mountains."

"He asks about you. How, he wonders, do you speak some words of his tongue?"

"Tell him I was once a friend of an Eno named Potaka."

The Catawba looked at me several times as Jublain explained how Potaka and I had become friends, and how we had traded there.

"Tell him we are his friends and we would like to be friends of his people. Tell him that when he is well enough we shall, if he wishes, help him to return to his people."

Several times I sat with him then, each time learning a few words or phrases that I might use in speaking his language. Yet I am afraid he learned my language more swiftly than I learned his. There came a day when I took him with me and showed him about the small fort.

Wa-ga-su looked at everything, but he was especially impressed with the cannon. "Big voice!" he exclaimed suddenly.

"Aye," I showed him one of the balls, but he was not so impressed as I had expected.

"Too big for man," he said, "throw away too much!"

Of course, he was right. I explained to him that the gun was for use against stockades or ships, and when he seemed to question the presence of the gun inside the fort I told him ships might come of men who were not friendly to us.

"Wa-ga-su," I said, "someday I shall go to live in the mountains."

"Is good," he said. "I show you."

He drew lines in the dust to show me where his country lay, and the rivers that bordered it. He showed me as well the trading paths leading cross the country that were used by all Indians. Little by little, each of us learned more of the language of the other, and he warned me that his enemies would be searching for him, and even now might be lurking in the woods around us.

"What enemies come after you?"

"Tuscarora . . . they are many. Great fighters."

"You are safe here, Wa-ga-su. And when you are well, we will take you to your people or put you far upon the way."

Little by little I got the story of his escape. They had captured him while hunting, had tortured him for three days, making each day worse. Then they had tied him to a stake for burning. Using his two feet he had edged a burning brand around, working with the still unburned end, and tilting it, got it to fall against the rawhide that held his ankles. His legs free, he had somehow gotten free his hands, sprang through the flames at the back, and run into the woods. They had immediately followed, but he eluded them. Then, wounded, sick, exhausted, he had fallen down near the edge of the swamp, where, smelling blood, the alligator had come for him.

With the coming of night the great gates to our fort were closed and barred. The smaller gate which opened on the river side was also barred. Two sentries walked the walls at night, and a system of signals was arranged with those men who remained aboard the *fluyt*, where a watch was also kept.

Nothing in my nature permitted me to trust to fortune, for it was my belief that good luck came to those who work hard and plan well. So far we had remained free from trouble with Indians. Hopefully, it would remain so.

Each night a different man was officer of the watch, a duty I divided with Jublain, Pimmerton Burke, and Sakim. On this night, Pim was on duty, and he awakened me at a few minutes past midnight.

"Barnabas? Can you come?"

"What is it?" As ever, I was immediately awake.

"I don't know. But you'd better come."

He disappeared soundlessly. I got up and began quickly dressing.

"What is it, Barnabas?" Abigail was awake.

"I don't know. But I fear it is trouble, for Pim is not easily alarmed."

Taking up my pistols, buckling on my sword, and then taking a musket, I slipped out into the night. Behind me I heard Abigail stirring about. I mounted the ladder to the wall.

A guard loomed beside me. It was a man I knew as a Newfoundlander, a good, sturdy man, Ned Tanner. "They're out there, Cap'n," he whispered, "and it is I who thinks there's a-plenty of them."

"Stand by, then."

Walking on around the walk below the wall to the other guard, I found Pim Burke.

"Tanner says there's a lot of them out there. What say you?"

"Aye," the guard, a swarthy, husky chap from Bristol, spoke softly. "They've something in mind, Captain. They've been all about below the walls."

Listening, I could hear the movements of men, but what they planned I could not guess. "Pim," I said, "do you go below and roust out six good men. Let the others rest, if they've the will to. It may be a long day before us."

Now to take a stockaded position is not an easy thing if the defenders be alert. With cannon, it was a simple thing, without them almost impossible without negligence on the part of the defenders. Yet the very fact they had not yet attacked spoke of some preparation, which implied some knowledge of making war and strong positions. This implied there might be a white man among them.

151

The Spanish, who had settlements in the land of Florida, were not happy with England's attempts to settle Virginia, and it might be that a small party of Spanish were directing this effort. Of course, that was pure speculation, I had no facts.

A glance at the stars told me almost an hour had gone by since I had first been awakened. The ladder behind me creaked as the men climbed to their positions.

With moving about upon the walkway and listening, much time had passed, yet I had no idea of what they planned. Below me at least two and perhaps more of them were moving about, perhaps only seeking to find a way to enter.

I spoke softly. "What is it you want?" And I used the Catawba tongue.

There was abrupt silence.

"We do not sleep," I continued, "but we wish no trouble. If you would talk, come to us in the light, and we shall speak. If you come by night, we have no choice but to believe you enemies."

Again a silence. Then a voice, "Release the Catawba. He is ours."

"He is his own. You do not have him. We do not have him."

"Put him outside, and we will take him and go."

"He is a good man. He works beside us. We will not put him away. He has come to our village for protection."

"Then we shall take him. I, whom am Naguska, say this."

"You are a Tuscarora?"

"So it is."

"The Tuscarora are a proud people. They are fine warriors. But I am English. We do not surrender those who have come to us for aid."

"So be it." He seemed not too displeased. "You will die for it. All of you."

Then, surprisingly, he said in English, "You are a weak people, you English. And you tell lies about your country beyond the water. You are a small people. You cannot hunt. You have no fur. You have no big trees. You have

152

only your big canoes and a hunger for things that belong to others."

"You speak English?"

"My father was English. He taught me many words before I saw his weakness. He was no warrior. He was no hunter. He could do nothing . . . nothing that becomes a man."

"In our land only some men are warriors, and there is little game, so few of us are hunters. We obtain what is needed by barter."

"Bah! It is a woman's way! A warrior takes what he needs!"

"Who was your father?"

"He was nobody. He could only scratch marks upon paper, upon bark, upon whatever he had. He told me they were charms, so we did not burn them, but they did him no good."

"He is dead?"

"Long ago. It is well that he died. I had great shame to have no other father."

"I thought with you it was the mother's brother who was important to the boy?"

"Well, it was so. My mother's brother was a great warrior!"

He seemed willing enough to talk, and while he talked there was no fighting. I whispered as much to Pim, but advised him to be doubly alert.

"Come to the gate by day, and come alone. I would speak with you, Naguska."

"By day? By day you shall all be dead. Or prisoners, to die by the torch."

"You said your father made marks upon paper and bark. Do you have that paper and the bark? I should like to see it."

"I have them. I know where they are hidden. My father was a weak man. He could use no weapon, he could not hunt. He was much laughed at for his weakness. With him always it was only what he could put upon paper."

I heard a series of strange sounds. I tried to identify them.

153

Suddenly, I knew! Ladders! They had ladders!

Along various spots in the wall were small bundles of grass and twigs that could be quickly lighted. Taking one from its cubbyhole, I struck a light and touched it off with a spark. As it sprang into flame, I held it over the wall.

In the brief flare of light a dozen savage, painted faces glared up at me, then the ladders started to rise.

An arrow struck near me. Aiming at the nearest man's chest, I fired.

They came with a rush.

△ **18** △

"Ladders!" I shouted the word so all would know what to expect.

Ladders. I had never heard of an Indian using such things, yet Naguska was only half Indian, and he might have learned many things from the father he seemed to despise.

There was a burst of firing. Somebody dropped another lighted bundle, and then another. Two Indians were attempting to take a wounded man away, and a ladder dropped into place near me. I grabbed the top of it and shoved it from the wall. One man let go and fell off, another one rode the ladder back toward me.

My blade was there to meet his chest as he fell against the wall. For a moment his face was very near to me, and then I was drawing the blade clear.

Other men were climbing up from below. The whole lot of our men had been brought up by the firing but, suddenly, there was a lull.

"More bundles!" I shouted. "Don't let them get away with the ladders!"

Here and there a shot followed. Then all was silence. Around us the velvet of night lay gently. A faint breeze stirred in from the sea, and there was left a smell of burned wood, grass, and gunpowder.

Then there was another aroma . . . fresh coffee! Some of the men had not tasted it, for the substance was new in England, yet Abigail had long been familiar with it from her travels on her father's ship in the Red Sea and the Indian Ocean.

There was a cup for each of us, and a pleasant, warming drink it was.

Jublain and Pim came to me. "Will they attack again, think you?"

"I do not know. The ladders failed only because we were alert, but they will think their medicine was bad. We must wait and see."

The attack had lasted only minutes, and now all was still. We drank more of the coffee and some men returned to their rest. A slow hour passed by, and then another. There was a faint gray light in the east, or perhaps I but wished it so.

Watkins came to me beside the parapet. "There's two ladders outside near the gate. Request permission to go out and get them."

I hesitated. To open the gates was a risk, but I wished to keep as many ladders from their hands as possible. Always before Indians had failed to succeed in attacks against stockades unless they could get in before a gate was closed.

"How many men will you need?"

"Twelve, I think. Two men for each ladder, the others to stand by in case of attack."

"Very well. Only it must be done quickly. At the first move from them retreat within the gate and close it."

We waited . . . the creak of the heavy gates was unnaturally loud in the stillness. Surely, the Indians could hear it, but what would they think? That we were pursuing them?

Yet Watkins and his men moved swiftly indeed. Within minutes the gates had swung shut again, and at least two of the ladders were within.

He came to me. It had grown a little lighter and his

grin was easy to see. "There was a third we could not carry so I almost cut the rawhide bindings through," he said. "Wait until they try climbing that one!"

Watching toward the dark line of forest, I thought of Naguska.

The threads that hold a man to leadership be thin indeed, and he had trusted his success to a new thing, an un-Indian thing, and it had failed. Some of them were sure to think that it was this strange thing that led to their defeat, they would blame him. I could not but feel regret for him, for he seemed an able man, although I was sorry he respected his father so little.

Yet, might it not be that he secretly loved him? That all this was a mask, a thing to shield him from such an emotion? For few of the Indians we had met thus far regarded the father with veneration, for the maternal uncle was he who drew the respect we gave to a father.

We waited, and waited, yet no further attack came, and slowly the sky grew lighter.

Here and there we saw patches of darkness on the grass, left by the blood of a victim, but there were no bodies, alive or dead. All had been spirited away in the darkness. We found four more ladders, one abandoned almost at the edge of the brush.

How well for us and all who lived behind stockades that this new way of war had failed them. I wondered how often it might have happened—that a truly great discovery was cast aside because of initial failure. The ladders were well-made, the uprights notched slightly, and the crosspieces bound in place with rawhide.

Abigail had breakfast ready when I came below. She had not waited for the main table to be set, knowing I would be hungry. I told her of Naguska, and she looked at me, smiling with amusement. "You are a strange man, Barnabas, for you seem almost regretful that he failed, when his success might have meant death to us all."

"It was a new idea to them, Abby, the ladders. And he must have argued many hours to convince his warriors of their worth."

I reflected.

"Yes, I do feel regret for him, and someday I hope we can meet again . . . under other circumstances. I would know more of this father of his. How he came to be here and what his name was. And whence he came."

Sakim and Pim came in to share coffee with me, and I told them of my thinking. "How strange it is to think that all our knowledge, all our skills can seem worthless to a people not accustomed to them."

Sakim shrugged. "It was ever so. Long ago I was on a ship to the Moluccas, and we stopped by an island to trade. No steel was known there, nor any metal at all. The tools, axes, knives . . . all were of stone.

"One such was beautifully made and I wished it for something to take home with me, and offered to trade a steel hatchet for his of stone. He looked at my hatchet, turned it over, used it, looked astonished at how easily it cut, then returned it to me and took up his own. He would not trade. He wanted what was known and familiar, not this strange tool of whose properties he knew nothing."

Sakim sipped his coffee. "It is good," he said, "but thin to my taste. I must show you someday how it is made in my country."

He put down his cup. "I have come tonight to talk to you of that."

"Of your country? My father knew a little, but too little. Peter talked some of the Eastern lands, but I know too little except that spices come from there, and gold and tea and coffee and much else."

Sakim smiled, and turned his cup upon the table. "Much else, indeed." He looked at me, his black eyes amused and a little doubtful, I thought. "That young man, Naguska. I am very like him in that I, too, have learning that may be despised, as his was."

"How so? I despise no learning, Sakim. That you know."

"Perhaps, my friend, and that is why I have decided to tell you what I have told no man since my first captivity to Europeans. It was easier to let them believe I was a Moor, for all understood what was a Moor, and to explain what I really was . . . it would have been useless, and worse, puzzling.

"Men do not like puzzles, Barnabas. They prefer categories. It is far easier to slip a piece of information into a known slot than to puzzle over the unknown."

"You are not a Moor? But you are a Moslem?"

"Many who follow Mohammed are not Moors, nor even Arabs. They were a conquering people, those Arabs who came out of their deserts after the death of Mohammed, and they carried the sword and fire to many lands, including Persia, one of the oldest, and I, who now call myself Sakim, came from a far place known as Khurasan, from the city of Nisphapur.

"It was the home of my father, and of my father's father as well, and who knows how many others? We were scholars, sometimes of the law, often of medicine, always of philosophy.

"In the study of medicine we were far advanced, for were we not the heirs of Greece? But we had learned from India as well, and from Cathay. In Bagdad alone we once had sixty-five hospitals divided into wards for the separate treatments of various ills and diseases, with running water in every room . . . and that was in the eighth century . . . eight hundred years ago."

"So what happened?" Burke asked skeptically. "I have seen none of this great medicine."

"Genghis Khan came . . . you have heard of him? And something like a hundred years later, Timur the Lame. He who in the West is called Tamerlane.

"You think you have seen war . . . Timur made pyramids of skulls and the streets ran red with blood . . . several times over a hundred thousand were put to the sword. No man truly knows how many, but he killed all . . . at first.

"Later, when he became wiser, he tried to save the artisans and the scholars, but too many had died. The hospitals were destroyed, the books burned, the teachers slain.

"Those two conquerors set civilization back five hundred years, my friends, and only a few survived. Several were ancestors of mine who fled into the hidden fastnesses of the Pamirs, and others into the far desert, the Takla-makan.

"There they treated the ill, they taught their sons and grandsons, and in time returned to Nisphapur and to Marv and to Meshed.

"In my time I studied in Nisphapur and in Marv, then in Isfahan and Constantinople, but by that time the urge was upon me to travel to the westward, so I set sail from Constantinople for Tripoli. Our ship was taken by pirates . . . I was enslaved . . . was taken by other pirates then freed, and when we met I was a sailor, only wishing to go home."

"And now you are here," Abigail said.

"I am here," he said simply, "and would be used. My skills rust. I thought at first to say nothing, but when Wa-ga-su was brought in, I thought then to speak, but hesitated."

"We have little medicine," I said.

"There are herbs and there are minerals. I can make my own. Lately I have seen herbs in the swamps and along the hillsides like those I know."

"Collect them, then," I said "Gather your herbs. Find your minerals. What help you need, we will give. By the look of today there will be many times when a man is needed who knows of medicine."

I stood up. "It is a bright day, and much is to be done. Be careful, Sakim. There will be Indians about. I give you one other chore . . ." I pointed at Lila. "Teach her what you can. She knows much of herbs. She will help you."

When Pim stood beside me in the yard he said, "Do you think he lies?"

"No . . . I believe him. There are stranger lives men have led. We are fortunate, Pim. We have a surgeon, a physician! No doubt he will keep some of us alive. If he saves only one, it is good. Sakim and I sailed together before this, and he proved a good man. And loyal."

Each day now was a day of work, and Wa-ga-su was

quick to see how little we knew, and how much we needed to know. He led us to likely spots in which to find nuts, berries, and edible roots.

In several places along the banks of streams we found thickets of blackberries, dewberries, and persimmons. We picked and picked until every receptacle we had was filled. Here and there we found nuts, although the season was still early for many of them.

Wa-ga-su drew in the sand a picture of his country for us, a vast area drained by the Catawba River, and lying between two other rivers. It lay at the farthest point, right at the foot of the mountains, and perhaps into the mountains themselves. That he did not make clear.

He showed us how to add the meal of ground nuts to thicken soup or stew, using walnuts, chestnuts, or hickory nuts, and how to search for and find clams along the shores.

John Tilly, who had been in command aboard the *Abigail*, went in a boat to search for clams and to catch fish out on the sound and along the sandy shores.

Suddenly Watkins came to me. "Barnabas." He spoke softly not to alarm the others. "Tilly's comin' back. He's comin' fast!"

We hurried to the river where Tilly had gone at once to the *Abigail*, dropping off two men. As we waited, he came to the landing with the other two.

"Ship off shore," he said shortly, "I made her out with my glass. The *Jolly Jack* . . . of London."

Nick Bardle. . . .

My old enemy was returned. Once he had kidnapped me, several times had tried to kill me, and he had killed Brian Tempany, Abigail's father.

I went to look.

His vessel was not large but was heavily gunned, and highly maneuverable. He would have a large crew, perhaps three times the men we could muster.

"Tilly," I said, "get the *Abigail* in good position then prepare for battle."

We had six guns in the fort and we brought them all

160

to bear on the river, leaving only the swivel-guns and our light arms to repel an overland attack.

Abigail looked pale and frightened. "Don't worry," I advised, "we'll handle him."

She nodded, but I could see she was worried, but no less than I, for if the attack stretched out too long we should lose much good working time before the cold weather set in. And during the past days, some of the leaves had begun to turn and there was frost upon the lowlands, and the morning mists were thicker.

I looked downstream where we would see Bardle's sails first, and I felt a little shiver go through me. I, too, was afraid, for it was no longer as it once had been, when only I could suffer from my mistakes. Now there were others, these who had entrusted themselves to me.

"I am not thinking of me," she said suddenly, "nor of you only. I am thinking of your son."

"My son . . . ?"

I looked at her stupidly.

"What did you say? My son?"

I am sorely afraid I shouted those last words, and they all turned, those who stood along the wall watching, those who manned the guns.

And then as realization dawned, a cheer went up.

My son!

"Cap'n?" It was Jublain. "Here she comes!"

Her masts showed against the sky above the green of the forest, a thinning forest, where the leaves had begun to fall. Her masts, then her bow, then a fores'l.

"Tom," I called to Watkins. "Your gun only . . . fire!"

△ 19 △

Watkins put his match to the touch-hole. There was an instant of pause, then the gun belched flame and smoke, leaping as if to spring from its carriage, and we saw the ball strike the butt of the bowsprit and scatter splinters in every direction. There was a great splitting and a crash as the yard came down and the bowsprit hung all askew, held only by the rigging.

Taking our shot for a signal, the gunners aboard the *Abigail* let go with a four-gun broadside that caught the *Jolly Jack* head on.

Then, with the *Jack* broadside to us, we let go with the remainder of the fort's guns, only an instant before the *Jack* fired its own broadside.

A momentary advantage had been ours. Bardle had apparently only seen the *Abigail*, and if he knew of the fort's existence he did not guess it was armed as it was from the guns of the ships we had taken.

Watkins' first shot had taken them unawares, throwing them off just in time to permit the *Abigail* to fire.

The glory of the sunlit morning was blasted by cannon-fire, and the beauty of the oncoming ship was shattered by our fire. Before the powder smoke obscured the scene I saw a great section of the *Jack*'s rail burst into fragments, and another ripping a hole in a sail. Others fell harmlessly into the water.

Great clouds of smoke billowed up from their guns and ours. There were splintering crashes, and the awful red lightning of the guns mingled with the thunder of them and the whine of flying splinters and the shouts and screams of men.

Through a haze of smoke I glimpsed the *Jack* falling back, guns firing. Suddenly the thunder of the guns ceased and there was an unbelievable silence. And then groans, cries, and calls for help.

Our massive gate was battered to splinters. One gun had been blasted from its carriage, and I saw Abigail and Lila bending over a man who lay sprawled on the ground. Then I saw another, as they ran from the first to the second.

Two men were being helped down ladders, both wounded. Another man, his arm dangling, was going down a ladder by himself.

Through the smoke I could see the topm'sts of the *Abigail*, and as the smoke lifted could see she had been hulled at least twice and was down by the head. Men were working about the deck, so some at least had survived. Even as I looked, one of the guns fired another shot.

Jublain came to me. "Two dead, Barnabas, and seven injured . . . one of them seriously."

He waved a hand at the gate. "I've started repairs, and we'll need them quickly if he tries to come back. I think the *Abigail* is in bad shape."

Jeremy Ring came up the ladder. "Jeremy, take Waga-su. He can probably guide you through the swamp to a point where you can see the *Jolly Jack*. Take a telescope. I want a report on her condition as soon as possible. Don't let yourself be seen."

Through my own glass I studied the *Abigail*, and it gave me a twinge to see her. I could never stand to see a fine ship damaged, for they are things of such beauty, white sails against the sky, prow lifting and dipping in the sea. They are living things.

One of the holes in her hull was barely above the waterline, the other higher, probably in the gundeck.

"Recharge all guns," I said. "Two gunners stand by, the rest get to work helping with the gate."

I went down the ladder to the common room. Sakim was there at work with Lila.

One man already had his arm set and was sitting to one side with a glass of ale in his hand. He grinned at me. "Good fight!" he said.

The only seriously injured man was a youngster. A fragment of metal from a bursting shell had ripped the side of his neck, another piece imbedded itself in his thigh. He had bled badly.

He looked up at me. "I'm sorry," he said.

"Sorry? You did very well," I said. "Sakim will take care of you."

It had needed no more than a minute or two for me to see that Sakim worked swiftly, surely, and with confidence. I had no further doubts.

There had been a surplus of poles cut when the stockade

was under construction, and from these a new gate was being made.

Food was being put on the table when a messenger came from the *Abigail*. The hole in the hull had been temporarily repaired and the water was being pumped out, but extensive repairs would yet be needed before she was seaworthy again.

There was no word from Pim Burke and Wa-ga-su regarding the *Jolly Jack*. Abigail was in our cabin meanwhile, and I sat down there.

"Did you mean it?" I said, "A son?"

"Well," she hesitated, "a child, anyway. I can't promise a son."

"It would be easier for a son," I said. "Here."

She nodded seriously. "You know, I never thought of that until now. It is one thing for a boy to grow up in this wilderness. But a girl? Here . . . so far from everything. Could she become a lady?"

"Wherever she grows up," I said, "your daughter would be a lady."

We talked of that, and of other things, and with one ear listened for the trouble we knew would come.

Pim Burke came in. He accepted a flagon of ale and sat down opposite me.

The *Jolly Jack*'s not badly hurt. Bowsprit gone, sprits'l and sprit-tops'l gone. Some damage to the bow. Most of her bulwark amidships is gone, and up to when we left they'd buried three men over the side."

He swallowed some ale, and wiped his mouth with the back of his hand. "Her main-tops'l yard is gone. Crashed to the deck. Several guns or gun-carriages damaged, but she's able to go to sea."

He paused. "I wonder if he knows how shallow the water is out there in the sound? He might run aground."

"I hope he doesn't," I said frankly. "I want him out of here."

"Aye, I was thinkin' on that." Pim looked up at me. "You plannin' to stay here?" He paused again.

Outside the wind stirred slightly. I could hear the men working to repair the gate.

"I'm going to the mountains, Pim," I said, "when spring comes."

"They'll not all go with you, Barnabas," he said quietly. "There's been talk. Some think we should take the *Abigail* and go a-pirating, and some are for trade, but many are restless now that the work's finished."

It was no hard thing to understand. They were far from others of their kind, and we'd seen no ships but Bardle's.

The sound was shallow. There were places where, if a man was careful, he could guide a vessel through the water and into the rivers in safety, yet there were shoals here and there, and floods from upriver kept them changing.

A large vessel could not well navigate in the sound unless during a time when the rivers were in flood. Abigail, if well-handled, could do it.

"Who's the leader of those who would be pirates?" I asked.

"Jonathan Delve."

"I well knew the man. A good gunner, a fierce fighter, and a tall, sallow-cheeked man with a spotty black beard and always-watchful eyes.

"So Delve's their leader now?"

"Aye. He says nothing of you, mind you. Delve is a wily one, and you'll not catch him out. Only he's talking of going a'pirating . . . of ships to be had off the coast. He's already come to me twice, wanting a boat with which to explore. I think he's got something on his mind, Barnabas. I've watched him . . . and listened. He's been on this coast before."

"How many of them are there?"

Pim shrugged. "It could be five, it could be more . . . They're restless, like I said."

Pim paused, drank some ale, and then said, "Delve came up with something . . . pointblank. Asked me if I'd ever heard of a man named Chantry."

"Chantry?"

"Aye. You mayn't have heard of him, being in the fens, like. He was talked about along the waterfront of Bristol,

165

and in the dives. He was Irish, they say, but there seems some mystery about him. He had great skill with arms, but was a trading man . . . or so it seemed. He put money in a voyage to America, and went along."

"What happened to him?" I asked.

"Well, he was lost ashore. Indians attacked a watering party and he was killed with the others and the ship pulled off . . . only he wasn't dead."

"So?"

"He showed up again in Bristol, a-sailing of his own ship, but how he come by it or a crew, no man could say. He unloaded a few mast-timbers, sold some fresh-water pearls and some dried fish, but when he pulled out of Bristol his ship was still deep in the water. There was a lot of talk. You know how it is around the harbor dives. Was it treasure he had aboard? Where did he get his ship and his treasure, if any? Where did he get a crew? And where had he been all that time?

"The next thing known is that he slipped out of harbor, and when we heard of him again he'd set himself up in western Ireland. Living like a King he is, him and the girl."

"Girl?"

"Aye. He was married to her, they say. Some say she was a Spanish lass, and some say an Indian But she was beautiful, rarely, wonderfully beautiful . . . and different."

"He was a lucky man, then. Fortune and a beautiful woman," I said.

"Aye," Pim said, "I should be so lucky! But that is not all of the story. There was gossip about it, and Delve has heard it all. Chantry had looted a Spanish galleon of its treasure, they say. Some say he captured it, some that he found it deserted but for the girl. He took a ship-load of treasure from it."

"It's a good story."

"Aye, but the story that Delve likes is that he only brought back a small part of the treasure—that his ship wasn't large enough to take the whole, and that the biggest part of the treasure is still in the bottom of the ship."

"And where is the ship?"

"Run ashore on some island or other, laying there for the taking."

"How long ago was this?"

"Some years back . . . maybe twenty . . . I don't know. Point is, from the description they got, they think it is somewhere near here. The story is told of some barrier islands, and sounds into which rivers flowed."

I shrugged. "Pim, this whole coast is like that, for miles and miles." Nevertheless I was remembering a ship in which I had taken shelter, a ship almost buried in sand on the shore of a river islet . . . a ship that might be buried or swept out to sea by this time. I said nothing.

"Put a couple of men to watch the *Jolly Jack*, Pim. Have them report her every move." I got up, thinking of Delve, and well knowing the lure of gold. I might lose almost all who were with me, leaving us vulnerable for any attack.

Now many things that had been keeping their shadows in the back of my mind came to the fore. What future, beyond the promise of land, could I offer those with me?

Other colonists would eventually come . . . but when? How long, I thought, must we wait? Most of us were young, but I think that no two men age at the same rate, or learn equal sums from experience. Some men learn by their years, others simply live through them.

I found Jublain at once. It took me only a moment to explain.

"Aye," he said gloomily, "I have had a feeling about Delve, but he has had a feeling about me, so I'd likely be the last he'd speak to."

That night, the *Jolly Jack* sailed away, to the great relief of all.

It was only later that I discovered Delve had spread the word very well indeed. On the morning after, he came to me with three other men.

Delve hooked his thumbs in his belt. He was smiling, a kind of taunting, challenging smile it was. "We be going to hunt for gold," he said. "We've heard there's a treasure ship nearby, run aground and beached."

167

"I know of no such treasure ship," I replied.

Jeremy Ring and Jublain had come to stand beside me.

"Aye, well, mayhap you've your own reasons for not sharing your knowledge with us," he said, still smiling. "But mayn't we hunt on our own?" His sharp little eyes probed mine. "Unless you would try to stop us."

"Why should I do that? Go ahead. You've my permission, if it is needed. Only those who go do not return."

He chuckled. "Like that, is it? Well, it's not likely we'd need to return. You'll give us food then?"

"For six days only. We can afford no more. After that you'll be on your own. I'll give you rifles and ten balls per man, and the powder for it, and where you go after that is wherever you like, but I'll have no quitters with me."

I looked him square in the face.

"You'll stay now, or you'll go and not come back. You came knowing what lay ahead, and now at the smell of gold, which probably isn't there, you'd go. Well, go and be damned!"

"You talk very big for a man who'll soon be alone."

"He'll not be alone," said Jublain. "I'll be with him."

"And I," Ring added.

"You're fools then," he said. "There'll be few else."

"That may be," I replied, "but there may be more loyal men here than you think."

For the first time I saw doubt in his eyes, but he shook it off. The dream was more pleasant to believe than to doubt.

The taunting expression came to his face. He wanted to get back at me, to hurt me, worry me, anger me. "Well, Barnabas, if there's no gold I can always join Nick Bardle."

"Why not? There's always room on a gibbet."

He turned sharply away, and Jublain made as if to start after him. "He needs killing," he said, when I stopped him.

"No doubt, but here is a good time to be rid of any

troublemakers. I want nobody with me who will not go the distance."

Yet there were steps I could take, and I took them. Recharging several pistols and a musket, I kept them at hand, and suggested to Jublain, Jeremy, and Pim that they stay close about.

Delve went to the edge of the wood with a dozen others and there was much talk going on.

"Pim," I said, "do you go to the *Abigail*. Tell Tilly what goes on, and tell him to stand by for trouble and allow no one aboard unless with an order writ by my hand."

Aboard the *Abigail*, I felt sure John Tilly would stand.

Pim was back within the hour. "They'll stand for you," he said, "every man of them."

"Good! Now let us close the gate."

We did so, and Jeremy went to the walls where he could keep a lookout, and a weather-eye on the dissenters.

When they were up and coming to the gate in a group, Ring called softly and I came up to the wall with him. Wa-ga-su came to me and wished to know what it was that had happened, and I explained to him. He shook his head in amazement, but went back to squat against the wall and watch.

Jonathan Delve was in the lead. When they came up to the gate and found it closed, they stopped, obviously surprised.

"Well, men, what is it?"

"Open the gate!" Delve shouted. "We want our belongings. We are going for the gold."

"It shall be as agreed," I said. "I think you go upon a fool's errand. Yet you shall have what I promised."

Then we lowered over to them the muskets and the food, and with much angry grumbling and shouting they marched away.

Some we did well without, yet others were good men led astray by a promise of gold. We stood together upon the walls, making a brave show of it, but we knew all too well that we were too few to defend the fort against

169

a strong attack as Bardle might make. Not to mention the Indians.

"Do you think they know how many have gone? The Indians, I mean?" Jublain asked.

"If they do not know, they will. There will be tracks left, and they will follow and observe. I think our friends have not chosen wisely."

I was already thinking of what was to come. We had a winter to get through before we could march to the mountains.

In the following days we stayed close by, gathering food, drying the meat from our hunting, gathering clams along the shore, fishing. Always, two of us remained within the fort, and now the great gate was always closed, and we used the smaller gate. It was easier to open and shut as well as to guard.

"I fear for them." Tilly had come to the fort to eat, leaving Blue in command of the *Abigail*. "They will find much trouble at Roanoke, unless they have great luck."

The lost colony. Would the same fate overtake us?

There was time then to get out the maps and charts and pore over them, to speculate on what lay beyond the blue mountains and the best way to reach them. Wa-ga-su had a quick intelligence, and grasped at once almost any idea that was not totally beyond the range of his experience. Our needs he understood at once.

He would guide us to his home country. He would show us a way into the mountains, but when we offered him a chance to go along, he refused.

"Have you thought of a voyage first?" Tilly suggested. "We have many timbers cut for masts, many skins, and much potash. It would be a valuable cargo."

"I cannot risk England," I said.

"Then what of the Spanish islands? Or France?"

Uneasily, I considered the subject. It was true we had a full and heavy cargo. Our work would be for naught if we left it on the ground and went away to the mountains.

170

The decision would have to be mine. To go meant to move, to move meant to risk the sea, conflict, and possibly capture and death.

John Tilly wished to go. There were good reasons for it and Abby, I knew, would leave the choice to me.

The rain fell softly, whispering gently down upon our roofs, beating a soft tattoo upon our walls. It would be wet in the forest, wet upon the trails, and out beyond the Banks would be the cold gray wintry sea, rolling its combers down from the northland. The great breakers would be snarling along the sand. Again I seemed to feel the tip and bow of a deck beneath my feet.

Once more the lights of a harbor seemed to beckon to me, once more the sound of music and laughter.

Tomorrow, I promised myself, I would decide. . . .

Our walls were strong here, our food supply good. Out there? No wall could stand against the sea, and good ship though we had, there were ships that were faster, more heavily gunned.

The weight of the burden lay heavy upon me. Now that I must decide for others, my decisions came not so quickly, for any move might mean the death of my wife, of a friend, or the loss of our ship.

Yet each move one makes is a risk, and if one thinks too long one does not move at all, for fear of what may come, and so becomes immobile, crouched in a shell, fearful of any move.

I would sleep the night, I would think much upon what I might do, but I think the decision was already made.

We would go to sea once more.

△ **20** △

Our first task was to bring closer to the fort the *Abigail*, and to careen her there so her bottom might be scraped free of encrusted barnacles. If this was not done, not only would her bottom soon be damaged but her sailing speed would be slowed, and this we could not have. In many a situation to be encountered at sea, only speed could lead to safety.

By night I sat over my table, working upon our meager supply of paper to see what could be done as to armament and cargo. Again and again I went over the stowage of that cargo to keep our vessel seaworthy and in balance, for the stowage of cargo is no simple matter.

Tilly, Ring, and Jublain were often with me. Tilly was the most knowing as to stowage and the management of such cargo. Jublain knew the most of the use of ordnance, and Ring, to my surprise, knew much of marketing.

On the latter, I consulted often with Abigail, too, for she had made many voyages with her father and had heard him talk of trade and the market in many lands, and also the talk of those who consorted and traded with him.

Meanwhile I went over my charts and considered much as to exactly where we should go. England would have been my first choice, but England meant almost certain prison for me. It would likely be fully as dangerous for us to approach any other port in Christian Europe. Yet I thought much of the harbors of Brittany, where many ships were built, where we of the fens were known, and where there was ever a dearth of timber for the masts of ships. Yet Brittany was no market for potash, and I hoped to dispose of our cargo at one move. Into port quickly, a quick sale, a quick escape and back to our fort, should best suit all our purposes.

The coasts of Barbary were another thought, but they were notorious for pirates, who had little timber and who would be likely to take both our cargo and ship. Yet I liked not the thought of supplying masts for pirates who had enslaved many an English seaman.

"What then of Ireland?" Abby suggested, and it gave me good pause.

What, indeed? There had been some building activity there, or so I had heard, in those parts not affected too much by the fighting.

172

Thus Ireland was a chance . . . and Brittany, another.

Any voyage was a risk, for with every day of sailing we would be coming closer and closer to the shores of England and the danger from English ships.

Yet our ship was a *fluyt*, of a neutral country, a type of ship they would have little reason to attack or disturb. We might just bring it off.

"What do you think of England?" I asked the others.

Jublain shrugged. "I think it would be a mistake. It is too close, too dangerous. Mountjoy's ships would be around the coasts, for there was talk of Spanish soldiers helping the Irish. They would suspect every ship."

"Why *not* to England?" Pim Burke suggested cheerfully. "Barnabas need not appear. We could sail right into Bristol harbor, sell for a good price where the masts are most needed, and the potash can be traded, and then be out and gone."

"It is too risky," Jublain objected.

Pim was always the daring one, willing to skirt the very edge of danger, yet his idea had merit.

"Why not Ireland?" asked Jeremy Ring. "I'd rather see the timbers go there than to Spain or to the Moors. We could take them to the Indies, but they would bring much less."

"That's true," I agreed. "I had been thinking of that."

Jublain was typical of the professional soldier. He fought always to win. No unnecessary risk, although he would hesitate at nothing when in combat, always playing the percentages. He was one to want the margin of safety always on his side, to take every precaution, then go ahead.

"Ireland it will be," I said, "for a first attempt. I know a bit of the Irish coast now."

"Where in Ireland?" Ring asked.

"Glandore is small. There would be no market there, but there's a place nearby . . . called Kinsale. Do you know it?"

"Aye," Jublain said, "and a likely place it is. Well, why not? It is your neck they have measured for the hemp, not mine. Although crossing the ocean to any port at this time is a chancy thing."

"We'll sail to the Azores," I suggested, "by a warmer if longer route, and then to Ireland."

A word here or a word there, and the choice might have been otherwise. Upon such slender threads are the lives of men suspended.

Now there was much to be done. The hull of the *Abigail* had been well scraped and treated by the time our decision was made, and the loading of cargo begun: mast-timbers, shingles, potash, the few furs and hides we had taken, and a few freshwater pearls.

We had a supply of food, far more than needed to supply our ship, so like the squirrels we dug holes and buried some food in the cool ground—mostly nuts, that would care for themselves, buried in barrels and casks.

At last, we cast off from the moorings made to trees, and floated slowly downstream, putting on more canvas to catch the wind.

When I glanced back, the fort stood silent and alone upon its low hill. Wa-ga-su stood beside me. I wondered at his thoughts, this strong, quiet savage going out upon the water and sailing to a land he had never seen and could scarcely imagine. Yet he seemed calm.

"We will come back, Wa-ga-su," I assured him.

He said nothing, merely stared at the receding shores. This was not his country, yet it was a land he knew, and from it he knew the way to his own people.

John Tilly took over the watch and I went below.

Once more I got out my charts of the Irish coast, yet even as I stared at the chart I was not seeing it, for my thoughts had turned to Ireland itself rather than the chart before me.

In 1597 the Irish had rebelled against the English, and led by O'Neill, Earl of Tyrone, as well as Red Hugh O'Donnell, they fought a shrewd and cautious campaign, attacking moving columns, staging ambushes and sudden raids upon camps. It was the kind of warfare for which the Irish fighting man was suited, and with which the Earl of Essex was unable to cope. Finally, a truce was declared and Essex returned to England to find the Queen in a fury over the truce. He was replaced by Lord Mountjoy, and beheaded not long after . . . or so we had heard while in Wales.

What might have happened since then, we had no idea. Months had passed, and we had no recent news. Our best opportunity was to work in toward the coast of Ireland and try to bespeak a fishing vessel or a trader for information.

Glandore was no fit harbor for our commerce. Cork was too big, and the danger of being trapped in that harbor was greater, due to its conformation. Studying the chart and talking with Tilly and Ring, who both knew the coast, we decided upon Kinsale.

We set our course for the distant islands, and the seas were gentle, the winds not strong, but steady. Twice we sighted other sails, and once a ship headed to us, but the *fluyt* was a good sailor and we hoisted all her canvas and pulled swiftly away.

Gulls accompanied us, and porpoises dove and played around our bow, seeming to enjoy the company of the *fluyt*. Nearing the Azores we sighted too many vessels for comfort, and pulled away from them and set our course northerly.

"Do you know Kinsale, Jublain?" I asked.

"I know it. A good little place on the river Bandon with a fine, safe harbor." He looked at me. "It is worse than Cork, if you're thinking of a trap."

"Aye, but quieter than Cork, I think, and an easier place."

He agreed, but with misgivings. Only Pim took the voyage lightly, for all were afraid for me. This I sensed, knowing the Queen wanted none of them but Black Tom Watkins, to whom the voyage was a very real danger.

Wa-ga-su had developed into an efficient seaman, intrigued by all the activities aboard ship, and aware of our apprehension as we neared Ireland.

It was my hope to come up out of the sea and sight the Old Head of Kinsale first. As it was a bold headland, with sharp cliffs, I'd no idea I could miss it. And I did not, for we sighted it at dawn and moved in at once toward the entrance. I could see the dark outlines of De Courcy Castle, and I had a man aloft and two in the bow to watch for rocks. There was one that lay two cable-lengths southwest-by-south from Hangman's Point, covered with three feet of water at low tide, and we slid past it easily on the west side.

Suddenly, Jublain hailed me. "Barnabas! Look!"

Look I did, and beheld a half-dozen ships lying at anchor before us . . . and every one of them flying the flag of Spain!

More than that, the flag flying above the town of Kinsale was Spanish, too.

In the distance we heard the boom of cannon.

Jublain came quickly to the deck.

"Barnabas, I like not the look of this! It were better by far that we leave now. At once!"

"How?" I protested. "Those are warships. If we attempt to leave, they will follow."

"What do you propose?" Tilly asked.

"That we brazen it out. That we approach boldly, as if all was planned. This would seem a bad time to be here, however, and a poor time for marketing timbers."

"May another man speak?" Jeremy said. "Look yon . . . a fire has broken out in the town. I think Kinsale is under attack. But under attack by whom? The Irish, who are Catholic? I think not. Essex was here. He failed. Then Mountjoy was sent. It may be that the Spanish have sent a fleet to help the Irish, and they have landed here."

"A foolish place to choose," I said. "The fighting is to the north, I think."

"Who expects all men to move wisely?" It was Jeremy again. "And I doubt that these knew aught of Ireland. Spanish ships are here. The town is in their hands, and the town is under attack. Obviously it is under attack by Mountjoy and the English."

He paused. "Do you speak the Dutch tongue, Barnabas?"

176

"A few words. I fished once with a Dutch sailor who lived briefly among us."

"I speak it," Jublain said. "Tongues are as easy to me as blades, and when a man fights on the continent he speaks many tongues."

"Then we must convince the Spanish we are Dutch, until such a time as we can escape."

There was a shout from the bow: "A boat is coming!"

We were abreast of the Upper Cove, and the marking on my chart was for four fathoms. "Let's go forward," I said to Tilly, "and drop a rope ladder for the boat."

The officer who came aboard was elegantly dressed, but one glance at his clean-cut jaw and his quick steps assured me that this was no perfumed popinjay.

"Captain Alonzo de Valdez," he said. "What is your ship? And what do you do here?"

Jublain introduced himself, then said, "Our captain and owner is Barnabas de Sacketi. We were bound for La Rochelle and heard the Spanish fleet were needing supplies and spars. We directed our course to this place."

He looked from one to the other of us, his eye sharp and curious.

"The name of your vessel is what?"

"*Abigail*," I said, speaking in the Welsh I had from my mother. "It is named for my wife."

Abigail, looking lovelier than I'd seen her of late, came from the cabin. She held out a slender, white hand to Valdez, who bent above it gracefully.

After a few minutes of polite conversation, he said to Jublain. "Inform your captain that he comes at a bad time. Kinsale is beseiged by Lord Mountjoy and the British."

"And the Irish?"

"Coming up behind him. There will be a battle shortly." He shrugged a shoulder. "It does not look well. The Irish have won many battles, but their style is not ours, and at formal warfare . . . I am not sure. Lord Mountjoy is formidable."

"Ask him about the timbers," I murmured to Jublain. Jublain spoke to him and Valdez nodded. "Yes, I believe so." I understood enough to know what he was saying even before Jublain translated for me. I had been observing some of the vessels at anchor, three with damaged spars.

"It is possible we might purchase them," concluded Valdez.

When he was gone, we looked at each other and Jublain shrugged. "A fine young gentleman, and were it only up to him . . . well, we might manage it. However, there is this in our favor. I think they wish no more trouble than they already have."

"We are armed," I said. "I saw him looking at the guns. He also noticed our position. If there is trouble with us, we could do much damage before they sank us." I hoped I was right.

Some of the noise of the guns was smothered by the bulk of Compass Hill.

What we could see of the town was much damaged. One street seemed to run around the hill, with steep, slippery lanes going up its side. Many of the houses were built with large balcony windows overlooking the harbor. On the opposite shore were two other villages which, Jeremy told me, were Cove and Scilly.

Actually, despite its approach, the harbor was large, commodious, and capable of handling a considerable number of ships.

Standing by the rail I studied the town and our situation. If the Spanish chose to take our ship and ourselves as prisoners, there was little we could do. We might run for the harbor entrance, but the guns of the ships . . . warships all of them . . . would surely do us damage beyond recovery.

Jublain had learned from Valdez that the force was under the command of Don Juan D'Aquila, and numbered 4,000 men.

We waited, a long, slow afternoon, for permission to go ashore, well aware of how delicate was the balance.

As it was obvious the Spanish ships themselves needed replacements for spars smashed in battle, our cargo might be timely. Yet what I feared was that they would simply take the ship, the cargo, and ourselves, throwing us all into irons.

It was dusk when Valdez returned. Obviously, he was disturbed, but not by us, as I first assumed.

"The timbers? May I see them?"

With him was a sturdy Basque, a craftsman, without doubt. And so he proved, for when we unbattened the hatches and took him below his manner was brusque, and no foolishness about him. He looked over the timbers, climbed down upon them, walked along them, and muttered to himself.

His report to Valdez was stated flatly, in a very few words.

Valdez was obviously pleased. He turned quickly to us. "He says your timbers are excellent! Just exactly what we need." Then his smile vanished. "The price?"

Aristocrats, I knew, did not like to bargain, yet our position was uncertain, and what we needed was good will if we expected to get out alive and with our *fluyt*.

I spoke briefly with Tilly, who knew better the price than I, and then I had Jublain tell him: "We appreciate your situation, but we would not wish to profit by it. Pay us what they would cost in Spain."

Unwittingly, I had not only said the right thing but had raised the price on the timbers, for they were at this time much more in demand in Spain than in England.

At our table I received an order from him. "For the money," he told me, "you must go ashore." He wrote down the directions. "Present this order at the ship chandler's shop and you will be paid at once."

He turned to go, then stopped and looked back. "Your wife is very lovely." He spoke in English, looking directly at me. "I would not have her life endangered. When you have your money . . . go. Go at once."

He went over the side and down the ladder to his boat, and they pulled away. He seemed in a very great hurry.

Our hatches open, we rigged our gear to get out the timbers and drop them in the water over-side, where they would be towed to the ships needing them. We worked swiftly.

"Tilly," I said, "stand by to get under way immediately on my return. Get all the timbers they bought into the water as quickly as possible. We will heave in the anchor if there is time, and if there is not we'll simply cut loose. I have an idea Valdez was trying to tell us they are through here."

"The guns now are louder," Pim said. "You wish me to go with you?"

"No. I shall take Jeremy." Turning to Jublain, I suggested, "Tilly will work the ship, you will handle the direction of the fighting, if any. If I am not back by an hour after dusk, cut your anchor and get out . . . fast. Do not worry about me."

I turned back to Ring. "Jeremy, bring two pistols as well as your blade."

He grinned under his moustache. "I have four tucked behind my sash, and a dagger as well."

Hurriedly, I went below. Abby was waiting, her eyes wide, her cheeks ashen. "Do not be afraid. And if I am not back by an hour after dusk, Jublain is to take the ship to sea. Do you understand?"

"We will wait."

"No." For the first time I spoke harshly to her. "You will go. It is you, and not only you, for now there is our son." I paused for a moment. "Get out . . . get away. I will join you somehow."

For a moment I held her, then tore myself loose lest I should weaken.

Jeremy was already in the boat. I swung over the side and dropped in beside him. We pushed off. While we went ashore, Blue was to remain with the boat, hiding deep in the shadows.

"How far have we to go?" Jeremy asked.

"Almost an English mile," I said.

Suddenly, there was a heavy boom from seaward. Turning, aghast, we stared back toward the harbor entrance. Slowly but surely, a great ship was coming down the harbor . . . and she flew the flag of England.

180

There was another boom, and the explosion of a shell scattered fragments and flame aboard the Spanish ship nearest to her.

"Come . . . we'll have to hurry now," I said, refusing to look back again, or turn my head.

Blue left us ashore.

The sun was gone behind the hill, a cool wind blew along the waterfront, and we hurried, running and walking toward the street named on the order. A native had given us directions.

"You're going through with it?" Ring asked.

"Why not? We delivered the timbers, and we need the money."

"And if he will not pay?"

Suddenly, before I could answer, there was an explosion within the town. A great light shot into the sky and vanished, there was a dull rumble of falling timbers and debris, and we saw great crowds of men fleeing down a street.

There were flames everywhere now, and the deafening sound of muskets. Behind us we could hear the boom of guns from the ships.

We pushed through a crowd of rushing, shoving men and turned into the comparative quiet of the side street.

A man ran past me, his face white, his eyes distended. I do not think he even saw me. A woman with a child cowered in the corner of a stone building, half hidden behind a barrel. It was as safe a place as any.

As we came upon the ship chandler's shop, the front of the shop was smashed by a cannonball. We forced open the door.

Inside, on the floor, a man lay dead, his skull crushed by a falling timber. Clutched in one hand was a sack which he had begun to fill with gold from an open strong box.

Near him lay a bundle of papers. They were signed *Diego de Guzman.*

"It is he," I said. "Our paymaster is dead!"

Jeremy Ring flashed a smile. "His gold is not. Do we collect it?"

"Of course." I tucked the order for payment into the dead man's pocket. "There, senor. The order is yours, the gold is ours.

"Take the box," I said, "perhaps we shall be overpaid a little, but who will care?"

Jeremy dumped the gold back into the strongbox.

He tilted the box. "It is heavy."

"It will be lighter," I said, "when we spend it. But then," I added, "gold is forever heavy." Yet I was not looking at Jeremy Ring when I spoke.

Four men had burst into the door, swords in their fists, stopping suddenly upon seeing us.

"We will have the box," said the first. He was a blond and square-faced man of forty-odd with a livid scar across his brow and going into his hair. His face seemed familiar though I knew for a fact I had never seen him before.

Flames crackled and a nearby man cried out in pain. It was almost dark, and I had not noticed him in the leaping shadows. Out upon the bay, a big gun cleared its throat with a gush of flame.

My father's blade was in my hand when I looked at the square-faced man. " 'At midnight,' " I said, " 'in the flames of a burning town!' " I could hear my mother's voice. I felt as though another force had entered my body.

His ugly scar went a deeper red; the flames played a shadow game across his craggy face. His eyes went wide and he stared at me. "My God!" he said, and we crossed our blades.

△ **21** △

Oh, he was a strong one! The instant our blades crossed I knew he was good . . . and dangerous. No stronger wrist had held a blade against me since I last had fenced with my own father.

182

"'At midnight in a flaming town!'" I repeated, and he faltered, but only a little.

"Are you the one?"

"I am . . . are you ready to die?"

"What man is ever ready?" He moved in, thrust, stooped suddenly and slashed a lightning stroke at my legs. Only I sprang back, and was smiling as he came to me again.

"My father taught me that one," I said.

"Your father? Must I fight him, too?"

"You fought him once," I said, "and bear the mark."

He was wary, pressing, but wary. I heard a pistol go off nearby, and from the tail of my eye saw a man sprawl dead, then saw another shot, and yet another.

"Ah? Was it he? But she said she had no husband!"

"She found him then," I said, "when he put his mark on you."

High mounted the flames, roaring, crackling, burning all about us. Red light gleamed in his eyes, reflected from his face, and the pall of smoke lay heavy over all. Our blades caught the glow and shone back the light. They clashed and joined, and the man and I stood like brothers close together, our swords uniting us. Then a quick disengagement.

"Finish him, Barnabas. We've far to go and the ship, by your order, will not wait."

Our blades crossed, I thrust, he parried, and I felt the thin line of pain as his blade caressed my skin and left a streak of blood for marker.

He was strong and very quick, a superb swordsman. Was he too good? Would we both die here?

No! There was Abby out there, and had it not also been foretold that I would have four sons?

Sweat streaked my face. Blood ran down my side. I moved warily.

"She was a grand, beautiful lass," he said suddenly, "with a fine lot of courage in her. Not a bit was she afraid, but she stood and told me to my face what would come."

"And well she knew," I said. "For she had the blood of Niall"

183

"Aye." The blond and savage man moved in quickly, his blade like the flash of lightning in a far-off storm. "It took me a fair while to learn who *he* was! "

Suddenly his eyes lifted from our blades to mine, an instant only, "But she was wrong, for it is you who die this night, Son of Hers! *You!*"

He thrust low and hard, but my father had taught me that, too, and my blade was double-edged. I parried . . . quite gently, and lifted quick my blade . . . not gently.

My sword-edge missed his belly I'd intended to open but cleft his chin . . . clean through as you'd slice a cheese. And then the smallest thrust forward and my blade was four inches out the back of his neck. He fell, almost twisting my father's sword from my hand, but I put my foot on his chest and drew out the blade.

The man was dead.

We went away then, dragging the strongbox, which was heavy enough for four men, and then Jeremy found a barrow and we loaded it in.

We ran, pushing the barrow at a stumbling run, first me, then Jeremy. We passed dead men and fleeing women and children, and then we reached the shore.

Blue was there. He had thrown matting over himself and the boat to conceal them from eyes who might want to escape across the channel.

We climbed in with the box and shoved off. Blue dipped deep the oars and the boat shot forward, and we looked once more at our ship.

"The devil!" Jeremy said. "She's moving!"

"Is she?" I looked. Was she? For a moment I could not tell, and then . . . yes, she was, moving outward! She had caught the tide and was letting it take her, no sails lifted to attract attention, just a hand at the whip-staff.

"Let me spell you, Blue." I moved to the oars. He let me have them, and I put my back into it and the boat leaped forward. The tide was helping us, too. I glanced at the sky. There were stars, but it was fainting light, also.

We were gaining on the *Abigail*, and nearing the British warship.

We came alongside, and hailed, and somebody tossed us a line which we made fast to the boat. Then some tackle and we sent the chest up, and then a quick scramble and we were aboard, too, and picking up the ship's boat.

Yet scarcely was I aboard when a hail came from the starb'rd side. "Heave to! We're coming aboard!"

Tilly crossed to me quickly. "It's the Royal Navy. What shall we do?"

"Heave to, instantly, and do our best. We're a Flemish ship with a largely British crew who were almost trapped by the Spanish until the coming of the navy gave us a chance to escape.

"Tell him that. It is all we can do. Keep Watkins and Wa-ga-su below and out of sight. If we have to, we'll bring Wa-ga-su up and be returning him to America as an emissary for Raleigh to the Indians, where he'll land his colony."

"You think quickly," John Tilly said dryly. "I hope it works."

"So do I," I said. "Otherwise it's Newgate for me."

The officer came over the side, a neat, trim-looking man, a fighter by the look of him and one who knew his business. "What ship are you?" he demanded.

Of course, he had seen the name on the hull, but it was a formal question.

"The *Abigail*, Captain." He was no captain but the unofficial promotion would do us no harm. "A Flemish ship with mostly an English crew. Thank God you came when you did. We'd sailed right into a trap."

"What do you mean?" The officer's eyes were missing nothing, but John Tilly was the typically stalwart British merchant officer, and must have pleased his eye.

"We're from America, seventy-two days at sea, and needing fresh water. We knew Kinsale Harbor, and when we saw Old Head we thought we were safe. We came right on in, and the first thing we knew we were under the guns of a Spanish fleet.

"We went ashore to plead our case, hoping to be allowed to go, and then the attack came and our boat came back to the ship just as you fellows were coming in.

"By the lord, Captain, you were a sight for weak eyes! When we saw that British flag and heard those guns . . ." Tilly mopped his brow with a handkerchief. "What can we do for you, Captain?"

"Where are you bound?"

"Falmouth, Captain, to discharge and load supplies for America again. We've an Indian aboard . . . one of the savages, you know, but he's a fine chap, and a great help to us. We're taking him back to speak to his colony for Raleigh. He's a good fellow and we've treated him well. We believe he will speak well to his chiefs when we get him back. It will ease the way for us."

"Your name?"

"John Tilly, sailing-master."

"I am Ephraim Dawes, first officer of Her Majesty's ship, the *Sprite*. Let me see your manifest."

Tilly led him to the cabin while I kept out of sight. It was unlikely that he knew me, but he would certainly know my name, for such a story as the possible discovery of King John's treasure would be bandied about.

Leaning on the rail, watching the water, I suddenly heard a faint rustle close by. Warily, I put a hand to my sword. The sound came from the ship's boat we'd hoisted aboard. I waited, and suddenly glimpsed a white hand on the gunwhale, then a head lifted enough for the eyes to see over and then, quick as an eel, a boy went over the gunwhale, paused, then darted for the shadows.

The last thing I wished was to create a disturbance that would lead to further delay in getting the British officer ashore, so I made no move.

A boy? A small man? Or perhaps a girl?

Hesitating only an instant, the boy ducked down the scuttle and vanished. Unquestionably, whoever it was had somehow hidden himself carefully aboard the ship's boat . . . perhaps with Blue's knowledge, possibly during Blue's momentary absence. Only one such possible hiding place offered itself . . . the small compartment forward where the sail was stowed.

John Tilly and Dawes emerged from below. Tilly walked with him to the ladder where several British sailors were gathered.

"You're free to go," Dawes said, "but keep a weather eye out for Spanish vessels. There are a few about."

And then Abby came out on the deck. She looked quickly around, saw me, and started toward me. "Barnabas . . . ?"

Dawes froze. Slowly he turned, staring at me. My clothes had been badly dealt with in the trouble ashore. I'd been somewhat singed, and I was dusted by falling plaster and wet from spray. I looked anything but a ship's officer.

"You, there! What's your name?"

"Crocker's the name, beggin' your pardon." I touched my forelock with diffidence. "Barnabas Crocker."

"This lady called you by your first name?"

"Aye, my family served her'n for nigh a hundred years, though we be from Yorkshire."

I'd worked with Yorkshiremen and was handy with the accent . . . at least to a degree.

"Where are you from, Crocker?"

"Filey was my home, an' well I wish I was back there now."

He studied me for a moment, then turned and went down the ladder. When his boat pulled away we stood for a moment, watching.

"Get some sail on her, John," I said quietly, "but not too quick with it until we're a bit further along. Then we'd best make a run for it."

Abby came to me. "Barnabas, I am sorry. I just didn't think."

"There's no harm done." I glanced up at the sails. The wind was strong and they were drawing well. Soon we would be out at sea, and with any kind of a lead the British could not overtake us. Yet I had said we were going to Falmouth and the more I considered it the more I liked the idea.

We had shingles, potash, and furs below, and might get as good a price at Falmouth as elsewhere. And it was an easier place to leave than Bristol. With every hour in these waters I was risking my freedom and the future of our project, but we had already made a goodly sum from our timber venture. What the chest contained we had not yet determined, but it was more than the worth of the timbers we sold.

Yet we still needed supplies, both for the homeward voyage and for our stay in the new land. Tools, also. And clothing.

John Tilly came to me. "Falmouth it is," I said. "A quick sail in, we'll dispose of the cargo to the first buyer, then buy our supplies and sail. I want to be in port no more than two days."

"That is very quick," he said, considering.

It had to be. That British officer might get to thinking, and putting one thing with another, might come back for another look. At the moment we were nothing in his plans. With parties of sailors ashore, and a chance of further battle with the Spanish, we were only an incident in his life. It was unlikely he'd give us a thought until the situation at Kinsale was settled. With luck, we'd be in Falmouth, out, and gone by then.

The *Abigail* slipped quietly into the harbor at Falmouth and dropped her hook. The gray battlements of Pendennis Castle, now in the process of completion, loomed over the harbor.

Jublain stood beside me, looking shoreward. "It is the Killigrews you must see here," he said, nodding toward the town. "If they are not off a-sailing after Spanish ships themselves, they will welcome you, I think. See the big house there? Close to the shore? That is Arwennack, the Killigrew home.

"Oh, they be a salty lot! They'd take your ship right from under you if you have not an eye upon them, yet they are respecters of boldness and courage.

"Speak to Peter, if you can. He's no longer young, but an able man, and you'll be safer talking to him than any of the others. Moreover, although he's a Queen's man he's damnably independent, and he's not likely to report your presence or hold you for the Queen's officers."

"You know him?"

"Served with him once. He'll remember me, I think."

"Let's be ashore then."

Peter Killigrew received us in a low-beamed room with a huge old fireplace. He took his pipe from his teeth and placed it on the table.

"Your name?"

"Barnabas Sackett, master of the *Abigail*. I'm fresh into your harbor with shingles, potash, and furs. I'd like to sell what I have, load supplies, and be off. It is," I added delicately, "my impression that I do not have much time."

"Sackett, is it? Are you the one they are hunting up down the land?"

"I am. I was told you were a fair man, and an independent one, and I have some'at to sell and much to buy. From you, if you'll but have it that way."

"They say you've found King John's treasure?"

"Balderdash, Captain Killigrew. Pure nonsense. I found some gold coins and discovered there was a market for antiquities. Here and there I'd stumbled upon ruins in the forest and up on the downs, so I got a manuscript by Leland . . . he walked over the country hunting such places. . . . Then I went to a place I remembered and commenced digging. I found some more, but it was pure chance."

Killigrew made a rumbling sound in his chest. Then he said, "Luck! I've no faith in luck, Sackett! Luck comes to a man who puts himself in the way of it. You went where something might be found and you found something, simple as that.

"All right, Sackett. I like the way you stand, the way you talk. What is it you need?"

I handed him my list. "I'll treat you fair," he said. "You'll pay 10 percent more than I'd sell for here, but that's some'at less than you'd pay in Bristol or London."

He pushed some papers on his desk. "I'll have lighters

189

alongside within the hour. I'll pay the going price for your potash. The shingles and what timber you have left, I'll pay premium for. They are hard to come by."

He turned in his chair and rang a small handbell. When a servant appeared in the door, he said, "Send Willys to me . . . now."

He pointed to a chair. "Seat yourself Sackett." He stared at me from under heavy brows. "So you're going back to America?"

"It is true."

"Fine! You've a fine ship there. Load her with mast timbers and send her back. I'll buy them, and whatever else you have to offer, and if you take any prizes, bring them to me."

"I will do that," I said quietly, "and I am grateful."

He got up suddenly. "Let us walk down to the inn. I'll have a drink with you there. Could have it here, but I need the air. Need the walk. Don't move around so much as I used to.

"Raleigh's land, is it? Well, well! Savages there? You've seen them? Are they truly as fierce as we hear?"

I shrugged. "Some are, some aren't. They are good fighters, and some are good traders as well. I hope to be friendly with them."

"It is well. Send your ships to Falmouth. We'll treat you fair and ask no questions, nor make a report. Why, 'tis foolishness, this talk of treasure! I believe no part of it, for you acted no part like a man with gold."

We sat over our ale and talked, of ships and the Queen, of Raleigh and Essex and Mountjoy, and of Kinsale that had fallen, and of the actor Shakespeare, and a likely man I found him, Peter Killigrew.

The *Abigail* lay still upon the crystal water of the bay when I returned, and the lighters were alongside, out-loading our goods, and Abby was at the rail.

She looked anxiously into my eyes. "Barney, I was that worried! I was afraid they'd taken you for the Queen."

"Not them." Suddenly, I remembered. "Abby, have

190

you heard anything unusual aboard ship? Or seen anyone not of the company?"

She looked at me oddly, and I explained. "A boy?" she asked. "Who came aboard in Kinsale? Oh, Barney, let's find him!"

"We must. I'd not like to be taken up for kidnapping." I called to Jeremy. "Stand by the scuttle, will you? I shall go below."

"What's up?"

When I explained, he shrugged. "It's just another lad, wishing for the sea, no doubt."

When I was in the darkness of the hold, I spoke out. "Lad, I saw you come from the boat last night. Come out now, for we're sailing to America in the morning, and there'll be no place there for lads whose family will be wanting them."

There was silence, then slowly from among some bolts of sailcloth, he stood up. We eyed each other in the dim light.

A fine, likely-looking lad he was, slender, but with good shoulders upon him, and a clear, clean-cut face with a shock of handsome hair. The skin of his face and of his hands marked him for gentry.

"Who are you, lad?"

He stared at me, brave enough, but frightened, too. "I am of Ireland," he said, "and my kinfolk are killed. I am alone, wanting only to get to France where there are others of my kind."

"To France, is it? You'd fly away and leave your land behind? We've enemies in France, boy."

"You have, if you're English, as I've no doubt you are. I've none, for it's Irish I am, and they are friendly to us there."

"Aye, so I've heard. You are Papists, Irish and French. Well, come on deck. You'll be hungry, and Catholic or Protestant, you'll be ready to eat. I'll have no lad hungry aboard my ship."

"It is very kind of you."

Yet he watched me warily, and I was sure he had no trust in me. So I commented, "Boy, you've the manner and style of a lad well-raised, so I'll trust that you've honor as well."

He turned on me, drawing himself up a little and looking directly at me. "I have, Captain. In my family, honor comes first."

"Do you know the name of Barnabas Sackett?"

"I do not."

"Well, the name is mine, and a good name it is as names go, but I am wanted by the Queen's men. It is a mistake, but the devil of a time I'd have proving it, so come the dawn I shall be away upon the sea to America."

"America?" he was startled. "I had thought—"

"Aye, no doubt you had expected aught but that. Well, America it is, and I shall not come back. Nor did I think that you'd such a voyage in mind when you came aboard."

"To get away, Captain. That was all I wanted. Had they found me they'd have slain me . . . upon the spot. I am—"

I lifted a hand. "Tell me nothing. It is not needed. I know something of the troubles of the Irish, and have naught against you, m'self, nor does anybody aboard, but there's some as might in the towns about here. Was I you I'd get far from the sea."

"You do not go to France, then?"

"To America only, and we'll touch no land, God willing, until we reach there. If you go ashore, lad, it will be here, in this place."

He stared off into the distance, frightened a little, but not wishing to show it.

"Say nothing of who you are, lad. Tell nobody you are Irish for a great while. There be many a lad adrift in England now. Mayhap you can get yourself apprenticed—"

"I am a gentleman! "

"Aye," I agreed grimly, "but would you rather starve a gentleman or live fat an apprentice? Lad, I know none here, but I'll set you ashore with a good meal inside you, a bait of food to last you, and enough money to buy an apprenticeship in a trade you welcome."

Startled, he looked at me. "You'd give me money?"

We went on deck and to the cabin then, where Lila fed him well, with some talk from Abby and me.

"My name?" He hesitated. "My first is Tatton. I'll not be telling the other."

A handsome lad he was, with clear hazel eyes, and a warm smile. Such a lad as someday I hoped my son would be, but we put him ashore in Falmouth with five gold coins sewed into his waistband and a packet of food.

He waved to us from the shore road before he started off, and we saw him no more, a fine, sturdy lad, walking away toward a future no man knew.

△ 22 △

Dark flowed the waters of the Chowan River, dim the shadows in forest and swamp, sullen the light upon the empty hill where once our fortress stood. The timbers we had hewn with our hands, the joints we had fitted with loving care, the huge gate with its repairs . . . all were gone.

Burned. . . .

"Do you see anything, Jeremy?"

Ring was studying the forest and the riverbanks through his glass.

We stood together on the poop, watching the banks slide by in the fading light of an aging day, seeing the red touch the hills with warning. Abby was beside me, large now with child, and John Tilly, calm, serious, a little worried, I think, for he approved not of our going. Jublain had told me at last that he had not the stomach any longer for the wilds. "I fear you must go from here without me, Barnabas."

Well enough I understood, and blamed him not a whit. There were other places for him, and other climes. In a way I was relieved, for I much wanted a good friend who knew where we were and what we did.

At the last I had decided to leave the ship to Tilly, for Jublain wanted it not, only passage back to Europe or to the French lands to the north. Pimmerton Burke, Tom Watkins, and Jeremy Ring would come with me, and others had chosen also to attempt the wilds. Jublain assured me he would come again on another voyage, but within days now we should be pushing upstream with Wa-ga-su as our guide.

We had hoped to find the fort intact, but it was gone, burned. Had they found the food caches? We did not need the food now but a time might come, and it was a comfort to know it was there.

We went up the hill in the morning under a sullen sky of clouds with lightning playing, and we stood among the charred timbers and felt a sadness upon it, for what man does not love that which he himself has built?

The earth above the caches was grown now with grass. If the food had been found it was long since. The nuts, at least, would keep.

We returned and went back aboard and sat at table with few words between us. "Is it all gone?" Abby asked.

"Burned," I said, "a few timbers and ashes. Grass grows where our house was, and where the wall was built. I think it must have been but a little while after we sailed."

"Nick Bardle?" she asked.

"Indians, I think. Bardle would not burn it. He would rather leave the timbers for further use sometimes, if along this coast he needed a spar. Scoundrel he may be, but he's not a wasteful man."

So we talked a little then, of old times and new times, of the *fluyt*, and all the while we tried to avoid the thought of good-bye.

For good friends we were and the time for parting near, and no one wished to be the first to speak of an end to what we had together.

Jublain was my oldest friend among them, of a chance meeting when he helped me escape my first serious trouble. Now I would see him no more. Or would I? Who can say, in such a world?

Yet the urge was on us, and on Abby no less than I,

the urge to see beyond those blue mountains, to find a new land, to break new earth, and see our crops freshening in the sun of a new spring. For land beyond the mountains is ever a dream and a challenge, and each generation needs that, that dream of some far-off place to go.

We had crossed an ocean to come . . . why? What drove us more than others? Why did Pim come with us and not Jublain? Why Jeremy Ring of the dashing manner and not John Tilly?

Thus far we had come together, and now some strange device, some inner urge, some strange thread grown into our beings was selecting us to move on westward.

Selecting? Or was it we ourselves who chose? Never would I cease to wonder at why one man and not another.

We had made our last purchases from Peter Killigrew, three light, strong boats that we carried on our decks for launching. Now we put them ready, and sliding down the river we went along to that other one to the south, a somewhat larger river, and so Wa-ga-su said, a larger one.

Much time I spent with Wa-ga-su. He knew my chart at once, put a finger on the sounds, and traced the rivers. Here and there he showed me changes in the river or parts that had been wrongly marked.

"Each year I shall come once along the coast," John Tilly said, "and shall tell others to keep an eye out for a signal from you."

Once more upon the map I showed him the area in which I planned to settle. "Of course, there is no way of knowing until upon the ground, yet I shall follow this river, I think, to the place where it comes from the mountains. Then I shall look for some valley, some cove, some sheltered, defensible place, and there we will settle.

"We have the tools, the seed corn, and much ammunition. We will plant our seed in the spring, and we shall try to find minerals, not gold so much as the useful minerals, and there we will claim land. I shall even mark out some for you if you should change your mind."

"Barnabas?" Jublain put a hand on my arm. "Cannot I, even at this last moment, persuade you not to do this thing? It will be long before other white men come, and longer before they reach the mountains. You will be very few, and you will be alone. Think of Abigail . . . without women, without the friendships, the comforts . . ."

"Lila will be there. We will make friends among the Indians."

"You hope! Well," he shrugged, "so be it. Perhaps it be your destiny, Barnabas. But if you have sons, send at least one of them home to England. There will be no education here for them."

"We will teach them. I have books. Yet, that is one thing you can do, Jublain. Do you remember where we first cached our furs? In the cave?"

"I do."

"If you come this way, bring books, wrap them well in oilskin, and hide them there. It may be that one day we shall return to the coast, and we will look for them."

Again we shook hands, and then we talked of other things, and at the last, when our ship was anchored off the river mouth, and our three boats were lowered and well stowed with our gear, two boats to be rowed, and one towed behind, Sakim suddenly came from below.

"With your permission," he said quietly, "I shall go with you. You will need a doctor where you go, and your wife will need one. I would like to come."

For a moment I could not speak. I simply held out my hand and he took it, so our party was thus the stronger, and stronger by as able a man as I had known.

In the first boat were Wa-ga-su, as our guide and interpreter, Abby, Lila, Sakim, Pim Burke, Black Tom, and myself.

In the second boat were: Tim Glasco, a square-built, strong young man, blond and cheerful, who was a journeyman blacksmith; John Quill, who had been a farm boy on a great estate in England; Kane O'Hara, who had been a mercenary soldier; Peter Fitch, a slender, wiry, tireless man who had been a shipwright and a ship's carpenter; Matthew Slater, a farmer; and Barry Magill, who had been a cooper and a weaver; and Jeremy Ring.

196

Abby kept her eyes firmly set on the river before us, her face slightly pale, her eyes large and solemn. Lila gave never a backward glance, nor had she ever, I think, once her mind was set upon a way to go.

As we moved upriver, I assayed again the strengths and weaknesses of our party. We were strong in body and spirit, I knew, but we faced our first winter in the wilderness, yet winter on the coast might be even fiercer.

We saw no Indians, we saw no wild game. The boats moved slowly and steadily upstream, holding well to the center of the river except when we could escape the direct current and move in shallower, quieter water near one shore or the other.

Each man pulled an oar, myself not excepted. Only Wa-ga-su, who sat in the bow, was free of that labor, because we wished his eyes and attention solely for the river and its banks.

On that first day we made what I felt was ten miles. Toward dusk, Kane O'Hara killed a deer, and Sakim speared a large fish. We moved to an island and made a small camp with a carefully screened fire.

The river flowed softly seaward, a faint wind rustled the leaves, then was still. Our driftwood fires threw a warm glow upon the faces of the men as they gathered about, eating and talking. Our boats had been drawn into a small cove, sheltered by trees and moss hanging from their branches. Peter Fitch had remained aboard, and I walked down from the fire to talk with him, and to listen to the night.

An owl flew by on slow, prowling wings. "Big one," Fitch said.

"Yes, it was." I hesitated. "Why did you come, Fitch?"

He looked around at me, and seemed a little embarrassed. "I did na wish to go home wi' empty hands," he said, "for I made big talk of what I'd do when away upon the sea. Back yon in the village, I had dreamed dreams of going to battle and winning a princess, maybe, or a lot of gold.

"Well, I've been four years gone and nothing to show for it but scars and the memories of bad times.

"Bad times were never in the dreams. Oh, I kenned enough to know there's many a slip, but I had high hopes, and they laughed at me for big expectations.

"Maybe it come of a-settin' in the chapel listening to the sermon, and thinkin' more on that chap buried in the stone box beside the altar. They had his figure carved in stone atop it, although I knew little enough about him who was buried there. He'd built the church himself, there at Acaster Malbis . . . that was our village . . . back in 1306 or some such time. He came of a Norman family who'd come with William the Conqueror, and they had lands from him.

"The name of the first one was Sir Hugh de Malebisse, which somehow became Malbys or Malbis, and they do say that when he came over he had little but a name and a sword, although there may be no truth in that.

"But I'd set there thinking of what he won with a sword, and it seemed to me that what one could do another might. Captain Sackett, I talked big. I can't go home with empty hands."

"Why should you?" I said. "There will be land here for all, and once located, we shall scout each his piece, and all adjoining they'll be."

"I'd like that. Will there be a stream on it? And trees?"

"Aye. We'll see to it."

Turning away, I added, "Keep a sharp eye and a listening ear or you'll not make it. The savages don't even need to see the color of your hair to want it."

There was a good smell of food in the air, pleasing because it was of the country. The cooks had boiled venison and wild turkey together, which all relished.

Seated, Abby and I ate and talked of our son to be . . . or daughter. And with our food we drank the water of the Roanokes, as fresh and clear as water could be. We talked of our home in the blue mountains, the home that was to be, and they were fine, bold dreams we had.

Wa-ga-su came suddenly from the darkness and spoke softly to me, and I did not move, but reached out with my sword-case and touched Jeremy upon the shoulder. He glanced from me to Wa-ga-su and got up slowly, walking to the pot for another helping, then back to us.

"Three canoes," Wa-ga-su said, "twenty, thirty men. They are on warpath."

"Jeremy," I said, "as quietly as can be, send Slater, Magill, and Black Tom Watkins to the boats to join Fitch, and do the rest move one by one to the shadows and to the fallen trees near the boats. Leave the fires burning."

"What is it, Barnabas?" Abby asked.

"There will be a fight. Get to the boats, you and Lila."

No sound disturbed the quiet night. Men walked away and darkness remained. The men looked to their muskets. As for myself, I put three pistols in my belt and carried a musket also.

The night was still. Somewhere a night-bird called.

They came with a rush.

They came with savage yells, intending to strike terror to our hearts, and had they found us unawares or sleeping, the yells and the sudden attack might have done so. Nor was the attack so well planned as I thought them usually to be. They had seen our fires, and without closer inspection, decided we must be gathered around them. They must have waited some time.

When they finally charged toward the firelight, spears and tomahawks poised to strike, they came upon emptiness. One warrior, quick to perceive, had turned sharply back when Slater shot him.

It was taken as a signal, and all of us fired. And in an instant they were gone . . . vanished.

Three bodies lay upon the earth, two obviously dead, the third only wounded. Yet he lay still.

I could see his eyes. They were open and alert, although he had been hit hard.

We reloaded our guns. The night was so still I could hear the rustling water among the reeds at the shore. Pim was beside me and I whispered to him, telling him to get the boats afloat and all aboard.

He slipped away. There was still the faint smell of powder smoke mingled with the dampness of mud, wet foliage, and the smoke from our now dying fires. Behind me I heard faint movements, and Glasco came up to my side. "I don't like it," he muttered. "It was too easy."

"You're right. We're going to pull out. I'd rather row all night than lose a single man."

From down the shore we heard a splintering crash, then another, and then a third.

Then all was silent again.

At the last moment, with all aboard, I waited . . . listening. There were faint, whispering movements, then silence. Overhead there were stars.

My hands touched the rough bulwark, and in utter silence we moved away. So silently that I heard but once the sound of a paddle.

"Will they follow?" I asked Wa-ga-su.

"No canoe," he replied.

"But they must have canoes."

"No canoe," he replied, and I detected a smug satisfaction in his tone. "I fix."

The oars dipped deep, and we moved off into the night. Abby was close beside me. I put my hand over hers and she leaned her head against my shoulder.

"Tired?" I asked her.

"Yes . . ."

"You've a right to be tired. We'll find a good place and rest."

"No, it's all right, Barnabas. I'll be all right." She paused a moment. "There is so little time before winter comes."

It was in all our thoughts. We were alone in an unknown land, with danger all about, and no hope of rescue if aught went wrong. We had cut all ties, but we floated together in the vast interior of this green strange land.

We were moving toward the mountains where it would be cold during the winter, and we had meat to kill, fuel to gather, shelters to build. Our only security lay in ourselves, in what we were, and what we would become. But had I chosen from thousands those who were with me, I could not have chosen better.

Leaving the bow, I went back to take the place of Tim Glasco at an oar, and after a half hour I shifted across the boat to give Kane O'Hara some rest.

When I returned to the bow, Abby was asleep, as was Lila. I moved alongside Wa-ga-su. "Tell me about the river," I suggested.

"There are villages," he replied. "One of them we will see tomorrow or the day after."

"Are the Catawbas a strong people?" I asked.

He shook his head somberly. "We are strong, but we have lost many men in war with the Iroquois, and we have been driven from our country in the north. The Iroquois fight everybody, kill everybody. Very savage, those people."

He spoke English well enough, after his months with us, and I spoke a good deal of his language.

"Then the Cherokee attacked us and we were driven to the place we live now. We will go no further. We will fight them again and again, but we will not leave."

"Are all of your people here?"

"No . . . some are still in the north, but they will come."

"Wa-ga-su, we have told you how many are the English. Soon they will come here. Many will come. Some will return, some will die, but more will come. We would be friends to your people. Think on this, and say what you think to your people."

"You wish me to say it is good for Catawba to join with the Queen's men?"

"I cannot advise you, Wa-ga-su. Much harm may come from it. What is right for us is not always right for you, and those of us who come are hungry for land—"

"There is enough for all."

"That may be. I do not know if there is ever enough. And there will be trouble with the English and the French and the Spanish even as there was trouble with the Iroquois."

Wa-ga-su was silent.

We continued to row.

The first light of dawn was upon the water, vaguely yet, but swirls of water could be seen and ripples, and the trees began to outline themselves against the morning sky. One last star hung in the sky like a far-off lamp.

Turning, I spoke to Jeremy, who was at the tiller. "There!" I pointed. "We will eat and rest."

We went up to the shore in the dawning, and beached our boats on the water, not too firmly, and tied them with slipknots, and a man remained armed with a musket in each boat. The rest stepped ashore and I walked along, gathering bits of brush and bark as I went. Others picked up driftwood, and behind some of the logs and rocks we found a smooth place some twenty feet across. Pulling some rocks together for a crude fireplace, I shredded some bark in my hands, put it down, and added twigs. Spilling a thumbnail of powder on the flattest piece of bark, I removed the charge from my pistol and, cocking it, pulled the trigger. A spark leaped into the powder and in an instant the fire was going.

Wa-ga-su had disappeared into the brush. I warned the others, so that a hasty shot might not kill him, and walked back to the boats.

"Keep down," I said, "and keep your eyes open. They can be all around before you see them."

Matt Slater went down to the stream to fish. There was a deep pool just below where the boats lay and he cast his hook there.

We ate and then slept on the grass with two men guarding; then those men slept and two more took over. Wa-ga-su returned. He had seen many deer and turkey tracks.

Shortly after noon we started upstream again, this time using sails, as there was better wind. It was not much, but it saved us all the labor of rowing or poling against the current. We moved up slowly. When we camped at dusk we were more than twenty miles from the scene of the fight.

Day after day, we pushed on. The stream grew narrower, the water, if possible, clearer. We hunted with our bows and arrows, killing turkeys aplenty and an occasional deer.

And all of us were changing. We were better hunters. We had become stronger and more confident. Traveling along a stream as we were, there was always game, and there were many fish. If the Indians fished with bait, they did so rarely, and the fish were easily taken.

At sundown on the tenth day, Lila came to me. "We must rest soon," she said. "I think we have not much longer to wait."

"She is right," Sakim said. "I think within the week."

Glancing west, toward where the blue mountains lay, I tried to calculate. If it was smooth water, not too many curves . . . and if there were no waterfalls, could we reach the mountains in two weeks?

Sakim shrugged. "We will see."

Lila turned and walked back to Abigail, and I made a round of our camp.

I mentioned two weeks to Wa-ga-su, and he shook his head no. "More far away," he told me.

He waved ahead and to the south. "The cold will come. Sometimes snow. Much ice on rivers. I think it is best you stay with my people. The Catawba is good farmer. Much grain. You stay."

There was hypnotic fascination in the journey by river. We moved along one bank or the other, choosing where the current was least strong, and often our way was overhung with the branches of huge old trees. At other times we were far from the banks, moving along in the brightest sunlight.

It was already cold at night.

Several times we saw deer swim across the stream ahead of us, and once we killed one for meat. Several times we killed turkeys, and once a bear.

We saw few Indians but were quite sure they saw us, and looked upon us with wonderment and curiosity. Yet as the distance grew we became more confident, more excited by what lay before and around us.

By night our flickering campfires lighted the wilderness, and sometimes we sang the old songs from home. Kane O'Hara had a fine voice, as did Jeremy. Of my own singing the least said the better. I liked to sing, and would have sung always, but my voice had no quality.

Much was I learning, for Wa-ga-su pointed out trees and plants used by the Indian for medicine or food, and also much about Indians themselves. The Catawba and the Cherokee were ancient enemies, and the legends among the tribes were that both had come from the north, although long, long ago and before any white man had been seen, even before De Soto or Juan Pardo.

There were mornings when the sunlight sparkled on every ripple, and shadows dappled the banks, and there were days when the rain fell in sheets and we could see only a few yards before us. Sometimes we were hard put to avoid huge drift logs that came down upon us, but each day we moved farther, each day we progressed some little bit.

"It takes a long time," Peter Fitch mumbled, one day. "I would na have believed 'twas any so far, or there was so much empty land in the world."

" 'Tis a miracle," Slater agreed, "and they do say there's more beyond the mountains."

Suddenly, Fitch caught my arm. "Captain, would you look now? What is that yonder?"

We had camped that morning under some great old trees on a broad flat bank of the river. Beyond the trees there was a wide savanna or plain, and out upon it lay a huge beast, a great, hairy black monster of a thing. As we watched, he got up suddenly, lunging to his feet and staring at us. His broad flat face, thickly matted with hair, was toward us, and his beard almost touched the ground.

Suddenly others like him began to appear.

Wa-ga-su came up beside me. "Good meat," he said. "Good hide also. You kill?"

I had to think twice about that. I'd seen some bulls in my time, but nothing quite like this one, nor nearly so big. And there was wonder in me if a bullet could bring him down, but Wa-ga-su assured me the Indians often killed them, sometimes with arrows, but occasionally with spears.

At his urging I rested my musket on its wiping-stick, aimed, and fired.

The huge beast moved not a whit, but continued to stare at me, finally jerking his big head up and down as if irritated by me or perhaps the bullet. I had begun at once to recharge my gun, and at the shot, O'Hara and Pim had come quickly from the trees, they being closer.

The beast then took a step toward me and suddenly bent at the knees and went down, then rolled over. The others did not run off or even seem to notice, not having heard such a sound before, and not connecting it with any danger to them.

Wa-ga-su was now pointing at the nearest cow, and truth to tell she had turned partly away from me so I had an excellent shot at the space behind her left shoulder. Knowing full well that I had many mouths to feed, I took rest and fired again, with equal good fortune. It must be admitted that neither beast was as much as fifty yards away and in plain sight, nor were they moving. But he was standing and looking, she grazing. Now, seeming to scent blood, the others moved off a little, looked back, then walked on across the savanna, and calling the others, we moved out to butcher our beasts.

Quill and Slater were expert at butchering, so leaving them to the task—with Wa-ga-su to advise and Fitch to help—I put Barry Magill at the edge of the woods to keep an eye out for trouble from inland while the others worked.

Abby was lying on a pallet near the fire and I went and sat down near her, holding her hand. She looked very pale this morning and I was frightened to see her so, and guessing how I felt, she squeezed my hand. It was getting very close to her time.

Watkins and Glasco were fishing, Pim putting a splice in a rope we had broken negotiating a falls, where we had to remove our boats from the water and take them overland, tugging and hauling them, then returning for our baggage and carrying that on our shoulders.

Suddenly there was a low whistle from Magill, and instantly, Glasco and Watkins took up their muskets. Pim stepped to shelter behind the bole of a huge tree while Black Tom and I went through the woods.

Our butchers had stopped cutting meat and were standing erect. Magill had his musket leveled, and Fitch was kneeling behind the carcass of the bull, holding his own musket.

On the crest of the low rise where we had first seen the buffalo stood several Indians. Each carried a bow and a spear as well, with a quiver of arrows behind each left shoulder. As we watched, another Indian appeared, then another, and another.

My musket was in my hands, and I waited, watching.

When at last they ceased to appear, at least thirty warriors lined the crest.

Against them we could fire three shots before they would be upon us.

<h1 style="text-align:center">△ 23 △</h1>

They stared upon us, and we upon them, and then Wa-ga-su stepped suddenly forward and called out to them in his own tongue.

Instantly they were alert. One of them came a few steps forward, peering at him. Wa-ga-su spoke again, and motioned them back, wisely guessing that any sudden advance might bring gunfire.

He walked toward them, speaking the while, and they waited for him. Suddenly they were all about him, showing great excitement. They seemed to know him, and yet I could not be sure.

He turned then and came to me. "They are my people," he said. "They are Catawba." Then he added, "They hunt for meat, but they have killed nothing."

"Wa-ga-su, the cow we must have, and the hides of both, but I would not see your people hungry. They may have the bull."

Walking out to the butchering, I explained to Quill, Slater, and Fitch. "Skin out the cow," I said, "and get the meat and hide. I think we will make some friends here."

At Wa-ga-su's invitation, they descended upon the bull,

and in no time at all fires were going and meat was roasted.

Lila met me at the edge of the clearing. "I think we must stay here," she said. "Her time is upon us."

Thoughtfully, I looked around. The grove of trees where the boats were drawn up was lovely, a peaceful place, open to the sky and with a good clear lookout in all directions, as well as a good field of fire.

There was water, fuel, and as evidenced by the buffalo, there would be game. If my son was to be born, it would be better here.

"Is this your country?" I asked Wa-ga-su.

"No . . . but my people are great hunters and wanderers. They travel far."

"They have women and child with them?"

"Many." He motioned toward the southwest. "Over there." Then he added, "You have given them much meat. They are pleased."

"If they are your people," I said, "they are our people."

The remark pleased him, and he repeated what he had said before, that it would be well for us to live with his people until the winter had come and gone.

"It may be," I said, "if it pleases your people. But we must try to find a place near the mountains . . . in a small valley, with water and timber."

"There are many, and many more over the mountains."

"What people live over the mountains?"

He shrugged. "All people hunt there, no people live."

Together we went back to our camp. The fire was burning, the boats tied along the bank now, and an awning of sailcloth had been raised, under which Abby was lying.

Sitting down beside her, I told her we would remain where we were until our child was born, and I told her of the Indians, whom she had not yet seen, and of the buffalo I had killed.

"It is a good place," I said, "and we can hunt nearby and gather fruit and nuts to help our eating. It is such another place as this that we will find."

"Why not here, Barnabas?" she asked me.

"No. It is lovely, but it is not the blue mountains. I

think in those mountains we will find a place we love, and another place, as well."

"Another?"

"Someday we may wish to move on, or our children. We must think of our children. The land we have passed through is too fair a land to lie empty as it is, and more men will come and settle there."

Abigail was listening, a smile on her face.

"There are mines to be opened here. I have heard much of metals the Spanish found. And the furs we can trade with Peter Tallis."

Holding her hand, I talked long of what we must do, of the planting of grain, the saving of seed, the planting of fruit trees and vegetables.

Sakim came up to join us. "There are many plants here that I know, plants used for medicine in other countries."

Around the campfire, we talked. "It would grow whatever we need. Is it not so, John?"

John Quill nodded. "It is true." He looked around him and shook his head. "I cannot believe it, Captain. So much land, and so few people, when in our country people long for the land and have none, for it all belongs to the great lords. Even the wild game is theirs."

"Aye," Tom Watkins agreed, "but trust not the red man. Have you seen their eyes when they see what we have? Each of our boats becomes a treasure ship to them, worth as much in their eyes as the richest Spanish galleon is to us."

Tim Glasco spoke then. "We have come far, and we follow wherever you go, but what is it you plan?"

So I told them, talking quietly, of the valley I sought. A place with good water, good land, and timber for fuel and for building. Then to build first, as before, a stockade and shelter, and then to survey for each a square mile of land.

They stared at me. "A square *mile?*"

"Aye, and why not? There is land in plenty, and each should have, if we can arrange it so, some stream frontage, some timber, some meadow. But at first I think we should remain together, inside the stockade at night.

"During the day we can work our land. Perhaps a piece close by that belongs to all, and which all work, and then each his own, further out. Within the stockade we must have stores, a granary, and the blacksmith shop, and a shop where Magill can weave and make barrels for us.

"There, with luck, we can build a small community, a world of our own. We will also trap fur, and when we have sufficient we will go down to the sea and trade, for more ships will come, and colonies will be established."

Well I know that what I said would require doing, and no easy thing it would be, and also now that we had come to a stop . . . or soon would . . . there would be more chance of trouble among us. Circumstances had tended to weed out many of those who might cause problems, but being human, there would be differences of opinion, for the ideal situation may exist but not ideal people. Wise I might not be, but I was wise enough to know that I myself would make mistakes. I was subject to anger, to sorrow . . . I do not think to discouragement.

If we lived among the Indians we would soon become Indians, and it seemed best that we keep to ourselves, be friendly, exchange gifts and favors, and with the buffalo bull we had begun well, for the bringer of meat is welcome at any fire.

Up to now we had been fortunate, but now we faced a winter, perhaps not a hard winter, for from what Wa-ga-su had said the winters were not bad . . . except occasionally. Nonetheless, we would need fuel, food, and shelter, and much hard work to have them.

All of us would change, and I myself had already changed, for suddenly I had become a leader of men who depended upon me to lead them well. Now I had to think carefully, and to plan, I had to be sure the work was evenly shared, and the food as well. I wished not to interfere with the Indians nor their way of life, but to learn from them. They knew the plants and animals of this country, they knew the seasons and how high up the rivers a man could go by boat. Whatever their thinking they had found a way of life in tune with the country, a way that seemed good with them.

Abby was not one to lie long upon her bed, and soon she was with Lila, cooking, sewing, and mending garments for the other men as well as myself. Her time was soon, and I walked into the forest alone, worried, thinking of her, and knowing little of such things as births, yet glad of the presence of Lila and Sakim.

Dark flowed the river past our grassy banks, whispering through the reeds and rustling in eddies near the roots of old trees. Dappled was the water with light and shadow, and above the water the changing leaves, for frost had come and brought autumn colors to the forest. Soon the leaves would be gone, and the trees bare until spring.

The forest aisles were a place for thinking, for all was still, with only the rustling of small animals and birds. There was little time left to us to find our winter haven and prepare for the cold and storms, so little time. And yet it would be best to wait, to wait just a little longer.

My thoughts prowled the forest and saw in the mind's eye the place we might find, and one by one I went through the moves to be made, so many at work on a stockade, so many on shelters, and so many for hunting and gathering. And there must be changing about to give all a taste of each.

A move well planned is a move half-done, and I tried to think through every phase. We would go, I decided, a little farther by water.

It was a Catawba who warned us.

He came suddenly, running from the trees beyond the clearing, screaming *"Occaneechee!"* And he ran toward us, darting swiftly from side to side. I saw an arrow strike near him and grabbed my musket at a rush from the trees along the shore.

Turning, I fired from my hip at a charging Indian and saw the bullet strike him, yet his step scarcely faltered. Even in that desperate moment I felt awe at the man's courage and his strength. He came on, and I dropped my musket and fired a second time, with a pistol.

210

He staggered then, but came on, and I killed him with a knife, breast to breast.

There was firing everywhere, and then a sudden charge from the Catawba, taking the attackers on the flank. Their presence was a total surprise, and the Occaneechee attackers broke and fled. Turning sideways, I lifted a pistol, brought it down in line, and shot another as he fled into the trees.

We moved out then in a rough crescent, those of us who could. I recharged my musket and pistol and sank my knife hilt-deep in the soft, black loam to cleanse it of blood, and we went after them. There was still a bit of fighting here and there. I saw an Indian bending a bow at me and fired quickly . . . too quickly.

My shot barked the tree at his head but he was no squirrel and merely sprang away, his arrow wasted into the brush.

Another came at me with a spear, but I parried the thrust with my musket barrel and sprang close, grasping the musket in two hands, shoulder-high, and driving the butt into his face. He took the full force of it and went back and down, and for a moment there was fierce fighting on all sides, but when the attack broke I called out, "Fall back on the camp! Fall back!"

Some heard my hail and passed on the call, and slowly we did fall back, for I had no desire to waste our strength by scattering in the woods.

Quill came from the brush near me, and then O'Hara a bit farther along. Glasco, Peter Fitch, Slater. . . . Anxiously, I counted them off as they gathered, moving back, pausing here and there to recharge their muskets.

Barry Magill was the last to come, bleeding from a gash on the face. Now all were present but Jeremy.

"Ring?" I asked.

"He did not come," Pim said. "He stayed in camp."

"Jeremy?" I could not believe it.

"Aye," Pim said, and there was an odd look to his eyes that puzzled me.

The Catawba came back, too. Not a few of them with scalps. We had struck the Occaneechee a blow . . . five men dead, and no losses to us, despite their surprise. But we had been thinking of this for weeks, and were ready. And the Catawba were always ready.

Two Catawba were wounded, only one seriously. We had come off better than we deserved, but somehow the attackers had not known of the presence of the Catawba, who were old enemies and fierce fighters. It was their sudden attack that had saved us.

"I want to see Jeremy Ring," I said, and he heard me speak and came toward me.

He bowed low, sweeping the ground with his ragged plume. "I regret my absence," he said with mock seriousness, "and nothing less could have kept me from your side, but I thought it best to stand by your kin," he said.

"My kin?" I stared at him, stupidly.

"Your wife," he said, "and your son."

△ **24** △

So my son was born on a buffalo robe in the heat of an Indian battle, under a tree by the side of a stream in a wild and lonely land, and he was given his name by a chance remark, a name he would carry forever. For we called him Kin, and thought of no other, and kin he was to all of us, to the meadow, the woodland, and the forest.

Abby was healthy and strong, and came from her labor smiling, proud she had given me a son. For a second name we called him Ring, for the man who had stood above them, sword in hand, musket and pistols hard by, stood there in case any Indian should break through our ranks and come upon them.

Kin Ring Sackett ... the name had a sound, and it was a sound I loved.

Lila brought him to me, my hands still hot from battle, the smell of powder smoke about me, and I took him carefully, for I'd no knowledge of babies, and held him gently and looked in his face, his eyes squinted and dark, his face still red and pinched, but he looked at me and seemed to laugh and grasped my thumb and tugged strongly. Oh, he was a lad, that one!

Two days later we left our river camp and moved up the river. For three full days we moved, but the water was becoming less for the season was late and the rains had not yet come. We beached our boats at last in a small bayou, unloaded them upon the shore, then drew them deep into a forest of reeds and hid them there.

We cached some goods on the spot, and hid them well, then moved out upon the trading trail, carrying the rest, and my own pack the heaviest of all. Yet strong I was to bear it, and the more willing that now I had a son, the first of my name to be born in the new land, a son who would know no civilization, but only the wilds.

He would grow up on woodland paths, riding rough water in a canoe down lonely streams and hunting his own meat in the wilderness. Looking about me I knew I could wish no better life for any man than that I was giving to him. A lonely life, but a wild, free life.

"There must be more than that, Barnabas," Abby said. "He must learn to live with civilized men also, for how can we know who will come to these shores and live upon these hills?"

The way we went was long, but the Catawbas traveled with us, returning to their country, and I set myself to learn from them, their language, their customs, their knowledge of wood and savanna. Never would I learn all they had to teach, for so much was natural to them that they assumed all would know it, things so obvious in their way of life that they would never think of teaching anyone, presuming knowledge.

We traveled slowly with them, for they hunted and gathered along the way, and late though the season. I relished the slower travel for the chance it gave to know the country.

The path we took was an ancient trading path that led across the country with many branches. Traders were usually respected and left to travel unmolested, as trade

213

was desired by all, yet there were always renegades, out-law Indians or war parties from afar that might not respect the trade route.

Wa-ga-su was much with us, and I began to notice a certain aloofness toward him by the others of his people. He seemed moody, sometimes puzzled, often downcast.

"What is it with my friend that he is troubled?" I asked.

He glanced at me, then shook his head. After awhile he said, "When I went away I was a great man among them. They loved and trusted me. No man was greater on the hunt, none brought more meat to the village, and none was greater upon the path of war. Now all is changed."

"What is the trouble?"

"They no longer trust me, Sack-ett. I told them of the great water, and they shook their heads in doubt, then of the great stone cities you have, and of the many people who live without hunting . . . they think me a liar, Sack-ett.

"My words are no longer heard in the village. When I speak they turn their backs upon me. They believe me a liar or that the whites have bewitched me.

"You see, they think you a small people, a weak people, even though your firearms make you great in battle. They say, 'Why do not they trap their own furs? Hunt their own game? If they do not, it is because they can not. There-fore they must be a weak people.' "

"I am sorry, Wa-ga-su. It might be the same with my people if I told them of the vast lands here, with so few people, of the great rivers, the tall trees . . . they might not believe me, either."

"Yes, I think it is so, Sack-ett. We grow wise, you and I, but in wisdom there is often pain. No man of my people has traveled so far. None but me has crossed the great water, none but me has seen the great cities and the horses and carriages. But if they will not believe what I have seen, if I am no longer great among my people—then I am an empty man, Sack-ett.

"Who is it for whom one becomes wise? Is it not for

the people? For his people? Do I become wise only for myself? I become wise to advise, to help . . . but they do not believe and my voice is only an echo in an empty canyon. I speak for my ears only and the sound is hollow, Sack-ett."

"You have a place with us, Wa-ga-su, a place as long as you live."

"Ah? I thank you. But of course, it is not the same, is it?"

We walked on together and the great forest was green about us.

"They believe the horses, do they not?"

"Horses they have seen, or their fathers or grandfathers have seen. The Espanish men had horses. I have heard it there is a people beyond the mountains have horses, but only a few taken from the white men or left behind by them."

"What game lies beyond the mountains, Wa-ga-su?"

"The buffalo are there, the deer, the mountain cat, a still bigger deer, and there is the animal with the long nose and big white teeth."

"What?"

"It is true. I have not seen it myself. My grandfather told us of them. They were a large animal that men used to hunt. They had great teeth . . . curving like so, and a long nose like an arm. They were very hairy."

The elephant? Here? It was not possible. There were elephants in Africa, and my father told me of the Carthaginians using them in war against the Romans, and the bones of still more ancient ones had been found in Europe. But here?

"You know of the great sea beyond the mountains?"

He shook his head. "There is a sea to the north, very far off. There is a sea to the south, also very far, but beyond the mountains there is no sea. There is only land."

No great western sea beyond which lay Cathay? No land of Cipango? Wa-ga-su must be mistaken. All the best minds said there was a sea beyond the mountains.

For days upon end we walked. We carried our burdens and we hunted for game, and somehow we lived, and

215

somehow at last we came to the land of the Catawbas, after fording another great river. We moved into the foot-hills of the mountains, and Wa-ga-su led us to a small valley, its steep sides heavy with forest, and a stream that ran though the meadow at the bottom.

Abby came up beside me and stood, looking about. "We will stop here," I said, "and here we will build our home."

"Our home, Barnabas?"

"For a time, Abby. For a time . . . there are still the mountains . . . and the land beyond."

△ 25 △

Once again we were at work, felling trees, hewing them into timbers, building a series of cabins and the stockade that would surround them. Tom Watkins and Kane O'Hara went to the woods, a-hunting. Near the slope of yellow mountain, in an open meadow, they killed two buffalo. This meat we dried against the winter's coming.

Our skills were the greater for what we had built before, and the houses and stockade went up easier, despite our lesser numbers.

Kin had filled out amazingly, and was a laughing, energetic little fellow as befitted the first of our name to be born in the new lands. Abby was much with him, and Lila with them both.

Peter Fitch, who was the best of us all at timber work, having been a shipwright, paused in his work one day. "I think of Jonathan Delve," he said. "I did not like the man. There was a cross-grain of evil in him, but he was strong."

"He was that," I agreed.

"And dangerous," Peter added.

"Aye. He is well gone."

Fitch stooped to take up his broadaxe. "If he is," he said.

I had turned away, but at that I stopped. "You do not think he is?"

"If he finds not what he went after, he will think of you. He will know you had some money from furs and timbers, and he will come to believe the story of King John's treasure. He will also begin to wonder why you go west into an unknown land.

"He will not believe you are what you are. He believes all men are evil, that all will steal, connive, do whatever is necessary to obtain wealth. He will think you very shrewd. He will say to himself, 'He goes to the western sea, there to build a ship and sail away to the Indies or Cathay.'"

I shook my head. "The Indians know of no western sea, and when Hawkins' men marched up the country, they saw no western sea, nor heard of it. Some say they walked from Mexico to the French lands in the north, some say only from Florida, but they covered a deal of country."

"No matter. Let the Indians believe what they wish, and you as well, but Delve will believe what pleases him best. He hates you, Captain, as he hates us all. Mark it down . . . we have not seen the last of Jonathan Delve.

"He proposed to us once to leave you and join Bardle, or to open the gates to Bardle when he attacked."

Later, talking to Jeremy and Pim, I spoke of Fitch's words. "Aye," Jeremy agreed, "I have been thinking of the man. It is far to follow, but who knows?"

Yet there was little time to think of such things. When men live by hunting it is a constant task with all our mouths to feed, and usually the Indians who came visiting. The amounts of fresh meat they could put away was astonishing.

Often I went with Abby and Lila to the woods, gathering nuts, and whenever we went, Kin was along, carried by one of us.

We learned to make clothes of buckskin, and moccasins such as Indians wore, and we learned to know the roots and leaves that could be eaten, although with winter coming the leaves were few and no longer tender.

Barry Magill set up shop in a corner of the yard and went to work at his trade. Barrels were needed for storing nuts and fruit. Yet the barrels were only one of the things he made, for he made several brooms, buckets for carrying water, two rakes for raking hay, and sap buckets for the gathering of sap from the sugar maples.

Black Tom came in one day with a smooth section of slate about four feet square. "It's big," he said, "but I figure you might cut it up to make slates for the young un. I see some chalk rock down the valley a ways, too."

He rubbed his palms on the front of his pants. "No use him bein' without eddication. No tellin' what will come to pass in his time, and a body should know how to read, write, and do sums."

"Thank you, Tom," I said, and he went away vastly pleased.

Wa-ga-su was with us much of the time, and he went often to the woods with Sakim.

Soon the stockade was built and the cabins roofed, a larger stockade then before. Building with logs was a foreign thing to we of England, yet my father had seen it done by men from Sweden, as had Jeremy Ring. The timber was present, and land must be cleared for planting, so we were able to accomplish the two tasks at once. Yet never were we to feel secure.

The Catawbas were our friends, but they had warred against nearly all the tribes at one time or another, and as we were the friends of the Catawbas we were regarded as the enemies of others, although we had no such feeling or desire. Most to be feared were the Cherokees from the south or southwest, and the Tuscaroras from the north.

There came a day when I had taken my rifle from the hooks above the door, and with Kane O'Hara and Pim Burke I went far into the mountains.

"Do not be afeered," I told Abby, "if we come not back this night. We must look about and find a way into the farthest mountains, as well as to scout the land. We may lay out a night or even two."

"Well . . . have a care," she said, and went to join Lila, who muttered something about "going gallivanting."

We went up the bottom of Muskrat Creek and crossed the southern tip of the Chunky Gal Mountain and over the bald peak known to the Indians as Yunwitsulenunyi, meaning "where the man stood." Wa-ga-su had told us the story that once a great flying reptile with beady eyes and furry wings had dived down suddenly from the sky and seized a child. This happened several times and the Indians cleared the mountaintops with fire and set up a watch to warn them of the flying beast. Then its den was found in an inaccessible place on the side of the peak and the Indians invoked their gods to strike the monster dead, and the gods responded with crashing thunder and vivid lightning and the monster was set aflame, writhing about in its agony.

The Indian on watch on that bald peak fled in terror and so for surrendering to his fear the gods turned him to stone, and there he remains to this day, the so-called Standing Indian.

We killed a brace of wild turkeys and camped that night against the rock face of a cliff in a corner away from the wind, and shielded by several ancient hickories. Our camp was on a river I thought to be the one called Nantahala, but we were high up and in a lonely place.

"It is far from London," Jeremy commented.

"Do you miss it?"

"Not I . . . I was nothing there, a soldier without a cause, a sailor without a ship. This . . . this is grand, beautiful! Had I not come here I should never have known it existed."

Dark bent the trees above us, flickering the flames and their shadows; the fire crackled, and a low wind moved through the trees, mourning for a summer gone. We huddled above our fire yet thought how beautiful was fire, how much a companion on the long marches and the lonely nights . . . even the bright dawns, with meat cooking.

We slept that night with the stars seen through the branches, with the sound of things that move in the night, and the little sounds the mountains make, the faint creakings and groanings and rattles of changing temperature and wind.

Before first light Jeremy was gathering dry branches, and Pim had gone to the stream for fish.

On the morning of the third day we started back. I had brought with me several well-tanned deerskins, and upon these I made a map of the country so far as we had seen it. The route by which we returned was different from the outer route. This was only partly because we wished to see new country, but it was never well to retrace a path where an enemy might lie in wait.

During the weeks that followed we made several such trips, and upon one of them Abby joined me. She was a good walker, and loved the country as much as I, and we brought Kin with us, carrying him Indian-style. Many of the mountain tops about were bare of trees, and this we could not understand although Pim Burke believed the Indians might have burned them off to offer a better view of the country around. Of this I was not too sure, for over much of it one saw only the tops of trees while enemies could move close under their cover.

Cold winds blew down from the north. We built our fires higher, and had no trouble finding the chinks in our log walls that had been left when we applied mud to the cracks. The cold wind blew through each of them and made us only too aware.

Meanwhile we gathered fuel, hunted a little, and cleared ground for spring planting, moving rocks into piles, cutting out the larger roots until we had several acres ready.

With the onset of colder weather we went into the higher mountains and set out traps.

"What of the furs?" Slater asked.

"We will go to the coast," I said. "Tilly will return with the *fluyt*, or other ships will come. We will go downstream by boat, sell our furs and what else we have, and then return here."

Often, I talked with Wa-ga-su about the lands beyond the mountains, and from his memory he dredged tales told by Catawba wanderers from other eras. Returning to the long-nosed animals, I learned again from him that no Catawba he had heard of had actually seen such an animal, but there were stories of them and he believed they might exist beyond the mountains.

Yet the stories, he agreed, might be very old, told of a time long ago.

We had climbed one day high up on Double Mountain, Wa-ga-su, Jeremy Ring, and Tim Glasco. Abby was with us, and we had stopped, enjoying the cold with its freshness and the smell of pines and cedar.

Suddenly Wa-ga-su said, "We go now. Indian come."

Experience had taught me to react quickly. I wasted no time in asking foolish questions. I said not what nor where, but catching Abby by the arm, started off the bald where we were and into the brush.

Below us was a level stretch of ground and on the far side a huddle of boulders, cast off by the mountain into a jumbled shape. There was a small spring there, as we had lately learned, and Wa-ga-su led us there, at a fast trot.

We had almost reached it when there was a sudden whoop behind us and a flight of arrows, yet we scrambled into the rocks and I turned at once to look the way we had come.

Nothing. . . .

Wa-ga-su had retrieved one of the arrows. "Seneca," he said, "very old enemy of Catawba."

There were four muskets amongst us, and Jeremy and I each carried two pistols. "We must not let them catch us unloaded," I said. "Wa-ga-su, do you fire with me. Let Jeremy and Tim hold their fire while we reload."

Several times I glimpsed movement at the forest's edge, but they were wary. I think they knew not how many we were, but guessed at once where we lay, for the rocks offered a good position, and perhaps they, too, although from far away, knew of the spring.

Abby put Kin in the shelter of some rocks and we lay still, waiting. A Seneca near the edge of the timber lingered too long in one place, and Wa-ga-su fired.

We saw the Indian stagger, then fall. A chorus of angry

yells sounded again and there was a flight of arrows, and two of them fell within the cluster of rocks.

It was not a circle, rather a mere cluster perhaps sixty feet long, half again as wide, with some rocks looming up in the center. Kin lay in a narrow crack in one of the largest of these.

They circled closer, daring us to fire. An Indian darted into the open, then dove back to shelter. Several times they darted out, trying to draw our fire. It was obvious they had encountered guns before, probably from the French or English far up the country from which they had come, for the home of the Senecas was several hundred miles away to the north. Yet Wa-ga-su assured me they often raided the Catawba as well as other peoples of the area.

The Catawba, he said proudly, were such noted warriors that every Seneca wished to kill one, to have his scalp to boast of.

Suddenly, they charged. The distance was scarcely twenty yards, and there were at least a dozen. Wa-ga-su had reloaded. He fired first, catching the big Indian in mid-stride. Deliberately, I held my fire, then when they had come on two strides further, I fired. Passing my musket back to Abby to reload, I drew both my pistols.

Jeremy fired, then Glasco, and I fired a pistol. Four Senecas were down and the attack broke, the Indians scattered in all directions. Wa-ga-su fired again . . . missing.

Yet they had managed to carry off three of their men. Two others lay exposed. One was in plain sight upon the grass, the second lay over a slight rise and we could see only his hand, although the rise was of a few inches only. Yet the hand did not move.

The cold wind blew, a few spatters of rain fell. "Keep your powder dry," I said, needlessly, for we all understood the necessity.

Five Indians down . . . it had been a costly attack for them.

"How many were there?" I asked.

Wa-ga-su shrugged. "I think not many, but they are

222

strong fighters. We must watch. They will try to get others and return."

Wa-ga-su lay quiet, watching. I could not but reflect on what our coming had meant to him, and what he had gained in knowledge he had lost in prestige within the tribe. He had no place among them now, for his word was doubted. At the same time, they could see that he stood high with us, as indeed he did.

He had indeed traveled farther, perhaps, than any member of his people. He spoke English very well, for he had much opportunity. That he was a man of keen, active intelligence was obvious.

Rain began to fall, a light, misting rain. I took a blanket and covered the crack where Kin lay. He laughed at me and waved his arms, making small noises. In one hand he clutched an arrow that must have fallen near him. When Abby saw it she was frightened and hastily took it from him lest the point be poisoned.

Suddenly a Seneca darted from the brush. I fired, but he dropped as my musket came up and the shot was a clean miss. The Seneca lay on the grass, nowhere visible, yet there. He lay perfectly still, and we watched, determined to get him when he should rise from the ground.

Only he didn't rise. Some minutes later, Ring nudged me and pointed. The hand that we had seen was gone. Somehow the Seneca had succeeded in retrieving that Indian, and had vanished with him.

The other lay in plain sight. We waited. "Two muskets," I said. "We must get him."

Suddenly, Wa-ga-su darted from the rocks. He ran swiftly forward, dropped flat beside the dead Indian, and with his knife made a quick circular cut, then grasping the hair he jerked off the scalp.

Rising to full height, he shook the bloody scalp and shouted taunts. Instantly, there was a flight of arrows, but he wheeled and ran, darting this way and that, to the shelter of our rocks.

I had heard of scalp taking, but had not seen it done before.

Slowly, the winter passed. The springs which had frozen into crystal cascades over the edges of cliffs— sheets of glistening ice that could be seen from afar —now began to melt. The ice disappeared from the higher courses of the rivers, and the water began to rush with greater speed.

There were several bales of furs, a few freshwater pearls, and many skins, including four great buffalo hides.

"We will go to the coast," I said that night when all were together. "With luck we shall meet Tilly and the *Abigail.*"

"Who will go and who will stay?" Fitch asked.

"All will go who wish it," I replied. "We should go down very swiftly, but the return will be slower."

"I do not know," John Quill said. "I may stay. I have found land that I like, and I may build my own cabin, plow my own land." He looked up at me. "I never owned my own land, Captain. I farmed all my life on land owned by others.

"It is good earth. I like to see it turned by the plow, I like to feel it in my fingers. It is fine soil, and it will grow a fine crop."

"Aye," Slater agreed. "I feel the same. I have laid out a square mile alongside John's, and I cannot believe it. I walk through the forest, along the banks of the stream, and I see blackberries growing in thickets, and nuts falling from trees, and it is mine."

"The Catawbas," I said, "can teach you much of planting. You are farmers, but they know this land, this climate. It is well to listen. I think you each know more than they, but what they can teach is important, so learn from them."

Quill nodded. "I have talked with their head men. I have agreed to give them one-third of my crop for five years and then the land is mine. Slater did the same."

"You will go or stay, Slater?"

"I feel as John does. I will stay. I wish to get in a crop, and to know my land better."

The others would come, and we talked much of the

224

going, for there were other streams down which we might go to the coast, others that called for a shorter trip overland, and we could build boats or rafts for the trip.

In the end it was decided to go back the way we had come, but then to sail down the coast, and return up one of the nearer rivers.

Lying abed, and before sleep came, Abby and I talked of this. "I want to go," she said, "but so much can happen. I worry about Kin."

"He will travel well," I said, "and it is our way. He can learn no younger."

The wind whispered around the eaves, a soft wind, a spring wind. I stirred uneasily. Was I doing the right thing? Should I dare such a long trip?

Yet we all needed a change, we all looked forward to seeing a ship from home.

Three days later, at the break of dawn, we started our trek to the boats.

△ 26 △

The water was a mirror, polished and perfect. Only our oars made a ripple, only our oarlocks a sound. A gull sailed by above, no wing moving, and our boats moved slowly outward from the land, moved toward the Outer Banks lying warm in the mid-day sun.

There was no ship upon the water, no sign of sail against the sky. Here all was quiet, and we watched, straining our ears for something beyond silence.

How many ships had come this way in times past? How many an eye had looked across this empty water? For no man may know the history of the sea, nor does the sea have a memory, or leave a record, save its wrecks.

To cross the wide ocean must never have been a problem. All that was needed was the courage, the desire, for men had sailed farther, long before. The Malays had sailed from their islands south of the Equator, from Java and Sumatra to Madagascar. And Cheng Ho, the eunuch from the court of Imperial China, had sailed five times to Africa before Columbus or Vasco Da Gama.

What wrecks might be buried in the sand out there where the warm Gulf current from the south came up to meet the cold Arctic current from the north? What unknown ships might here have ended their days?

Hanno had sailed around Africa . . . and where else? For long the Phoenicians and the Carthaginians had kept the Straits of Gibraltar guarded so that no other ships but theirs might sail to the seas beyond, and thus to the markets they wished to keep for themselves. In later times men had begun to call the Straits the Pillars of Hercules, whereas, in truly ancient times, the Pillars had been far to the east, on the coast of Greece. But this men had forgotten, and names are easily transferred, one place to another.

Of these things I had learned much from Sakim, who was a scholar, a wise man in his own land, and versed in many sciences.

The Philistines, he told me, were a sea people who came to the shores of what they call the Holy Land from somewhere to the west. They sailed over the seas in their high-prowed boats to attack the shores of the Levant and of Egypt, and they settled there and brought the first iron known to that coast.

Many nations had sailed far upon deep water before them, and even before the sailors of Crete and Thera, called Atlantis by some, had gone west of Africa.

The idea that the world was flat was never put forth by a seafaring man. It was a tale told to landsmen, or to merchants who might be inclined to compete for markets, for in those days the source of raw material was closely guarded.

Coming up to the inner shores of the Outer Banks, I remembered the sunken ship and the alligator, and wondered idly what had become of Jonathan Delve . . . and of Bardle, too, for that matter.

The thought of Bardle was worrying. If he should

appear now, with a ship, we would be helpless before his guns. Yet it was unlikely he would spend much time along these shores, and after months of absence he would not expect to see us again.

A low, sandy shore lay before us, topped with brush and some scattered groves of trees. These Outer Banks stretched along the coast for a great distance . . . nearly two hundred miles, I had heard, but I suspected it was not quite so far.

We took shelter in a deeply notched bay of fair extent almost exactly opposite the tip of the mainland that extended down from the north into the smaller sound. The Bank was at that place scarcely more than a mile wide, and we had drawn our boats close in shore. We waded to the beach.

We made camp there.

For days we camped on the beach, keeping always a lookout on the farther shore, but we saw no ship. Yet it was a quiet time, enjoyed by all. With Abby I took long walks along the shore where one could see for miles. We searched the shore for whatever the tide might have washed up. Obviously, no Indian had been along for some time for we found a cask of good brandy, and the wreck of a lifeboat still containing a sail and a boat hook. We found several gold coins, the skeleton of a man, half buried in sand, many logs, ships timbers, and other debris. We found three boxes, close together on the sand, with water-soaked clothing, all of which we took back to our boat for ourselves or the Catawba. Despite all this, for miles the beach was bare and empty.

We kept our fires low, used dry and relatively smokeless driftwood, and kept a sharp lookout at all times.

Each day brought an increase of doubt and worry. Despite the pleasure of camping, it was beginning to pall, and still no ship came.

Was our voyage downriver all for nothing? Should we wait longer? Or once more return to our fort?

Then on the twenty-fourth day, while we were gathering driftwood, I looked up and saw the ship.

She was not more than a mile offshore, and feeling her

way south. I looked at her long through my glass, and Jeremy studied her as well.

"British," he said, after a bit, "let's give her a hail."

"We shall," I said, "and then do you, Pim, O'Hara, and Magill stay from sight. Peter and Sakim can stay with the boats, and also keep out of sight. I'll meet them with Watkins and Glasco."

"If it is going aboard a ship there is," Abby said, "we shall go as well. I want Kin to see a ship, and all of us to have a bite of English food."

"All right," I agreed reluctantly, "come along."

Yet I took the time to charge two pistols and conceal them under my buckskin hunting shirt, and my knife as well. My sword and my musket were in plain sight.

The ship hove to, then dropped her hook and put a boat over the side. We waited, standing on the beach.

There were seven men in the boat. The man in command was a burly, smiling fellow with a cheerful face. "Well! Isn't this a pretty sight! English, I'll wager, and castaways."

"We've furs to trade," I said. "And we are here willingly, and do not wish to be picked up."

"Ah? Well, of course not. But the master asks that you come aboard . . . be his guests. Have a meal, and then back to the shore you shall come." He glanced curiously up and down the empty beach. "Although why you'd like this better than old England, I can't guess."

He looked around. "Furs, you say? Well, the captain's the man for that. He'll trade. Come! Supper is waiting, and the captain ordered up the best when he saw you through his glass. 'Women,' the captain said, 'it's a bit of time since we've seen the whisk of a skirt, and two such lovely wenches—women—I've never seen!' "

We scrambled up the ladder and over the side, and as I came over, a hand reached out for my musket. I pulled it back, smiling. "I will keep that," I said. "There's redskins ashore and there might be pirates as well."

A huge man, as large as two of me and fat, came down the deck. "Let it be Joshua! Let it be! The man's a

228

guest aboard here, and welcome to his arms if he wishes!"

He held out a huge hand. "Wilson here! Captain Old-fast Wilson, master of the *Lion*, out of Portsmouth! How do you do? Your name would be?"

"Barnes," I said, "and this is Mrs. Barnes. We are," I lied, "settlers on this shore. Is this one of Raleigh's ships?"

"It is not. It is my own ship." He glanced from me to Watkins and Glasco. "Settlers, you say? I did not know there were any such, since Grenville's men were lost and the Raleigh settlers vanished from Roanoke."

"Our ship was a Flemish galleon—"

There was a movement behind me, and then a man stepped around to face me. It was Emmden.

"He lies! That is Sackett! Barnabas Sackett, and it is the Queen herself who wants him!"

"Of course, it is!" Wilson was smiling smugly. "I glimpsed you once in London, m'boy! Saw you fair! Even from the glass I was certain sure 'twas you. By all that's holy, this is a good day! A reward from the Queen herself, and—"

"Cap'n?" Joshua said. "He said he had furs to trade."

"Ah? Furs, is it? Well, a fair trade we'll have. Do you be telling us where the furs are now. You tell us, and you'll eat well and sleep well aboard this ship! Otherwise, it's the blackest corner of the hold and a weight of chains for you, and certain drowning if we sink. What'll it be m'boy? Irons or the furs? Treat me right, and I'll do the same by you!"

"Well," I said reluctantly, "do I have your word on that? I have but six bales—"

"Six?" The greed shone in his eyes. "Why, of course! For six bales you have my word on it, and the best of quarters for you and your lady as well. Even for the wench yonder." He indicated Lila.

"There's no hope for it, Abby," I said, shrugging. Then I added, "There's a ship's boat across the island, and the bales on the shore hard by. If you send a boat, I'd be glad to show them—"

"Na, na, m'boy! I'd not be troublin' you." He pointed a finger at Black Tom Watkins. "We'll send that one.

229

He'll know where they are, an' he'll lead us right to them. He will if he wants to live without fifty lashes a week until he dies.

"Do na think I'm a hard man, m'boy, but there's a world of deceit and evil about us, an' a man does have to protect himself, now doesn't he?"

He glared at Tom. "What's your name, man?"

"Watkins, and I'll gladly show you where the furs lie if you'll let me become one of your crew or drop me in the nearest port. I've had my fill o' that," he jerked his head toward the shore. "Savages by night an' no drop of ale by day. I'll show you, certain sure I will!"

"Joshua," Wilson turned on us, "do you take them below. Keep them together for the non, and if there's no furs, well, we'll have a bit of their hide. Hers, too." His eyes glinted. "No doot 'tis a pretty hide, but will show the better for some blood on it. Do you take them below."

They had taken my musket and a hand had jerked away my sword, but there was no further search and I'd the knife handy and two pistols.

Pistols were not that common thing about and I doubt they gave it a thought, with me so obviously armed with musket and sword. Put us all together, they did, and in a small cabin near the main one, and we stood crowded there, scarce room to turn about.

"What now?" Lila said. " 'Tis a brave man I know you are, but what is one against all, and only Glasco aboard to help."

"And what of Tom?" Abby asked, holding Kin close. "Is it true that he's turned upon us?"

"Of course, the blackg'rd has!" I spoke loudly, and then, ever so softly, "I'd trust him with my life!"

"You have," Lila said. "Be sure of that!"

"Aye," I said, "and I'm trusting another man as well, a wise and a shrewd one, that Jeremy Ring!"

△ 27 △

Two pistols I had, but that meant but two shots, and then it was the knife until death.

Where had they put my sword and musket? In the main cabin, I was sure. That sword had been my father's, and I wanted it back again. Yet now I would have accepted any sword, any weapon.

Looking quickly around the small cabin, I saw nothing. Yet they had put us hastily there, not thinking, and there might be something about. Leaning toward Lila, I urged her to look.

Softly, she began, feeling the man's bunk, searching the drawers of his small cabinet. A compass, a Bible, a small, much-worn booklet on navigation, a sewing kit. . . nothing more.

"Lila," I said, "the pillow."

She looked. Pillows were a not often thing aboard ship, but this man loved his comfort, slight as it was, and he had a pillow, a soft, downy pillow with a faint, fishy smell. Gull feathers, no doubt, and made by himself.

She looked under it, but I shook my head and made a move to indicate holding it over her face. Lila got the idea at once and took up the pillow, placing it on the small stand near her.

Jeremy Ring was a quick-thinking and shrewd young man, and I was guessing he would at once surmise something wrong when he saw the boat returning without us. Truly, my life and those of my family and Lila were in his hands. His, and those of Tom Watkins.

Yet I had no wish to trust to any man when so much was at stake, and there was every chance we might ourselves do something. I liked not the look of the man Oldfast Wilson.

Well, I'd two shots. If the worst came for it, he would get the first one. If we could get a guard to open the door, and I could distract his attention, then Lila and her pillow might well do the rest.

If a man or woman is inclined to murder or violence, owning a gun is not important. There are always a dozen things about with which a man can be killed. For myself, I'd no wish for any of it. I'd been controlling my temper better these days, with hopes I might someday conquer it altogether. For I'd always been inclined to go into fierce although not unreasoning rage. It was a serious fault, and I'd worked hard at controlling myself, for giving away to anger is a weakness in a man.

We heard no sound except those made by the ship herself, and occasional movements above deck. Abby clutched my hand. "Barney," she whispered, "what will happen?"

"Trust to Jeremy," I suggested. "If there's a fight we've some likely lads ashore there, and if they fail, then we've to do something ourselves."

Waiting was a hard thing. Abby put little Kin down on the bunk, and he seemed happy enough, unaware of what was taking place.

A long time passed, and then we heard steps upon the deck outside, and the door was opened. It was Joshua, and he held a pistol in his hand. "Cap'n Wilson wants to know how far they had to go? They've been a long time aboot it."

"Well," I edged to the side of the door away from Lila, "they'd to cross the bank, y' know. 'Tis maybe a mile, but walking in deep sand is slow. Going and coming, that's two mile. They'd to unload the furs from the boat and carry them across. Six bales, and each bale a load for two men, I'd say."

Deliberately I put my shoulder against the door so he had to turn to face me and turn his shoulder to Lila. The pistol was aimed right at me, and at such range he could not miss. Lila was hesitating, and I said, suddenly, "Whatever they do, they'd best do it!"

I snapped the last words and slapped the pistol barrel with my right hand just as Lila clapped the pillow over his face. Yet all did not go as I hoped.

Slapping the pistol barrel, my hand did not make firm contact, knocking it only slightly aside. And as Lila clapped the pillow over Joshua's face she jerked him back, off balance. The gun blasted and something stung my cheek and brow, and then Lila was holding Joshua tight and I had wrested the gun from him.

There was a pounding of feet on the deck as someone came running, but I stepped over Joshua. Abby caught Kin up and followed, and we made for the deck. Lila dropped Joshua, now unconscious or dead, but she did not neglect to strip him of the now empty pistol and his cutlass, and well I recalled that with a cutlass she was not one with whom to trifle.

Abby turned swiftly toward the door of the main cabin at the end of the passage and opened it. I was facing the opposite way, toward the deck. A man lunged into the opening, a bare blade in hand, and thrust hard at me.

The door was narrow, and as he thrust, I fired. The bullet took him in the chest and smashed him to a dead stop. Then his eyes seemed to glaze over and he fell toward me. I thrust the empty pistol in my belt and caught up the cutlass and went through the door to the deck.

Facing me were a dozen men, and not one of them was Wilson. I'd the cutlass and one shot. Lila came up beside me, with her own cutlass.

"Drop it!" He was a burly, black-bearded fellow with a bend in his nose. "You'll get nowhere with this!"

There are times to fight and times to talk. The two of us might account for three or four of them before they had us, but behind us were Abby and Kin.

"Joshua," I said, "is dead. By this time your crew are dead or prisoners. I've two dozen men ashore there, and more than a hundred Indians. Put a boat in the water, and we'll go. Try to keep us and we'll leave you for the Indians."

"Captain?" The big black-bearded man called out. "Captain Wilson?"

He was looking over my shoulder. Fear went over me like a dash of icy water on a wild night at sea. Wilson had been behind us, in the main cabin!

I stood fast, but I was frightened. Abby was back there, Abby and Kin. They were behind me, and Wilson behind them, yet if I turned to look, we all were lost.

"There's no use to call him," I said. "Get the boat in the water if you wish to live, and—" I added—"if any of you wish to cross the blades with Lila, be advised she's stronger than any two of you, and better with her blade than any four—"

"Five," Lila said coolly. "I've marked that many for my own. Do you take the rest."

It is not good for a man to think too long if he must act, and too many ideas had been thrown at them, each causing doubt and hesitation.

Joshua dead . . . where was Captain Wilson? Indians ashore, the boat crew possibly captured or dead, two blades and a pistol facing them—and at such range where at least one man must die before blades could be crossed.

They hesitated, and in so doing lost their advantage.

Quickly I stepped forward, Lila beside me, and they backed up, warily. There was no command, each waited for the other to act, and still no word from the cabin behind us.

Torn with fear, I dared not look around or lose my slight advantage. What was happening ashore I knew not, nor where stood Abby with my child.

Suddenly there was a shout and a crash behind me, a boat bumped the ship's side, and the men before me, half started forward at the shout from the cabin, half turned toward the ship's side.

Holding my fire, I thrust quickly at the nearest man. He tried to parry the blow, but his reaction time was too slow although he partly parried it. The point of my blade, and a good six inches of it, went into his thigh. With-

234

drawing quickly, I cut sidewise at a second man, who leaped back and tripped over a third.

Suddenly men were swarming over the side, and the first over, sword in hand, was Jeremy Ring. None of the ship's crew were armed with pistols, as was natural, and all of my men were.

There was a scream behind me and, wheeling, I leaped into the passage and in two steps was at the door of the main cabin. It stood open and beyond the table stood Abby, holding Kin. Her face was very white, her eyes wide and cool, and she was facing Oldfast Wilson.

His face glistened with sweat, his shirt was wet, and there was a smell of brandy in the room.

"I'll kill you, you—!"

My pistol I had thrust into my waistband, and my point was low. I was deceived by the man's huge size, and never suspected the quickness with which he moved. He turned like a cat and struck out hard with the telescope he clutched in his hand.

The blow caught me across the knuckles and my cutlass went to the floor. He leaped at me, and my reaction was the instinctive one of a man with a knowledge of fisticuffs. I struck, left and right, into his face.

Blood splattered, but the next minute he had me wrapped in those huge arms. "Now!" he gasped, "I break your back!"

His strength was enormous. He had seemed huge and fat. He was all of that, but he was also a man of unbelievable strength. His huge arms wrapped around me and he began to crush. Desperately, I hooked short, smashing blows at his face, and every blow crushed and split the skin, but oblivious to my blows he tightened his grasp. I felt a streak of agony go through me. I struggled, fought to break his hold and could not. I felt my breath going. He was leaning his huge weight on me now. His mouth was wide and gasping. Blood trickled from lips broken by my punches.

I thrust a thumb into his cheek and dug my fingers into the flesh below his ear and behind his jaw. With all my strength, I ripped at his cheek. Something broke

235

and began to tear and he screamed. With a tremendous heave I threw him from me and struck hard with my right hand, and the blow caught him on his upraised chin.

His head went back but, mad with fear, I smashed again and again at his face and body. Hitting his enormous body was useless. I might as well have pounded a huge leather sack filled with wheat. So I struck again and again at his face and he fell back and I staggered, catching myself on the doorjamb.

Somebody caught my arm and I jerked free, turning to see Jeremy Ring.

"All is well," he said. "We have the ship."

△ 28 △

"Sail, Ho!"

The call came from the deck, and as one person, we left the smashed and bloody cabin and went to the deck. A fine tall ship was bearing down upon us, flying the flag of Britain. I swore softly, bitterly. I had never thought, as a lad, to look on that flag with anything but respect and affection.

"Stand by," I said. "I do not mean to be taken."

They were lowering a boat, and in a few minutes it was nearing our side. Six men were pulling at the oars. A stalwart, square-shouldered man sat at the tiller.

As they came alongside, he asked, "Is it all right to come aboard?"

"It is," I said.

My men were walking about, picking up dropped weapons. There was a splash of blood here and there and the crew of the ship or what remained aboard had been herded into the waist, where O'Hara and Magill stood guard over them.

As the officer came over the side, I said, "We've had

a bit of trouble here, gentlemen, but it is all over now. What can I do for you?"

"We need water," he said, "and seeing you hove to, we thought you might know where it could be had, or might be watering yourself."

"There is fresh water ashore," I said, "and I'll gladly guide you to it, and help you with the watering. As you see," I swept an arm at the deck and the ship's crew, "we've had a spot of trouble here. I am a settler ashore, and came aboard this ship to trade six bales of furs. The master of the ship and his crew attempted to steal my furs and my wife."

He looked around, his face grim. "Well, he didn't, did he?"

"We had more men ashore than he reckoned with, Captain."

"May I see the furs?"

"You may. They are close to the spring where you will get water." I indicated a spot on the shore. "If you will go there, I'll join you."

He hesitated. "You've come well out of this. I hope there is to be no more violence."

Suddenly his head turned sharply, and I looked. Old-fast Wilson leaned against the jamb of the door, his face battered and bloody. His mouth gaped wide where I'd torn his cheek.

"My God in heaven!" The captain of the ship turned to me.

"We had a fight, Captain. The man is uncommonly strong."

"He beat me, damn his soul. Beat me." Oldfast Wilson shook his big head in bewilderment. "I thought no man could do it."

"We're going ashore now, Wilson, and we're taking some powder, shot, and about six hundred pounds of food. If you'll tell me how much I owe, I'll pay."

"Take them and be damned! I'll not touch your money!" He turned his head. "He's Barnabas Sackett, Captain. Wanted by the Queen. I thought to take him back to England."

237

The captain of the new ship shrugged. "I'm not a warship, only a peaceful trader bound for the Indies. I shall buy his furs if the price is right. I do not know that the Queen wants this man, nor have I been asked to search for him. Nor am I aware of his crimes, if any. He has approached me with courtesy, and I shall respond in the same way."

Two weeks longer we waited, and saw no sign of the *Abigail*. There was no more time to be spent, so we took our boats and started up a stream that emptied into the sea somewhat to the south of our former route.

And it was then that the fever took me, fever and chills. For days I was ill. Sometimes we lay up along shore, often we pushed on, but Abby was ever at my side and ever in command. She who knew much of men and ships, and in this my illness, took over. When there was doubt, she resolved it, when there was a decision to be made, she made it.

With her father, aboard ship, Abby had learned much of such things, and understood the necessities of command. So it was fever and chills, chills and fever. And no sooner did I start to get better than Tom Watkins was down with it. Sakim understood it well enough, for it was an illness found in many tropical lands, he said.

For several days we laid up, resting, at a place called Cross Creek. It was a meeting place of many trading paths, but no Indians came while we were there, or if they did, they avoided us.

Lila made a loblolly that she had learned from the Catawba, a dish made with Indian corn and dried peaches. Kane O'Hara killed a buffalo and Jeremy a deer, one of the largest I have ever seen, with a noble rack of horns.

Finally we could walk about, although very weak. Each day I tried a few more footsteps. I was constantly worried about our crops, about the fort, and the worry that must beset Slater and Quill, for we had long overstayed the expected time.

Then there came a day when I determined to wait no

longer, but to return to our boats and proceed up the river. We began loading, packing the carrier-boat carefully, then the others.

We were just pushing off when four Indians came from the forest and stood looking upon us, and something in the looks of one immediately drew my attention.

"Potaka!" I called.

He stepped into the water and waded toward me, hand outstretched. "Sack-ett! It is you!"

The Eno laid hold of the gunwale with both hands. "Where is it you go, my friend?"

"To the land of the Catawba," I replied. "We now live there, although we plan to go beyond the blue mountains."

"Ah? It is ever beyond the mountains with you, Sackett. But we will come also. The Catawba are our friends."

With four more rowers it was no time until we reached a point from which we could leave our boats. Once more we concealed them near the opening of a small creek where there was a reed-choked backwater, drawing them well back into the reeds and covering them with others to hide them well. Into each boat we put some water to keep the bottom boards from shrinking. Once more we shouldered our burdens and began the overland trek to the fort, a much shorter distance now due to the fact that the river we had used had taken us closer to Catawba country.

On the first night out Potaka came to me, much disturbed. "Many warrior come this way," he said.

"Who?"

"Tuscarora . . . maybe thirty mans . . . no woman, no child."

A war party then . . . headed toward the Catawba, toward our fort.

"When?"

"Four days . . . I think. Maybe three days."

It was bad news. Traveling at the speed with which a war party could travel they must have arrived in the fort area as much as two days ago.

The four Eno scattered out and went through the

239

woods. They could fight and would fight, but they were no such warriors as either the Tuscarora or the Catawba. When they returned they reported no sign of Indians.

We moved on, traveling more swiftly. My strength was returning, and Black Tom Watkins could walk once more, yet neither he nor Fitch were well men, and we had to move warily so as not to be surprised by the returning party.

Desperately, I wished to forge ahead, but dared not leave my family at such a time. We kept close, with Enos out ahead and behind.

The months had made me into a woodsman, more so than ever I have been, and Jeremy also. The gay young blade whom I had first met at the down-at-heel inn in London now wore buckskins. The hat with the plume had been put aside for another hat, and he wore moccasins instead of boots. Kane also, had become the complete woodsman, and the others to a degree.

Suddenly we broke out of the woods and the fort lay before us, charred by fire, but standing.

"Kane? Barry? Stay with my wife." Pim, Jeremy, Glasco, and I moved out in a wide skirmish line, our muskets ready.

Sakim and Peter brought up the rear, and the Indians scattered wide on our flanks.

There was no sound from the fort.

No hail from the walls, no welcoming smoke . . . only silence and the wind.

The grass bent before it, the leaves stirred upon the trees. Each step I took brought me nearer . . . to what?

The gate of the fort stood open, the bar lay on the ground inside. My eyes searched the battlements but nothing moved. We moved toward the gate.

"Sakim? Fitch? Stay outside. Watch the woods. I am going in.

"Pim, after a minute, come in . . . and you, Tom."

Musket ready for a sudden shot, I stepped inside. All was still. No sound disturbed the fading afternoon, and then, at the door of our cabin, a body.

240

Scalped . . . and dead. Several days dead, but the weather had been cool.

It was Matt Slater.

Matt Slater, who so loved the land, and who had, at last, wide acres of his own. A square mile of forest, meadow and fields traded for a plot, six by three.

There was no sign of Quill.

"Scatter out," I said. "We've got to find Quill."

"He may be a prisoner."

"If he is," I said, "we'll go get him. No matter how far we go, or how long it takes."

Our cabin had been looted, our few possessions gone or broken. The same was true in every room until we mounted the ladder to the walk. We saw several patches of blood, dark stains now, some visible on the earth below, some upon the walk. The ladder to the blockhouse had been pushed over, and evidently whoever had made the stand within had fired along the walk on either side, keeping the Indians at a distance.

Pushing gently on the door, I found a timber wedged against it, but managed to get a hand through and moved it enough to open the door.

John Quill sat facing the doorway, his head on his chest, his musket across his knees. There were eight other muskets within the room, all placed in position near loopholes or the door.

Kneeling beside him I touched his hand. Turning sharply I said, "Get Sakim up here! He's alive!"

△ 29 △

We buried Matt Slater on the land he loved, and buried him deep in the earth. We planted a tree close by his head that its fruit might fall where he lay. His years had been given to raising crops, and seeing the yellow grain bright in the sun, so we put him down where the seasons pass, where his blood could feed the soil. We left him there with a marker, simple and plain.

HERE LIES

MATTHEW SLATER, A FARMER
A FAITHFUL MAN WHO
LOVED THE EARTH
1570–1602

John Quill recovered, though wounded sorely, and told us a little of what had transpired.

They had come suddenly in the dawn, killing a Catawba who had brought meat to the fort, and the gate had been closed against them before they could take his scalp.

Then began a desperate fight, two men against thirty, and they ran from wall to wall, firing here, firing there. The Catawba warriors were far from the village on a hunt, but the old men fought and the women fought, and John Quill and Matt Slater defended the fort.

It was after sundown before they came over the wall and Slater went down fighting four men, and John Quill retreated into the blockhouse where they had gathered food and powder for a stand. Alone, he fought them all through the night and another day. They tried to fire the blockhouse but the timbers were damp from recent rains and would not burn.

"Six men I know I killed," John Quill said, "and mayhap another went, and finally they gave up and one shouted at me in English and told me to come to them, that the tribe would welcome me. They told me I was a great warrior—" John Quill looked at me. "Captain, I am only a farmer. It was all I ever wished to be, like poor Matt, who had his land only to lose it."

"He will never lose it," I said. "He had it when he died, and he had the memory of it in his soul. Nothing can take that from him."

"He was a brave, fine man," Abby said gently, "as you are, John. Our country needs such men to build it and

242

make it grow. God help us always to have them, men who believe in what they are doing, and who will fight for what they believe."

"Aye," I said, "no man ever raised a monument to a cynic or wrote a poem about a man without faith."

So we came back to the fort after our journeying, and with my own hands I carried on the farming of Slater's crops. He'd planted them well and cultivated them a mite before passing on, and it was no trouble to keep up the work he'd begun.

We were all of us growing into the land, finding our living from it, and learning where the berries grew thick upon the bushes and where the nuts fell and the pools where the trout loafed in the shadows.

Man is not long from the wilderness, and it takes him but a short time to go back to living with it, and we had the Catawbas to guide us. Peter Fitch took an Indian girl to wife, a tall well-made girl with four warrior brothers.

We went often to the far hills that spring, wandering deep into the mountains and living off the country, for there was always fresh meat for a man good with a gun, and there was no need to be belly-empty if you could shoot.

One day Kane O'Hara asked leave to be gone awhile. He took his musket and went over the mountains, and some said that would be the last of him, but I thought it would not and said so, but the womenfolk worried.

It was many weeks later when he came back, and when we saw him coming down the mountain, straight and tall as always, we saw he wasn't alone. Somebody walked beside him, and when he came closer we saw she was a Spanish girl from a Florida settlement.

"Kane," I asked, "did she come willing?"

"She did," he said, "but you can ask her yourself. I took meat to her town, and I speak her tongue from a time when I was a prisoner there, and I broke some wild horses for them—"

"Horses?"

"Aye, they've horses. I made to fetch some, but hadn't nothing to trade for them and they are wary of letting them go. Toward the end they got suspicious of me and did not believe what I said. Only Margarita believed me and said so, and when I left she came with me."

He looked at Abby and smiled. "It is all right, Mistress Abby. We stopped at an Indian village where there was a priest, an Irish priest from the Spanish lands who was teaching the Indians the ways of God, and he married us, all fitting and proper."

"What of her folks?"

"We sent them word by the priest. He was stiff about a marriage without her father saying it was proper, him knowing the family and all, but a nudge with a pistol and a reminder that if he did not marry us we'd be wedded Indian fashion, and he came through shining with a proper ceremony."

When the year ended we went down the river again, all of us going this time, with Kin doing his own walking and Abby having her hands full with Brian . . . named for her father . . . whom she carried when Lila could bear to let go of him.

Kin walked along with us, and bawled when he was picked up to be carried and insisted he carry his own pack, so we made a small one for him.

One of our boats was gone when we came to them, but we took the other two and went down the river after a few repairs. There were more of us now but we knew the country better and knew woodland travel.

We built a raft to tow our load of furs, for it was large, and we'd more pearls, mostly gotten by trade with the Indians, and some by capture. There'd been fights with the Cherokees, the Creeks, and the Tuscarora, and one day a captured Shawnee told us there had long ago been a great bunch of white men who lived on a river across the mountains, but they had fought often with the Shawnee and the Cherokee, too, before the Cherokee came so far south. Finally, the white men had been killed, but some of their women had been kept by Indian men, and a few of the survivors had come to live with the Shawnee.

It was a long story, but there were many such, and

from time to time we heard stories of white men who had been in the country before us.

We had come down all the way to the Outer Banks again when we saw a canoe coming toward us. It was Potaka again. He had a strange-looking creature with him, a long, thin man with a beard who kept saying over and over, "Barnabas, Barnabas." And it was Jago, who had sailed with us on the *fluyt*.

The Indians had found him, months before, roaming in the woods, and had cared for him as they did all mad men, for so they thought him to be. And truly, he was wandering in his mind.

"Jago," I said, "I am Barnabas."

"You said to ask for you," he said simply, and was content.

That he had been through some terrible ordeal was obvious, and his body bore the scars of torture, most likely by Indians. And from where he had been found and what he could recall it must have been the Tuscarora . . . but there was no certainty of this.

After he had rested with us, he slowly began to recover. Always a hard worker, he was no different now. Bit by bit we learned a little. He had been on a ship that somehow had been attacked by Indians when laying off shore. Some of the crew, including himself, had escaped. Some of the Indians had been carried out to sea on the ship, and when his own party ashore had somehow been separated, he had wandered in the forest, subsisting on nuts and roots until captured by the Indians. How he had gotten free of them, we could not learn.

For three weeks we waited, and saw no sail. Yet once again we enjoyed our sojourn upon the beach, and the change of diet provided by the sea. It was a pleasant, easy time. There was game in the woods and the fish were running well and the only Indians we encountered were friendly and inclined to trade.

Kin, I think, was the happiest of us all. He ran along the shore . . . miles of almost straight beach, all open to sun and sky. He was brown as an Indian, tall for his age, and a quiet, serious child.

On our fourteenth day we saw a sail, but it passed us by. Several days later we saw another. Warily, it came closer, and through our glasses we could see a man studying us through his own spyglass. He took soundings, then anchored and put a boat over.

Several men took to the boat and, when nearing shore, one of them suddenly stood up and waved.

It was John Pike.

When the boat came closer he leaped over the side and came splashing to us, his face lit with pleasure. "Barnabas! And Mistress Abigail! It is good to see you!"

We welcomed him to our campfire and he sent the boat back for wine and ale.

"I have done well," he said after awhile. "The *fluyt* is now part mine and I also own another ship now, which trades abroad."

He held Brian on his lap as he talked. "Barnabas, if you'd like the boys to go to school in London, let me have them. I'd treat them like they were my own."

That Pike had done well was obvious. He was a man of business, prosperous, yet still adventurous. But he should have known I would not thus part with my sons.

Later, he took us aboard his ship. He lingered for several days, taking on fresh water, trading with Indians and with us, and catching a supply of fresh fish as well as some game from the forest.

To Abby and Lila he gave some bales of assorted dress goods, and to me, canvas, tools, and seed for grain and vegetables. He had planned well, and what we might have thought of needing, he could supply.

On the last day, Jeremy Ring said suddenly, "Captain Pike, I would be pleased if you'd fetch your Bible."

Pike looked up, surprised, at Jeremy.

"I want to get married," said Jeremy quietly, "to Lila."

Astonished, I looked at her. She was blushing, her head hanging.

"Lila!" Abby exclaimed. "Is this true? Why didn't you tell me?"

Blushing furiously, Lila said, "I didn't know. He didn't ask me."

"You knew how I felt," Ring said.

"Yes, yes, I did." She glanced at him, suddenly shy. "I did."

"Well, then?"

"Yes . . . I will. Of course, I will."

The ceremony was brief, and we all stood on the shore with a light wind blowing, ruffling our hair and blowing the women's skirts, and Captain Pike read from the Bible.

When it was over I said to Pike, "You'll send the news? You know the Icelanders? They will take the word of Lila's marriage to Anglesey. Tell them she has married a good friend and a good man."

"I will that."

"And John Tilly? What of him?"

"Why, we're partners! I thought I had told you. He commands the *fluyt* when she's at sea. We trade in the Spanish Indies. It's risky, but we've some friends who like to profit a bit in the trade themselves, and although we have to avoid Spanish warships we make a good thing of it."

"Slaving?"

"Not us. The Arabs and the Portuguese have that business, and we wish for none of it. They intrigue with the warlike African tribes who sell them their prisoners . . . the ones they themselves used to enslave or kill.

"But I am a free man and would see all men free. John Tilly believes as I do, so we have no conflict. Slaves are not an easy cargo. I prefer sugar, rum, or timber . . . fur if they can be had."

He sat on a hummock of sand. "You have been to your mountains? And what lies beyond?"

"More mountains, and then lowlands again, and lovely timbered valleys and meadows. These I have not seen, but the Catawba tell me they are there."

"There is much fighting among the Indians?"

"An Indian boy is not a man until he is a warrior. To

be a warrior he must fight, take scalps, count coup. And they do not forget old enmities."

At last he got up. "Now we must sail. This coast makes me nervous, too." He looked at me with keen, thoughtful eyes. "You will stay here? Raise your boys here?"

"Now, at least. When they grow older we will see the bent of their minds."

He took my hand, then started to leave. He had gone several steps when he stopped and turned.

"Barnabas? Do you remember Delve? Jonathan Delve? He was with you awhile, I believe?"

"What of him?"

"Around a year ago he came down to the coast and was taken aboard a vessel as a castaway, he and several others. He told the ship's master of a valuable wreck of which he knew. When he got the captain ashore, some more of his men were there and they ambushed and killed the captain and several of his crew. Two escaped."

"So?"

"He took the ship, and since has become a pirate and a dangerous man. It is reported that when drinking he talks often of you. For some reason you are on his mind."

"We will be careful."

Pike walked away over the sand, and I stood and watched him go. He had ships at sea, a reputation as a successful man, no doubt. Would I trade that for what I had?

I would not.

Feeling better, I walked back to Abby. "We will go home now," I said.

△ 30 △

Where go the years? Down what tunnel of time are poured the precious days?

We are young, and the fires within us burn bright.

All the world lies before us and nothing is too great to be done, no challenge too awesome.

Then suddenly the days are no more, the years are gone, and the time that remains is little, indeed.

Kin has grown tall, as fine a woodsman as I know, and as good a man. Brian is the thoughtful one. Each book I have he has read and reread, and soon, I know, he will go from me to a wider world. Regret is in me that he would leave, yet happiness, too, for he has his own life before him in a bigger world if not a better one.

Yance? What shall I say of Yance? His heart is pure, his strength the greatest of them all, I think. Yance is strong, he is rough, he is always wrestling, fighting, climbing, doing, changing.

He is a good son, faithful to his mother and to me. To his brothers, he is loyal. Yet he acts before he thinks. He is a bundle of muscle and impulse, a swift runner, a dead shot with any weapon, and a dangerous man because of it.

He listens when I speak, and he obeys. Yet sometimes he acts before I have a time to speak.

And then there is Jublain . . . named for my old friend but called Jubal.

He is the truly quiet one. A ghost in the woods, he moves like a shadow, and lives much with the Indians. He is gone for weeks, then comes and squats against the wall and listens to the talk and is gone again.

To me he gives love and respect, to his mother, adoration, and that is as I would have it.

We none of us know how far he has gone or what he has seen, for he rarely speaks of it. Sometimes stories come to us . . . an Indian from the west once came among us, looking for him. Jubal had been gone for weeks, and the Indian told us by sign language that Jubal had been far beyond the great river that divides the country in two . . . we had not known that.

Kin has no wife, nor has Brian or Jubal. Yance does, of course. He went far to the north last year and came upon a colony that had settled there several years before. For days he scouted about, watching the people go about their work. He had done the same at Jamestown when he grew old enough to go so far from home, for Raleigh had at last planted his colony and my boys used to go down to the place where they were and lie in the woods and watch them to see how they lived.

Yance had done the same at the place in the north, the place they were calling "New England."

That group landed in 1620 . . . thirteen years after the Virginia colony was finally established at Jamestown. Yance had been curious, as were all the boys, for the tales they heard from their mother and me, as well as the others of our group, were not enough. Only Yance went so far north.

He usually went alone or with a Catawba or two. He had gone several times with their war parties against the Iroquois or the Cherokee . . . with whom, in fact, the Catawba were often friendly.

Yance found the place called New England, already scattering out from the original settlement. He went into the village bringing meat. My boys always brought meat when they went anywhere, including their home.

He made friends, for he was genial, agreeable, and a hard worker, but for them he was too filled with good spirits, too energetic, and not God-fearing enough in their way. So one day when he had offended they put him in the stocks. It took nine men to do it, but they did it.

Only that night a girl stole her father's key and came down and set him free. He built a careful fire against the stocks and burned them down, but by the time the fire was discovered Yance was in the hills, and being Yance, he took the girl with him, and she, being the kind of a girl he would choose, came willingly.

Oh, she was a lovely one! Gay, filled with good spirits, singing always . . . and not always hymns, for she took readily to our wild English ballads of lost loves, highwaymen, and the fairs.

For we sang much in our hills, the gypsy songs, the Scotch Highland songs, the Irish songs.

There was always the fighting, for the Indians came

250

against us, and no morning sun arose without its risk, no day in the field without its danger.

The Catawbas were firmly our friends as they were to be the friends of the white man always. As warriors came from afar, hoping to kill a Catawba and have the scalp to boast of in the villages, so they came to fight us also as our name grew.

We were fighters all. John Quill, who had made his great defense of the fort after the death of Slater, was remembered by our enemies, for they gloried in the strength of any fighting man, enemy or friend.

But time has a way of stealing strength from a man, and even before that, his swiftness and agility. One day they came upon Glasco, working at his forge.

The boys were off hunting. I with my wife and our new daughter was at the river . . . only Tim Glasco was there. Usually an uncommonly wary man, that time he was not wary enough, and they came very close. He heard them, got off a quick shot and laid about him with his hammer and tongs.

They got an arrow into him, but he did not drop. They rushed him, and he swept two of them, right and left, into the dust. One went down from the red-hot tongs, another from a freshly sharpened spit for roasting meat.

Still they came, and they killed him.

We heard the shot from afar—Wa-ga-su, Pim Burke, and I, leaving Kane O'Hara with the women.

Too late. Glasco was down and his scalp taken. He was not quite dead, and somewhere he had picked up some Indian thoughts. "Get them," he whispered hoarsely, "and my hair back. I'll have my own hair upon my head when I cross the divide."

With Jeremy, Pim, and Kane O'Hara we set out after them, and we fled them down the nights and down the days, and across the rivers that men had given names, over the Broad and the Wateree, across Rocky River and Coldwater Creek to a skirmish on Long Creek, and then on to the Yadkin.

Suddenly, on the Yadkin, they turned to fight, and out-

251

numbered we were, but better shots. And two warriors died and lost their hair before we moved again.

Through the woods and across the savannas, through blackberry patch and under the hickory trees, and suddenly before us we heard a burst of firing, and then another, and we closed in swiftly to see the Senecas trapped in a bend of Lick Fork of the Dan. We saw one man down in the water, another trying to crawl a bank in a trail of blood, and we closed in swiftly.

From the bank beyond, a huge warrior suddenly stood up and shouted a challenge, and from the brush leaped Yance. He rushed forward, knife in hand, and the two met there in the open glade in a fierce and desperate fight. The big Indian threw his tomahawk. It caught Yance on the shoulder and the big Indian went in as Yance started to fall. But as the Indian charged, Yance kicked up both feet and boosted the Indian clear over his head. Then, swift as a striking snake, Yance turned on him and buried a knife in his chest.

The Catawbas, who ran the war trail with us, took many a scalp that day, and evened the score for their own people slain. And when the scalps were taken, we turned our backs and started slowly home.

My sons had been hunting the Blue Ridge, looking for caves of which we had heard, caves in which white men were said to be buried . . . men from some long-ago time before the beginning of years.

An Eno found them there and told of the war party of Senecas heading south upon a raid, and so they had come down from the high-up hills, too late to help defend our settlement, but in time to intercept the Senecas' return.

From far away they had heard shooting, then saw the Senecas coming across a savanna, and moved to meet them on Lick Fork.

Yet when we returned, Glasco was dead, only hours before.

"I wish he could have known," I said. "We brought back his hair."

"He knew," Lila said. "I told him. For I saw it as in a

dream, saw Yance come charging with a knife in his hand, saw blood upon his shoulder, saw him go down, then come up and turn, and saw his shoulder move."

She went to Yance and uncovered his shoulder. There was a deep gash there, the bleeding stopped with moss. "Come," she said, "we will make it clean." And he went with her, as he had when a child.

Abby stood waiting, her face still, her eyes round and serious.

"Barnabas," she said, "we must go down to the river. I would speak with you there."

I knew it would be a serious talk, for long it had been since she'd called me aught but Barney.

And when we sat together on the bank, she said, "We have a daughter, Barnabas, and she will be a beautiful girl."

"She is your daughter," I said.

"It is a wild land here. What will be her future?"

Uneasiness stirred within me, and for the first time I truly felt fear. "I do not know," I said, "but by the time she is grown—"

"It will be too late, Barnabas. Our daughter will not become a hunter or a fighter of Indians. She must have education, she must know another world than this."

My fingers felt the grass. I pulled a blade and tasted it and waited, my heart beating slowly.

"You have your sons, and they will grow your way. I want our daughter to have another choice. If she stays, who will she marry? One of your wild wilderness men? Would you have her curing buffalo hides, growing old before her time?"

"What else can we do?" I asked, though in my heart I knew the answer.

"In all things, Barnabas, I have done as you wished, for in all things they were what I wished as well. In this I do not know, and you must help me. I do not know, Barnabas, but I am filled with misgivings."

"You would take her from me? Soon Brian will go to England to study law. Already Sakim has taught him mathematics and logic, government and philosophy. I have learned much from Sakim, for I, too, have listened when he taught. Yet I am no scholar, and but a simple man."

Abby put her hand over mine. "Not so simple, Barnabas, but so wise, so strong, and yet so gentle. You forget that I have known you for a long time. And a good time," she added quietly, "a very good time. And I do not want to leave you."

It was there. The word had been said.

"Where would you go?"

"To London, at first. Perhaps to Paris. I would need time, Barnabas, for I have been long away. I would need to learn again how to behave as an English lady."

"You have always been a lady."

"You could come with us, Barnabas. You could come. Elizabeth the Queen is dead. A man sits now upon the throne. The old suspicions would be forgot."

But even as she spoke, we knew I would not go. I would never leave again for so long the shadow of those mountains I had found at last.

"After this?" I swept my hand at the mountains, fields, rivers. "No, Abby, our duties divide. Yours will take you to England with our daughter, mine will keep me here.

"Perhaps the boys no longer need me, but they know I am here. I am an anchor, I am a single, positive thing. I am a focal point, if no more. A balance wheel, a hub about which they may revolve, and I will be here for them to come to if they are hurt. I would not have them without that.

"They may never need me, but as long as I am here, they are not lost. If I can be no more to them, I will be their Pole Star."

"The Senecas will come again, Barnabas, and the Shawnees."

"Of course . . . I know that. I would miss them if they failed to come, and they would miss me if I was not here to greet them."

I stood up, slowly. "Abby, we will arrange it. We will go down to the sea once more, and we will find a ship, and you may go to England.

"When she has seen the world, when she has learned what it holds, then bring her to me again and let me see what my daughter has become.

"At least . . . do not let her forget me."

△ 31 △

Yet suddenly there came news of such evil portent that new fears beset our colony. On the 22nd of March, the Indians had raised up and killed several hundreds of the colonists in the land called Virginia.

That particular colony was some distance from us and we had but little knowledge.

From time to time we had word of them from Indians passing, or the observations of Kin or Yance, and we knew of harsh times they had, with a shortage of food and much illness. The site of the town they had formed, called Jamestown, was not the best one and, as we had discovered to our cost, there was much fever on the coast close to the swamps.

After some beginning trouble between Powhatan, of whom we often heard but knew little, and these colonists, troubles between them had simmered down, largely to the strong stand taken by a Captain John Smith, a man of Lincolnshire who had fought in wars upon the continent.

The story as we heard it from the Catawbas was thus: A war captain called Nemattanow, who was called by the colonists "Jack of the Feather," because of his feather adornment, had persuaded a man named Morgan to go into the woods with him for trade or hunting or something of the kind. Nemattanow had often been in Morgan's house, and coveted many of the things he saw there. Later, in the woods, he murdered Morgan and returned to the cabin wearing Morgan's cap. Morgan's boys suspected what had happened and tried to entice the Indian to the presence of a Master Thorpe.

An altercation developed and Nemattanow was shot and wounded. The boys put him in a boat to take before the governor. Feeling his death was near, Nemattanow, who the Indians believed could not be hurt by a bullet, pleaded with the boys not to tell how he was killed, and to bury his body in the white man's cemetery so his death would not become known.

Oppecancanough, who was king of those Indians, was much angered when he heard of the death of Nemattanow, but made great signs of love and peace to the colonists so that no danger was felt, and due to the fact that no war had been entertained for some time, few of the colonists were armed, there being few swords, and fewer guns except for fowling pieces.

Yet Oppecancanough informed his people of what was planned, sending presents of venison and fowl to various colonists with much evidence of good will, and sometimes sitting to breakfast with them. Then, suddenly, on the 22nd of March they arose and slaughtered three hundred and forty-seven men, women, and children, striking so quickly that few knew what happened, killing them often with their own tools, then hacking and defacing the bodies.

One Nathaniel Causie, who had come with John Smith, seized upon an axe when attacked and clove the head of one of his attackers, whereby they fled, and he escaped, though injured, for they hurt none who did stand to fight or were upon their guard, killing only those they caught unawares and unarmed.

By this time the colonists were established for one hundred and forty miles along the river, on both sides, and the Indians, because of their nature of living off the country, must themselves be in groups of thirty, forty, or sixty. Yet the whole plot had been so carefully arranged that each group of Indians was aware, and many more than the three hundred and forty-seven might have been killed had not one Indian, friendly to a man named Pace, informed him of the plot. Pace had informed the governor, after rowing in haste down the river.

Six of the council were slain, George Thorpe, Nathaniel

Powell, John Berkeley, Samuel Macock, Michael Lapworth, and John Rolfe, this Rolfe having married an Indian named Pocohontas.

The unrest occasioned by this disaster was sure to put many Indians to flight, and there would be trouble along the paths.

Yet the news included more than the story of massacre and that was that several ships had arrived, bringing more settlers. It was a chance that could not be missed.

"We will go, Abby. Peter has two boats finished and a third well along in the building. If we all pitch in to help, that boat should be ready for the river in a few days. We will go down the river . . . the Cape Fear, I believe they call it now . . . and go up the coast to Jamestown.

"Peter wishes to sell his boats, and there should be a market for them there. We can carry our furs, robes, and grain."

We were three large boats and one canoe when we started, with Kin, Brian, and Yance in the canoe, Jeremy, Pim, and myself in the first boat with the women, Kane O'Hara and Tom Watkins in the second, Jubal and Waga-su in the last and most heavily loaded.

We went up the coast from the rivermouth, staying inside the banks when possible, and came finally to the Bay of Chesapeake and the Potomac River.

We came to the landing at Jamestown to see three ships in the river and much busied they were with lowering cargo to boats—and one ship lying close in alongside a dock, being a craft of such shallow draft.

A man of some presence watched us come close along and called out, "What have you there?"

"Corn and hides," I said, "and some furs. We be seeking out someone who would buy."

"Corn? You will be speaking to the governor of that. We have had losses here."

"Aye," I said, "we heard of that and came along to help. We ask but a fair market price. As for that," I added, "we would sell the boats, too."

Climbing up on the dock, I was followed by Brian and

Kane O'Hara. He glanced from one to the other of us. "It is that you plan to settle here?"

"No. We've good places yon, and crops put in, but we heard your troubles and had this grain put by."

"If you sell your boats, how then will you get home?"

"Overland," Brian said. He was a fine, handsome lad who spoke well, indeed. "That is, some of us would, sir. My mother, sister, and I would ship for England."

"I am Captain Powell," he said, "William Powell. We are on short rations here, and the governor will be pleased to see you."

He bade me come with him to meet the governor, Sir Francis Wyatt, an uncommonly shrewd man, and intelligent enough to ask few questions. I spoke him fair, using my own name, and hoping the years would have erased it from memory, as it seemed to have done.

"We are obliged, Captain," he said to me. "You could have come at no better time. Now what are you asking per bushel?"

"As I told Captain Powell," I said, "we came to help, not to profit by your troubles. We will take the fair market price and no more."

"Commendable," Wyatt said dryly, "and unusual." He turned to Powell. "Will you see they are put up properly?" Then he smiled at me. "If you would wait outside? I wish to speak to Captain Powell."

Here it comes, I thought. The next thing is an order for my arrest. We went outside, but I did not move from the door. Inside, I could hear Powell say, "Do you believe them, Sir Francis?"

"Believe them? I have no idea whether they are telling the truth or not, Captain. I have a colony on the verge of starvation, and am not inclined to ask any questions at all. They have grain. We need grain. They will sell it at a reasonable price. I will pay their price. Furthermore, I will let them go back to their homes with thanks, and hope they come to us again. Such men we can use."

"I could use them," Powell said grimly. "Did you look at them, Sir Francis? That's the strongest, toughest, most able lot of men I've seen in many a year. At least two

258

of the older ones have been soldiers or I miss my guess."

He shook his head. "I have an idea who they are, Sir Francis. I think it's that lot we've been hearing about, from up at the edge of the mountains."

"It well may be." Sir Francis got to his feet, for I heard his chair shove back. "Make no report on this, Powell. In London they will only want to know that we fed our people. How it was done will not interest them.

"We will buy their grain. We will house them at the expense of the colony, and we will speed them on their way. Who knows when again we may need help?"

Powell chuckled, then said, "Sir Francis, if we've to fight the Indians again, just let me recruit that lot. I'd ask no more."

Powell came out. The cabin he then took us to was well-built and strong, and there was a small tavern, or what passed for one, close by.

"Captain Sackett," Powell said, "there are presently three ships in port, two of them loading for the West Indies. The third has just recently come in, but I don't much like her looks. I'd hesitate, if I were you."

"What's wrong with her?"

Powell studied his nails thoughtfully, then he said, "She's too heavily armed for a merchant ship, and if I ever saw a craft with a pack of rascals for crew, that's it. And that Captain Delve—"

"*Delve*, did you say? *Jonathan Delve*? A kind of a taunting look to his eyes?"

"You know the man?"

"I know him," I said grimly, "and I don't like him. I'd heard he was a pirate, and I agree with your judgment of him."

Powell looked thoughtful. "We're not heavily armed here, and a ship like that could be a trouble to us, so I want nothing more than to see him gone."

When Powell was gone I explained to the boys who Delve was. That he had survived so long was evidence of his cunning.

"Kin," I suggested, "the man does not know you or

259

Brian. Go down along the river and see what you can learn, but stay away from him and don't get into trouble."

"He's an evil man," Abby said.

"He is that, and I would like it better if you and he were not on the same sea. He has been a pirate, and probably is yet, and more than likely has come in for supplies while he looks over what ships may be worth the taking."

"Did you see his vessel?" Jeremy asked, wryly. "She's got thirty-six guns, and she's fast."

"Fast she may be," Yance said quietly, "but she's at anchor now. They don't move very fast with an anchor in the mud."

"What are you suggesting?" Pim asked.

Yance grinned slowly, looking up from under his thick brows. "Well? If she worries us, let's take her, and remove the worry."

I shook my head. "That would be piracy on our part. So far as we know he has done nothing."

"If you'd have sent me," Yance said, "I'd have seen to it."

"That's why I didn't send you, Yance." I smiled at him.

Yet but part of my thoughts at this moment were upon Jonathan Delve. The presence of the man and his ship were but a minor irritation compared with the fact . . . and it was a fact . . . that Abby and I would soon be apart.

My mind almost refused to accept it. She had been so much a part of my life that I could scarcely imagine being without her, though I fully understood how she felt.

Noelle was but ten. Her feminine associations had been good. Yance's wife, although a gay, fun-loving girl as exuberant as he himself, had come from a sedate, religious upbringing. Kane O'Hara's wife, of Spanish background, was even more so.

Peter Fitch's Catawba wife moved with a grace and conducted herself with a decorum that would have done credit to any great lady. She had taken on European ways easily and naturally while losing none of her own, and it was a rare thing, I thought, who had little experience after all, that so many women could live together . . . or near to each other, without friction.

John Quill had been almost a second father to Noelle. A man married to his farm, he thought of little else, yet he was forever bringing her the largest strawberries, birds' nests, or flowers from the woods or the edges of his fields.

It had been a good life we lived, and what school we had was conducted by the various wives and by Sakim, whose depths of knowledge none had ever plumbed. Like the boys, Noelle had grown up on stories known to the Catawba and the Cherokee, to the Irish (from Kane O'Hara) and Sakim's stories of Scheherazade. Sakim read also from the *Katha Sarit Sagara,* the so-called "Ocean of Story" as gathered together by Somadeva, a court poet to King Ananta of Kashmir, and his queen, Suryavati.

Often I wondered what their vision of life must be, learning, as they had, from such oddly dissimilar storytellers. They had learned the Catawba story of the beginning of things. Kane O'Hara told them stories of Cuchulainn or of Conn of the Hundred Battles, and of the Irish kings who lived on Tara. From Jeremy they had stories of Achilles and Ulysses and of Xenophon's retreat of the Ten Thousand. From Sakim, stories of Ali Baba and Sinbad, of Rustum and his fabled horse, Raqsh, who killed a lion to protect his sleeping master.

From Abigail they had the story of God and of Jesus and Mary, and from Sakim, of Allah and Mohammed, and from Sweet Woman the story of Wakonda the Sky Spirit. From Barry Magill they learned something of weaving, from Peter Fitch a love of good wood and the uses of it, and from John Quill a love of the earth and the magic of making things grow.

What was left for me? A little of each, and the pointing out of things along the trail, and something of England's history, of the Normans, the Danes, and the Celts, of the Norsemen and their raids and wanderings.

Yet there were strange gaps in their knowledge, realized suddenly when after hearing the story of Rustum and Raqsh, Noelle asked me, "Papa, what is a horse?"

△ **32** △

The cabin with which they provided us was no place for a man, what with all the sewing and stitching, and the talk of the women as they stitched skirts and petticoats, and tried on and fitted, and exclaimed over this and that. For neither Abby nor Noelle had the proper clothes for shipboard nor for landing in England, either.

Kin returned and we sat against the log wall outside the cabin. "Jonathan Delve has something on his mind," he said, "but nobody has a notion of what. This much I did learn. He was taken by a British warship and was in Newgate for a time, and somehow bribed his way out."

"He is not idling here for nothing," I said.

"Aye, that he is not. Brian is just now sitting over ale with a sailor who's been aboard her, and if I know Brian he will soon have all the man knows."

Kin ran his fingers through his long hair. "Pa, we may be late tonight. There's some looking about we'll do."

"Be easy with it, son. The British are no fools, and are sharp upon the form and manner of things."

A thought came to me. "Where's Yance?"

"Him?" Kin said, almost absent-mindedly. "He's helping the blacksmith who is behind in his work. You know Yance. He must be busy all the time."

Aye, I knew him. Busy indeed he was, but with what? Yance was never one to be idle but often enough his busy-ness was trouble.

However, the day was a quiet one, and I enjoyed sitting in the sun and watching what went on about us, for it had been long since I'd seen any settlement but our own. From time to time some of them would stop to pass the time with me, and so I heard much of the story of the early settlement of Jamestown, which had been only a shadow-tale until now.

Indians had told us a bit here or there. How the colony came near starving, and how many had died. And how at last John Smith was given the command he should have had at the beginning and then all began to come right. They told us also of some of his explorations up the coast, and how he had gone to islands far off the north coast to another settlement for supplies.

That night, warm, bedded down, I lay awake beside Abby and looked up in darkness at the hand-sewn rafters. A knowing hand had shaped them, a knowing hammer drove the pegs. There is a quiet beauty in such things as these, a beauty more than paint or chisel make, the beauty of quiet men, making strong things for their own use, shaping each piece with loving fingers.

At last I slept, awakening slightly when the boys came, and wondering in my half-sleeping way why they came so late when the dawn was in the sky.

Captain Powell came the next morning.

"If there's trouble," he asked, "will you and your lot fight with us? For Captain Delve is with us still and a ship comes in this morning with a thousand weight of powder aboard, and as much of shot and lead. She'll have clothing aboard, and seed and much for which we've waited."

"When she leaves, where does she sail?"

"To London, Captain Sackett, straight to London town."

"Will she carry my wife and my daughter and my son Brian?"

"She will if you help us. For I fear that Delve means to take her. We've lately discovered he's low on powder, and needs all she carries for whatever it is he's about, and he has put his ship around this morning and his guns aim at the town."

"We'll stand by you," I said.

"Aye," said Kin, "that we will, if needed. But do not

worry, Captain Powell. Arm your men and have them stand by, too. But they need fear no cannon fire."

"No cannon fire? He has thirty-six guns, man. Can you mean to say no cannon fire and him with thirty-six guns?"

"Aye." Kin smiled his slow smile and looked up, his gray-green eyes alight in his lean brown face. "And not a one of them will fire. Last night we went aboard, my brothers and I, with O'Hara and Jeremy Ring and Mr. Burke, and while two of us guarded the doors just in case, we spiked every gun!"

"*Spiked* them!" Powell exclaimed. "How could you, with men on watch, and—"

"We be woodsmen, Captain Powell, who move quietly even among Indians. They heard us not. One man on watch was put quietly to sleep. The other . . . well, I regret to say it, but one was strong and made a fight and took the blade like a good lad. He's down in the river now, drifting toward the sound.

"Some guns we merely spiked and in some we wedged cannonballs tight against the base of the bore, and hammered them home snugly with wooden wedges. Oh, we made a few sounds then, but those aboard were snug asleep after all their rum, and we not too much worried.

"What's needed now, Captain, I leave to you, but if it were me I'd draw Delve's teeth by taking what powder he has left. We'd not want him chasing after a ship that carries our mother and sister, although Brian can care for himself."

"Whose idea was it," I asked, suspiciously, "to go aboard at all?"

Kin smiled, "Why Yance's of course, but it appealed to us, too. Would you have had us done other than what we did?"

"You might at least have awakened me," I grumbled.

Kin chuckled. "It would have worried Ma. Then, too, you older men need your sleep."

He ducked when I struck out at him, and laughed at me with tender eyes.

I thought of my father, of Ivo Sackett. He would have loved them, too.

"Captain Powell?" It was a soldier at the door. "Captain Delve is coming ashore, and he has twenty men with him."

"Summon the company. Muskets charged and ready. I will meet them here."

So we took up our muskets then and went down to the water with Captain Powell, and when the men came ashore we moved in around them, with muskets and pistols, sixty men to their twenty, and all armed and ready.

Jonathan Delve was an older man now and the mark of Satan was on him. He started to bluster and threaten, but I spoke to him quietly.

"You'll surely remember me, Delve. You served under me once, and a poor sort of man you were. And by the look of you, you're no better now."

He started to speak but I cut him off.

"You'll threaten no man here, nor raise your voice on the streets of the town. You and your men are prisoners, and Captain Powell will provide you with comfortable quarters while they go through your ship. We hear you've a spot of powder left, and we'll be having it."

"You'll be damned if—!" He started to bluster.

"It is you who'll be damned, Captain Delve. Don't threaten us with your guns. By now your men will have discovered that your guns are spiked."

"Spiked!" His voice was hoarse with rake. "You're a liar, Barnabas Sackett! How could—?"

"My boys are woodsmen, Delve. They were aboard last night." A movement caught my eye, and turning my head from him I saw a ship coming up the river. "Here comes your quarry now, with cargo for Virginia. You'll not mind waiting ashore until she's gone, will you, Delve?"

Now there was a hint of panic in his eyes. "What are you trying to do, Sackett?"

"It is not me." I indicated Captain Powell. "You must speak to this officer, or to the governor."

So they were disarmed and taken away to be locked up. We walked to the riverfront, the boys and I, to watch the ship come in, yet there was no joy in me to see her, fine craft though she was, for Abby would be going away, and my little girl with her.

Would Noelle have the gift? We had never talked of it, although sometimes she looked at me so solemnly, so strangely that I was sure she knew.

In the better of the several ordinaries that had sprung up, I was invited to a glass of wine with the governor, Sir Francis Wyatt. He gestured to a seat opposite him. "Captain Sackett, I hear you will be leaving us soon?"

"I will."

"Your wife, I hear, is returning to England?"

"With my son, Brian, and my daughter, Noelle. This is not the land to bring up a young woman, and my son wishes to read for the law."

"Commendable." He turned his glass on the table. "Sackett, if you will permit me? I have asked no questions as to your background or your reasons for settling here. You realize, of course, that the land you occupy is the King's?"

"I suppose that is the official interpretation," I replied quietly. "However, I must suggest a thought. The land lies in the realm of the Catawba. So far as I am aware none of that land has to date been purchased, nor has it been yielded. Moreover, the Catawba has been a friend of the white man. At least," I added, "to the Englishman."

"What you say is true, no doubt, yet the grant given stretches to the western ocean. I do not wish to create an issue where none yet exists, Sackett, and certainly you have been most helpful. Most men under the circumstances would have demanded the highest price for their grain."

"It is not our nature to take advantage."

"You wish no favors in return?"

"None. If you wish, however, you might write some letters of introduction for my family, and especially for my son. It is not easy for a young man to make his way without friends."

"It shall be done. My family home is at Boxley Abbey. A letter will accompany your ship to England. I shall

266

also address several members of the company on your behalf."

He leaned back in his chair. "None of us knows what the future holds, and by all appearances I shall be governor here for several years. It may be that we will again need your help."

"You have only to ask."

"Thank you. I would also take it kindly if you would keep me informed on any exploration you do into the mountains, or beyond them. And perhaps you can help us develop our relationship with the Catawba. I understand they are a strong people."

"They are among the most noted fighting men in the country, Sir Francis. And, as it happens, most of their enemies are our enemies, too."

I paused. "You understand, Sir Francis, that I left England rather hurriedly."

He lifted a hand. "Please! No more of that. You are a settler here. You have proven useful and helpful. I wish to know nothing more. I am a practical man, Sackett, and I am interested only in the interests of the colony." He glanced at me curiously. "You have been here a long time?"

"More than twenty years."

"You realize that, officially, no one has been here so long?" He refilled his glass. "Of course, for some time there have been stories of white men in the back country. You knew that, I suppose?"

"There were such rumors when first we came here, Sir Francis. I am sure that we were not the first. We found initials carved upon trees, and stories among the Indians of white men. And such stories were here before the lost colony of Roanoke vanished.

"Juan Pardo heard such stories. It is likely that Ayllon's captain, Gordillo, also did. Estevan Gomez was along this coast in 1525, and contributed much to the mapping of it. And I have had access," I said, "to many maps. No matter how far back you go, you still find rumors of white men. It is obvious the sea was crossed many times, perhaps continually over long periods of time. The Phoenicians never divulged their sources of raw material or trade goods."

We talked long, and Sir Francis asked many searching questions about the soil, the game, the minerals. I told him we had found but little gold, but several mines of both iron and lead, and that we cast our own musket balls and manufactured our own powder.

When I returned to our cabin, Pim Burke was waiting for me. He looked uneasy, and that was unusual.

"What is it, Pim?"

He looked shame-faced, then said, "Barnabas, I—" he paused. "Well, I have been offered a post. I shall be clerk and interpreter, and do some trading as well. There's a grant goes with it, Barnabas, and I'm growing no younger."

"None of us are, and I'd advise you to accept."

He looked relieved. "I don't want to seem disloyal— I mean, just when you are losing so much."

"Nonsense! If I had heard of it first, I would have suggested it to you. By all means, Pim, take it. You may be of more use to us here than at the colony. Besides, I am thinking of going over the mountains."

"Well . . . if you do not object, Barnabas. My first loyalty is to you."

I put a hand on his shoulder. "We have come a long way together, Pim. We are friends, you and I, and where we are you will never find a wife, and you should have one. You deserve one."

"Well, to tell the truth—"

"There's a girl?"

"A widow, Barnabas. Young, and with a bit put by, and I've a bit, as you know . . ."

"By all means! But Pim . . . ?"

He looked at me. "The emerald? I've told only one person." He suddenly looked shy.

"So be it, then," I said. "Let us keep in touch, and wherever I may be, Pim, you have a friend."

We shook hands and he went his way, hurrying a little as if he feared he might turn back.

That night I lay awake, having said nothing to Abby

of Pim's going. She would regret him, regret his being from me, for he had been a good friend and loyal but I had been much put out these past months, seeing no future for him in what we did.

Land, yes. We had bargained with the Catawba for land, and he had his piece as I had mine, yet it is an empty life for a man alone, although it seems not so when a man is young.

Yet I wished he had not mentioned the emerald. We had found several . . . he had one, I had four. Three of these I had given to Abby and one to Brian. They would serve as something in case of need, and any one of the stones was rich enough to buy an estate if need be.

Pim's emerald was not a large one, but struck me as exceedingly fine.

We had heard rumors of a few small diamonds being found in the lower foothills, but of this we had no positive knowledge.

At last the day came. Several times I had met with the master of the *Eagle*, a solid man, and by all accounts, a good seaman. I had twice been aboard his ship, and she was finely kept with a competent-appearing crew.

At dawn I was up and outside, looking at the weather. A fair day . . . yet a gloomy one for me.

Abby came out shortly afterward and walked beside me. We stood at the river, saying nothing, my hand touching hers or hers mine. But no words came to us.

We talked of her returning, yet I think neither of us believed in it. There was still a chance the warrant for my arrest might lie dusty in some drawer to be taken out and used, and both of us knew that a frontier girl of ten does not become a great lady in three years or four.

At the end, we kissed lightly and she said, "Be careful, Barnabas," and little Noelle clung to my hand with tears in her eyes.

Brian stood tall, as I expected him to, and gripped hard my hand. "I will make you proud of me, Father."

"I am already proud," I said quietly. "Take care of your mother and sister."

The other boys stood around, looking awkward and feeling worse. Lila kept saying over and over that she should be going with them.

"You've Jeremy to think of," Abby said quietly, "and your own children."

"Come back, Abby," I said. "Come back."

"Wait for me, Barney, for I love you. I do, I always shall, and I always have since that very first night when you came in from out of the storm."

I stood on the bank then, and watched the *Eagle* sail down the river, and suddenly I knew in my heart with an awful desperation that I would not see any of them again.

Lila took my hand and gripped it hard. "They will be all right. They will be all right. I see a safe voyage and a long life for them."

She said nothing of me, or of my life.

△ **33** △

The place on Shooting Creek was not the same. Time and again I found myself turning suddenly to exclaim over a sunset, the dappled shadow of tree leaves upon the water or the flash of a bird's wing . . . and Abby was not there.

The blue of the mountains seemed to draw closer, and more and more my eyes turned westward. . . .

Yet there lay the mountains, vast and mysterious, with unknown valleys and streams that flowed from out of dark, unbelievable distances, and always beyond, the further heights, the long plateaus, the sudden glimpses of far, far horizons.

Jubal slipped silently into the cabin as I sat over Maimonides, reading.

"Pa? There's talk in the villages. They're coming after you again."

"You'd think they would tire of it."

270

"You're a challenge, Pa. You don't realize how much, for their best warriors have tried, and they have been killed or suffered from wounds. You have become a legend, and some say you cannot die, that you will never die, but others believe they must kill you now, it is a matter of honor. They will come soon. Perhaps even tonight."

Jubal nodded, then he spoke suddenly, as if with an effort. "Pa? You don't mind it? That I am not like the rest?"

"Of course not. You're a good man, Jubal, one of the very best. I love you as I do them."

"Folks crowd me, Pa. I like wild, lonesome country. I like the far-looking places. It ain't in me to live with folks. It's the trees, the rivers, the lake and wild animals I need. Maybe I'm one of them . . . a wild animal myself."

"I'm like that, too, Jubal. Almost as much as you. And now that your mother is gone, I could walk out that door and keep going forever."

We were silent for a time. The fire crackled on the hearth and I closed my book. The firelight flickered on Jubal's face, and moved the shadows around in the back of the room, and my eyes wandered restlessly over the stone-flagged floor, over the hide of the bear I had killed in the forest on the edge of the rhododendrons. I remember I had recharged my musket and then slid down the rugged slope, where flowering sand-myrtle clung to the crevices, to stop beside the carcass of the bear.

My shot had gone true and the bear had dropped. They were never so difficult to kill if the shot was placed well, and a raven had flown over, looking with a wary eye at me and on a second flyby with a hopeful eye at the bear's huge size. For that raven well knew I'd take the hide and some choice cuts, but I'd never carry that six hundred pounds over the ridges between myself and home.

"Pa? Aunt Lila told me once, you had the gift."

"We are of the blood of Nial, Jubal." I glanced at him. "Do you have it, too?"

"The Indians believe I do."

271

"Do you know about me?"

"I . . . think so, Pa."

"Do not speak of this, Jubal. It is enough for you and me and Lila. I am not distressed, for there is a time for each of us, and we are rarely ready.

"One thing I know. I am still too young to rust. When spring comes and my crop is in once more I shall make a pack and walk over to see some of your western lands before I die."

"I've been beyond the mountains," said Jubal, "and have ridden the rivers down. I've been to a far, far land where the greatest river of all flows south and away toward the sea, sometimes I think I'd like to get a horse and ride off across those plains forever, going on and on just like that river goes.

"Beyond the bunch-grass levels where the buffalo graze, there are other mountains, or so the Indians say, mountains that tower their icy summits into the sky, and I've gone that way, but not yet so far.

"The Indians there live in tents of buffalo hide, and I've fought with them, hunted with them, slept in their lodges, and I could live their way and find happiness, I think. They've got horses, the southern Indians do, got them from the ranches down Mexico way."

"They do not have horses further north?" I asked.

"Not yet, but they'll have them soon, and Pa, when an Indian gets a horse he becomes a different man. I've seen it. The Comanche and the Kiowa have the horses, but the Kiowa haven't been long upon the western plains, for they have just come from the mountains further west.

"The Indian in America is like the people you told us of in Europe and Asia, always at war with one another, always pushing into new lands and pushing off the people who were there, or killing them."

"People are much the same the world around, Jubal. We are no better and no worse . . . nor are they. The Picts were in England and the Celts came, and long after them, the Anglos, Saxons, and Danes. And when they settled nicely down, the Normans came, took all the land from the people of England, and handed it out in parcels to the men who came over with William the Conqueror. It is the old story. To the victor belong the spoils.

"For the Indian has done the same thing to other Indians. In Mexico the Aztecs were a savage people who conquered an older, more civilized people, and then marched out like the Romans and tried to conquer all about.

"Cortez found willing allies because many of the Indians of Mexico hated the Aztecs.

"It was the same in Peru. The people we call the Incas suddenly went on the march and welded together a vast empire of tribes and peoples, and it was done by conquest. Yet it is not only men who do this. Plants do it also. When conditions are right a new type of plant will move in and occupy the ground."

"Pa? There's been white men out yonder. After I crossed the big south-flowing river I went by canoe up a river that flows down from the west, and in wandering the country north of there, I found some great stones with writing on them, writing just like on some of the old, old maps you have from Iceland."

"Runes?"

"Yes. No two ways about it, Pa. They've been there."

Long we talked while the fire burned down and the coffee turned cold in the cups. It was the most Jubal had ever talked, I think. The sound of his voice was warm in the room, and when at last he stood, he said, "Sleep lightly, Pa, for the Indians will come when their medicine speaks, and those who sleep too soundly may never awaken."

He went outdoors then, for he rarely slept inside even in the coldest weather. Taking wood from the bin, I built up the fire, and when the wood caught I went outside and walked over to Jeremy's.

Lila was kneading dough. Jeremy was weaving some cloth, for Barry Magill had been teaching him the trade.

"Sit you," Lila said. "The pots on. It's sassafras tea, if you'll have it."

"I will," I said, and then to Ring, "Jubal's here. He says there's been a gathering of warriors to the north and

273

the talk in the villages is that they will come again . . .
perhaps tonight."

"We will need two men on the walls, then. Barry and
Tom for the first watch?"

"Aye, and Sakim and Kane for the second. We'll save
the last for ourselves."

" 'Tis then they'll come, Barnabas. I was thinking back,
just now. Do you remember the sailor's wife who let us
rooms? Mag, wasn't it?"

"I think so. Aye, I recall her well. I hope her man
came back and that she had a dozen sons. She was a
good woman."

"I'd like to see Jublain again. He was a good man with
a blade, Barnabas. The best I ever know . . . excepting
you."

"And you."

"Well . . . it was a skill I had. I could ride, too, but
how long has it been since I've seen a horse?"

"You'll be seeing them again. There's a Spanish man
below the Santee who has nine horses to sell or trade.
He's going back to the old country and he wants to live
well. He cannot take the horses for the trouble and the
expense, and nobody would wish them to go, yet his own
people cannot pay the price. He has said he will bargain."

"When?"

"I've sent Kin and Yance."

Jeremy Ring gathered up his work and put it aside,
drinking the last of his tea. "I'll go over to John Quill's
now, but I do not think he'll leave his place. He's built
three cabins now, two burned by Indians, and his crop
burned three times, so he's sworn that the next time he
will stand them off or die."

I went to warn Black Tom. He had been early asleep,
and he rolled out and pulled on his clothes, a cutlass,
two pistols, and a musket, and climbed the walls. Sakim
followed, for he would stand the watch until Barry was up.

The night was cool. The stars were out but clouds were
moving in. It would be a dark, dark night.

Kane O'Hara and his wife came in from their cabin at
the edge of their fields. Kane had taken to smoking

tobacco, having been taught by Wa-ga-su, who was still much with us.

It seemed strange, at such a time, not to have Abby to think of.

The wind seemed unusually cool off the mountain. Was this to be the night?

"No . . . not yet." I spoke aloud, and Kane O'Hara, who stood near me, glanced over.

"Just thinking aloud," I said. He nodded. "I do it, too, when my wife is from the house."

We watched the stars disappear beneath the oncoming clouds. The night was dark and velvet with stillness. I moved, and the planks beneath my feet creaked slightly. A vagrant breeze stirred the leaves of the forest, then passed on. We listened to the sounds, for these were our woods and we understood them well. For never are the sounds of the forest quite the same, one place to another, and if the ear is tuned to listening it distinguishes each whisper from others in the night.

Leaving Barry and Tom on the wall, I walked back to my cabin.

On the wide bed I lay alone, thinking of Abby, of Abigail. I remembered the things she had said, the lift of her voice and the quiet, intimate sound of it in the night. I thought of the times when our children had been born, and how frightened I was when the second one came.

Why it was, I never knew, but upon that night I felt suddenly isolated, terribly alone, and I tried to get someone to stay with me—even a little longer, for Abby had been lying in Lila's cabin where she could be cared for better and watched over in the night.

All the terrible aloneness I had ever felt crowded around me then, for this was her time, and there was nothing I could do, I who would have done everything. John Quill had stopped by that night with a piece of venison from a kill and I talked to him until he almost had to pull himself away.

There was no reason for my fears, for the child came easily, with no complications.

Sometime I fell asleep, and was awakened by Sakim's hand on my shoulder. "It is time, I think."

"Is there any sign of them?"

"Perhaps . . . a little change in the sounds . . . but very little. Come! I have coffee."

Coffee was still a rare thing, but we had acquired a taste for it from our captured cargo, long ago, and when that was gone we had gotten our supplies from slave ships bound for the West Indies. Sometimes we were without, but used ground beans or whatever was available.

Our kitchen table was scoured white. That had been Abby's doing and I had done nothing to mar its perfection since she had left. My meals I had taken on a bench outside the door, and used the table only when writing or reading. Which led me to think . . . I had to see if John had poured candles for us. Mine were getting fewer and fewer.

Sakim filled our cups. "It is good, old friend, that we are together. I see you have been reading Montaigne. Earlier it was Maimonides . . . I wish I might introduce you to Khaldoun . . . Ibn Khaldoun. His *Muquaddimah!* That you must someday read. He was of the greatest of our thinkers . . . not the greatest, perhaps, but one of them. A most practical man . . . like you."

"I? Practical? I only wish I were. There is a madness in me at times, Sakim, and much of the time I am the least practical of men."

"Drink your coffee. There is bread made from the meal of corn here. Lila would be desolate if she thought you had ignored it."

"Not Lila. You forget how she is. She does what needs doing and is not hurt by being ignored. I learned long ago that in her own way our Lila is a philosopher."

"Well . . . I only hope Jeremy realizes. Yet it is easy to philosophize about marriage when one is unmarried. Let us eat our cornbread. If we are to talk nonsense it is better to eat while doing so, then the time is not entirely wasted."

Sakim put down his cup. "Our good Khaldoun has much

to say on the subject of eating. He maintains that the evidence shows that those who eat little are superior to those who eat much, in both courage and sensibility.

"Yet we readily accept the idea that a fat man is wise. Was he not wise enough to provide for himself? But we hesitate to ascribe piety to any but the lean. A fat prophet could never start a new religion, while a lean, ascetic-looking one could do it easily.

"A prophet should always come down from the mountain or out of the desert. He should never arise from the table.

"Also, he must have a rich, strong voice, but not one too cultivated. We tend to dislike and be suspicious of too cultivated a voice. A prophet's voice should have a little roughness in the tones."

"We had better get to the walls," I said, a little roughness in my own voice. "It grows a little thick in here. At least, when I read Montaigne I can close the book when I am tired of listening."

"See? I drop my pearls and they are ignored. Well, so be it."

We climbed the ladder in darkness, feeling our way from rung to rung. Kane O'Hara loomed beside us. "Nothing," he said. "But the crickets have stopped."

As he left, he added, "If you need me, raise your voice or fire a shot. I shall not sleep, only nod a little over the table."

"I'll remain here," Sakim said, to Kane. "But don't eat all the cornbread."

The posts that made up the palisade were of uneven lengths and were deliberately left so, as that made it more difficult for attackers by night to recognize a man's head. The poles averaged between fifteen and sixteen feet above the ground with a walk running around the wall ten feet above the ground except at the gate itself. Two ladders led from the ground to the walk, and there were two blockhouses projecting from the walls to enable defenders to fire along the walls. The second blockhouse had been added sometime after the first, as we were continually trying to improve our situation.

Jeremy was charging the extra muskets.

No stars were visible now. The wind was picking up, which made the detection of any approach a doubtful thing. It was intensely dark, yet our eyes were well accustomed to the night. So far as I had been able to learn, no Indian had succeeded in taking a fortified position such as ours, but I knew the dangers of over-confidence, and tried to imagine how they might attempt it.

A dozen times they had attempted this fort with no success. If they tried again, it must be because they believed they could succeed.

Something struck the palisade below me. . . .

Further along something else seemed to fall, and something snake-like whisked along the walk and disappeared over the wall.

Not quite over. It was a knotted rope, and the knot caught in one of the interstices between two posts. Instantly, I heard moccasins scrape against the logs outside, and almost at once a head loomed over.

His weirdly painted face was just inches away from mine and my reaction was instantaneous: a short, vicious smash in the face with the butt of my musket.

He had not seen me at all, and had thrust his head forward to look, so he took the full force of my blow and hit the ground with a thud.

"Ropes!" I shouted. "They're climbing ropes!"

Reversing my musket, I fired at a second head that was looming over the wall some twenty feet away, and which I could scarcely make out.

It was hand to hand then, and a bitter fight it was. Three Senecas, for such they proved to be, actually made it over the wall. One we shot as he dropped to the ground inside, another was killed with a sword thrust.

What was happening beyond my vision I'd no idea. It was no time for looking about. A big Indian leaped over the wall just before me, a lithe, splendid-looking rascal, although dimly seen. He no sooner lighted on the balls of his feet than he lunged at me, knife in hand.

My musket was empty and I'd put it down. There was no chance to draw a gun from my belt, and he held the knife low and came in fast. With a slap of the hand I drove the knife-wrist aside and out of line with my body, grasped the wrist, put a leg across in front of him, and spilled him to the walkway.

He hit hard, but was up with a bounce and came at me again, more warily this time. There was time to draw a pistol, but he had no such weapon. So I drew my own knife, the knife of India given me by my father long since. The Indian thrust well, but I parried and also thrust. He'd some knowledge of knife-fighting but none of fencing, and the point of my blade nicked his wrist.

He pulled back suddenly, blood upon his hand, then feinted and dove at me, grabbing at my legs. My knee lifted and caught the side of his head as he came in, and the nudge was enough to put him over the edge.

He fell ten feet but landed standing up. He came back up instantly, and I leaped at him. He sprang back, but not soon enough and I hit him and knocked him back to the ground. I jumped down to continue the fight. I hit him with my fist under the chin.

He staggered. The force of my fist had hurt him. I hit him twice more. He was totally unused to the boxer's style and the blow in the wind hurt him anew. Again I hit him and he fell back into the dirt. I grabbed him up by the lot of necklaces at his throat and slammed him hard against the gate.

He hit with tremendous force, and I thought he was out. I found his knife on the ground.

The first light of dawn was in the sky and I saw him plain. He had got up and was running away. I took the knife and threw it at him, yelling, "You'll need that!"

He turned and caught it from the air as one might catch a ball. "I will bring it back!" he shouted, and was gone.

For a moment I stood stock-still, staring after him. He had yelled in *English!*

"Wait!" I shouted, but he was gone and away.

My shout was the fight's end, and I walked slowly around, making a circuit of the walls. Kane had taken an arrow through his upper arm and Black Tom Watkins had a bad knife cut. Jeremy hadn't a scratch but it developed that I had three—a slight puncture wound and two slight cuts, troublesome if not cared for.

We believed that three of them had died, but as they had taken the bodies away we could not be sure.

What had turned the tide was not of our doing. For just at the moment of the hardest fighting, Kin, Yance, and a dozen Catawba, aided by Wa-ga-su, had come storming up and broke the back of the attack upon us.

Moreover, Kin and Yance were riding horseback!

△ 34 △

How swiftly roll the years! How lonely keep the nights!

At last I am westward going, over the blue mountains into the land beyond, and long have I dreamed of this! How many, many times have I looked with longing at those smoky mountains against the sky?

Pim Burke is back, if only for a little time. His fair lady proved unfair. She took his emerald and what gold he had and fled upon a ship for England, and may no good come to her.

Yet he is back, and for that I am grateful. He will stay but for a little while, for he returns to the coast to set up an inn in one of the new towns. It is a business at which he will do well.

John Quill has been to Williamsburg to make a claim for his grant of land. He has spoken for his piece here, and for another on the Chowan, and has persuaded Jeremy to do the same.

Kin and Yance have again gone beyond the mountains following a path of the Indians, worn by the feet of centuries going yonder. Soon I shall be meeting them, for it is into this land I am going at last.

Not in two years have we seen Jubal. Somewhere he roams beyond the great river of De Soto, somewhere across the vast plains that lie yonder toward the sun, and I think he will stop no more until he walks the shining western mountains of his dreams, and this I understand, for I have followed my dream of mountains, too. And so must it be for each generation, for they must ever look to the mountains, ever seek to pass over them.

Their bodies will mark the trails, their blood will feed the grass, yet some will win through and some will build and some will grow. . . .

Brian is reading law at the Inns of Court in London, a handsome gentleman, they say. And Noelle is a young English lady now, a beauty and a girl of spirit. A fine horsewoman, an elegant dancer. Does she ever remember our blue mountains? Or long for her father, who remembers her small hands in his hair, the first tears in her eyes, and the laughter never far from her lips? When William dies, the old fenlands will be hers.

We write, our letters crossing on the *Abigail* and other ships. And I continue my trade with Peter Tallis.

And Sakim, our teacher, our physician, our friend . . . one day word came from his own land, and I know not what it said, but he came to me with a farewell, and between two suns he was gone.

Now, I Barnabas Sackett, no longer a young man yet not quite an old one, am bound, west again. Black Tom Watkins rides with me. My old companion from the fens now rides the high ridges where waits the wind. At the last, when Jeremy would have come, Lila would have none of it, and for once he listened well.

Now the shadows rise from the valleys, and another night comes creeping. We have all day followed a trail made by buffalo, who wind the contours of the hills and seem ever to find the easiest way.

The Shawnees speak of this as the dark and bloody ground, and no Indian now lives here, although they come to hunt. Yet there are evidences of ancient habitation . . . stone walls, earthworks, and some things found in caves. In one of the old forts Tom found a Roman coin.

Preposterous, you say? I only say he found a coin,

lost by someone, not necessarily a Roman, yet perhaps someone who traded with a Roman, for the greatest myth is that of the discovery of any country, for all countries were known in the long ago, and all seas sailed in times gone by.

We are alone, Tom and I. Soon we will camp. Yet I am restless upon this night and if there were a moon would be for moving on.

Twice in the past few minutes I have glanced along our back trail, yet have seen nothing . . . yet something is there, bear, ghost, or man . . . some thing.

Ah! A wind-hollowed overhang, a sort of half-cave, with great slabs of broken rock lying about, and some few trees and many fallen ones. "Tom? If there's water, we should stop here."

While he searched about, I sat my saddle. Dusk was upon us and the trails were dim. . . .

Tom came from the darkness. "There's a good spring, Barnabas. This is the place."

Ah? This is the place? The words have a sound to them. Tomorrow we will meet the boys in the cove that lies ahead, the cove where grow the crabapples of which they have spoken.

Swinging down, I stripped the gear from my horse and drove deep the picket-pin to let him graze. While Tom gathered wood for the fire, I staked out his horse.

Firelight flickered on the bare rock walls. The broiling venison tasted good. Kneeling, I added fuel to the blaze. The warmth was comforting, and suddenly I was glad to be resting, for we had come a far piece since the dawning.

No sound in the night but the wind, no whisper but the leaves. The higher ranges lay behind us. The crab-apple cove lay just below. Beyond that a long, long valley that ends or seems to end at a river, a strong-flowing river that goes, they say, to the great river of De Soto. Jubal has ridden that river down. He has spoken of it to me.

Tom handed me a chunk of venison. "Indians say there were white folks here, in the long ago time. Chero-kees say they wiped 'em out. The Shawnees say the same. Likely somebody from one tribe married into the other an' carried the tale, or maybe they came together on the war party."

The wind moaned in the pines and the land was dark around us. The fire fluttered in the wind, and I added fuel. I should not be looking into the flames . . . the eyes adjust too slowly to darkness, and somebody, I think, is out there, waiting.

Somebody, perhaps, and some . . . *thing.*

This was my land. I breathed deeply of the fresh, cool air from off the mountains. This was what I had come for, this wide land, those tall boys who rode down the mountain paths toward me. It was a land for *men.* Here they could grow, here they could become, here they could move on to those destinies that await the men who do and are.

My father had given me much, and I had given them a little of that, I think, and a wide land in which to grow. Had I done nothing else, I left them this birthright . . . for I knew that out there beyond the great river, beyond the wide plain, beyond the shining mountains . . . beyond . . . there would be, for the men of this land, forever a beyond.

Many would die . . . do not all die, soon or late? Yet many would die in combat here, many would die in building, yet each in passing on would leave something of himself behind. This land waited long for the hard-bellied men to come, waited, snugged down for destiny. Hard though the years may be, and the moments of doubt, there will always be the beyond.

I looked again to the stars. Even there . . . even out there, given time. . . .

Black Tom Watkins stirred the fire again. He added sticks. "You got the notion something was behind us out there?"

"Bring the horses close, Tom. Yes I think there is something out there. Yet even so, I'd like an early start. We are to meet the boys in the cove where the crab-apples are."

283

He looked around at me. "D' you reckon we'll make it, Barnabas?"

"Do you wonder, Tom?"

He was silent, and the fire crackled. Somewhere out there the wind moved through the trees. "I reckon not, Barnabas. I reckon I knew from the moment we straddled a horse for this ride that we wasn't goin' but one way this time."

"We've ridden a good trail together, Tom, a long ride since that night on the edge of the fens."

"Aye, an' the boys are old enough now to git on without us." He looked up at me, embarrassed. "Barnabas, I hope you won't mind, but sometimes I think those boys are my own."

"That's the way I want it, Tom. You've been a second father to them, and a fine example."

"Example? Me?"

"You're a man, Tom Watkins, a man to ride down the warpath with . . . or any path. You were there when the long guns spoke, and you were beside me when the blades were drawn . . . and when they were sheathed . . . and you never shirked a job that needed to be done."

"Lila knew, didn't she? That why she wouldn't let Jeremy come?"

"She knew."

He brought the horses closer to the fire, and I walked out in the night and listened. Suppose I was wrong? Well, then . . . we'd meet the boys tomorrow.

I went to the spring and drank deep of the cold, cold water.

When I straightened up, I heard the faintest of sounds. My musket lifted and I faded deeper into the shadow of a boulder. A quick glance showed me Tom was gone . . . the fire flickered alone. Suddenly, off to my left a shadow shifted and I heard the blast of Tom's musket. The shadow stopped, then fell forward . . . and then they came swiftly, silently, and there were too many.

My musket accounted for one. A warrior loomed up from the shadows almost at my feet, and I shot him with a pistol, then ran forward, clubbing my musket to stand over Tom.

An arrow struck me. I felt the blow, then a stab of pain.

They were all around me then. The musket wrenched from my hands. My knife was out . . . that knife from India and a gift to my father, and from him to me.

It swung up and in. I heard a gasp and an Indian fell from me. Suddenly, with all my strength I swung into them, stabbing, slashing. Fire was kicked into the grass and a great flame went up, crackling and angry.

A huge warrior loomed before me, striking with a club. I went in quickly, under the blow. I put the knife into his ribs and he fell from me, jerking it from my grip. He fell and I swung a fist and knocked another sprawling, then stooped to withdraw the knife and felt a tremendous blow on the skull.

I was bleeding, I was hurt. I went down again, got up again. I grabbed a pistol, but the hammer clicked. Tom still had one unfired. I lunged for his body, knocked an Indian sprawling and threw three from me. Coming up with Tom's pistol, I fired into the Indians who loomed before me, then clubbed the pistol and struck another. I was down. An Indian loomed over me with a lance. I struck it aside and grasped it, pulling myself up. They fell back in a circle, staring at me, and I stood weaving before them, the lance in my grasp.

They were going to come for me again. I reached down and caught up my powder horn, pulled off the stopper and threw it into the fire. There was an explosion and a puff of fire shot out, and the Indians leaped back.

Tom, who had evidently been knocked out, came up then, and for a few minutes we stood back to back. I retrieved my knife and we fought, working our way back toward the cave mouth.

"Barn . . . I'm goin', I—"

He went down again but I caught up his cutlass. For a minute or more I held them off with that swirling, thrusting blade, but I was weaker.

I was bleeding . . . I was hurt.

Suddenly, I was down. There was a thrown lance in my chest. I tried to move, could not.

I gripped the knife. "Come on, damn you! I can kill another of you!"

They stared at me, and drew slowly back. I was dying and I knew it.

They knew it, too.

Suddenly one of them dropped to his knees and began to sing a death-song.

My death-song. He was singing it for me.

Turning my knife, I handed it to him, hilt forward. "Th . . . anks," I said.

Or thought I said.

"Ab—? Abby? I—I wish—"

In the dust, my finger moved . . . stirred.

Kin . . . Yance . . . the boys and Noelle. Had they found a path, as I had? Did they know the way to go?

Who would live to tell the story—our story?

My finger wrote in the dust. I looked, my gaze blurred.

I had written: *Give them tomorrow.* . . .

Dead I was, yet not quite dead, for I felt the Indian stoop above me, covering me gently with a blanket.

There was a whisper of moccasins, withdrawing. . . .

The dawn wind stirred the corner of the blanket. One of the horses whinnied . . . for a long, long time, there was no other sound.

In the lodges of the Senecas there was silence. And into the darkened lodge of the old chief the four warriors came and they stood tall before him.

For a long time they stood in silence, arms folded. Then one said, "He is finished."

"You have his hair?"

"We were twelve. Four came away. We left his scalp with him . . . and the other, also."

Another spoke. "We covered them with blankets, for they were brave."

"He was ever brave." The old man was silent. "You have done well."

286

And when they had walked from the lodge the old man took a pinch of tobacco and threw it into the fire. Then sadly he said, "Who now is left to test our young men? Who now?"

ABOUT LOUIS L'AMOUR

"I think of myself in the oral tradition—as a troubadour, a village taleteller, the man in the shadows of the campfire. That's the way I'd like to be remembered—as a storyteller. A good storyteller."

It is doubtful that any author could be as at home in the world created in his novels as Louis Dearborn L'Amour. Not only could he physically fill the boots of the rugged characters he writes about, but he has literally "walked the land my characters walk." His personal experiences as well as his lifelong devotion to historical research have combined to give Mr. L'Amour the unique knowledge and understanding of the people, the events, and the challenge of the American frontier that have become the hallmarks of his popularity.

Of French-Irish descent, Mr. L'Amour can trace his own family in North America back to the early 1600s and follow their steady progression westward, "always on the frontier." As a boy growing up in Jamestown, North Dakota, he absorbed all he could about his family's frontier heritage, including the story of his great-grandfather who was scalped by Sioux warriors.

Spurred by an eager curiosity and desire to broaden his horizons, Mr. L'Amour left home at the age of fifteen and enjoyed a wide variety of jobs including seaman, lumberjack, elephant handler, skinner of dead cattle, assessment miner, and officer on tank destroyers during World War II. During his "yondering" days he also circled the world on a freighter, sailed a dhow on the Red Sea, was shipwrecked in the West Indies and stranded in the Mojave Desert. He has won fifty-one of fifty-nine fights as a professional boxer and worked as a journalist and lecturer. A voracious reader and collector of rare books, Mr. L'Amour's personal library of some 10,000 volumes covers a broad range of scholarly disciplines including many personal papers, maps, and diaries of the pioneers.

Mr. L'Amour "wanted to write almost from the time I could walk." After developing a widespread following for his many adventure stories written for the fiction magazines, Mr. L'Amour published his first full-length novel, *Hondo*, in 1953. Mr. L'Amour is now one of the four bestselling living novelists in the world. Every one of his more than 90 books are still in print and every one has sold more than one million copies. He has more million-copy bestsellers than any other living author. His books have been translated into more than a dozen languages, and more than thirty of his novels and stories have been made into feature films and television movies.

His hardcover bestsellers include *The Lonesome Gods; The Walking Drum*, his twelfth-century historical novel; *Jubal Sackett; Last of the Breed;* and *The Haunted Mesa.*

The recipient of many great honors and awards, in 1983 Mr. L'Amour became the first novelist ever to be awarded a Special National Gold Medal by the United States Congress in honor of his life's work. In 1984 he was also awarded the Medal of Freedom by President Ronald Reagan.

Mr. L'Amour lives in Los Angeles with his wife, Kathy, and their two children, Beau and Angelique.